MAGU CROEN
RHAG POEN

MAIR WYNN HUGHES

Argraffiad cyntaf—Gorffennaf 1994

ISBN 1 85902 152 2

ⓗMair Wynn Hughes

Dymuna'r cyhoeddwyr gydnabod cymorth adrannau'r Cyngor Llyfrau Cymraeg.

Argraffwyd gan
J.D. Lewis a'i Feibion Cyf., Gwasg Gomer, Llandysul

1.

Neidiodd Bethan ar ei heistedd yn y gwely a rhoddodd hwb hapus i'w chwaer.

'Cysgadur!' meddai. 'Rydyn ni'n mynd adre heddiw. Wyt ti ddim yn cofio?'

Trodd Ceren yn gysglyd mewn ymateb a chladdodd ei hun yn ddyfnach o dan y dillad.

'*Ceren!*'

Ond fe wyddai Bethan nad oedd fawr o ddiben ceisio deffro Ceren o'i thrymgwsg. A dim ond saith o'r gloch oedd hi wedi'r cyfan. Fe fyddai'n awr arall cyn y deffroai ei chwaer o ddifri.

Ysgydwodd Bethan ei phen. Fedrai hi ddim aros yn ei gwely eiliad yn rhagor. Ddim heddiw, a'i mam a'i thad yn cyrraedd y bore 'ma. Gwasgodd ei breichiau amdani'i hun wrth ddychmygu'r Sierra coch yn troi ym mhen y stryd. Fe fyddai'i mam yn eistedd yn y sedd ffrynt a'i llygaid yn dawnsio'n hapus wrth weld y ddwy ohonyn nhw'n disgwyl yn yr ardd. Ac fe fyddai'i thad yn taro 'Bib-bib' ysgafn ar y corn fel y llywiai'r car i'r dreif.

Roedd hi wedi cael llond bol ar aros hefo Anti Catrin. Dim byd ond gwnewch hyn a chofiwch wneud y llall yn dragwyddol. Ond fe fyddai popeth yn newid heddiw—wedi i'w rhieni gyrraedd.

Cododd Bethan a throedio ar flaenau'i thraed am y ffenestr. Agorodd y llenni. Roedd yr haul yn tywynnu, a'r lawnt ben bore yn garped o berlau gwlith. Gwisgodd yn frysiog.

Cychwynnodd yn ddistaw i lawr y grisiau. Daria! Fe gwynodd y trydydd gris yn swnllyd fel arfer. Rhewodd. Gobeithio na fu'r sŵn yn ddigon i ddeffro Anti Catrin, meddyliodd. Gwrandawodd yn betrusgar cyn ymlacio ac estyn ei throed am y gris nesaf.

Ond!

'Bethan! Ceren! Y chi sy 'na?'

Agorodd drws y llofft a daeth Anti Catrin i'r golwg. Roedd hi mewn gŵn nos blaen gyda choler uchel a rhes o fotymau i lawr at ei thraed. Roedd ei gwallt brith wedi ei dynnu'n rholyn tynn y tu ôl i'w phen, ac roedd golwg ymholgar ar ei hwyneb.

'Bethan? Ble'r wyt ti'n mynd?' holodd. 'Wyt ti wedi molchi cyn gwisgo amdanat? Chlywais i mo dy sŵn di yn yr ystafell ymolchi.'

Ochneidiodd Bethan o dan ei hanadl. Doedd neb fel Anti Catrin am ffwsio a deddfu.

'Mi wna i yn y munud, Anti Catrin,' meddai. 'Eisio mynd allan am ei bod hi'n fore braf oeddwn i.'

(Ac am fod Mam a Dad yn dŵad heddiw meddai'n ddistaw wrthi'i hun.)

6

'Mi fydd y bore braf yno'r un fath wedi iti molchi,' meddai Anti Catrin. 'Dos rŵan, a rho grib trwy dy wallt wedyn.'

Trodd Bethan yn anfoddog i gyfeiriad yr ystafell ymolchi. Roedd Anti Catrin yn poeni am fod yn dwt a theidi byth a beunydd, cuchiodd wrthi'i hun. Pa ots ei bod hi heb ymolchi? Pwy oedd i wybod, na sylwi, am ychydig wedi saith yn y bore?

A châi hi ddim mynd allan am oesoedd rŵan. Ddim wedi i'w modryb ddeffro. Na. Fe fyddai eisio gosod y bwrdd brecwast. Eisio estyn lliain o'r drôr a'i daenu drosto a gosod cwpanau a phlatiau yn eu lleoedd priodol, a napcyn mewn cylch arian wrth ochr pob un. A rhoi marmalêd mewn dysgl fach wydr ar ganol y bwrdd, a dau baced grawnfwyd fel milwyr ochr yn ochr ar y dde.

Ac yna fe fyddai eisio deffro Ceren a gofalu ei bod yn molchi a chribo'i gwallt yn dwt, a bwyta brecwast yn dair sidêt hefo'i gilydd wedyn. Ac fe fyddai'n rhaid helpu i glirio'r bwrdd a golchi'r llestri. Ac erbyn hynny, fe wyddai Bethan y byddai'r bore tawel a welodd hi o ffenestr y llofft wedi diflannu'n llwyr.

Fe ddeuai fen y dyn llefrith i dinc dincian ei ffordd i lawr y stryd a'r bachgen papur newydd i chwibanu o ddrws i ddrws. Ac fe fyddai pobl yn cychwyn i'w gwaith gan refio'u ceir a chlepian drysau.

'Jest eiliad . . .' cychwynnodd Bethan gan betruso wrth ddrws yr ystafell ymolchi.

Yna brathodd ei thafod. Roedd ei mam wedi pwysleisio fod yn rhaid iddyn nhw fod yn enethod da, a chofio pa mor garedig fu Anti Catrin yn eu cymryd am bythefnos gyfan yn ystod gwyliau haf am ei bod hi a Dad yn llawn eu trafferth hefo'r estyniad newydd gartre.

'Iawn, Anti Catrin,' meddai'n ufudd wrth gofio.

Pa ots, meddyliodd Bethan. Dyma'r bore olaf. Fory, fe fydden nhw ill dwy'n deffro gartre. Yn deulu unwaith eto. Mam a Dad a Ceren a hithau. Ac mi fyddai gan y ddwy ohonyn nhw lofft bob un o hyn ymlaen.

Gwenodd Bethan fel yr arllwysodd ddŵr i'r basn. Roedd hi'n dyheu am gael gweld ei llofft newydd. Daliodd ei phen yn gam a gwnaeth lygaid bach arni'i hun yn y drych fel y ceisiodd ddychmygu sut un fyddai hi. Papur wal pinc a gwyn fyddai ar y muriau, wrth gwrs. Bu ei mam a hithau'n ei ddewis yn siop fawr yr Arcêd. Ac mi aethon nhw ymlaen i'r siop ddodrefn hefyd, a phrynu bwrdd gwisgo a wardrob a chwpwrdd cist.

'Rwyt ti'n ddeuddeg oed rŵan ac yn ddigon hen i ddewis trosot dy hun,' dywedodd Mam gan afael amdani'n sydyn a'i gwasgu ati.

'Bodlon?' gofynnodd wedyn wrth adael y siop.

'O, Mam!'

Fe deimlai Bethan yn rhy hapus i anadlu bron y funud honno. Gwenodd wrth gofio. Yna taflodd ddŵr brysiog tros ei hwyneb a'i dwylo a brysiodd i ddeffro Ceren. Roedd heddiw'n ddiwrnod *grêt*!

Ac wrth y bwrdd brecwast, roedd hi wedi methu'n lân â pheidio mwmian canu o dan ei gwynt. Hyd yn oed wrth olchi'r llestri hefo Anti Catrin.

'Mi fyddan nhw yma cyn cinio, yn byddan?' meddai wrth sychu'r plât olaf.

Am eiliad, fe dybiodd hi fod gwên fach yn llygaid ei modryb fel y trodd i edrych arni. Ond penderfynodd mai dychmygu wnaeth hi gan fod llais Anti Catrin yn undonog sych fel y gwasgodd y cadach llestri a thywallt dŵr o'r ddysgl.

'Byddan. Mae'n well i ti a Ceren bacio'ch pethau. Mae'n siŵr y byddwch chi ar dân eisio mynd.'

'O . . . na. Rydyn ni wedi . . . mwynhau . . .'

Baglodd Bethan wrth feddwl sut i ddiolch a hithau ddim wedi mwynhau dim, jest. Wel, doedd dim modd iddyn nhw, yn nac oedd? Roedd Anti Catrin yn disgwyl iddyn nhw aros yn yr ardd a bihafio'n deidi, yn disgwyl iddyn nhw gerdded yn ufudd pan aent gyda hi i'r parc, a byth i faeddu'u jîns na bwyta hufen iâ, na gwneud ffrindiau hefo'r eneth honno a wenodd arni droeon ym mhen draw'r stryd.

Pletio'i cheg wnaeth Anti Catrin wrth ei gweld, a galw ar Ceren a hithau i frysio 'mlaen a pheidio â loetran.

'Ond roedd hi am fod yn ffrindiau, Anti Catrin,' grwgnachodd hithau'n wgus.

Ond sôn am bobl lawr dre ddim yn gofalu am eu plant, a bod edau a nodwydd yn ddigon rhad wnaeth Anti Catrin, nes bod Bethan yn teimlo fel sgrechian. Ac er ei bod hi wedi gweld yr eneth wedyn, chafodd hi wneud dim ond gwenu'n glên arni a dilyn Anti Catrin fel ci bach wrth gortyn. Roedd Bethan ar dân eisio mynd adre.

Dringodd y grisiau gyda Ceren i ddechrau pacio.

'Pa bryd mae Mam a Dad yn dŵad?' holodd Ceren yn hiraethus gan eistedd ar y fainc ffenestr yn y llofft a phwyso'i thrwyn ar y gwydr.

'Cyn cinio, siŵr,' atebodd Bethan. 'Yli, rho dy bethau yn dy gês.'

'Munud,' meddai Ceren gan anadlu'n drwm ar y ffenestr a cheisio gwneud patrwm yn y cwmwl wedyn.

'Gwna rŵan, a phaid â baeddu'r ffenest,' meddai Bethan.

Ond ni chymerodd Ceren sylw.

'Wyt ti eisio i Mam a Dad fynd hebddot ti, ta?'

bygythiodd Bethan yn ddiflas. 'Mi fyddan nhw ar frys eisio cychwyn yn ôl, cofia.'

'Rho di nhw imi.'

'Na.'

'Plîs.'

'Na.'

'Ond fedra i mo'u plygu nhw. Maen nhw'n ormod i'r cês.'

'Na.'

Fe wyddai Bethan fod ei llais yn codi'n ddiamynedd. Ond pam roedd angen i Ceren fihafio fel babi er mwyn cael ei ffordd ei hun?

Daeth Ceren oddi wrth y ffenestr.

'Plîs, Bethan,' meddai gan wasgu'i breichiau am ganol ei chwaer a gwenu'n gariadus arni.

Roedd Bethan ar fin ysgwyd ei phen. Ond fedrai hi ddim ffraeo hefo Ceren heddiw. Ddim â hithau mor hapus wrth feddwl am weld Mam a Dad. Gafaelodd yn nillad Ceren a'u plygu rywsut rywsut i mewn i'r cês.

'Rydw i'n synnu atat ti,' meddai llais Anti Catrin o'r tu ôl iddi. 'Nid fel'na mae plygu dillad.'

Teimlodd Bethan y gwrid yn dringo i'w hwyneb, a saethodd olwg sarrug ar Ceren. Ond roedd honno'n rhy brysur yn bihafio fel babi i sylwi.

'Y fi'n methu, Anti Catrin,' meddai.

'Rwyt ti'n ddigon hen i ddysgu,' meddai Anti Catrin yn siarp. 'Rŵan!' Rhoes hwb bach iddi i

11

gyfeiriad y gwely. 'Dechrau arni. A helpa dithau hi'n iawn, Bethan.'

Trodd Anti Catrin ar ei sawdl. Syllodd Bethan ar ei chefn fel y diflannodd i lawr y grisiau. Doedd gan Anti Catrin ddim hawl, meddyliodd yn sydyn. Ddim hawl i siarad fel'na hefo nhw, na hawl i gyffwrdd pen ei bys yn Ceren. Pedair a chwarter oedd hi, ac wedi arfer cael Mam i'w helpu.

Trodd i edrych ar ei chwaer. Roedd honno'n sefyll a'i phen i lawr a'i gwallt melyn syth yn cuddio'i hwyneb. Crio, ta gwenu oedd hi? Gwenu, penderfynodd Bethan yn ddiflas. Roedd Ceren yn mwynhau ei chael hi i drwbl.

Ond cododd Ceren ei phen yn sydyn a gafael yn llaw Bethan.

'Rydw i'n falch fod Mam a Dad yn dŵad. Wyt ti? Mae Anti Catrin yn dweud y drefn o hyd.'

Nodiodd Bethan.

'Ond mae hi wedi bod yn garedig yn ein cymryd ni,' meddai gan gofio geiriau ei mam.

'Hy!' Gwnaeth Ceren sŵn fel rhochian yn ei thrwyn.

'Sssh! Beth petai hi'n dy glywed di?'

Ond roedd yn rhaid iddi chwerthin. Doedd neb tebyg i Ceren am rochian yn ei thrwyn. Roedd o'n sŵn uchel a hir ac anfoesgar, fel gollwng gwynt o falŵn anferth. Yn fuan, roedd y ddwy yn lladd eu hunain wrth chwerthin ar y gwely ac wedi anghofio popeth am bacio'r dillad yn y cês.

Roedden nhw'n gorwedd yno'n gyrff llipa pan ddaeth sŵn car o'r tu allan.

'Hei! Maen nhw wedi cyrraedd,' meddai Bethan yn falch.

Neidiodd y ddwy oddi ar y gwely a rhedeg yn bendramwnwgl i lawr y grisiau.

'Enethod!'

Galwodd Anti Catrin yn awdurdodol uchel o'r gegin. Ond anwybyddodd y ddwy y llais.

'Mam! Dad!' bloeddiodd Bethan gan agor y drws a'i thaflu ei hun trwyddo.

Gwrthdrawodd â rhywun a safai ar stepan y drws. Gafaelodd breichiau cryfion ynddi, a chlywodd lais dwfn yn holi.

'Ydi Miss Preis i mewn? Miss Catrin Preis?'

Edrychodd Bethan i lygaid caredig plismon. Ond roedd rhywbeth od yn ei lais, ac yn ei lygaid hefyd. Rhywbeth na fedrai Bethan ei adnabod yn iawn. Fe roes ei chalon dro sydyn, ofnus.

'Anti Catrin? Ydi. Roedden ni'n meddwl mai Mam a Dad oeddech chi,' eglurodd yn gloff.

'Eich mam a'ch tad?'

Roedd rhywbeth odiach yn llais y plismon. Tynnodd ei gap a'i ddal yn ei ddwylo.

'Ydi'ch modryb . . . ?'

Daeth cryndod rhyfedd i goesau Bethan.

Cryndod a ledaenodd trwy'i chorff nes cyr-raedd at ei gwddf.

'Be sy . . . ?'

Ni fedrai ynganu'r geiriau. Ni fedrai wneud dim ond edrych i fyny i wyneb y plismon a thybio gweld rhyw neges ofnadwy yn ei lygaid.

Daeth Anti Catrin i'r lobi gan sychu'i dwylo.

'Peidiwch â chadw eich rhieni ar stepan y drws . . .' cychwynnodd.

Yna gwelodd y plismon ac edrychodd yn ymholgar arno.

'Miss Catrin Preis?'

Nodiodd Anti Catrin.

'Ga i air hefo chi? Ar eich pen eich hun?'

Brathodd Anti Catrin ei gwefus, ac wedi un edrychiad craff ar y plismon, trodd at Bethan a Ceren.

'Ewch i'r lolfa, a chaewch y drws,' gorchmyn-nodd.

'Ond, pam? Be sy?' holodd Bethan a'i thafod yn sych.

Cymerodd Anti Catrin arni ei bod heb ei chlywed. Gafaelodd yn ei hysgwyddau a'i hebrwng yn ddiseremoni trwy'r drws a Ceren gyda hi.

'Arhoswch yna,' gorchmynnodd.

Agorodd Bethan ei cheg i holi eto, ond roedd lwmp mawr trwm yn llenwi'i gwddf, ac ni allai orfodi'r geiriau heibio iddo.

14

'Pam mae Anti Catrin wedi'n cau ni yn fan'ma?' holodd Ceren yn gwynfanllyd.

'Be wn i?' atebodd Bethan yn sydyn ffyrnig. Trodd oddi wrth ei chwaer fach gan daflu'r geiriau dros ei hysgwydd.

'Be-th-aa-n!'

Dechreuodd Ceren grio. Fe deimlai Bethan fel crio hefyd. Doedd hi ddim yn siŵr pam. Ond . . . ond . . . roedd hi'n siŵr fod rhywbeth ofnadwy wedi digwydd. I'w rhieni.

Roedd murmur lleisiau'n codi a gostwng yn y lobi, a'r ofn yn cynyddu bob eiliad yn ei chorff hithau. Beth oedd wedi digwydd? Pam roedd Anti Catrin wedi'u hel nhw i'r lolfa mor sydyn, a pham na ddeuai hi atyn nhw i ddweud beth oedd yn bod?

Ymaflodd Ceren yn ei llaw.

'Am be maen nhw'n siarad, Bethan?' holodd yn ofnus.

Ysgydwodd Bethan ei phen heb ateb, dim ond gafael yn dynn yn llaw ei chwaer a gwasgu.

'Aawww!' cwynodd Ceren.

Ond ni chlywodd Bethan hi. Hoeliodd ei llygaid ar y drws. Fe agorai yn fuan ac fe ddeuai Anti Catrin trwyddo i ddweud . . . be?

'Gollwng, Bethan!'

Cipiodd Ceren ei llaw ymaith a throdd yn guchiog tua'r ffenestr.

'Mi ddeuda i wrth Mam. Ac wrth Dad.'

Ceisiodd Bethan wenu fel yr aeth gyda hi at y ffenestr. Roedd ei thraed fel creigiau o drwm, a sŵn tonnau'r môr yn byddaru'i chlustiau. *Beth oedd wedi digwydd*?

Caewyd drws y ffrynt. Gwelodd Bethan y plismon yn mynd i'w gar. Eisteddodd yn sedd y gyrrwr am rai munudau heb gychwyn y peiriant. Cynyddodd y cyffro annifyr o'i mewn hithau. Pam na ddeuai Anti Catrin i ddweud rhywbeth wrthyn nhw? Roedd unrhyw newydd yn well na dim.

Trodd fel yr agorwyd drws y lolfa'n ddistaw. Safai Anti Catrin yno. Roedd golwg ansicr ar ei hwyneb. Cliriodd ei gwddf yn swnllyd ond ni ddywedodd air.

'Be sy, Anti Catrin? Beth oedd y plismon eisio?' Baglai llais Bethan.

Daeth Anti Catrin ymlaen atynt. Rhoddodd ei breichiau am ysgwyddau'r ddwy a'u tynnu ati.

'Rhaid ichi fod yn enethod dewr iawn,' meddai.

Safodd yn ddistaw am rai eiliadau fel petai'n methu dweud gair arall.

'Pam?'

Fe wyddai Bethan fod ei llais yn dianc oddi wrthi. Yn codi'n uwch ac yn uwch.

'PAM?'

Llyncodd Anti Catrin boer araf.

'Mae eich rhieni wedi cael damwain. Damwain car ar y ffordd yma.'

Gafaelodd yn dynnach ynddynt a'u tynnu ati.

'Maen nhw yn yr ysbyty . . .'

Daeth bloedd sydyn oddi wrth Ceren.

'Rydw i eisio nhw. Rŵan. Dim eisio iddyn nhw fod yn yr ysbyty.'

Roedd y lwmp yng ngwddf Bethan yn ymledu at ei stumog.

'Ydyn nhw wedi brifo lot? Gawn ni fynd i'w gweld nhw?' holodd. 'Gawn ni? Plîs?'

Tynhaodd braich Anti Catrin amdani.

'Ddim ar hyn o bryd, Bethan,' meddai. 'Fel y dywedais i, mi fydd yn rhaid ichi fod yn enethod dewr. Mi a i i'r ysbyty ar unwaith, ac mi gewch chithau aros hefo Mrs Jones drws nesa. Mi ddo i'n ôl cyn gynted ag y medra i.'

Safodd Bethan yn fud fel y prysurodd ei modryb o'r ystafell. Clywodd ddrws y cefn yn agor, ac ymhen munudau hir daeth llais Mrs Jones o'r lobi.

'Wrth gwrs, mi gân nhw aros hefo mi. Rhyw-beth fedra i'i wneud, mi wyddoch hynny. Diar, diar, tydi pethau'n digwydd mor sydyn! Wn i ddim sut y gwnaiff y pethau bach ymdopi. Na'u tad chwaith.'

2.

'Gym'rwch chi rywbeth bach i de?'

Roedd llais Mrs Jones yn orgalonnog. Fel petai'n ceisio cymryd arni nad oedd dim yn bod. Felly y bu hi trwy'r amser. Yn siarad . . . ac yn gwenu . . . ac yn cynnig bwyd a diod iddyn nhw, a throi'r teledu ymlaen. Ac yn ysgwyddo cwestiynau ymaith nes bod Bethan yn swp sâl.

'Dydw i ddim eisio dim, diolch,' meddai.

Pam na ddeuai Anti Catrin yn ôl? Neu pam na ffoniai i ddweud rhywbeth? Roedd ei thu mewn yn un cwestiwn mawr.

'Ga i fisged sinsir?' gofynnodd Ceren. 'A diod oren? Plîs?'

'Cei siŵr,' oedd yr ateb parod.

Trodd Bethan i ffwrdd. Roedd hi'n wfftio at Ceren yn sôn am fisgedi sinsir a diod oren. Oedd hi wedi anghofio fod rhywbeth wedi digwydd? Rhywbeth ofnadwy! Pam nad oedd hi'n poeni fel hithau yn lle mwytho cath Mrs Jones a siarad lol yn ei chlust? Fel petai hi wedi anghofio popeth am y plismon a'r ysbyty a brys Anti Catrin i fynd yno.

Fe deimlai Bethan fel gafael yn ei chwaer a'i hysgwyd, ond roedd hi eisio ei gwasgu ati hefyd, a theimlo fod Ceren yn rhannu'r ofn a lenwai'i thu mewn hithau.

Daeth dagrau i'w llygaid a rhwbiodd nhw i

18

ffwrdd yn frysiog. Fe ddeuai ei rhieni'n ôl yn fuan. Wrth gwrs y deuent. Mi fyddai popeth yn iawn wedyn. Fe safai Mam yno'n chwerthin yn braf tra eglurai Dad mai damwain fach gawson nhw. Wedi torri braich a chael sgriffiadau i'w coesau. Neu daro'u pennau a chael rhwymyn i ddiogelu'r briw, efallai. Dim byd mawr.

Ac wedyn, fe ddywedai'i thad fod yn rhaid iddyn nhw gychwyn am adre'n syth bin. Am eu bod nhw wedi gwastraffu amser yn yr ysbyty yn cael Pelydr X ac yn cael eu harchwilio gan y meddygon. Fe fyddai'n chwerthin ac yn dweud fod angen iddyn nhw frysio gan fod tacsi'n disgwyl yn y dreif. Am fod y Sierra wedi'i ddryllio yn y ddamwain.

Caeodd Bethan ei llygaid yn sydyn dynn, a gwasgodd ei dwylo i bocedi'i jîns. Doedd hi ddim am feddwl am ddryllio. Ddim fel yn y ddamwain honno a welodd hi ar y teledu. Car wedi'i ddryllio'n chwilfriw a ... a ... neb wedi ...

'Well i tithau gymryd rhywbeth, Bethan,' meddai Mrs Jones. 'Fydd dy fodryb ddim yn hir eto, mi gei di weld.'

Ond roedd meddwl am fwyta tamaid yn drech na Bethan. A pham roedd Mrs Jones yn sôn am Anti Catrin, ac yn sôn dim am Mam a Dad? Beth oedd wedi digwydd? A pham roedd Anti Catrin mor hir? Roedd hi'n bnawn rŵan.

'Yli chwarae mae hi,' meddai Ceren gan giglan wrth weld y gath yn pawennu'r papur.

Trodd Bethan at y ffenestr ac edrychodd tua gardd Anti Catrin. Rhoes ei chalon sbonc sydyn. Roedd car o flaen y drws. Ers pa bryd?

'Maen nhw wedi dŵad!' gwaeddodd.

'Diolch, Mrs Jones,' gwaeddodd wedyn cyn agor y drws a chychwyn rhedeg i dŷ ei modryb. 'Tyrd, Ceren!'

'Arhoswch.'

Fe wyddai fod Mrs Jones wedi gweiddi rhyw-beth arnynt. Ond doedd dim ots. Gafaelodd yn llaw Ceren a'i llusgo hi i fyny dreif ei modryb. Agorodd y drws a baglu'n ffrwcslyd i'r lobi.

'Mam! Dad!' gwaeddodd gan ruthro am y lolfa.

Arhosodd yn stond. Roedd ei thad yn eistedd ar y gadair. Roedd ei ben yn isel yn ei ddwylo ac roedd o'n . . . *crio*! *Ei thad yn crio*! Yna cododd ei ben a'i gweld hi a Ceren. Crynodd ei wefusau fel yr agorodd ei freichiau.

'Bethan! Ceren!' Roedd ei lais yn floesg.

'Dad!'

Taflodd Bethan a Ceren eu hunain amdano.

'Dad!'

Yna gofynnodd Ceren y cwestiwn yr ofnai Bethan ei yngan.

'Ble mae Mam?'

Symudodd Anti Catrin yn anniddig wrth y lle tân.

'Peidiwch â phoeni'ch tad rŵan,' meddai.

Roedd ei llais hithau'n floesg hefyd.

Ysgydwodd eu tad ei ben a thynhaodd ei freichiau amdanynt.

'Na,' meddai. 'Rhaid inni wynebu pethau hefo'n gilydd.'

Arweiniodd y ddwy at y soffa ac eisteddodd arni gyda nhw. Roedd sgriffiadau ar ei wyneb a rhwymyn am ei wddf a'i arddwrn.

'Mae Mam . . .' cychwynnodd. Baglodd ei lais. 'Mae Mam wedi . . . wedi . . .'

'Wedi be?' holodd Ceren yn ddryslyd.

Ond fe wyddai Bethan. Roedd hi'n cofio'r car hwnnw yn rhacs gyrbibion ar y teledu. Caeodd ei llygaid wrth feddwl am ei mam yng nghanol y ffasiwn lanastr. Dechreuodd sgrech dyfu yn rhywle tua'i stumog; sgrech a gododd yn sŵn ofnadwy yn ei gwddf, ac a ffrwydrodd allan yn grio poenus.

Roedd hi'n gwybod fod ei thad a Ceren yn crio hefyd. Ond rywsut, dim ond ei chrio hi oedd yn bwysig. Châi hi byth weld Mam eto. Châi hi byth ddewis papur llofft a dodrefn newydd hefo hi. Na byth rannu hanesion ysgol, na swnian arni am jîns hefo label ffasiynol arnyn nhw chwaith. Na byth . . . Boddodd yn yr wybodaeth. Roedd ei mam wedi *mynd*!

Clywodd lais ei thad wrth ei chlust.

'Dyna oedd orau, meddai'r meddyg. Faset ti

ddim yn licio gweld dy fam yn diodde, yn na faset? A dyna wnâi hi wedi damwain o'r fath.'

Ond mi fasa hi *yma*, meddyliodd Bethan. Fel yr ydych *chi* yma. Fasa hi ddim wedi'n gadael ni.

Roedd ei thad bron â chrio eto. Fe deimlai Bethan y dylai ddweud rhywbeth wrtho. Ond, beth?

'Ble mae hi rŵan?'

'Hefo Iesu Grist,' meddai Anti Catrin. 'Dyna mae'r Beibl yn ei ddysgu inni.'

'Ond ble mae *hi*? Y hi ei hun.'

Gwylltiai Bethan wrth Anti Catrin am nad oedd hi'n deall. Ond fe ddeallai ei thad yn iawn.

'Yn y mortiwari. Dyna lle maen nhw'n rhoi . . .'

'Ond i ble wedyn?'

'Bethan . . .'

Roedd rhybudd yn llais Anti Catrin. Ond roedd angen gwybod ar Bethan. Doedden nhw erioed am adael Mam yn y mortiwari. Hen le unig heb neb i wylo drosti hi.

'Gaiff hi fynd adre? Gawn ni i gyd fynd adre?'

Edrychodd Anti Catrin a'i thad ar ei gilydd. Yna ysgydwodd ei thad ei ben. Roedd loes ar ei wyneb.

'Rydyn ni am ddefnyddio'r Capel Gorffwys,' meddai. 'Dyna fydd orau, Bethan. Mi . . .'

Ni allai ei thad orffen. Cododd ar ei draed gyda chymorth ffon.

'Mae'n rhaid imi ddechrau trefnu. Ffonio
. . .'

Yn sydyn fe wyddai Bethan beth y dylai ei
wneud. Yn y dyfodol. Pan oedd y tri ohonyn
nhw gartre unwaith eto. Y hi a'i thad a Ceren.
Fe fyddai'n rhaid iddi hi ofalu amdanyn nhw.
Yn union fel y byddai ei mam yn ei wneud. Ac
roedd hi'n ddigon hen, doedd? Yn ddeuddeg
oed.

Trodd at Ceren.

'Mi eisteddwn ni yma tra byddwch chi'n
ffonio,' meddai.

Gafaelodd yn ei chwaer a'i thynnu'n glòs i
gylch ei braich.

'Mi fyddwn ni'n iawn yma,' meddai.

Gwenodd ei thad yn ansicr arni.

'Gwell i'r ddwy ohonyn nhw fynd yn ôl at Mrs
Jones,' meddai Anti Catrin. 'Tan amser
gwely.'

Edrychodd Bethan arni fel petai'n rhywun
dieithr. Doedd gan Anti Catrin ddim hawl i
ddweud wrthyn nhw beth i'w wneud. Dim ond
modryb oedd hi. Y hi a'i thad a Ceren oedd yn
deulu.

'Na, Anti Catrin,' meddai. 'Rydyn ni am aros
yma i helpu Dad.'

Agorodd Anti Catrin ei cheg i orchymyn yn
wahanol. Ond caeodd hi drachefn wrth i'w tad
ddweud,

'Ia, hynny fydd orau inni i gyd, Catrin.'

Ystumiodd Anti Catrin ei hysgwyddau, ond ddywedodd hi ddim gair ymhellach. Gafaelodd Bethan yn dynn yn llaw Ceren. Dim ond y nhw ill tri oedd yna bellach. Dad a Ceren a hithau.

3.

Estynnodd eu tad ei ddwylo i gyffwrdd eu gwalltiau, ond roedd ei feddwl ymhell.

'Ia, arhoswch chi yma tra bydda i'n ffonio,' meddai'n drymaidd.

Trodd am y lobi gydag Anti Catrin, a daeth murmur eu lleisiau isel trwy'r drws cilagored.

'Be wnei di hefo'r ddwy?' holodd Anti Catrin. 'Eu gadael yma?'

Tynhaodd Bethan ei bysedd am rai Ceren. Roedd arni ofn cael ei gadael yma gydag Anti Catrin. Beth petai rhywbeth yn digwydd i'w thad hefyd?

'E—eisio Mam,' wylodd Ceren yn sydyn isel.

Trodd a chladdu ei hwyneb yn ysgwydd Bethan. Turiodd ei bysedd yn dynn gïaidd i'w braich fel y dechreuodd grio o ddifri.

'R—rydw i e—eisio M—mam!'

'Paid â chrio, Ceren,' meddai Bethan. 'Yli, mi wyliwn ni'r teledu tra bydd Dad yn ffonio.'

Cododd a phwyso'r botwm. Yna eisteddodd wrth ochr ei chwaer a'i gwasgu ati.

'Mi gei di ddewis beth i'w wylio.'

Datgysylltodd Ceren ei hun ac eistedd i fyny ar unwaith. Roedd hi wrth ei bodd yn chwarae â'r teclyn bach rheoli sianelau. Chwaraeodd ei bysedd—un, dau, tri, pedwar—trosto tra cadwai'i llygaid ynghlwm wrth y sgrin.

'Cartŵn, Bethan,' meddai'n fodlon.

Fel arfer, fe fyddai Bethan yn mwynhau cartŵn hefyd. Ond nid heddiw. Ddim â'i thu mewn yn wagle colledus, a hithau'n ceisio ymgodymu hefo'r wybodaeth na welai hi mo'i mam byth eto. Byth!

Dechreuodd trobwll dyfu o'i mewn. *Doedd ei mam ddim yma*! Fyddai hi byth yma eto. Fe ddiflannodd i'r nefoedd bell y soniai Anti Catrin amdani. Ond os oedd yna Iesu Grist a nefoedd, pam roedd yn rhaid iddo ddwyn eu mam a hwythau i gyd ei hangen hi? Gwasgodd Bethan ei dwylo'n ddyrnau fel yr ymladdodd yn erbyn y dagrau a losgai ei llygaid.

Roedd yn rhaid iddi fod yn wrol a chryf. Er mwyn Ceren a Dad. Ond . . . ond doedd hi ddim yn gwybod sut i fod yn wrol a chryf a hithau ar goll y tu mewn.

Ceisiodd glustfeinio i gyfeiriad y lobi, ond roedd sŵn y teledu'n rhwystr.

'Tro fo i lawr, Ceren,' hisiodd.

'Pam?'

'Am fy mod i'n dweud.'

'Nid chdi ydi'r bòs. Mam ydi'r . . .'

Dymchwelodd wyneb Ceren.

'Ble mae Mam?'

Pam na chaeai Ceren ei cheg yn lle arthio ar yr un peth o hyd? Fe deimlai Bethan fel gafael ynddi a'i hysgwyd nes bod ei dannedd yn clecian. Byddai'n eitha gwaith â hi am ofyn cwestiwn mor ddwl. Roedd Mam wedi ... wedi ...

Gwasgodd Ceren ati'n ffyrnig.

'Mae popeth yn ôl-reit, Ceren fach,' meddai.

Ceisiodd wneud ei llais yn feddal gariadus fel y byddai llais ei mam. Ond fedrai hi ddim. Roedd y dagrau'n codi cryndod arno.

Beth oedd Dad yn ei wneud? Pwy oedd o'n ei ffonio? Bygythiai'r dagrau yng nghornel ei llygaid. Ond doedd hi ddim am adael iddyn nhw lifo. Dim ond y hi oedd gan Dad i'w helpu rŵan. Doedd yna neb ond Dad a Ceren a hithau ar ôl, ac mi roedd Ceren yn rhy fach i ddim.

Daeth Anti Catrin i'r lolfa. Agorodd ei cheg i ddweud y drefn wrth weld y llun ar y sgrin, yna gwasgodd ei gwefusau drachefn.

'Peidiwch â throi'r sŵn yn uchel,' gorchmynnodd.

Aeth allan gan gau'r drws yn dynn ofalus ar ei hôl.

Fe deimlai Bethan fel neidio ar ei thraed a dobio'r drws yn ddidrugaredd. Roedd hi eisio bod yn y lobi hefo'i thad. Roedd hi'n dyheu am deimlo cysur ei fraich amdani ac am gael

26

clywed ei lais yn ei sicrhau y byddai popeth yn iawn—mai hunllef oedd y cyfan. A bod Mam yn disgwyl amdanynt yn rhywle. Ond, wrth gwrs, roedd hi'n gwybod nad oedd hynny'n bosibl. Roedd Mam wedi marw.

Daeth sŵn car o'r tu allan. Cododd Bethan i edrych trwy'r ffenestr. Roedd dyn mewn siwt dywyll a golwg galarus ar ei wyneb yn cerdded tua'r drws. Gwgodd Bethan. Pam roedd yn rhaid iddo fo edrych yn alarus? Doedd o ddim wedi colli neb.

Symudodd at ddrws y lolfa a chlustfeiniodd. Clywodd ganiad y gloch ac Anti Catrin yn ei wahodd i'r tŷ. Roedd ei lais yn ddwfn ac yn diferu o gydymdeimlad.

'Profedigaeth sydyn ofnadwy . . . Cydym-deimlad dwys . . . Trefniadau.'

Safodd Bethan yno a'i dwylo ynghlwm. Fe deimlai ar wahân i bopeth. Fel petai hi wedi ei chau mewn cwpwrdd a'r allwedd wedi ei thaflu am byth. Pam na ddeuai rhywun i egluro beth oedd yn digwydd?

'Ddim yn iawn gwrando tu ôl i ddrws,' meddai Ceren. 'Mam yn dweud . . .'

Cwympodd ei hwyneb yn ddagrau eto.

'B-ble mae h-hi, Bethan?'

'Wedi . . . wedi . . .'

Llyncodd Bethan boer heibio i'r lwmp yn ei gwddf. Dydi o ddim yn deg, meddyliodd. Fedra i ddim egluro am nad ydw i'n gwybod y geiriau iawn. Dad ddylai ddweud. Mae o'n gwybod.

Symudodd i eistedd ar y soffa unwaith eto gyda'i chwaer. Rhoddodd ei braich yn dynn amdani.

'Dydi hi ddim yma rŵan, Ceren,' meddai'n ofalus.

'Pam nad ydi hi?'

'Am ei bod hi wedi . . .'

'Ond roedd hi wedi *addo* dŵad i'n nôl ni.'

Oedd, roedd hi wedi addo, meddyliodd Bethan. A phan fyddai ei mam yn addo, fe fyddai hi'n cyflawni hefyd. Ond, fedrwch chi ddim cadw addewid pan ydych chi wedi marw.

Canodd cloch y drws eto a daeth rhagor o leisiau o gyfeiriad y lobi.

'Y pethau bach. Ble maen nhw?'

Fe lanwodd y tŷ hefo pobl yn mynd a dod. Teulu, cymdogion i Anti Catrin, ffrindiau, y gweinidog. Sut roedden nhw i gyd yn gwybod? Roedden nhw'n eistedd ar gadeiriau ac yn yfed te ac yn gwneud wynebau sobr, ac yn siarad yn ddi-ben-draw.

'Ewch i'r gegin, enethod,' gorchmynnodd Anti Catrin gan eu hebrwng yno a pharatoi i gau'r drws arnynt.

'Ond be am Dad?'

'Mae'ch tad yn brysur rŵan. Rho ddiod oren i Ceren, Bethan.'

Gwgodd Bethan. Gwna hyn, gwna'r llall eto.

Rhywbeth i'w chadw hi a Ceren ar eu pennau eu hunain. Agorodd yr oergell yn bwdlyd a thynnu'r paced sudd oren ohoni.

'Hwda.'

Estynnodd wydriad i'w chwaer.

'Pam 'dan ni yn y gegin? Pwy ydi'r bobl 'na?'

Dechreuodd Ceren grio eto.

Daeth Anti Catrin i'r gegin a thebot yn ei llaw. Edrychodd yn graff ar wyneb Ceren a throdd at Bethan.

'Ewch i fyny i'r llofft, 'ych dwy,' gorchmynnodd.

Meddalodd ei llais.

'Mi fydd yn well ichi yn y fan honno.'

Pam mae'n rhaid ein hel ni o un lle i'r llall? meddyliodd Bethan yn wgus. Roedd hi eisio dweud yn blaen wrth Anti Catrin.

'Ein mam ni sydd wedi marw. Mam Ceren a fi. Mae ganddon ni hawl i aros.'

Ond ddaru hi ddim. Gafaelodd yn llaw Ceren a'i harwain i fyny'r grisiau'n ufudd er bod ei thu mewn yn ferw gwyllt.

'Mi fydd Mam yma yn y munud, yn bydd, Bethan?' meddai Ceren a'i llygaid yn llawn dagrau.

'Ddim heddiw,' atebodd hithau.

'Ond rydw i eisio Mam. A Dad.'

Roedd Ceren yn mynnu troi'n ôl ar y grisiau.

'Plîs, Ceren? Tyrd.'

'Na.'

'Plîs?'

Ceisiodd Bethan gofio sut y byddai'i mam yn perswadio Ceren. Cyfrif gyda hi, 'tê? Cyfrif a chanu,

'Un dau tri
I ffwrdd â ni,
Gris i chdi
A gris i mi.'

Gwenodd Ceren ar unwaith.

'Eto, Bethan. Eto.'

'Tyrd. Mi orweddwn ni ar y gwely ac edrych ar lyfr Twm Tomato wedyn.'

Ymhen hir a hwyr, fe ddistawodd popeth i lawr y grisiau. Roedd Ceren yn hanner cysgu erbyn hyn a llyfr Twm Tomato yn babell bigfain ar ei brest.

Symudodd Bethan ei braich yn araf rhag ofn iddi ddeffro, a brathodd ei gwefusau wrth deimlo'r pinnau bach yn ei bysedd. Rhwbiodd nhw i leddfu'r boen a chododd yn ddistaw. Agorodd y drws a cherddodd trwodd i'r landin. Edrychodd tros y canllaw.

Safai ei thad yn y lobi. Roedd yn pwyso yn erbyn y wal a golwg ddigalon arno.

'Dad!' galwodd Bethan gan gadw'i llais yn isel rhag deffro Ceren.

Brysiodd i lawr y grisiau a'i thaflu ei hun i'w freichiau. Gwasgodd yntau hi ato heb ddweud gair. Safasant yno am eiliadau hir.

Yna, fe'i daliodd oddi wrtho.

'Rhaid imi fynd yn ôl adre,' meddai. 'Mae llawer o bethau i'w trefnu eto, Bethan.'

'Mae'n cesys ni'n barod.'

Ysgydwodd ei thad ei ben a thynhaodd ei fysedd ar ei hysgwyddau.

'Rhaid ichi aros yma hefo Anti Catrin, Bethan. Rydw i'n dibynnu arnat ti i edrych ar ôl Ceren. Mae hi'n fach, a fedra inna ddim . . .'

Tyfodd ofn yng nghalon Bethan.

'Ond fydd dim rhaid inni aros yma am *byth*, yn na fydd? Ddim hefo Anti Catrin? Fedrwn ni ddim.'

Ddywedodd ei thad yr un gair.

'DAD!' erfyniodd hithau a phanig yn tyfu o'i mewn. Doedd o 'rioed am eu gadael yma am byth?

Daeth llais Anti Catrin o'r tu ôl iddynt.

'Paid â phoeni dy dad rŵan, Bethan. Mae ganddo ddigon i'w wneud.'

'Rwyt ti *yn* deall, on'd wyt ti?' meddai Dad. 'Mae'n well ichi yma hefo Anti Catrin.'

Dychwelodd y lwmp anferth i wddf Bethan. Roedd eu tad am gefnu arni hi a Ceren. Doedd o ddim eisio nhw wedi i Mam farw.

4.

Roedd meinciau hir yr amlosgfa yn oer i eistedd arnynt. Eisteddai Anti Catrin yn gefnsyth un ochr iddi, a'i thad yn wargam yr ochr arall. Ond rywsut, roedd hi, Bethan, ar ei phen ei hun.

Oedd, roedd hi'n teimlo caledwch oeraidd y fainc oddi tani ac roedd hi'n ymwybodol o Anti Catrin a'i thad o boptu iddi hefyd. Ond breuddwyd hunllefus oedd y cyfan. Breuddwyd y byddai'n siŵr o ddeffro ohono'n fuan.

Sut y gallai ei mam fod mewn bocs hir ar allor amlosgfa, a hithau'n ei gweld o flaen ei llygaid y funud 'ma? Yn ei chofio'n fyrlymus hapus fel y soniai am yr estyniad newydd ac am ddewis papur a phaent, a dodrefn a llenni. *Fedrai*'r hunllef ddim bod yn wir. Yn na fedrai?

'*Ein chwaer annwyl . . . ym mlodau ei dyddiau . . . mor frawychus o sydyn . . .*'

Roedd rhywun yn crio'n ddistaw y tu ôl iddi, ac Anti Catrin yn dal ei hances yn glòs wrth ei cheg. Edrychodd Bethan ar ei thad. Roedd o'n edrych i lawr ar ei ddwylo ac yn plethu ac ailblethu ei fysedd. Ac roedd deigryn unig yn powlio'i ffordd i lawr ei wyneb.

Fe deimlai Bethan fel crio hefyd, rywle yn ddwfn yng nghyfeiriad ei stumog. Ond fedrai hi ddim. Ddim heb weiddi sgrechian.

Gafaelodd ei thad yn dynn yn ei llaw fel y

swniodd yr organ yn deimladwy dawel. Cododd yn anystwyth a'i thynnu hithau ar ei thraed hefyd. Tynhaodd ei fysedd ar ei ffon fel y daeth siffrwd dillad o'r meinciau y tu ôl iddynt, a thwrw traed ar y llawr blociau sglein.

Beth oedd yn digwydd? Arweiniodd ei thad hi'n araf at yr allor. Fe wyddai oddi wrth ei wyneb fod ei gefn a'i goes yn brifo. Safodd gyda hi i edrych ar yr arch dderw a'r dorch flodau a oedd yn drwch lliwgar arni. Roedd ysgrifen ar y plât arian. Enw ei mam. Elisabeth Rees. Sefydlodd ei llygaid arno, ond doedd yr enw'n golygu dim iddi. Mam oedd Mam, nid yr Elisabeth Rees 'na a'i henw ar focs.

Ochneidiodd ei thad.

'Tyrd, Bethan,' meddai'n ddistaw.

Cerddodd Bethan yn ufudd gydag ef tua'r coridor. Roedd blodau yno hefyd. Torch ar ôl torch ohonyn nhw yn forder lliwgar ar y llawr. Ac roedd yno ddau lyfr mawr agored ar fwrdd, ac enwau pobl wedi marw ar y tudalennau agored. Yno y byddai Mam hefyd.

Anadlodd Bethan yn ddwfn wedi cyrraedd yr ardd y tu allan. Roedd arogl ysgafn blodau ar yr aer. Roedd hi'n falch o adael awyrgylch yr amlosgfa, ond doedd hi ddim eisio gadael ei mam yno chwaith.

Gwelodd y bocs unig a'i dorch flodau o flaen ei llygaid unwaith eto. Edrychodd ar ei thad. Fe ddiflannodd y deigryn, ond roedd ei lygaid yn goch llaith, a phwysai yn drymach ar ei ffon.

'Gadael y fechan gartre wnaethoch chi? Dyna oedd orau, yntê?' meddai rhywun.

Ceren? Roedd Bethan wedi anghofio am Ceren. Am beth roedd hi'n meddwl y funud yma, tybed? Oedd hi'n hiraethu am Mam, ynteu oedd hi'n chwarae'n ddi-hid hefo cath Mrs Jones?

Roedd torf o bobl yn crynhoi o'u cwmpas, a phob un yn estyn llaw ac yn cydymdeimlo. Roedden nhw'n ysgwyd eu pennau ac yn edrych yn sobr, ac yn siarad mewn lleisiau isel.

'Mae'n ddrwg iawn gen i . . .'

'Mae'n ddrwg iawn gen i . . .'

Roedd lwmp ofnadwy yn tyfu yn ei gwddf. Pam nad âi'r bobl yma adre?

'Ydych chi rywfaint esmwythach, Huw?'

Teimlodd Bethan yn ddig am eiliad. Pam roedd yn rhaid holi am gyflwr ei thad, a Mam wedi marw? Sut y gallai un ddod trwy ddamwain yn holliach bron—ac un arall ddim? Efallai mai ar ei thad roedd y bai.

Safai Anti Catrin ychydig oddi wrthi. Roedd hi'n siarad hefo perthynas pell iddyn nhw. Anti Dwynwen. Honno fyddai'n anfon cerdyn Nadolig a thocyn llyfr i Ceren a hithau bob blwyddyn.

Llifodd eu geiriau tuag ati.

'Wn i ddim be wnaiff Huw, wir,' meddai Anti Catrin. 'Rhaid iddo drefnu am y tymor nesa yn y coleg. Ac mae ganddo daith ddarlithio yn Ffrainc a'r Almaen ymhen pythefnos. Rydw i wedi cynnig cymryd y genethod, wrth gwrs.'

Byw hefo Anti Catrin? O, na! Sut y gallai ei thad gydsynio? Dad a hi a Ceren oedd yn deulu bellach. Doedden nhw ddim eisio neb arall.

Trodd ato'n fyrbwyll.

'Dad . . .'

Ond roedd ei thad yn dal i siarad ac ysgwyd llaw.

'Dad . . .'

Doedd dim ots ganddo. Roedd o'n rhy brysur yn derbyn cydymdeimlad yr wynebau sobr a edrychai mor gyfoglyd o deimladwy ar y ddau ohonyn nhw. Fedrai hi ddim stumogi rhagor. Trodd i redeg oddi wrthynt.

'Bethan!'

Roedd hi'n gwybod fod ei thad yn galw arni, ac Anti Catrin hefyd. Ond doedd dim ots. Roedd yn rhaid iddi fod ar ei phen ei hun yn rhywle, a hynny'n ddigon pell oddi wrth y llygaid caredig a'r lleisiau pitïo di-ben-draw. A doedd hi ddim am fynd at Anti Catrin, waeth beth ddyfarnai ei thad.

Rhedodd nes cyrraedd muriau sgwâr yng nghornel yr ardd. Roedd giât yn y wal. Agorodd hi'n ffrwcslyd a'i chael ei hun mewn cilan ddistaw. Syllodd ar y placiau bychain a oedd yn frith ar y muriau. Enwau . . . enwau . . . enwau. Pob un hefo'i ddyddiad geni a'i ddydd-

iad marw. Fedrai hi ddim dianc oddi wrth enwau oeraidd, marw.

Gwasgodd ei hewinedd yn gïaidd i gledrau'i dwylo fel y ceisiodd leddfu'r boen a dyfai o'i mewn. Un o'r enwau yma fyddai ei mam bellach. A doedd hynny ddim yn deg. Nid enw oedd Mam. Mam oedd hi. Mam fyw a arferai chwerthin a jocian a smwddio a golchi llestri, a swnian arni hi a Ceren i dacluso'u llofft a helpu yn y tŷ.

Agorodd y giât eto. Safai ei thad yno.

'Bethan,' meddai. 'Mae'n rhaid inni fynd.'

Edrychodd y ddau ar ei gilydd.

'Pam, Dad?' holodd Bethan. 'Pam roedd yn rhaid i Mam farw?'

Ochneidiodd ei thad, ac edrych arni a'i wyneb yn llawn loes.

'Wn i ddim, Bethan,' meddai'n drymaidd. 'Wn i ddim.'

'Fydd dim rhaid i Ceren a fi fyw hefo Anti Catrin, yn na fydd?' holodd Bethan.

Caeodd ei thad ei lygaid yn boenus.

'Efallai mai dyna fydd orau inni i gyd,' meddai.

'Ond mi ofala i am bopeth yn y tŷ,' addawodd Bethan. 'Am goginio a llnau a phopeth. Ond, plîs, dydw i ddim eisio byw hefo Anti Catrin. A dydi Ceren ddim chwaith.'

Nid atebodd ei thad am eiliadau hir.

'Mi gawn ni weld,' meddai o'r diwedd.

Teimlai Bethan weddill ei byd cyfarwydd yn llithro ymhellach o'i gafael. Doedd ei thad ddim eisio hi a Ceren wedi i'w mam farw. Llifodd atgasedd sydyn trwyddi. Mam ddylai fod yma'n fyw, nid ei thad. Fyddai hi byth wedi eu gadael hefo Anti Catrin.

Pigodd dagrau y tu ôl i'w llygaid. Nid un rhiant oedd hi'i eisio, ond dau. Roedd hi eisio dianc yn ôl i'r amser cyffyrddus clòs hwnnw pan oedden nhw'n deulu hapus gyda'i gilydd. Mam a Dad a Ceren a hithau. Ond fedrai hi ddim, yn na fedrai?

'Dydi o ddim yn deg,' meddai'i thad. 'Pam Mam?'

'Na, dydi o ddim yn deg,' meddai'i thad. 'Ond cofia di pa mor hapus fyddai dy fam bob amser. Cofia pa mor hapus oedden ni i gyd. Mae hynny'n rhywbeth i'w gofio am byth, Bethan.'

Rhoes ei thad ei fraich am ei hysgwydd a'i harwain trwy'r giât. Cerddodd y ddau'n araf am y car. Fe ddisgwyliai Anti Catrin yn y sedd ôl. Dringodd Bethan i mewn ati, ond wnaeth hi ddim edrych arni. Plygodd ei hun yn fychan bach yn y gornel a syllodd trwy'r ffenestr heb ddweud gair.

Roedd y car yn ddu a moethus. Eisteddai'r gyrrwr yn ddistaw barchus y tu ôl i'r llyw a'i thad wrth ei ochr. Doedd neb yn dweud dim.

Crynodd gwefus Bethan. Brathodd arni'n

ffyrnig ond ni allai atal y cryndod. Yna teimlodd fraich Anti Catrin yn ei thynnu ati.

'Cria di, 'mach i,' sibrydodd. 'Mi deimli'n
well wedyn.'

Ymlaciodd Bethan yn erbyn y siaced ddu a
gadawodd i'w dagrau ei sgubo ymaith. Roedd
cysur yng nghynhesrwydd y fraich amdani ac
yn yr hances a estynnodd ei modryb iddi.

Yn fuan cyraeddasant dŷ Anti Catrin. Safai
ceir yn y dreif ac yn y stryd hefyd. Fe wyddai
Bethan fod yr un bobl yno'n disgwyl. Fe
fyddent yn yfed te a gwledda ar frechdanau
ham a theisennau bach. Llygaid a dannedd a
dwylo'n cyrraedd am ragor i'w fwyta fel petaen
nhw wedi anghofio'r amlosgfa a'r bocs hir ac
enw Mam arno fo. A fedrai hi ddim dioddef
hynny.

Trodd am y grisiau.

'Rydw i'n mynd i'r llofft,' meddai mewn llais
a heriai ei thad a'i modryb i ddweud gair yn
groes.

'Bethan . . .'

Estynnodd ei thad ei fraich i afael ynddi. Ond
roedd hi wedi cael digon ar bopeth. Ar
wynebau a lleisiau a llygaid tosturiol. A digon
ar ei thad ac Anti Catrin hefyd.

Carlamodd i fyny'r grisiau a chau drws y
llofft â chlep. Pwysodd ei chefn arno a'i llygaid
yn ddagrau llosg. Mam! O! Mam! Pam na
fuasech chi yma o hyd?

Ysgydwodd ei phen yn ffyrnig a symudodd i syllu arni'i hun yn nrych y bwrdd gwisgo. Doedd hi ddim yn adnabod yr eneth a syllai'n ôl arni. Geneth amddifad hefo wyneb llwyd a llygaid yn llawn dagrau. Ond Bethan Rees oedd hi'r un fath.

5.

Wnaeth ei thad ddim aros. Doedd o ddim yn caru Ceren a hithau ddigon i aros, dyna pam. Llithrodd Bethan yn is o dan y cynfasau a gadael i'r chwerwder lifo'n don trosti. Petai o'n eu caru, fel y byddai Mam yn eu caru, fyddai o ddim wedi'u gadael, yn na fyddai? Esgusion oedd ei eiriau.

'Rhaid ichi aros yma am ychydig, Bethan. Tria ddallt. Mae'n well i bawb fel hyn. Mi faswn i'n poeni petaech chi gartre ar eich pen eich hunain. Mae'n rhaid imi fynd 'nôl a blaen i'r coleg ar adegau, ysti.'

'Ond mi fedra i wneud pope . . .'

Pa iws siarad hefo rhywun a oedd wedi penderfynu peidio â gwrando? Roedd fel petai'n ei thaflu ei hun yn erbyn wal frics a honno'n ildio dim.

Ystwyriodd Ceren yn aflonydd o dan y cynfasau, a throdd i'w thurio'i hun yn glòs wrth gorff Bethan. Estynnodd hithau i'w thynnu ati. Fe ofalai hi na châi Ceren gam, addawodd yn ffyrnig.

Ond, wrth gwrs, doedd hi a Ceren ddim am aros yma. Ddim ond nes y deuai ei thad unwaith eto. Fe fyddai hi'n siŵr o'i berswadio, fe'i cysurodd ei hun. Gartref hefo'i gilydd y dylen nhw'u tri fod.

Teimlodd wresogrwydd cysglyd ei chwaer fach yn dynn wrth ei hochr, ac er ei bod hi'n berffaith sicr na chysgai hi'r un winc, **fe** lithrodd i gwsg annifyr lle'r oedd damwein**iau** a cholled yn un hunllef bendramwnwgl.

Anti Catrin a'i deffrodd fore trannoeth. Am eiliad gorweddodd Bethan yno'n swrth a'i llygaid yn crwydro'n ddioglyd o gwmpas yr ystafell wely. Roedden nhw'n mynd adre heddiw, on'd oedden? Adre i weld yr estyniad newydd, ac i edmygu'r papur wal a'r dodrefn a ddewisodd hi a Mam.

Mam! Llonyddodd ei chalon. Sut y gallai hi anghofio am *un* eiliad? Doedd Mam ddim yma. Fyddai hi byth yma eto. Llanwodd ei llygaid â dagrau llosg.

'Helpa Ceren i molchi, wnei di?'

Rhoes Anti Catrin law ysgafn ar ei hysg-wydd, ond roedd ei llais mor ddiddychymyg ag arfer. Llais dideimlad, heb falio fod Mam wedi marw.

'Ga i fynd i chwarae hefo Solomon eto heddiw?' holodd Ceren gan neidio ar ei heistedd.

'Solomon?'

Edrychodd Bethan arni am funud. Yna cofiodd yn sur. Cath Mrs Jones drws nesa, yntê? Dyna ddangos nad oedd ots gan Ceren am eu mam chwaith. Roedd fel petai pawb wedi cau drws ar y golled ac am fyw bywyd normal doed a ddelo. Roedd hi'n casáu pob un ohonyn nhw. Anti Catrin a Dad a Ceren. Doedd ganddyn nhw ddim hawl i anghofio.

Llygadodd ei chwaer fach yn flin.

'Cod,' gorchmynnodd gan daflu'r cynfasau o'r neilltu.

Am unwaith fe ufuddhaodd Ceren heb gwyno. Am ei bod hi ar dân eisio chwarae hefo Solomon, meddyliodd Bethan yn chwerw.

'Solomon am chwarae hefo fy mhêl fach goch i heddiw,' meddai Ceren. 'Mae o'n rhedeg ar ôl llinyn, ac yn cnoi a phaffio hefo fo wedyn. Mae 'na *hwyl* i'w gael wrth chwarae hefo Solomon, Bethan.'

Gwasgodd Bethan y cadach ymolchi a rhoes sgrwb cïaidd i wyneb ei chwaer. Y bitsh fach ddi-hid iddi.

'Saf yn llonydd, wnei di,' meddai rhwng ei dannedd. 'Sut y medra i dy molchi di, a chdithau'n gwingo?'

'Aawww! Mi ddeuda i wrth Mam ...' cwynodd Ceren.

Rhewodd ei cheg ar agor.

'Mam. Ble m-mae hi, Betha-an?'

Toddodd calon Bethan yn syth. Nid wedi anghofio roedd Ceren, wrth gwrs. Rhy fychan oedd hi, yntê? Cyrcydodd a'i thynnu ati. Claddodd ei hwyneb yn ei gwddf.

'Dydi hi ddim yma rŵan, Ceren.'

'Ond mi *ddaw* hi yma, yn daw?'

Sut y gallai hi ateb ei chwaer fach? Cofleidiodd hi eto. Yna cododd ar ei thraed gan geisio gwneud ei llais mor ddiddychymyg â llais Anti Catrin gynnau.

'Tyrd. Mi awn ni i lawr i frecwast. Mi fydd Solomon yn disgwyl amdanat ti.'

Gwenodd Ceren yn hapus.

'Fydd o, Bethan? Am y bêl goch hefyd?'

Brysiodd i lawr y grisiau. Dilynodd Bethan hi'n araf. Roedd y diwrnod yn ymestyn yn wagedd hir o'i blaen, a'r lwmp enfawr yn llenwi'i gwddf unwaith eto.

Fe wyddai fod Anti Catrin yn edrych arni fel yr eisteddai wrth y bwrdd brecwast. Ond doedd hi ddim am gyfarfod ei llygaid. Peth preifat oedd galar. Rhywbeth rhyngddi hi a'i thad a Ceren.

'Gymeri di dôst a marmalêd ar ôl dy rawnfwyd?'

Tybed oedd llais Anti Catrin yn feddalach nag arfer? Na, dychmygu wnaeth hi.

'Dim diolch.'

Roedd meddwl am fwyta'n ei thagu'n gorn. Edrychodd i lawr ar ei phlât. Wyneb ei mam a welai ynddo. Neidiodd ar ei thraed. Fedrai hi ddim aros yno eiliad rhagor.

'Dydw i ddim eisio . . .'

Rhuthrodd am ddrws y ffrynt a ffrwydrodd allan i'r dreif. Roedd yn rhaid iddi ddianc. Dianc ymhell bell oddi wrth Anti Catrin a Ceren ac absenoldeb ei thad.

'Bethan! Ble'r wyt ti'n . . . ?'

Ond ni chymerodd arni glywed. Rhedodd i lawr y dreif ac allan i'r stryd. Syllodd i'r chwith a'r dde gan fethu penderfynu ble i ddianc. Ond pa ots? Fe wnâi rhywle y tro. Anelodd am y parc ar frys gwyllt. Fyddai fawr neb yno yn y bore fel hyn. Dim mamau a choetsys, na phlant yn rhedeg a sgrechian chwarae o gwmpas y llyn. Dim ond tawelwch.

Trodd i mewn trwy'r giatiau a rhedodd ar hyd y llwybr. Dim ots i ble, dim ond iddi gael dianc oddi wrth bopeth. Brathai ei hanadl yn ei hysgyfaint, ond wnaeth hi ddim arafu. Roedd ei llygaid yn llawn dagrau, yn byrlymu'n gawod i lawr ei hwyneb.

Cyrhaeddodd y rhododendron a dyfai'n fur ym mhen pellaf y parc. Safodd am eiliad wedi'u cyrraedd gan ymladd am ei hanadl. Edrychodd yn ôl. Doedd neb i'w weld yn unman. Llonydd-wch. Heb neb na dim i amharu arno. Ymwth-iodd ei ffordd rhwng y perthi trwchus, a'i chanfod ei hun mewn cilan fechan gudd y tu ôl iddynt.

Gordyfai'r glaswellt yn sypiau heglog o dan ei thraed a chaeai'r perthi'n fur y tu ôl iddi, gan adael dim ond clwtyn o awyr las, berffaith ymhell uwchben. Ochneidiodd, a suddodd yn ddiolchgar i'r llawr. Caeodd ei llygaid tra treiglodd dagrau araf i lawr ei hwyneb.

Clywodd sŵn llechwraidd ychydig ar y chwith iddi. Agorodd ei llygaid a throi ei phen i syllu i'w gyfeiriad. Beth oedd yna? Llamodd ei chalon yn sydyn. Roedd hi'n siŵr fod rhywun yn edrych arni. Cofiodd am yr holl storïau brawychus oedd yn cael eu hadrodd ar y teledu ac yn y papurau newydd, a dringodd cryndod oeraidd i fyny'i hasgwrn cefn. Neidiodd ar ei thraed.

Crwydrodd llygaid Bethan yn wyllt tros y cysgodion a thynhaodd bodiau ei thraed yn ei hesgidiau fel y paratôdd i ddianc.

'Pwy sy 'na?'

'Fi.'

Ysgydwodd y brigau'n swnllyd wrth iddynt gael eu gwahanu. Ymlaciodd Bethan. Yr eneth honno a wenodd arni droeon ar y stryd oedd yno.

Edrychodd yr eneth arni o gil ei llygad a gwenodd.

'Beth wyt ti'n ei wneud yma?'

'O . . .'

Llifodd atgof yn don tros Bethan, a throdd i ffwrdd rhag i'r eneth ganfod ei bod hi'n crio.

'Wedi cael ffrae wyt ti?'

Ysgydwodd Bethan ei phen heb droi'n ôl.

Symudodd yr eneth i'w hwynebu.

'Hynna (gwnaeth arwydd dau fys) iddyn nhw ddeuda i.'

'Pwy?'

'Oedolion. Tadau. Malio dim ond am eu busnes eu hunain.'

Llyncodd Bethan. Un felly oedd ei thad hithau hefyd. Teimlai fel ffrwydro fel y tyfodd yr atgasedd ynddi. Fe adawodd Dad Ceren a hithau. A doedd o'n malio am ddim ond am ei bethau ei hun. Yr eneth yma oedd yn iawn. *Hynna* iddyn nhw i gyd!

Gollyngodd yr eneth ei hun rywsut rywsut ar y glaswellt.

'Mi fydda i'n dŵad yma o hyd, ysti. Pan fydd pethau'n ormod gartre.'

'Fyddi di?'

Nodiodd yr eneth gan dynnu glaswelltyn a'i gnoi'n synfyfyriol.

'Bydda. Be 'di dy enw di?'

'Bethan.'

'Mari ydw i. Byw yn y tai 'na y tu cefn i'r arch-farchnad.'

Edrychodd y ddwy ar ei gilydd am eiliadau hir.

'Faint ydi dy oed di?' holodd Mari o'r diwedd.

'Deuddeg.'

'A finna.'

Llygadodd Mari jîns a chrys chwys Bethan.

'Ti'n byw yn y rhan posh o'r dre, debyg.'

'Aros hefo Anti Catrin,' eglurodd Bethan.

'Honno welais i hefo ti? Trwyn yn yr awyr ac yn pletio'i cheg fel petai hi am ei wnïo fo. Snob.'

Gwenodd Bethan ar ei gwaethaf. Roedd Anti Catrin *yn* pletio'i cheg pan nad oedd rhywbeth yn ei phlesio.

'Pam wyt ti'n aros hefo hi? Gwyliau?'

Llifodd tristwch tros Bethan eto. Agorodd ei cheg i egluro, ond fedrai hi ddim dweud yr un gair. Dim ond agor a chau'i cheg a theimlo'r dagrau'n llifo'n afon i lawr ei hwyneb.

'Mam . . . wedi . . .'

Gwrthodai ei thafod siapio'r geiriau.

'Mam . . . wedi . . . wedi . . .'

'Wedi mynd? Fy mam inna hefyd. Cymryd y goes hefo'i chariad. Gwynt teg ar ei hôl hi ddeuda i. Doedd hi'n malio dim amdana i, a dydw inna'n malio dim amdani hitha. Malio dim am *neb*, yli.'

Roedd golwg styfnig ar wyneb Mari.

47

'Nid ... mynd. Marw,' meddai Bethan a'i gwefusau'n crynu. 'Ac mae Dad am inni aros hefo Anti Catrin. Y fi a fy chwaer fach.'

Rhwbiodd ei hwyneb i geisio atal y dagrau.

'Hwda.'

Estynnodd Mari hances iddi.

'Chwytha dy drwyn hefo honna. Sori am holi, 'tê.'

Eisteddodd y ddwy heb ddweud gair ymhellach a'u meddyliau ymhell.

'Mae gen i le dirgel,' meddai Mari o'r diwedd. 'Rhywle i fynd pan fydd Dad yn mynd trwy'i bethau.'

Ciledrychodd ar Bethan.

'Os lici di, mi ddangosa i iti. Ond iti addo peidio â dweud wrth neb.'

'Ôl-reit.'

Neidiodd Mari ar ei thraed.

'Tyrd, ta,' gorchmynnodd yn swta.

Dilynodd Bethan hi'n ddyfnach i'r llwyni rhododendron, ac ymlaen trwy ffens fratiog i ddryswch gardd a orchuddiwyd bron i gyd gan lwyni drain a mieri. Safai sgerbwd hen dŷ wedi mynd â'i ben iddo ym mhen draw'r ardd. Anwybyddodd Mari'r hen dŷ, a throdd i'r dde cyn diflannu i lawr ochr serth.

'Gwylia syrthio.'

Llithrodd a chrafangiodd Bethan yn wyliadwrus wrth ei sodlau. Teimlodd fiaren yn cydio yn ei jîns a gwyddai fod bachiad ynddynt. Ond doedd dim ots beth ddywedai Anti Catrin. Ei jîns hi oedden nhw. Jîns a brynodd Mam iddi. Daeth yr un hen lwmp i'w gwddf eto, ac ymladdodd yn erbyn y dagrau a fynnai lenwi'i llygaid.

'Dyma ni.'

Roedd llais Mari rywle islaw iddi. Edrychodd i lawr a'i chanfod yn sefyll ger hen sièd a orchuddiwyd gan eiddew trwchus.

'Fan'ma?'

'Ia. Tyrd i mewn.'

Gwthiodd Mari y drws ar agor a chamodd i'r hanner gwyll y tu mewn. Trodd i wylio wyneb Bethan.

'Grêt, 'tê?'

Lledaenodd llygaid Bethan fel yr edrychodd o gwmpas. Roedd nifer o gelfi yno. Hen fag cysgu, cadair a bricsen o dan un goes iddi, bwrdd chwarae cardiau a'i wyneb gwyrdd yn llwydni byw, a phwt o garped wedi hen weld ei ddyddiau gwell.

Ysgubodd Mari sbecyn o lwch oddi ar wyneb y bwrdd cardiau â'i llaw ac edrychodd **ar** Bethan yn fodlon.

'Grêt, 'tê?' meddai eto gan ei gollwng ei hun ar y llawr llychlyd. 'Neb ond y fi'n gwybod amdani. A chdi rŵan, wrth gwrs.' Pwyntiodd at y gadair. 'Gosod dy ben-ôl ar honna. Ond bydd yn ofalus. Coesau simsan ganddi.'

Pwysodd yn erbyn y wal a thynnu'i choesau ati.

'Mi fedrwn ni gyfarfod yma pryd bynnag hoffet ti,' cynigiodd.

Eisteddodd Bethan heb ddweud gair, a'i llygaid ar wyrddni'r eiddew a fygai'r ffenestr. Roedd yr hen sièd a'i thrugareddau bregus yr union le yr oedd hi'i eisio. Rhywle i ddianc. Rhywle i wfftio a chasáu pobl nad oedd wahaniaeth ganddyn nhw am farwolaeth ei mam. Dad a Ceren ac Anti Catrin.

Fe fedrai ei dychmygu ei hun yn eistedd yma am oriau.

'Be ti'n 'i ddweud? Cytuno?' holodd Mari.

'Iawn.'

'Beth am fory, ta? Yn y bore?'

'Ia.'

Dim ots beth ddywedai Anti Catrin. Fe fyddai hi'n siŵr o ddianc yma.

Edrychodd ar ei wats, a phigodd ei chydwybod hi. Roedd hi wedi rhedeg o'r tŷ ers amser brecwast. Fe fyddai Anti Catrin yn siŵr o boeni, er nad oedd ganddi hawl i ddweud dim. Efallai y byddai'n well iddi fynd yn ôl, a rhoi ar ddeall i Anti Catrin ei bod hi am gael rhyddid, nid carchar. A fyddai hi ddim yma'n hir, p'run bynnag. Fe fyddai hi a Ceren yn mynd adref yn fuan. Croesodd ei bysedd.

Llusgodd Mari y drws ar gau'n ofalus. Dilynodd Bethan hi i fyny'r llethr a thrwy'r ffens i ganol y llwyni rhododendrons.

'Aros eiliad,' meddai Mari. 'Dydyn ni ddim eisio i neb ein gweld ni'n dŵad allan, yn nac oes?'

Gwahanodd y brigau'n ddistaw a chraffu i'r chwith a'r dde.

'Neb,' cyhoeddodd.

Camodd y ddwy allan a cherdded yn fud am giatiau'r parc. Ciledrychodd Mari ar Bethan unwaith neu ddwy, ond fe welai oddi wrth ei hwyneb nad oedd am ddweud gair.

'Wela i di,' meddai'n ddidaro cyn troi ar y chwith a brysio ymaith.

'Iawn,' atebodd Bethan.

Trodd hithau i'r dde. Tynhaodd ei thu mewn fel y cofiodd am Anti Catrin. Byddai'n rhaid iddi ei hwynebu rŵan, ac ymddiheuro efallai. Ond doedd hi ddim yn edifar chwaith.

Dechreuodd ei stumog rwmblan fel y cofiodd na fwytaodd damaid o frecwast. Prysurodd ei chamau fel y trodd i'r dreif, yna arafodd nhw drachefn. Roedd Anti Catrin yn disgwyl ar stepan y drws.

6.

'Ble buost ti?'

Roedd y cwestiwn moel yn crogi rhyngddynt fel y safodd y ddwy wyneb yn wyneb o flaen y drws.

'Allan.'

'Allan ymhle?'

'Jest, allan.'

'Wyt ti ddim yn meddwl fy mod inna'n poeni?'

Dringodd y gwrid i wyneb Bethan. Roedd hi'n gwybod na ddylai hi fod wedi dianc fel yna, na diflannu am oriau chwaith. Ond doedd Anti Catrin ddim yn deall. Doedd neb yn deall. Gwgodd.

'Eisio llonydd.'

Meddalodd wyneb Anti Catrin ychydig, ac estynnodd ei llaw i afael yn ysgwydd Bethan.

'Rydw i'n gwybod fod rŵan yn amser anodd iti, Bethan. Mae'n anodd inni i gyd.'

Roedd Bethan eisio gweiddi'n ôl arni. Beth oedd hi'n ei ddeall am ddim? A pha amser anodd oedd o i Anti Catrin? Doedd hi ddim wedi colli'i mam.

'Tyrd. Mi anghofiwn ni am y bore 'ma. Ond rhaid iti beidio â diflannu heb eglurhad eto. Wyt ti'n dallt?'

Tynhaodd dyrnau Bethan, ond ddywedodd hi'r un gair. Fe gâi Anti Catrin weld. Doedd hi ddim am gymryd ei chaethiwo jest am fod Dad yn gwrthod mynd â nhw adre.

'Tyrd i'r tŷ rŵan. Mae'n siŵr dy fod ti eisio cinio.'

Roedd llaw Anti Catrin yn dal ar ei hysgwydd a'i llais yn rhesymol gyfeillgar. Ond doedd Bethan ddim yn teimlo'n gyfeillgar. Na, roedd hi'n teimlo'n ferw gwyllt o'i mewn.

Roedd Ceren yn eistedd ar y soffa. Roedd y teclyn bach rheoli'r teledu yn ei llaw a ffilm ar y sgrin. Gwenodd pan welodd Bethan.

'Fi a Solomon wedi chwarae,' meddai. 'Mae o wedi blino rŵan. Wnei di chwarae hefo mi ar ôl cinio, Bethan? Dweud stori? Jest nes bydd Solomon wedi deffro.'

Hy! Diolch yn fawr am ddim, meddyliodd Bethan. Rydw i'n ail i gath rŵan. Braint. Eisteddodd wrth ochr Ceren a cheisio magu diddordeb yn y sgrin. Criw o blant yn mynd ar wyliau hefo'u rhieni oedd yna. A geneth yn helpu'i mam i bacio. Teimlodd ei chyhyrau'n tynhau a'r un hen lwmp yn ei gwddf.

'Gwylio lol,' meddai gan gythru'r teclyn rheoli o law Ceren a'i ddiffodd.

Dechreuodd Ceren grio ar unwaith.

'Anti Catrin! Bethan wedi'i ddiffodd o. Tyrd â fo'n ôl. Does gen ti ddim hawl.'

Roedd Bethan eisio dyrnu'r soffa yn ei rhwystredigaeth. Doedd Ceren yn teimlo dim wrth weld mam i deulu hapus ar y sgrin?

Doedd hi ddim yn teimlo'r golled ofnadwy yn cnoi o'i mewn?

'O, hwda'r swnan,' meddai'n ddiamynedd gan daflu'r teclyn ati.

'Dyna ddigon, Bethan. Rydw i'n synnu atat ti,' meddai Anti Catrin o ddrws y lolfa. 'A dowch am ginio rŵan cyn iddo fo oeri.'

Diflannodd i gyfeiriad y gegin.

'Tyrd yn dy flaen,' gorchmynnodd Bethan yn ddiflas.

Safodd i ddisgwyl i Ceren ufuddhau. Ond roedd Ceren yn eistedd yno heb symud. Roedd ei phen i lawr a'i gwallt melyn yn cuddio'i hwyneb.

'Fyddwn ni'n byw yma rŵan, Bethan?' holodd mewn llais bychan bach. 'Am byth?'

'Na fyddwn siŵr,' meddai Bethan yn bendant. 'Mi fyddwn ni'n mynd adre toc, mi gei di weld. Wedi i Dad ddŵad.'

'O, Bethan!'

Yn sydyn fe hyrddiodd Ceren ei hun oddi ar y soffa i afael yn dynn yn ei chwaer.

'Ddim eisio aros. Eisio mynd adra at Mam a Dad.'

'Ond mae Mam . . .'

Ni allai Bethan fynd ymlaen. Oedd Ceren byth yn deall fod Mam wedi marw? Ac na ddeuai hi byth yn ôl? Teimlai dan bwysau wrth geisio egluro pethau i'w chwaer fach.

'Mae Mam wedi'n gadael ni, Ceren. Wedi cael damwain ac wedi brifo. Lot.'

Yna fe gofiodd am eiriau Anti Catrin.

'Mae hi wedi mynd at Iesu Grist. I'r nefoedd.'

'Pam oedd hi eisio mynd i fan'no? Mae o'n bell.'

'Ydi.'

'Rhy bell i ddŵad yn ôl?'

'Ydi.'

Gwasgodd Ceren ei breichiau am gorff Bethan.

'Gawn ni fynd adre'r un fath?'

'Cawn.'

Ystyriodd Ceren am ychydig.

'O!' meddai.

Yna,

'Rydw i eisio bwyd rŵan.'

Trodd am y gegin fel pe na bai dim yn bod. Dilynodd Bethan hi'n araf. Roedd wyau wedi'u sgramblo'n eu disgwyl ac Anti Catrin yn tywallt sudd oren i wydr Ceren.

'Mam wedi mynd i'r nefoedd, Anti Catrin,' meddai Ceren gan ei gosod ei hun yn ei chadair a llygadu'r wyau sgrambl. 'Ga i sos coch arno fo, plîs?'

Brathodd Anti Catrin ei gwefus fel y rhoes y gwydr o'i blaen a throi i estyn y sos coch.

'Do, 'mechan i?' meddai'n floesg.

Ond roedd Ceren wedi colli diddordeb.

'Am chwarae hefo Solomon munud,' meddai'n fodlon.

Efallai fod Anti Catrin yn colli Mam dipyn bach hefyd, meddyliodd Bethan. Ond nid fel yr oedd hi a Ceren yn ei cholli. Colled perthynas oedd o i Anti Catrin. Chwaer-yng-nghyfraith. Ond colli mam oedd o iddyn nhw.

'Rydw i am ailbacio'r cesys pnawn 'ma,' meddai'n sydyn. 'I fod yn barod pan ddaw Dad.'

Llonyddodd dwylo Anti Catrin.

'Pacio? Ond dydi dy dad ddim yn dŵad tan ddiwedd yr wythnos,' meddai.

'Ddim yn dŵad?'

Cododd llais Bethan.

Rhoddodd Anti Catrin ei chyllell a fforc yn deidi ar ei phlât.

'Yli, Bethan,' meddai. 'Rwyt ti'n ddigon hen i sylweddoli. Mae gan dy dad ddyletswyddau yn y coleg er ei bod hi'n wyliau. A thaith ddarlith-io'n fuan. Mae angen llonydd i wella a pharatoi arno fo rŵan.'

'Mi fasa fo'n gwella'n gynt petai Ceren a fi yna,' meddai Bethan a'i llais yn crynu. 'Ond does dim ots ganddo fo amdanon ni. Ein gadael ni yma hefo . . . hefo . . . '

Roedd hi'n mynd i ddweud dieithryn, ond fe'i hataliodd ei hun.

'Hefo fi? Y fi ydi'i chwaer o, a modryb i titha,' meddai Anti Catrin mewn llais rhesymol.

56

'Helpu'i gilydd mae perthnasau, Bethan. Pwy sydd well i wneud?'

'Ond rydw i a Ceren eisio mynd adre.'

Ochneidiodd Anti Catrin.

'Gawn ni weld be ddywedith eich tad ddiwedd yr wythnos. Ond mae ganddo ddigon i'w drefnu.'

Esgus ydi hynny, meddyliodd Bethan yn chwerw. Dydi o ddim eisio fi a Ceren wedi i Mam farw. Doedd neb eu heisio nhw. Ddim hyd yn oed Anti Catrin. Doedd hi ddim yn licio plant. Eu cymryd nhw am mai hi oedd unig chwaer Dad ddaru hi. Cododd lwmp i'w gwddf. Fedrai hi ddim eistedd rhagor wrth y bwrdd.

'Rydw i'n mynd i'r llofft,' meddai gan ruthro am ddrws y gegin.

Wfft i Anti Catrin os ceisiai ei hatal. Carlamodd i fyny'r grisiau a'i thaflu ei hun ar y gwely. Treiglodd y dagrau araf i lawr ei hwyneb.

Cofiodd am ei phwrs yn sydyn. Tybed oedd ganddi ddigon i dalu am y siwrnai adref? Cododd ei gobeithion. Mi fyddai'n rhy hwyr i Dad ddweud dim wedyn.

Dychmygodd gyrraedd adref ac agor y drws. Mi fyddai'r muriau cyfarwydd yn cau'n glòs amdani ac arogl lafant yn llenwi'i ffroenau. Fe fyddai'r bwrdd wedi'i osod yn y gegin a thusw o flodau ar fwrdd bach y lobi. Ac fe ddeuai Mam . . . Chwalodd y darlun yn chwilfriw.

Trodd ar ei bol a chladdu ei hwyneb yn y gobennydd. Pa iws breuddwydio am fynd adref? Estynnodd am ei phwrs a syllu ar y bunt unig a oedd ynddo. Dim digon i ddim. Roedd popeth ar chwâl wedi colli Mam. Dim cartref ... dim rhieni ... dim arian poced ... a neb yn malio.

Llusgodd ei thraed ar y carped fel y cerddodd at y ffenestr. Syllodd trwyddi a'i meddyliau'n gymysg. Yna agorodd y drws o'r tu ôl iddi a daeth Anti Catrin i mewn.

'Bethan,' meddai mewn llais isel teimladwy. 'Paid â chau dy hun yn fan'ma. Rydw i *yn* dallt, ysti.'

Daeth i sefyll ati.

'Mi wn i ei bod yn anodd iti dderbyn pethau. Ond dydi dy dad ddim wedi anghofio amdanoch chi. Eisio amser i drefnu mae o.'

'Ond trefnu be?' holodd Bethan a'i llygaid yn llawn dagrau. 'Hefo'n gilydd rydw i eisio bod, nid yma.'

Gafaelodd Anti Catrin ynddi a'i harwain i eistedd ar y gwely.

'Yli, y fi ydi unig chwaer dy dad. Yr un y medr o droi ati. Ond mi ddaw amser y byddwch chi hefo'ch gilydd eto.'

'Pryd?'

Ysgydwodd Anti Catrin ei phen.

'Wn i ddim. Ond rhaid iti ymddiried yn dy dad. A than hynny, aros yma hefo mi.'

58

Brathodd Bethan ei gwefus yn ansicr. Oedd Anti Catrin yn dweud y gwir? Ynteu tric oedd o? Rhywbeth i'w chadw hi'n ddiddan tra oedden nhw'n penderfynu beth i'w wneud hefo Ceren a hithau. A beth oedd am ddigwydd iddyn nhw pan âi Dad ar ei daith ddarlithio? Efallai y caen nhw fynd hefo fo!

Gwasgodd Anti Catrin ei hysgwydd am eiliad, cyn codi a siarad yn ei llais rhesymol arferol.

'Tyrd i lawr y grisiau rŵan. Be faset ti'n licio ei wneud y pnawn 'ma? Mynd am dro i'r parc?'

O na! meddyliodd Bethan. Cerdded yn deidi wrth ochr Anti Catrin a bihafio unwaith eto.

'Rydw i am fynd i gyfarfod Mari,' meddai.

'Mari?'

Edrychodd Anti Catrin yn ddryslyd arni.

'Wedi'i chyfarfod hi bore 'ma. Rydyn ni'n ffrindiau.'

'O!'

Roedd 'O' Anti Catrin yn llawn drwgdybiaeth.

'Does 'na'r un Mari yn byw yn y stryd yma. Stryd nesaf, hwyrach?'

Ddywedodd Bethan 'run gair.

'Well iti ddŵad â hi yma, felly. Mi wna i de ichi'ch dwy.'

Ond doedd Bethan ddim eisio gwneud hynny. Eisio gweld Mari i edrych a oedd hi'n deilwng i fod yn ffrind iddi oedd Anti Catrin. Snob!

'Fory, efalla,' meddai gan afael yn ei siaced.

Roedd hi'n falch o gael dianc o'r tŷ ac oddi wrth lygaid Anti Catrin. Roedden nhw'n boenus a beirniadol a thosturiol ac yn ... wyddai hi ddim beth rywsut. Doedd hi ddim yn deall sut y gallai hynny fod chwaith. Gwneud ei dyletswydd roedd Anti Catrin, 'tê? Helpu am fod Dad yn frawd iddi.

Anelodd am y parc unwaith eto. Ond doedd pethau ddim 'run fath y tro yma. Roedd y parc yn llawn o bobl. Yn blant a mamau a thadau, a neiniau a theidiau i gyd yn mwynhau haul y pnawn, a fedrai hi ddim dioddef gweld hapus-rwydd teuluoedd.

Trodd i gyfeiriad y mur rhododendron. Gwgodd. Roedd criw o blant yn chwarae o'i flaen. Fedrai hi ddim ymwthio trwyddo rŵan a diflannu i ddiogelwch y sièd yn yr ardd.

Trodd i eistedd ar fainc ger y llyn. Syllodd ar ei wyneb a'i meddyliau ymhell. Ddim yma yr oedd hi i fod, ond gartre gyda Mam a Dad a Ceren. Y cyfan ohonyn nhw'n deulu gyda'i gilydd, a dim unigrwydd yn agos atyn nhw. Roedd yr haul yn tywynnu'n boeth ar ei chroen, ond roedd hi'n oer oer tu mewn.

'Haia!'

Mari! Trodd yn falch.

'Ddim yn disgwyl dy weld ti mor fuan,' meddai honno gan ei gollwng ei hun ar y glas-wellt. 'Y fodryb 'na'n mynd ar dy nerfau di?'

Nodiodd Bethan. Ond er ei bod hi'n nodio, roedd yna un darn bach ohoni'n cywilyddio hefyd. Doedd Anti Catrin ddim yn ddrwg i gyd, yn nac oedd? Er ei bod hi'n ffwsio ac yn deddfu ac yn snob, roedd hi'n trio'i gorau weithiau.

'Mae hi eisio iti ddŵad i de.'

'Pam?'

'Eisio gweld sut un wyt ti.'

'Hy!'

'Ddoi di?'

'Pryd?'

'Fory.'

Trodd Mari ar ei bol a thorri glaswelltyn. Cnodd ef yn araf heb ddweud gair.

'Ddoi di?' holodd Bethan eto.

'Os doi di adre hefo mi.'

'Pryd?'

'Heddiw.'

Tro Bethan i fod yn ddistaw oedd hi. Efallai na fyddai Anti Catrin yn fodlon iddi fynd, meddyliodd yn annifyr. Ond doedd gan Anti Catrin ddim hawl i ddeddfu. A doedd dim angen iddi hithau boeni am Ceren chwaith. Roedd honno'n berffaith hapus yn chwarae hefo Solomon, on'd oedd? Gwthiodd y teimlad euog oddi wrthi.

'Iawn.'

Neidiodd Mari ar ei thraed.

'Tyrd, ta.'

Cerddodd y ddwy tua giât y parc.

'Fydd dy dad adre?' holodd Bethan.

Sut oeddech chi'n siarad hefo rhywun â'i wraig wedi'i adael?

'Gweithio, tydi?' atebodd Mari.

Ciledrychodd Bethan arni. Doedd hi ddim yn hoffi holi. Ond dyna ofnadwy oedd mam yn dianc hefo cariad arall. Ceisiodd ddychmygu pa un oedd waethaf. Colli mam mewn damwain, ynteu colli mam i gariad newydd. Colli oedd y ddau, penderfynodd.

Cyraeddasant y stryd o dai teras lle'r oedd cartref Mari. Roedd criwiau o blant yn chwarae ar y stryd, a rhai mamau'n sgwrsio ar y stepiau a arweiniai o'r clytiau gerddi at y drysau. Distewodd y sgwrs fel y nesaodd y ddwy, a gwyddai Bethan fod eu llygaid yn eu dilyn bob cam.

'Wedi cael ffrind newydd, Mari?' holodd un.

'Ddim o'r ffordd yma, yn nac ydi?' meddai un arall.

'Trwynau busneslyd,' brathodd Mari o dan ei gwynt.

Agorodd giât fach wichlyd a chamodd yn gefnsyth i fyny llwybr yr ardd. Edrychodd Bethan o'i chwmpas fel y dilynodd hi. Roedd border cul o flodau'n tyfu'n wyllt wrth y llwybr, a sgwâr bychan o wair trwchus ar y dde. Roedd chwysigod yn codi'n bennau ar baent y drws a'r llenni les yn geimion wrth y ffenestri.

Am eiliad, fe ddychmygodd Bethan wyneb ei modryb. Byddai'n siŵr o wfftio wrth weld y fath flerwch. Ond, doedd Anti Catrin ddim yn gwybod sut roedd pethau yng nghartre Mari, yn nac oedd?

Fel y cyrhaeddodd y ddwy at y stepiau, agorodd drws y tŷ nesaf a daeth dynes i'r amlwg. Roedd corff crwn cyffyrddus ganddi a gwallt cyrliog yn gwmwl o gwmpas ei hwyneb. Gwenodd arnynt, ond roedd tristwch ar ei hwyneb hefyd.

'Mi bicia i yna cyn i dy dad ddŵad adre, Mari,' meddai.

'Slwtan,' meddai Mari rhwng ei dannedd.

Edrychodd y ddynes i gyfeiriad Bethan a gwenodd.

'Ffrind newydd?' holodd.

'Mrs Morris,—dyma Bethan,' meddai Mari ond roedd gwg ar ei hwyneb wrth eu cyflwyno.

Fe deimlai Bethan yn annifyr. Pam roedd Mari mor anghwrtais a'r ddynes drws nesa yn trio bod yn gyfeillgar?

Tynnodd Mari allwedd o'i phoced ac agor y drws. Estynnodd i dynnu Bethan trwyddo cyn ei gau â chlep.

'Hynna i'r feudan. Trio stwffio'i ffordd yma am fod Mam wedi mynd,' meddai'n ffyrnig. 'Ei llygad ar Dad . . .'

'Ond, beth am ei gŵr?'

'Hwnnw? Efo Mam, tydi?'

Edrychodd Bethan yn syfrdan.

'Y ddau? Hefo'i gilydd?'

'Ia,' oedd yr ateb swta.

Roedd wyneb Mari'n fôr o surni.

'Sori. Wyddwn i ddim,' meddai Bethan yn gloff.

Roedd hi'n teimlo'n fwy annifyr byth. Bron nad oedd hi'n difaru dod yma hefo Mari.

'Dy dad ddim eisio chdi. Mam ddim eisio finna,' meddai Mari.

Am eiliad, roedd ei llygaid yn llaith a'i hwyneb yn llawn loes. Yna sythodd ei hysgwyddau a gwenu fel pe na bai dim yn bod.

'Dim ots, ysti. Dydw i'n malio dim.'

Caeodd Bethan ei llygaid am eiliad. Dim ots gan Mari am ei mam hi, ond *roedd* ots ganddi hi, Bethan am Mam. Ots ofnadwy. Roedd hi'n crio o'i mewn o hyd wrth feddwl na welai hi mohoni byth eto, ac yn crio mwy byth am i'w thad gefnu arni hi a Ceren, a'u gadael nhw hefo Anti Catrin.

'Tyrd i'r gegin,' meddai Mari.

Roedd arogl sglodion yn ymdroi yn y gegin gaeedig a llestri'n diferu'n bentwr ar y sinc.

'Gosod dy hun ar y gadair 'na,' meddai Mari gan lenwi'r tecell yn brysur. 'Coffi?'

'Diolch.'

Estynnodd Mari fygiau o'r cwpwrdd ac agorodd baced o fisgedi siocled.

'Dad yn rhoi arian siopio imi bob wythnos,'

meddai. 'Wedi cael llond bol ar gerdded siopa hefyd. Ond mae Dad a fi'n iawn heb Mam. A heb honna drws nesa.'

'Mi fydda inna'n dechrau siopio pan awn ni adre hefyd,' meddai Bethan. 'Mi ofala i am bopeth wedyn. Coginio—a llnau hefyd.'

'Llnau? Phw! Dydw i ddim yn gwastraffu llawer o amser hefo hynny rŵan,' meddai Mari. 'Mi driais i ddechrau, ond does ots gan Dad am ddim.'

Brathodd ei gwefus am eiliad.

'A rŵan, wel, mae o'n ormod o drafferth gen i, tydi?'

'Ond . . .'

Gallai Bethan ei dychmygu ei hun yn trefnu pethau i'r dim gartre. Fe fyddai cinio da ar y bwrdd pan ddeuai Dad o'r coleg, fyddai Ceren byth yn swnian, ac fe fyddai hithau'n glanhau a smwddio a gwneud teisen sinsir ac yn cadw pobman yn bictiwr o deidi. Yn union fel y byddai ei mam yn ei wneud.

Chwalodd ei stumog yn sydyn fel y cofiodd. Mam fyddai'n gwneud popeth fel'na llefodd llais o'i mewn. Mam fyddai'n coginio, ac yn magu Ceren a jest bod *yna*. Yn ffraeo ac yn deddfu weithiau hefyd.

'Efallai y daw dy fam yn ôl ryw ddiwrnod,' meddai, i gysuro Mari.

'Dydw i ddim eisio iddi ddŵad yn ôl. Mae Dad a fi'n iawn hefo'n gilydd—weithiau.'

Ond roedd mam fyw yn well na mam farw, on'd oedd? Ceisiodd Bethan ganfod geiriau i egluro hynny i Mari, ond fedrai hi ddim. Roedd wyneb Mari mor sur—ac mor benderfynol hefyd.

'Ers pa bryd . . .?' dechreuodd.

Brathodd ei gwefus. Na, ddylai hi ddim holi pethau fel'na.

'Ers pa bryd yr aeth Mam, wyt ti'n 'i feddwl? Chwe mis.'

'Am ei bod hi'n anhapus yr aeth hi?' mentrodd Bethan.

'Anhapus? Beth am Dad a fi?' Fflachiodd llygaid Mari'n sydyn. 'Fedr neb fod mor anhapus â ni rŵan.'

Cododd i gadw rhai o'r llestri oedd ar y bwrdd sinc yn swnllyd. Clepiodd ddrws y cwpwrdd arnynt a throi i wynebu Bethan.

'Rydyn ni'n iawn, Dad a fi,' meddai'n ffyrnig. 'Ond inni gael llonydd ac i Dad beidio â chael y felan.'

'Y felan?'

'Iselder. Am ei fod o'n methu anghofio. Ond sut medr o anghofio, a honna drws nesa yma byth a beunydd. Yn ei chynnig ei hun iddo fo.'

'*Mari!*'

'Wel, dyna be mae hi'n ei wneud, 'tê? Yn dod yma o hyd ac o hyd. Wedi colli un dyn ac eisio un arall.'

Disgynnodd Mari i'r gadair a golwg amddifad ar ei hwyneb.

'A dydw i ddim yn gwybod beth i'w wneud. Rydw i wedi blino gofalu am dŷ ar fy mhen fy hun, ac ar drio coginio a Dad byth bron yn bwyta. Dim ond eistedd yn y gadair yn sbio ar ddim byd. A honna drws nesa i mewn ac allan fel io-io, a neb yn malio amdana i.'

'Efallai mai unig ydi hi.'

'Mi geith fod yn unig yn ei thŷ ei hun.'

Rhwbiodd Mari ei llygaid yn ffyrnig.

Wyddai Bethan ddim beth i'w ddweud. A beth petai Dad yn cael iselder hefyd? Daeth lwmp oeraidd i'w gwddf wrth ddychmygu'r fath beth.

Sniffiodd Mari a phalfalu'n ddall am ei hances.

'Dim ots gen i, ysti. Dim ots gen i am neb.'

'Ond beth tasa dy dad yn gwaethygu? Mae pobl yn mynd i'r ysbyty hefo iselder.'

Gwasgodd Mari y mŷg yn ei dwylo.

'Wnaiff o ddim. Wna i ddim gadael iddo fo.'

Cododd yn ffrwcslyd a dal y mŷg o dan y tap i'w olchi.

'Rydw i'n iawn rŵan.'

Edrychodd ar y cloc.

'Mi fydd Dad adra'n fuan. Gweithio sifft yn y gwaith.'

Brathodd Bethan ei gwefus. Roedd popeth ar chwâl iddi hi a Mari. Fedrai Mari ddim gwella felan ei thad, a fedrai hithau ddim ateb Ceren pan oedd hi'n holi am Mam, na pherswadio Dad i fynd â nhw adre, nac ymdopi hefo byw am hir hefo Anti Catrin.

Estynnodd y distawrwydd rhyngddi hi a Mari. Dyna ofnadwy oedd cael tad hefo'r felan a mam wedi'i gadael. Ond roedd mam Mari'n fyw yn rhywle, on'd oedd? Doedd hi ddim wedi *marw*!

Edrychodd ar ei wats. Bron yn bump! Fe fyddai Anti Catrin yn dechrau poeni. Ond doedd waeth am hynny. Wnâi hi ddim gadael Mari.

'Dos di,' meddai Mari wrth ei gweld yn llygadu'i wats. 'Mi fydda i'n iawn. 'Run fath â phob diwrnod.'

Safodd Bethan yn ansicr. Roedd un hanner ohoni eisio mynd a'r hanner arall eisio aros.

'Siŵr?'

'Siŵr. Wela i di fory. Pnawn.'

'Reit ta.'

Trodd am y drws. Daeth cnoc arno ac fe agorodd fel y cyrhaeddodd Bethan ato.

'Y fi sy 'ma.'

Mrs Morris! Ciledrychodd Bethan ar Mari a gweld y disflastod ar ei hwyneb.

'Rhywbeth bach ichi i swper. Wedi addo i dy dad, Mari. Mi gadawa i o i gynhesu yn y ffwrn.'

Prysurodd at y stof a throi botwm y ffwrn fel petai'n berchennog arni. Yn sydyn aeth wyneb Mari yn fflamgoch. Trodd ar ei sawdl heb ddweud gair a diflannodd i fyny'r grisiau.

Ochneidiodd Mrs Morris.

'Dim ond trio helpu rydw i,' eglurodd. 'Ond mae Mari . . .'

Teimlai Bethan yn annifyr. Edrychai Mrs Morris fel petai bron â chrio. Ond doedd Bethan ddim am gydymdeimlo hefo hi.

'Mynd rŵan,' meddai gan deimlo'n rêl bradwr wrth feddwl am Mari yn unig yn y llofft.

Caeodd y drws yn ofalus a chychwynnodd am dŷ Anti Catrin. Am ychydig roedd hi wedi anghofio am ei cholled ei hun. Ond ddim ond am ychydig. Yn awr, roedd popeth yn ffrydio'n ôl iddi.

Colli Mam. Dad yn eu gwrthod. Ceren yn anghofio. Byw hefo Anti Catrin. Ond, colli Mam oedd y gwaethaf.

7.

Derbyniodd Anti Catrin hi'n ôl heb holi. Roedd Ceren ar ei bol o flaen y teledu, a'r bêl fach goch yn rholio o law i law ganddi tra gwyliai'r sgrin.

'Solomon wedi chwarae lot,' meddai. 'Am chwarae fory hefyd.'

Teimlodd Bethan yr atgasedd yn codi ynddi. Sut y meiddiai Ceren wneud dim ond gwylio teledu a chwarae hefo cath? Sut na chofiai hi fod Mam wedi marw? Bob munud o bob dydd. Fel y cofiai hi.

Toddodd ei chalon wrth edrych ar ei chwaer fach. Roedd hi mor ddiniwed ac ifanc. Geneth fach amddifad, fel roedd hithau'n amddifad—a Mari hefyd.

'Wyt ti eisio stori?' holodd gan ddisgyn yn glewtan ar y mat wrth ochr Ceren. 'Twm Tomato?'

Ysgydwodd Ceren ei phen heb dynnu'i llygaid oddi ar y sgrin.

'Cartŵn,' meddai. 'Wil Cwac Cwac.'

'Os mai fel'na rwyt ti'n teimlo,' meddai Bethan yn swta.

Anelodd am y llofft. Gorweddodd ar y gwely ac agor y llyfr hwnnw a brynodd hi dro'n ôl yn y siop bapur newydd. Ond fe fynnai'r geiriau lifo'n un. Gwasgodd ei llygaid yn flinedig. Mi fyddai hi wrth ei bodd yn darllen fel arfer, yn cael blas ar y stori ac yn ei dychmygu ei hun yn arwres y llyfr. Ac mi fyddai Mam yn chwerthin, ac yn bygwth sbectol iddi am fod ei thrwyn mewn llyfr o hyd.

Taflodd y llyfr o'r neilltu fel y galwodd ei modryb o waelod y grisiau.

'Bethan! Swper!'

Bu'n disgwyl i'w thad ffonio trwy'r gyda'r nos. Roedd o'n siŵr o wneud, meddyliodd. Ac mi gâi hithau gyfle i'w berswadio mai gartref roedd hi a Ceren eisio bod. Nid yma hefo Anti Catrin.

Fe wyddai fod llygaid Anti Catrin arni bob tro yr edrychai ar y cloc. Mor araf y symudai ei fysedd. Saith o'r gloch. Chwarter wedi. Hanner awr wedi. Amser gwely Ceren. Ond mynnai'r gloch gadw'n ddistaw er iddi ddisgwyl a disgwyl.

'Ga i ffonio, Anti Catrin? Plîs?'

Roedd yr un olwg boenus a beirniadol a thosturiol yn llygaid Anti Catrin unwaith eto. Fel petai hi'n deall yn iawn, ond ddim am ddweud.

'Cofia fod dy dad yn gweithio'n galed,' meddai. 'Mi fydd wedi blino . . .'

Gwasgodd Bethan y derbynnydd fel y pwysodd ar y botymau. Atebwch Dad, plîs! Rydw i eisio clywed eich llais chi. Rydw i eisio gwybod fod yr wifren yn ein cysylltu ni. Eisio teimlo'n ddiogel. Eisio gwybod na chawsoch chithau ddamwain hefyd, a 'ngadael inna heb neb.

'Hylô! 329406.'

Dad! Ffrydiodd gollyngdod trwy gorff Bethan. Dyna wirion fu hi'n poeni. Wrth gwrs fod Dad yn iawn.

'Hylô!' Daeth llais ei thad eto.

72

'Y fi . . . sy 'ma.'

Brwydrodd yn erbyn ei dagrau.

'Dad. Eisio . . . eisio . . .'

Roedd ochenaid yn llais ei thad.

'Bethan! Roeddwn i'n meddwl amdanat ti a Ceren.'

Ffrydiodd gollyngdod trwyddi.

'Oeddech chi? Oeddech chi, wir?'

Roedd distawrwydd yr ochr arall. Sbonciodd ofn i'w gwddf.

'Dad? Ydych chi yna? Dad?'

'Ydw.'

Roedd ei lais yn un ochenaid hir eto.

'Gawn ni ddŵad adre, Dad? Plîs?'

Ymledodd y distawrwydd rhyngddynt. Yn sydyn, fe wyddai Bethan fod ei thad yn crio. Dyna pam nad oedd o'n siarad. Roedd o mewn tŷ gwag . . . ar ei ben ei hun . . . yn lwmp o hiraeth fel roedd hithau'n lwmp o hiraeth . . . ac yn *crio*!

Gwasgodd y derbynnydd at ei chlust fel petai'n ceisio dod â'r llais yn nes. Dad! Rydw i eisio bod yna hefo chi. Rydw i eisio teimlo'n ddiogel hefo chi a gwybod na wna i eich colli chi hefyd.

'Dad! Gawn ni ddŵad adra?'

'Yn . . . fuan, Bethan.' Cliriodd ei thad ei wddf yn swnllyd. 'Ond . . . dim rŵan. Mi ddo i yna ddiwedd yr wythnos. Byddwch yn blant da i Anti Catrin.'

73

Daeth clic y datgysylltu. Safodd Bethan yn hir, hir, a'r derbynnydd yn ei llaw. Yna rhoddodd ef yn ôl yn ofalus araf a throi'n ddall am y grisiau. Teimlai'n wag o'i mewn. Yn wag o bopeth ond unigrwydd a cholled. A phethau gwag oedd y rheiny hefyd.

'Bethan!'

Yn sydyn, roedd breichiau Anti Catrin yn dynn amdani a hithau'n beichio crio a'i phen ar ei hysgwydd.

'Dyna fo. Dyna fo. Cria di.'

'Rydw i e-eisio M-mam. Ond w-wela i mohoni h-hi eto. Pam, Anti Catrin? Pam?'

Siglodd Anti Catrin hi yn ei breichiau.

'Wyddon ni ddim pam . . .' cychwynnodd.

Torrodd Bethan ar ei thraws.

'Ond pam na wyddon ni pam? Pam mae'n rhaid i bopeth gael ei ddryllio a ninnau mor hapus? Dydi o ddim yn deg.'

Daeth llais bychan ofnus o ddrws y lolfa.

'Pam nad ydi Mam yn dŵad, Bethan?'

Cwympodd wyneb Ceren yn ddagrau.

'Eisio i Mam ddŵad. Rŵan.'

Gwasgodd Anti Catrin ysgwydd Bethan cyn troi i afael am Ceren.

'Tyrd hefo mi i'r gegin i edrych be gawn ni. Bisged siocled, efallai. A chofia dy fod ti am chwarae hefo Solomon fory.'

Anghofiodd Ceren ei dagrau.

'Ydw, dydw?'

Cerddodd yn hapus am y gegin gydag Anti Catrin.

'Dos dithau i molchi dy wyneb, Bethan,' meddai Anti Catrin.

Dringodd Bethan y grisiau'n araf. Roedd hi'n teimlo'n well wedi crio ac yn agosach at ei modryb hefyd. Fel petai'r ddwy ohonyn nhw'n teimlo'r golled 'run fath, ac yn hiraethu'r un fath.

Ymolchodd, ac aeth i lawr i'r gegin. Roedd Ceren yn bwyta bisged siocled.

'Coffi, Bethan?'

Roedd llais Anti Catrin yn ddiddychymyg a dideimlad unwaith eto. Na, doedd Anti Catrin ddim yn teimlo'r un fath â hi, nac yn hiraethu'r un fath chwaith, penderfynodd Bethan. Cymryd arni roedd hi.

8.

Wfftiodd Bethan yn ddistaw bach. Te prynhawn! Dyna hen ffash. Fel pe baen nhw'r un oed â Ceren ac yn dwlu ar lemonêd a theisennau eisin a phethau plentynnaidd felly. Mi fyddai Mam yn paratoi brechdanau a choffi mewn mygiau mawr, a gadael iddi hi a'i ffrindiau eu cludo i'r llofft i wrando ar ddisgiau, a thrio dillad a steil gwahanol i'w gwalltiau.

75

Mam! Caeodd ei llygaid am eiliad fel y tyfodd yr hiraeth o'i mewn. Yna, rhoes glep i'r drws o'i hôl a chychwynnodd am y parc.

Roedd Mari yno o'i blaen. Brysiodd Bethan ati.

'Sièd?' holodd.

Nodiodd Mari heb ddweud gair.

Cerddasant ochr yn ochr am y llwyni rhododendron. Ciledrychodd Bethan unwaith neu ddwy ar wyneb Mari. Roedd hi eisio holi beth a ddigwyddodd wedi i'w thad gyrraedd adre, ond roedd y cuchio amlwg ar wyneb ei ffrind yn ei rhwystro.

'Dydi pethau ddim yn deg,' haerodd Mari'n sydyn gan anelu cic at dún gwag a adawyd ar y llwybr.

'Nac ydyn,' ochneidiodd Bethan.

Roedd hi'n meddwl am golli Mam . . . a Dad wedi'u gadael . . . am Anti Catrin yn oeraidd a chlòs bob yn ail . . . a Ceren yn treulio amser yn y drws nesa . . . a hithau'n teimlo fel crio a gweiddi a sgrechian a dobio a chicio nes y cymerai rhywun sylw.

Ymwthiodd y ddwy trwy'r rhododendron ac ymlaen at y llethr a arweiniai at yr hen sièd. Roedd haul y prynhawn yn grasboeth, a'r dail yn llipa llesg ar y brigau cyfagos. Caeodd pobman yn gysurlawn amdanynt.

Dilynodd Bethan Mari i hanner gwyll y sièd. Roedd yr awyrgylch oerllyd tu mewn yn gysgod rhag y gwres, ac yn gysgod rhag popeth a ddigwyddodd iddi hithau hefyd. Byddai wedi hoffi cau ei hun yno am byth. Ei chau ei hun oddi wrth ei cholled a'i chau ei hun oddi wrth Dad am iddo ei siomi hi a Ceren. Dyna wnaeth o. Cefnu. Gadael. Siomi.

'Wedi dŵad â hwn yma bora 'ma,' meddai Mari gan amneidio at fag plastig a orweddai ar wyneb y bwrdd cardiau. 'Cael arian siopio gan Dad.'

'Be?'

'Ble mae dy feddwl di? Wedi dŵad â hwn yma bora 'ma. Gwario hefo'r pres siopio gefais i gan Dad.'

'Ond arian prynu bwyd i'r tŷ oedden nhw,' meddai Bethan gan lygadu'r pacedi creision a'r bisgedi a'r caniau Coke a'r fferins a dynnai Mari o'r bag. 'Be ddeudith dy dad?'

'Dim byd,' meddai Mari'n wgus. 'Honna drws nesa'n dŵad â rhywbeth o hyd.'

'Ond os ydi dy dad yn rhoi arian . . .'

'Ydi. Am nad oes ots ganddo fo. Nid arian ydw i'i eisio, ond sylw.'

Mi fasa'n well gen i fod gartre hefo Dad, dim ots am faint y sylw, meddyliodd Bethan yn ffyrnig. Gartref rydw i eisio bod. Gartref hefo Ceren a Dad. Hefo'n gilydd. Yn deulu er bod un wedi mynd.

'Eistedda di ar y gadair, mi eistedda inna ar y

mat,' gorchmynnodd Mari. 'Hwda, wyt ti eisio diod?'

Gosododd ei hun yn gyfforddus ar y llawr ac agorodd baced creision yn freuddwydiol.

'Mi fedrwn ni aros yma yn hir,' meddai. 'A gadael i bawb boeni. Dysgu gwers iddyn nhw.'

'Ond . . .'

'Ond be?'

'Fasa hynny ddim yn deg.'

'Does 'na ddim yn deg i ni, nac oes?'

'Ond fedrwn ni ddim aros.'

'Pam?'

'Am . . . Wel, am . . .'

Ailosododd Mari ei hun ar y mat yn benderfynol.

'Eitha gwaith â nhw, ddeuda i. Mam a'i chariad, a Dad a honna drws nesa. Dysgu gwers iddyn nhw, 'tê? Dysgu gwers i dy dad ac Anti Catrin hefyd.'

'Na. Fedrwn ni byth. A does dim angen. Mi ddaw Dad fory, ac mi fydd Ceren a finna'n mynd adre hefo fo. Siŵr o fod. Wnaiff o ddim ein gadael ni hefo Anti Catrin.'

'Wyt ti'n siŵr y byddwch chi'n mynd?'

'Ydw.'

'Dyna ti, ta. Dim problem, yn nac oes?'

'Nac oes,' meddai Bethan yn bendant.

Ceisiodd reoli'r gwagle o gwmpas ei stumog, a chroesodd ei bysedd. Trio ei pherswadio ei hun roedd hi.

'O, paid â gwrando arna i,' meddai Mari'n sydyn.

Palfalodd am y gweddillion yng ngwaelod ei phaced creision.

'Mi gawn ni de bach sidêt hefo dy Anti Catrin, ac mi a inna adre i baratoi swper i Dad wedyn. Efallai y cawn ni lonydd gan honna drws nesa heno . . . ac efallai y bydd Dad yn ei hwyliau gorau.'

Gwasgodd y paced creision yn ffyrnig.

'Ac efalla y bydd y blydi Wyddfa'n lwmp o gaws bore fory hefyd.'

Disgynnodd distawrwydd rhyngddynt.

'Sut un oedd dy dad cyn i dy fam adael?' holodd Bethan o'r diwedd.

''Run fath â thad pawb arall, am wn i,' meddai Mari gan ystumio'i hysgwyddau.

Daeth golwg hiraethus i'w hwyneb.

'Licio chwerthin a thynnu coes. Gweithio o gwmpas y tŷ a chwibanu wrth beintio'r drws a'r ffenestri. Paent melyn hapusrwydd, medda fo.'

Hyrddiodd y paced gwag i'r gornel.

'Wel, mae ei felyn hapusrwydd yn chwysigod cyfoglyd rŵan, tydi?' meddai.

Gorweddodd yn ôl ar y mat ac edrych trwy'r drws agored i'r heulwen y tu allan.

'Mae'n braf yma, tydi? Cael llonydd gan bawb.'

Llonydd, meddyliodd Bethan. Oedd, roedd hi eisio llonydd. Ond roedd hi fwy o eisio rhyw-beth arall. Eisio bod gartre gyda Dad a Ceren roedd hi, nid teimlo bod darn mawr o'i bywyd wedi'i sgubo i ffwrdd i rywle. Roedd hi eisio gafael yn y darn bach oedd ar ôl, ac eisio ei wasgu a'i gofleidio nes bod y twll gwag o'i mewn wedi mynd.

Teimlodd yr un hen ddagrau yn pigo y tu ôl i'w llygaid, ond fe'u gorfododd ymaith. Doedd hi ddim am grio fel babi. Roedd hi am fod fel Mari, yn malio am ddim. A byw am yfory. Dad a Ceren a hithau.

Neidiodd ar ei thraed.

'Tyrd. Mi fydd Anti Catrin yn ein disgwyl ni,' meddai.

Camodd allan i'r heulwen ac anadlodd yn ddwfn i'w hysgyfaint. Doedd gan yr haul ddim hawl i dywynnu mor siriol a'i bywyd hithau ar chwâl. Edrychodd i fyny ar y belen ddisglair uwchben.

'Pa hawl?' sgyrnygodd rhwng ei dannedd.

Ond doedd hi ddim yn disgwyl ateb. Byd anghyfiawn oedd o. Byd lle'r oedd pethau ofnadwy fel marw'n digwydd, a neb yn gwybod pam.

Efallai mai ei bai hi oedd fod Mam wedi marw. Petai hi wedi bodloni ar rannu llofft hefo Ceren, fyddai dim angen estyniad, fyddai Ceren a hithau ddim wedi dŵad at Anti Catrin

. . . a fyddai Mam a Dad ddim yn teithio i'w nôl
. . . a fyddai'r ddamwain ddim wedi digwydd.

Ceisiodd wthio'r syniad o'r neilltu fel y dilyn-odd Mari i fyny'r llethr a thrwy'r mur rhodod-endron i'r parc. Tybed ai arni hi roedd y bai?

9.

'Hylô, Mari!'

Roedd llygaid Anti Catrin yn graff fel y llyg-adodd Mari o'i chorun i'w sawdl. Roedd hi'n gweld y jîns bratiog a'r crys chwys heb ei smwddio, meddyliodd Bethan yn sur.

Trodd Anti Catrin am y gegin.

'Mae te bron yn barod,' meddai. 'Dos i nôl Ceren o'r drws nesa, Bethan. Na, aros. Ewch i olchi'ch dwylo gyntaf, eich dwy.'

Edrychodd arnynt yn feirniadol.

'Wn i ddim be fuoch chi'n ei wneud i gael y ffasiwn olwg arnoch eich hunain.'

Pa hawl oedd gan Anti Catrin i siarad fel'na? Ac i edrych ar Mari fel pe bai hi wedi methu cyrraedd rhyw safon arbennig? Beirniadu heb wybod oedd hynny.

'Tyrd, Mari,' meddai gan ei harwain i fyny'r grisiau ac i'r ystafell ymolchi. 'Paid â chymryd sylw o Anti Catrin,' cysurodd ei ffrind. 'Un fel'na ydi hi.'

'Malio dim. Malio dim am neb, yn nac ydw?' meddai Mari.

'Nac wyt, siŵr,' cytunodd Bethan. 'Yli, brysia, inni gael nôl Ceren. Mi gym'rith oesoedd iddi ffawelio â Solomon.'

'Solomon?'

'Cath drws nesa. Hwnnw'n bwysicach na dim.'

Fe deimlai'n sur o'i mewn wrth gofio. Dim ond y hi oedd yn colli Mam, yn cofio amdani ac yn hiraethu. Smalio cydymdeimlo roedd Anti Catrin yn ei wneud . . . a chefnu wnaeth ei thad jest pan oedd hi ei angen fwyaf . . . a doedd Ceren yn gwneud dim ond baldorddi hefo'i Solomon hyn a'i Solomon llall yn dragwyddol. Doedd neb yn deall. Ddim hyd yn oed Mari, er ei bod hithau wedi colli'i mam hefyd. Ond colli person byw oedd hynny, nid colli rhywun wedi iddyn nhw farw. A doedd y ddau ddim 'run fath.

'Ewch i nôl Ceren rŵan,' gorchmynnodd Anti Catrin wedi iddyn nhw gyrraedd y gegin.

Cerddodd y ddwy am y drws nesa. Roedd Bethan yn benderfynol o afael yn Ceren a'i thynnu oddi yno gerfydd ei sgrepan. Efallai yr âi hi a Mari i'r llofft ar eu pennau eu hunain ar ôl te.

Pan gyraeddasant, roedd Ceren yn gorwedd ar soffa Mrs Jones, a Solomon ar ei glin.

'Eisio i Ceren ddŵad ar unwaith,' eglurodd Bethan. 'Te'n barod.'

'Ond mae Solomon yn cysgu,' cwynodd Ceren. 'Yn cysgu'n sownd.'

Edrychodd o dan ei haeliau ar Mari.

'Pwy 'di honna?'

'Mari. Wedi dŵad i de. A rŵan hyn ddeudodd Anti Catrin, Ceren.'

'Ia, 'mechan i,' meddai Mrs Jones wedi iddi ddweud "hylô" wrth Mari. 'Rho di Solomon ar y glustog. Mi fydd yma pan ddoi di'n ôl.'

'Ga i ddŵad ar ôl te?'

'Cei siŵr,' oedd yr ateb.

Fe deimlai Bethan fel ffrwydro. Roedd Ceren yn rêl babi'n meddwl am ddim ond am gath. Fe ddylai fod yn hiraethu ac yn cadw'n glòs ati hi, Bethan. Er, wrth gwrs, doedd hi ddim eisio babi o chwaer fach yn swnian byth a beunydd chwaith. Ond hefo hi y dylai Ceren fod. Dwy chwaer amddifad wedi'u gorfodi i aros hefo Anti Catrin. Dwy hefo'i *gilydd*!

'Tyrd,' meddai rhwng ei dannedd.

Gafaelodd yn ei llaw a diolch yn frysiog i Mrs Jones.

'Aww! Rwyt ti'n brifo'n llaw i. Mi ddeuda i . . .'

Arhosodd Ceren yn sydyn a'i hwyneb yn llawn gobaith.

'Ydi Mam wedi dŵad, Bethan? Wedi gadael Iesu Grist?'

83

Llyncodd Bethan y lwmp sydyn yn ei gwddf. Doedd Ceren byth yn deall. Rhoes ei braich am ei hysgwyddau a'i thynnu ati.

'Does neb yn dŵad yn ôl oddi wrth Iesu Grist. Maen nhw'n *aros*. Yn tydyn, Mari?'

'Ydyn.'

'Am byth?' holodd Ceren.

'Am byth.'

Edrychodd Ceren ar Mari.

'Mam chdi hefo Iesu Grist?'

Daeth Anti Catrin i'r drws cyn i Mari ateb.

'Dowch, wir,' meddai.

Roedd lliain gwyn a phinc ar y bwrdd a phopeth wedi'i osod yn deidi arno.

Crwydrodd llygaid Mari tros y llestri tsieni a'r brechdanau samwn a oedd yn sgwariau bychain ar y plât, a'r teisennau eisin a cheirios ar ganol y bwrdd, a llenwodd ei llygaid â dagrau.

'Mi fyddai Mam . . .' cychwynnodd cyn palfalu am ei hances a rhwbio'i hwyneb yn ffyrnig.

Edrychodd Anti Catrin yn graff arni am eiliad.

'Eistedd yn fan'na, Mari,' meddai yn ei llais dideimlad arferol.

Dim ots ganddi fod Mari'n ypset, chwyrnodd Bethan wrthi'i hun. Doedd ots gan Anti Catrin am ddim ond am gadw popeth yn lân a theidi, a pheidio â baeddu dillad a gwneud i'r cymdog-

ion siarad a phethau felly. Eu dioddef nhw yma
roedd hi, nid eu croesawu.

Gwgodd i'w chyfeiriad. Ond roedd Anti
Catrin yn estyn brechdanau i Mari, ac yn ei
hannog i fwyta hynny fedrai hi. Ac roedd tinc
caredig yn ei llais er nad oedd ei hwyneb yn
dangos dim.

Bwytaodd Bethan yn ddistaw. Ond roedd
Ceren yn llawn storïau am Solomon.

'Mae o'n chwarae hefo llinyn . . . a phêl goch
. . . ac yn cysgu ar y soffa . . .'

Roedd Bethan wedi cael llond bol.

'Ia, wel,' meddai Anti Catrin. 'Mi gei
chwarae hefo Solomon eto, Ceren. Aros yma
hefo Bethan a Mari am ychydig rŵan.'

'Ond mae Solomon . . .'

Roedd wyneb Ceren yn barod i gwympo'n
ddagrau ar unwaith.

'Wyt ti am sbio ar lyfr hefo mi?' holodd Mari.

Disgynnodd gên Bethan. Pam roedd Mari'n
cynnig a hwythau'u dwy eisio bod hefo'i
gilydd?

'Tyrd dithau i glirio'r llestri, Bethan,' gorchmynnodd Anti Catrin.

Dilynodd Bethan hi am y gegin yn wgus.
Fyddai Mam byth yn swnian am olchi'r llestri
pan fyddai ffrindiau'n ymweld. Ond roedd Anti
Catrin . . . Pletiodd ei gwefusau'n styfnig.

Caeodd Anti Catrin ddrws y gegin.

'Beth sydd wedi digwydd i fam Mari?' holodd.

'Yyy.'

Doedd Bethan ddim yn siŵr beth i'w ddweud. Sgwariodd ei hysgwyddau. Roedd hi am fod yn ffrindiau hefo Mari waeth beth ddywedai Anti Catrin.

'Wedi'u gadael nhw,' meddai'n foel.

'Dyna roeddwn i'n 'i feddwl,' meddai Anti Catrin. 'Beth am y gweddill o'r teulu?'

Roedd Bethan yn gacwn am iddi holi cymaint. Ond doedd hi ddim am gelu dim. Mi gâi Anti Catrin weld ei bod hi'n benderfynol o fod yn ffrindiau hefo Mari, waeth beth ddywedai hi.

'Dim ond ei thad. Ac mae'r felan arno fo. Cymryd dim sylw.'

Ochneidiodd Anti Catrin.

'Druan bach,' meddai.

Fedrai Bethan ddim credu ei chlustiau. Anti Catrin yn dangos cydymdeimlad! Un oeraidd, ddideimlad oedd hi, 'tê? Un sych grimp fel tôst wedi llosgi.

Cliriodd Anti Catrin ei gwddf yn swnllyd.

'Ia, wel. Mae llawer math o golled, Bethan.'

Yna gafaelodd yn y llestri glân a'u cadw'n ofalus yn y cwpwrdd.

Wrth gwrs, roedd Anti Catrin yn iawn. Roedd hithau'n gwybod bod colled Mari'n wahanol, doedd? Ond doedd hynny ddim yn gwneud colli Mam yn llai o beth chwaith. Estynnodd ei hances a chwythu'i thrwyn yn egnïol.

Roedd hi eisio ei thaflu ei hun i freichiau Anti Catrin . . . eisio crio a chrio nes chwalu'r lwmp anhapus o'i mewn. Roedd hi eisio teimlo bod *rhywun* yn barod i wrando a chydymdeimlo . . . eisio Dad . . . eisio Mam . . . ac eisio i Ceren hiraethu fel hithau.

10.

Deffrodd Bethan. Gorweddodd yno a'i llygaid cysglyd yn llygadrythu i dywyllwch dudew yr ystafell wely. Teimlai'n swrth a diymadferth. Fel petai pob asgwrn o'i chorff yn suddo'n ddyfnach ac yn ddyfnach i grombil y fatras, ac yn ei llusgo hithau'n ôl i'r cwsg roedd hi newydd ddeffro ohono. Ond eto, roedd rhywbeth yn mynnu ei chadw'n effro.

Dechreuodd Ceren ystwyrian wrth ei hochr a chwyno o dan ei gwynt. Os deffroai, fe ddeuai Mam yno i'w chysuro. I roi diod iddi a lapio'r gynfas yn glòs tros ei hysgwydd. Bron na ddeffrai hi Ceren rŵan er mwyn denu Mam yno atyn nhw, a chlywed ei chwerthiniad ysgafn fel y setlai y ddwy ohonyn nhw'n ôl i gysgu.

Gwenodd Bethan yn y tywyllwch. Na, gwell iddi beidio. Roedd Mam yn haeddu'i chwsg fel pawb arall. Roedd hi . . .

MAM! Cofiodd. *Roedd Mam wedi marw!*
Doedd hi ddim yma. Fyddai hi byth yma eto.
Tynnodd ei choesau at ei gên a gwasgodd ei
hun yn belen gron o dan y gynfas. Roedd ei
meddwl yn llawn atgofion. Mam yn mwmian
canu wrth dynnu'r deisen sinsir o'r ffwrn;
Mam yn gwthio'r hwfer, a'r dwster yn hongian
yn llipa o boced ei ffedog, a Mam yn dewis
dodrefn i'w llofft newydd hithau. Mam yn
deddfu ac yn dweud y drefn. Ond beth oedd ots
am hynny rŵan?

Pam roedd yn rhaid i Mam farw a'u gadael
nhw? Pam roedden nhw yma hefo Anti Catrin
a Dad yn malio dim?

Teimlai'r gobennydd yn wlyb o dan ei
hwyneb. Symudodd Bethan yn anniddig.
Roedd . . . rhywle . . . arall . . . yn wlyb . . .
hefyd. Y fatras? Symudodd law arbrofol a
theimlo gwlybaniaeth oeraidd, ond cynnes
hefyd rhyngddi hi a Ceren. Beth? Cododd y
gynfas ac arogli'r gwagedd rhyngddynt. Daeth
drewdod melys trymaidd i'w ffroenau. Am
eiliad, ni fedrai ddychmygu beth ydoedd.
Yna . . .

Cododd ar ei heistedd yn frysiog ac ymestyn
am y golau. Taflodd y gynfas a'r cwilt o'r
neilltu a llygadu'r clwtyn gwlyb aflan a
ymledai tros y fatras. Wedi gwlychu'r gwely!
Nid y hi. Ond Ceren. Ych-â-fi! Wedi pi-pi yn y
gwely. Ond fyddai Ceren byth yn gwlychu. A

rŵan, dyma hi wedi gwneud yng ngwely Anti
Catrin. Beth ddywedai hi? Fyddai hi'n wyllt
gacwn? Yn ddigon gwyllt gacwn i'w hanfon yn
ôl adre hefo Dad pan ddeuai?

Dechreuodd Ceren gwyno a cheisio tynnu'r
dillad yn ôl.

'Ceren! Deffra!'

'Ddim eisio.'

Ceisiodd Ceren dyrchu'n is yn y gwely. Yna
dechreuodd ei gwefus grynu.

'Dwi'n wlyb, Bethan.'

Agorodd ei cheg i floeddio crio.

'Sssh! Paid â deffro Anti Catrin. Yli, mi
newidia i'r dillad. Ddim ond iti beidio â
gwneud sŵn.'

'Ond . . . ond . . . rydw i'n wlyb.'

'Wyt siŵr. Anghofio deffro wnest ti. Hidia
befo.'

'Ga i'r drefn? Gan Anti Catrin?'

'Na chei siŵr.'

'Eisio Mam. Eisio hi rŵan, Bethan.'

Ochneidiodd Bethan. Ond ddywedodd hi'r un
gair. Ddim ond codi'n benderfynol a pherswadio Ceren i godi hefyd.

'Yli. Mae gen ti goban lân yn y cês. Tynn
honna.'

'Eisio i ti wneud,' meddai'n gwynfanllyd.

Brathodd Bethan ei gwefus yn flin. Eisio.
Eisio. Roedd hithau eisio hefyd. Eisio gwely

sych. Eisio llofft iddi'i hun. Eisio mynd adre.
Eisio Mam yn ôl.

'Wnei di ddim deffro Anti Catrin, na wnei?'

'Na.'

Taflodd y cwilt i'r llawr a dechreuodd
dynnu'r dillad gwlyb oddi ar y gwely. Gobeithio fod gan Anti Catrin blastig i ddiogelu'r
fatras, meddyliodd. Oedd, diolch byth! Ond
châi hi ddim dweud y drefn wrth Ceren, p'run
bynnag, penderfynodd. Doedd Ceren a hithau
ddim eisio bod yma. Ar Anti Catrin a Dad
roedd y bai. Fyddai dim ots am wlychu'r gwely
gartre.

'Dwi'n oer, Bethan.'

'Gwisga dy ŵn nos, ta. A dy slipars.'

'Wn i ddim ble maen nhw.'

Estynnodd Bethan nhw'n ddistaw.

'Aros yn fan'na tra bydda i'n nôl dillad glân,'
gorchmynnodd.

'Ddim yn hir, na fyddi?'

Roedd golwg ddigalon ar Ceren ar lawr y
llofft. Cofleidiodd Bethan hi'n sydyn.

'Yli. Dwy funud fydda i. Eistedda ar y gadair,
a chyfra i ddeg.'

'Fedra i ddim.'

'Medri siŵr. Rwyt ti'n cyfri i ddeg ers tro.'

'Ddim eisio ista. Eisio pi-pi.'

Gafaelodd Bethan ynddi a'i rhuthro am yr
ystafell ymolchi. Efallai y câi hi gyfle i nôl

dillad glân tra byddai Ceren yn eistedd ar y pan.

'Gwna di. *A phaid â gwneud sŵn.*'

'Ond ma' 'na sŵn wrth bi-pi.'

'Oes siŵr. Peidio fflyshio roeddwn i'n 'i feddwl.'

'O!'

Gadawodd Ceren yn eistedd a cherddodd yn ofalus ddistaw am y cwpwrdd dillad. Agorodd y drws a phalfalodd ynddo.

Daeth sŵn pwyso ac ailbwyso handlen o'r ystafell ymolchi a dŵr yn arllwyso'n bistyll sydyn i'r pan wedyn.

'Ceren!' hisiodd Bethan yn ddiflas. 'Mi ddeudis i wrthyt ti . . .'

Ond roedd yn rhy hwyr. Agorodd drws llofft Anti Catrin.

'Be sy? Be wyt ti'n ei wneud yn y cwpwrdd dillad, Bethan?'

'Yyy-yymm!'

Ond waeth iddi heb â chelu. Fyddai dim modd celu fore trannoedd p'run bynnag.

'Ceren wedi cael damwain fach . . .'

'Damwain . . .?'

Daeth bloedd o ddrws yr ystafell ymolchi fel y dechreuodd Ceren grio o ddifri.

'Ddim yn trio, Anti Catrin. Ddim yn trio.'

Taflodd Anti Catrin un cipolwg beirniadol i gyfeiriad Bethan, cyn prysuro ati.

'Tyrd, Ceren fach. Wrth gwrs doeddet ti ddim yn trio.'

Arweiniodd hi'n ôl am y llofft gan orchymyn,

'Estyn ddysgl a chadach a disinffectant, Bethan. A'r hen dywel o'r gegin gefn hefyd. A'r gynfas binc waelod o'r cwpwrdd wedyn.'

Ufuddhaodd Bethan gan wgu. Roedd Anti Catrin fel petai yn ei beio hi am i Ceren wlychu. Deffro wedi iddi wneud ddaru hi, 'tê?

Estynnodd bopeth yn ddistaw, a chynorthwyo Anti Catrin i sychu'r fatras ac ailwneud y gwely. Aeth cryndod sydyn trwyddi. Fe ddylai fod wedi gwisgo'i gŵn nos.

'I dy wely rŵan, Ceren,' meddai Anti Catrin. 'Reit i lawr o dan y dillad.'

'Bethan hefyd.'

'Yn y munud,' meddai Anti Catrin. 'Wedi iddi glirio tipyn bach.'

Gwisgodd Bethan ei gŵn nos a chludodd y ddysgl i lawr y grisiau wrth gwt Anti Catrin. Gobeithio nad ydi hi am ddechrau tantro a rhoi bai arna i, meddyliodd yn wgus. *Un gair, jest un gair* sydd eisio iddi'i ddweud. Dydw i ddim eisio bod yma, a does ganddi hi ddim hawl.

Ond rhoi'r tecell i ferwi a thanio'r tân trydan wnaeth Anti Catrin.

'Eistedd yn fan'na iti gael cynhesu,' meddai'n garedig gan estyn am y cwpanau.

Teimlodd Bethan y dagrau sydyn yn llenwi'i llygaid. Caredigrwydd oedd y peth diwethaf a ddisgwyliai gan Anti Catrin wedi smonach y gwlychu. Derbyniodd gwpan llawn yn ddiolchgar a llymeitiodd y te poeth yn araf.

'Wedi ypsetio mae Ceren, ysti,' meddai Anti Catrin gan eistedd yn y gadair gyferbyn. 'Effaith yr hyn a ddigwyddodd ydi'r gwlychu 'ma.'

'Pa bryd gawn ni fynd adre, Anti Catrin?' mentrodd Bethan.

Bu Anti Catrin yn ddistaw am beth amser.

'Wn i ddim, Bethan. Na wn i wir,' meddai'n drymaidd. 'Rwyt ti'n ddigon hen i ddallt fod pethau'n anodd iawn i dy dad ar hyn o bryd. Fedr o ddim canslo'r daith ddarlithio 'ma. Mae amserlen gaeth ganddo. A fedr o mo'ch gadael chi 'ych dwy ar eich pen eich hunain chwaith.'

'Pam na fedr o ganslo? Mae Mam wedi . . . Y ni sy'n bwysig rŵan. Ceren a fi a fo. Pam mae'n rhaid iddo fynd ar ryw hen daith ddarlithio? Mi fedr rhywun arall fynd.'

'Efallai y gwnaiff y daith les iddo, Bethan. Ei helpu i anghofio ychydig.'

Aeth ton chwilboeth trwy gorff Bethan.

'Anghofio? Does ganddo fo ddim hawl i anghofio. Ddim i anghofio Mam. Rydw *i*'n cofio, a Ceren hefyd.'

Nodiodd Anti Catrin yn bwyllog.

'Dyna pam roeddwn i eisio siarad hefo ti,' meddai. 'Am Ceren. Rhaid iti fod yn fwy o chwaer iddi, Bethan.'

'Mwy o chwaer?'

Doedd hi ddim yn deall. Sut y gallai hi fod yn fwy o chwaer? Siarad gwirion.

'Aros mwy hefo hi. Chwarae hefo hi. Mynd â hi am dro. Eistedd i weld y teledu hefo hi. Bod yn amyneddgar hefo hi.'

Dechreuodd y te chwildroi yn stumog Bethan. Ffordd arall o ddweud mai arni hi roedd y bai. Am y gwlychu. Am fynd allan hefo Mari. Am golli Mam. Am bopeth.

'Ddim eisio imi fynd allan hefo Mari ydach chi. Meddwl nad ydi hi'n ddigon da. Dyna be sy, 'tê? Yntê?'

Roedd hi bron yn gweiddi.

'Wel . . .'

'Waeth ichi ddweud y gwir ddim.'

'Trio dangos iti y peth gorau i'w wneud ydw i. Mae Ceren yn ypset . . .'

'Rydw inna'n ypset hefyd.'

'Wyt siŵr. Ond rwyt ti'n ddigon hen i ddallt.'

'Wna i *byth* ddallt. Byth ddallt pam roedd yn rhaid i Mam farw. Byth ddallt pam fod Dad yn fyw. Byth ddallt pam ein bod ni yma yn lle bod gartra. *Byth*!'

Sodrodd ei chwpan ar y bwrdd a rhuthro i fyny'r grisiau. Wnâi hi byth faddau i Anti Catrin am fod mor ddideimlad. Byth!

11.

Bu Bethan yn hir cyn cysgu wedi mynd yn ôl i'w gwely. Gorweddodd yno a'i thu mewn yn berwi ac ailferwi wrth gofio am eiriau Anti Catrin. Roedd hi wedi trio'i gorau, doedd? Wedi gwneud llw ei bod hi am ofalu am Ceren. Ond doedd Ceren ddim eisio'i gofal hi. Roedd chwarae hefo Solomon yn ddigon.

Cododd fore trannoeth yn teimlo'r un mor dymherus. Ond roedd Anti Catrin yn bihafio fel petai dim geiriau cas wedi bod rhyngddynt. Efallai'i bod hi wedi anghofio? Ond, na.

'Mi gei di chwarae hefo Bethan y bore 'ma,' meddai wrth Ceren wedi gorffen brecwast.

Cwympodd wyneb Ceren yn syth.

'Ddim eisio. Eisio chwarae hefo Solomon. Mrs Jones wedi addo.'

'Ddim heddiw, Ceren,' meddai Anti Catrin gan gadw'i llais yn rhesymol. 'Mi gewch chi chwarae yn yr ardd a dŵad am dro i'r parc wedyn.'

Cododd llais Ceren yn wylofain.

'Ddim eisio. Ddim eisio.'

Fe deimlai Bethan yn falch wrth ei chlywed. Eitha gwaith ag Anti Catrin am drio trefnu pethau i'w siwtio hi ei hun, heb feddwl am deimladau neb arall. Cuddiodd wên o dan ei bysedd fel y llymeitiodd weddillion ei choffi.

'Dim rhaid, nac oes? Dim rhaid chwarae hefo Bethan yn lle Solomon.'

Roedd wyneb Ceren yn goch gan dymer a dagrau. Dechreuodd strancio.

Ceisiodd Anti Catrin afael ynddi a'i chofleidio ond roedd corff Ceren yn dalpyn styfnig.

Yn erbyn ei hewyllys fe ddechreuodd Bethan gydymdeimlo, nid hefo Ceren, ond hefo Anti Catrin. Doedd hi ddim yn gwybod sut i drin plant yn strancio, yn nac oedd? Anwybyddu Ceren wnâi Mam bob amser. Gadael llonydd iddi strancio a chrio a cheisio cael ei ffordd ei hun, nes byddai'r storm drosodd. A pheidio byth ag ildio iddi.

'O diar! O diar!' meddai Anti Catrin gan geisio tynnu Ceren ati.

Ond roedd corff Ceren yn hollol anhyblyg.

'Dydw i ddim eisio chwarae hefo Bethan. Ddim eisio. Ddim eisio.'

Roedd Bethan wedi cael llond bol. Gafaelodd yn Ceren a'i thynnu oddi wrth Anti Catrin. Plonciodd hi ar y gadair.

'Aros yn fan'na nes rwyt ti wedi gorffen gwneud stŵr.'

Trodd at Anti Catrin.

'Gadael llonydd iddi fyddai Mam. Cymryd dim sylw. Mam . . . yn . . .'

Yna, rywsut, roedd hi ym mreichiau Anti Catrin.

96

'Sori, Anti Catrin. Doeddwn i ddim yn meddwl yr hyn ddeudais i neithiwr. Sori.'

'Dallt 'ngeneth i,' oedd yr ateb. 'Dallt yn iawn.'

Ond dyna oedd y broblem, yntê. *Doedd* Anti Catrin na neb yn deall. Doedden nhw ddim yn gwybod am y gwacter oedd y tu mewn iddi, na'r teimlad amddifad wrth wybod nad oedd Dad eu heisio nhw am fod Mam wedi . . . marw.

Yn sydyn hyrddiodd Ceren ei hun tuag atynt.

'Fi hefyd. Fi hefyd.'

Gafaelodd yn dynn yng nghoesau Bethan ac Anti Catrin a chladdodd ei hwyneb yn eu dillad.

'Mi fydda i'n hogan dda. Wir yr. Ond rydw i'n *licio* Solomon.'

Gwenodd Anti Catrin ychydig.

'Beth am iti aros hefo Bethan y bore 'ma?' cynigiodd. 'A chwarae hefo Solomon yn y pnawn?'

'Www, ia.'

Roedd Ceren yn wên i gyd ar unwaith.

'Mi faset tithau yn medru mynd at Mari y pnawn 'ma, Bethan,' meddai Anti Catrin. 'Mae'n dda iti gael ffrind 'run oed â ti.'

Edrychodd Bethan yn syn ar ei modryb.

'Ond . . . dydych chi ddim eisio . . .' tawelodd ei llais yn ddim.

'Ia, wel. Eisio'ch cadw chi'n glòs roeddwn i. Y ti a Ceren.'

'Ond rydyn ni'n glòs,' meddai Bethan mewn syndod. 'Mor glòs ag erioed.'

Ond fe wyddai nad oedd hynny'n wir chwaith. Roedd hi a Ceren yn rhan o deulu o'r blaen, doedden? Yn ddwy a mam a thad ganddyn nhw.

Erstalwm, roedd popeth yn ddiogel o'u cwmpas. Ond rŵan . . .

Tynhaodd Bethan ei gafael yn Ceren. Ei chwaer fach oedd hi, meddyliodd yn ffyrnig. Fe ofalai hi na châi gam.

'Dowch inni glirio'r bwrdd,' meddai Anti Catrin.

Roedd ei llais mor undonog a dideimlad ag arfer. Fel pe na bai dim siarad arbennig wedi bod rhyngddynt, neithiwr na'r bore 'ma.

Efallai mai felly oedd orau, meddyliodd Bethan, fel y sychodd y llestri a'u cadw yn y cwpwrdd. Peidio â dangos cariad na theimlad at neb. Chaech chi mo'ch brifo wedyn, na gadael i golled eich boddi mewn atgofion chwaith.

Wedi cael cinio, aeth i chwilio am Mari. Cerddodd yn gyflym heibio i'r rhes dai a'r criw merched ar stepan un o'r drysau, nes cyrraedd at y drws melyn a'r chwysigod yn frith arno. Curodd.

Dim ateb. Curodd yn drymach. Doedd bosib nad oedd Mari i mewn. Ciliodd ychydig ac edrych i fyny at ffenestr y llofft. Ond doedd dim symudiad yno chwaith.

Llifodd siom trosti. Roedd hi wedi meddwl yn siŵr cael cwmni Mari. Efallai ei bod hi wedi mynd i'r parc. Trodd yn ôl am y giât fach.

'Chwilio am Mari oeddet ti?'

Safai Mrs Morris drws nesa yno.

'Ia.'

'Dydi hi ddim yma ers y bore. Mi aeth ar ras wyllt. Os gweli di hi, deuda fy mod i wedi paratoi caserôl i'r ddau ohonyn nhw erbyn heno.'

'Ôl-reit.'

Trodd Bethan ar ei sawdl a chychwyn i gyfeiriad y parc. Mi fyddai Mari'n grac ulw pan glywai am y caserôl, meddyliodd. Tybed a oedd Mari'n iawn, a bod Mrs Morris a'i llygaid ar ei thad? Roedd hi, Bethan, yn gweld Mrs Morris yn ddynes iawn. Yn ddynes garedig.

Roedd yr haul yn boeth ar ei breichiau noeth fel y cerddodd trwy'r giatiau. Arafodd ei cherddediad a chymerodd seibiant bach wedi cyrraedd ymyl y llyn. Roedd awel ysgafn i'w theimlo a mwynhaodd ei gyffyrddiad oeraidd ar ei chroen chwyslyd.

Yna cofiodd am ei mam. Sut y gallai hi anghofio'r hyn a ddigwyddodd am eiliad? Doedd ganddi ddim hawl i anghofio nac i fwynhau. Safodd yno a'r hiraeth yn llifo'n don trosti. Mam. Teimlodd y dagrau'n pigo y tu ôl i'w llygaid, ond fe'u gorfododd yn ôl. Doedd pethau ddim gwell wrth ichi grio, yn nac oeddynt?

Cerddodd ymlaen am y mur rhododendrons. Roedd Mari'n siŵr o fod yn y sièd. Fe gâi'r ddwy ohonyn nhw eistedd . . . a siarad . . . a threulio amser yn gwneud dim . . . a chofio.

Arafodd ac edrych o gwmpas yn wyliadwrus. Rhaid iddi fod yn ofalus. Doedd Mari ddim am i neb ganfod eu cuddfan.

Llithrodd trwodd ac ymladd ei ffordd trwy'r llwyni ac ymlaen trwy'r ffens fratiog. Roedd drws y sièd yn gilagored.

'Mari!' galwodd yn ofalus fel y cyrhaeddodd ato.

Ni ddaeth ateb.

'Wyt ti yna?'

Pwysodd yn erbyn y drws a'i agor. Roedd Mari'n eistedd a'i chefn yn erbyn y wal.

'Hei! Pam na faset ti'n f'ateb . . . ?' cychwyn-nodd.

Yna fe'i hataliodd ei hun. Roedd llygaid Mari'n chwyddedig goch ac ôl crio ar ei hwyneb.

'Be sy?'

Cododd Mari ei hysgwyddau heb ddweud gair.

'Wyt ti'n sâl?'

Ysgydwodd Mari ei phen yn ddistaw.

'Be sy, ta? Dy dad?'

'Ia—aa.'

Roedd ateb Mari'n ochenaid hir.

'Dydi o ddim gwell. Eistedd trwy'r gyda'r nos heb ddweud gair. A ddaru fo ddim bwyta'i fwyd. Dim ond eistedd ... a sbio ... ac ochneidio, a'i lygaid o'n symud dim.'

Yn sydyn, trodd a chladdu'i hwyneb yn ysgwydd Bethan.

'Dydw i ddim yn gwybod beth i'w wneud. Mae gen i ofn. Ofn iddo fo ... iddo fo ...'

'Beth am Mrs Morris? Fedr honno ddim siarad hefo fo?'

'Honno? Dydw i ddim eisio iddi hi roi'i throed trwy'r drws. Busnesu, a thrio cael ei phig i mewn.'

'Ond mae'n ddrwg ganddi am be sy wedi digwydd, Mari. Doedd ganddi hi ddim help—na dy dad chwaith.'

Roedd wyneb Mari yn styfnig.

'Dydw i ddim eisio hi.'

Wyddai Bethan ddim beth i'w ddweud.

'Beth am fodryb neu ewythr, nain neu daid?'

'Sgynnon ni ddim.'

'Dim un?'

'Na.'

Bu distawrwydd hir rhwng y ddwy. O'r diwedd, ochneidiodd Mari a rhwbio'i hwyneb yn flinedig. Ceisiodd wenu.

'Waeth imi heb, yn na waeth? Wyt ti eisio creision? Halen a finegr ta caws a nionyn?'

Bwytaodd y ddwy heb siarad.

'Mi fasen ni'n medru byw yma, ysti,' meddai Mari'n sydyn. 'Jest y chdi a fi.'

'Ond . . .'

'Ond, be? Does neb yn malio amdanon ni, nac oes?'

'Mae Dad yn dŵad fory. Efalla y bydda i a Ceren yn mynd adra.'

'O!'

Roedd siom ar wyneb Mari, ond llygedyn o ollyngdod hefyd. Fel pe na bai hi o ddifri, p'run bynnag.

'Wnâi o ddim gweithio. Faswn i ddim yn gadael Dad,' meddai.

'Na finna'n gadael Ceren a Dad chwaith.'

'Na.'

Eisteddodd y ddwy'n dawedog eto. Yna edrychodd Mari ar ei wats.

'Well imi fynd yn ôl. Eisio paratoi swper—os gwnaiff rhywun ei fwyta fo.'

Cofiodd Bethan am Mrs Morris a'i chaserôl.

'Mi welais i Mrs Morris yn nrws y tŷ nesa gynnau. Eisio imi ddweud 'i bod hi wedi paratoi caserôl.'

'Tydw i'n dweud wrthyt ti?' chwyrnodd Mari. 'Ma'r blydi dynes fel barn. Stwffio hi a'i chaserôl.'

Caeodd ddrws y sièd â chlep wichlyd.

'O, tyrd yn dy flaen,' meddai'n flin.

Yna stopiodd yn stond.

103

'Wyt ti'n mynd fory? Wir?'

'Wel . . .'

'Ond wela i mohonot ti eto, felly.'

Yn sydyn roedd llygaid Mari'n llawn dagrau. Rhwbiodd nhw i ffwrdd yn ffyrnig.

'Fydd gen i neb wedyn. O, be 'di'r ots. Dydw i'n malio dim am neb.'

'Mi ddo i i ddweud wrthyt ti. Wedi i Dad gyrraedd.'

'Ddoi di?'

'Dof, siŵr.'

Dringodd y ddwy y llethr ac ymwthio trwy'r llwyni.

'Aros,' sibrydodd Mari. 'Jest rhag ofn.'

Sbeciodd trwy'r rhododendron, yna amneidiodd ar Bethan i'w dilyn.

'Wela i di fory ta?' meddai wrth giât y parc.

'Gweli.'

Ac er bod Bethan ar dân eisio gweld ei thad, ac eisio mynd adre hefyd, fedrai hi ddim peidio â phitïo ei bod hi'n gadael Mari.

Cerddodd ar hyd y palmant a'i meddyliau'n chwildroi o'i mewn. Mari . . . Mam . . . Anti Catrin . . . Ceren . . . Dad. Pam roedd yn rhaid i fywyd fod mor anhapus a chaled?

12.

Fe ddeffrodd Bethan yn gynnar fore Sadwrn. Gorweddodd am eiliadau hir yn syllu i gyfeiriad y ffenestr agored ac yn gwrando ar anadlu ysgafn Ceren ar y dde iddi.

Mae Dad yn dŵad heddiw, meddyliodd. Efallai mai dyma'r bore olaf imi ddeffro yn y gwely yma. Efallai y bydda i'n deffro yn fy llofft newydd bore fory, a Ceren yn ei llofft hithau.

Ond fedrai hi ddim credu hynny chwaith. Cofiodd am eiriau Anti Catrin. Fel roedd taith ddarlithio gan ei thad, ac na fedrai'r ddwy ohonyn nhw aros gartre ar eu pen eu hunain, na mynd hefo fo chwaith.

Dechreuodd Ceren symud a chwyno fel y gwnâi bob amser wrth ddeffro. Doedd hi 'rioed wedi gwlychu eto?

Rhoddodd Bethan law arbrofol rhwng y dillad. Na, roedd pobman yn sych! Plygodd tros ei chwaer fel yr agorodd ei llygaid.

'Dad yn dŵad heddiw, Ceren.'

'A Mam?'

Suddodd calon Bethan.

'Na . . . ddim Mam,' meddai'n drymaidd.

'Ond rydw i'i heisio hi.'

A finna hefyd. A finna hefyd, meddyliodd Bethan yn drist. Rydw i'n gweld ei heisio hi bob dydd. Mi roddwn i'r byd am gael clywed ei llais a chyfarfod ei llygaid wrth rannu jôc.

'Ydi Mam hefo Iesu Grist o hyd?'

'Ydi.'

'Ydi hi'n licio yno? Yn well na hefo ni?'

'Wn i ddim, Ceren.'

Ond *roedd* hi'n gwybod hefyd. Yma hefo nhw y basa Mam yn dewis bod.

'Hyd yn oed tasa hi wedi brifo'n ofnadwy, a byth am wella?' gofynnodd llais bach o'i mewn.

Caeodd ei llygaid rhag y darlun a dyfodd yn ei meddwl. Mam mewn gwely yn rhwymynnau i gyd. Mam yn methu siarad, methu cerdded, a methu gwenu. Mam hefo peipen yn ei bwydo a llinellau poen a digalondid ar ei hwyneb. Fedrai hi ddim dioddef ei gweld felly. Pwysodd yn ôl ar y gobennydd a chaeodd ei llygaid.

'Wyt ti'n cysgu?'

Agorodd ei llygaid eto i ganfod Ceren ar ei heistedd ac yn edrych i lawr arni.

'Na . . . jest . . .'

Fedrai hi ddim gorffen. Cododd.

'Tyrd i molchi. Mi fydd Dad yma ar ôl brecwast.'

Dilynodd Ceren hi'n ufudd. Ond roedd ei gwefusau'n crynu.

'Eisio mynd adra at Mam a Dad. Ddim eisio aros yma, Bethan.'

Pam roedd yn rhaid iddi *hi* drio darbwyllo Ceren? Dad ddylai egluro. Y fo ac Anti Catrin. Y nhw oedd yn gwybod sut. A wyddai hi ddim oedd hi'n credu mewn Duw ac Iesu Grist

106

chwaith. Ddim ar ôl iddyn nhw adael i Mam farw. Fyddai rhywun da ddim yn caniatáu hynny.

Dringodd y ddwy i lawr y grisiau ac i'r gegin. Roedd Anti Catrin wedi gosod y bwrdd yn barod, a llenwai arogl tôst eu ffroenau fel y cerddasant i mewn.

'Bwytewch eich dwy. Mi fydd eich tad yma toc.'

Doedd dim awydd bwyd ar Bethan. Roedd ei stumog yn corddi gormod. A'i thu mewn yn tynhau a thynhau hefyd, nes roedd yn gwlwm anystwyth.

Daeth sŵn car o'r tu allan a gwich y brecio.

'Dad!'

Neidiodd Ceren o'i chadair a rhedeg am y drws.

'Dad! Mam!'

Pletiodd Anti Catrin ei cheg ac ysgwyd ei phen fel y brysiodd am y drws ffrynt.

'Huw! Mi gyrhaeddaist di,' meddai.

Roedd Ceren wedi gwthio heibio iddo ac yn edrych i gyfeiriad y car.

'Ble mae Mam!' holodd yn ddagreuol.

Edrychodd eu tad ac Anti Catrin ar ei gilydd.

'Fel'na mae hi,' meddai Anti Catrin. 'Dydi hi ddim wedi sylweddoli.'

Fe deimlai Bethan fel rhywun dieithr yn sefyll yno a neb yn cymryd sylw ohoni. Roedd hithau'n ferch iddo, doedd? Ac wedi cael yr un golled â Ceren.

Yna roedd breichiau ei thad amdani ac yn ei gwasgu ato.

'Bethan. 'Ngenath i,' meddai a'i lais yn crynu.

'Dad.' Roedd dagrau bron â'i threchu.

Safai Ceren ar stepan y drws. Doedd hi'n dweud yr un gair, dim ond yn sefyll yno ac yn edrych o un i'r llall fel petai'n methu deall. Yna rhoddodd floedd sydyn a rhedeg fel bwled i gyfeiriad ei thad.

'Dydi hi ddim yma. *Ddim yma!*'

Cododd eu tad hi a'i chludo yn ei freichiau i'r lolfa. Eisteddodd ar y soffa a gafael yn dynn ynddi.

'Na, dydi hi ddim yma, Ceren,' meddai.

Dringodd bawd Ceren yn araf i gyfeiriad ei cheg. Eisteddodd ar ei lin heb ddweud gair, dim ond sugno, sugno a'i llygaid yn llenwi'i hwyneb yn sydyn.

Yna,

'Chwarae hefo Solomon,' meddai gan lithro oddi ar ei lin a diflannu am ddrws y cefn.

'Ceren . . .'

'Gad iddi,' meddai Anti Catrin. 'Mae hi'n fodlon yn nhŷ Mrs Jones.'

Roedd Bethan eisio gafael yn ei thad. Eisio gafael ynddo a byth ei ollwng eto. Ond fe deimlai swildod rhyfedd. Fel petai hi'n ansicr o'i chroeso, a'i thad yn rhywun dieithr iddi.

'Rydw i wedi dŵad â blodau,' meddai ei thad yn drymaidd. 'Ddoi di hefo mi i'r amlosgfa, Bethan?'

Oedd hi eisio mynd? Eisio gweld yr adeilad lle y gwelodd hi arch ei mam ddiwethaf? Y bocs hwnnw hefo Elisabeth Rees wedi'i sgrifennu ar y plât arian?

Ble'r oedd yr arch rŵan? Llosgi pobl roedden nhw mewn amlosgfa, yntê? Caeodd ei llygaid rhag y darlun o fflamau, a llosgi, a mynd am byth!

'Ddoi di?'

Nodiodd heb ddweud gair.

'Ia. Ewch chi,' meddai Anti Catrin. 'Mi fydd Ceren yn iawn hefo Mrs Jones tra byddwch chi.'

Trodd y ddau am y drws. Daeth gwaedd fel y rhwygodd Ceren ei ffordd o'r cefn a'i thaflu ei hun at ei thad.

'Chewch chi ddim mynd. Dwi'n dŵad adre hefyd.'

Plygodd eu tad a gafael yn dynn ynddi.

'Dim ond . . .'

Edrychodd yn fud i gyfeiriad Bethan ac Anti Catrin a llyncodd boer yn gynhyrfus.

'Fedra i ddim mynd â hi. Ddim i'r amlosgfa, Catrin.'

Ond roedd Ceren wedi plethu'i breichiau am ei wddf ac yn gwrthod gollwng.

'Mi ddo i hefo chi,' meddai Anti Catrin gan estyn am ei chôt.

Yn fuan roedden nhw yn y car.

'Welwn ni Mam?'

Tynhaodd dwylo'i thad ar y llyw.

'Na welwn,' atebodd yn floesg.

Roedd dwylo Bethan yn chwysu fel y troesant i mewn trwy giatiau'r amlosgfa. Roedd hi'n cofio. Yn cofio'r meinciau hir a'u caledwch oeraidd, yn cofio'r crio distaw y tu ôl iddi a llais soniarus yn geirio'n hunllefus . . . *'Ein chwaer annwyl . . .'* ac yn cofio'r arch dderw â'i phlât arian.

Plethodd ei bysedd yn nerfus fel y camodd allan o'r car. Gafaelodd ei thad yn y blodau a thynnodd botel ddŵr o'r bŵt. Yna arweiniodd y ffordd am furiau sgwâr y gilan yng nghornel yr ardd.

Agorodd y giât a'i dal yn agored iddyn nhw ddod trwodd. Edrychodd Bethan o'i chwmpas. Roedd hi'n cofio'r placiau a oedd yn frith ar y waliau, pob un hefo'i ddyddiad geni a'i ddyddiad marw. Cerddodd ei thad yn araf at y gornel. Gwasgodd ei fysedd goesau'r blodau fel yr edrychodd ar y plac newydd a osodwyd yno.

Safodd Bethan wrth ei ochr. Elisabeth Rees, dyna oedd ar y plac. Roedd Mam yn blac ar y wal bellach. Plac marmor oeraidd, ac enw yr un mor oeraidd a llwm arno. Enw a phlac na allai hi'u cysylltu hefo mam gynnes, gariadus, llawn chwerthin iach. Ond plac Mam oedd o.

Teimlodd wefr y colli a'r gwagedd o'i mewn fel y plygodd Dad i agor y botel. Tywalltodd ddŵr i botyn crwn a rhoi'r blodau ynddo. Yna'i osod gyferbyn â'r plac.

'Blodau pwy?' holodd Ceren.

'Blodau Mam,' meddai ei thad.

'Ydi hi yma?'

'Ydi,' oedd yr ochenaid ddistaw, o dan ei wynt bron.

'Yn lle?' holodd Ceren yn ddagreuol. 'Yn lle?'

Ni allai Dad ateb. Gafaelodd Anti Catrin yn llaw Ceren.

'Cofia am Solomon, Ceren.'

'Be mae Solomon yn ei wneud, Anti Catrin?' holodd Ceren.

Gwasgodd Anti Catrin ei llaw.

'Disgwyl amdanat ti, rwy'n siŵr,' meddai.

'Ia, 'tê?' meddai Ceren yn hapus. 'Mynd rŵan?'

Cerddodd y ddwy trwy'r giât ac i gynhesrwydd y bore heulog tu allan. Edrychodd Bethan ar ei thad. Roedd ei wyneb yn gaeedig bell fel y syllai ar y blodau.

'Dad!' mentrodd Bethan. 'Dad!'

Ni ddaeth ateb.

'Dad! Ydyn ni'n mynd adre heddiw? Y fi a Ceren a chi?'

111

Fe wyddai fod ei llais yn codi'n daer. Ond roedd hi eisio gwybod. Eisio gwybod *rŵan*!

Edrychodd ei thad arni fel petai'n rhywun dieithr.

'Be?'

'Dŵad adre. Heddiw. Hefo chi. Ceren a finna.'

Estynnodd ei thad i'w thynnu'n glòs.

'Fedrwch chi ddim. Mae'r daith ddarlithio a . . .'

'Mi ddown ni hefo chi. Fyddwn ni'n ddim trafferth.'

Ysgydwodd ei thad hi'n ôl a blaen yn ei freichiau am eiliad.

'Rhaid iti sylweddoli'r problemau, Bethan. Fedrwch chi ddim. Mae gen i daith flinedig ac amserlen dynn. Ciniawa a chyfarfod dynion busnes yn llenwi'r dyddiau. A be faswn i'n 'i wneud hefo chi? Eich gadael mewn gwesty ar ôl gwesty?'

'Mi arhoswn ni gartre, ta.'

Ysgydwodd ei thad ei ben.

'Bethan, Bethan. Fedra i ddim gwneud hynny chwaith. Rwyt ti'n *gwybod* na fedra i ddim. Wn i ddim lle i droi, a dyna'r gwir iti.'

Llenwodd y siom ei gwddf. Dim gobaith mynd adre. Dyna roedd o'n ei ddweud, yntê? Ond beth oedd am ddigwydd iddyn nhw?

13.

Cnociodd Bethan ar ddrws cartre Mari trannoeth. Ble roedd hi heddiw? Fe chwiliodd amdani yn y parc, ac yn y sièd hefyd, ond doedd dim golwg ohoni.

Cnociodd eto. Dim ateb. Efallai fod Mari yn y cefn, meddyliodd. Yn rhoi dillad ar y lein, neu rywbeth felly. Aeth rownd y gornel i'r ardd gefn.

'Mari!' galwodd.

Meddyliodd ei bod yn clywed ateb. Yn y tŷ? Pwysodd yn erbyn drws y cefn. Fe ildiodd o dan ei bysedd.

'Ble rwyt ti?'

Safodd yn stond ar lawr y gegin. Roedd Mari'n hanner gorwedd ar y llawr a chadair wedi'i dymchwel wrth ei hochr.

'*Mari*! Be wnest ti?'

Roedd wyneb Mari'n wyn gan boen.

'Cyrraedd i'r cwpwrdd top. Disgyn.'

Penliniodd Bethan wrth ei hochr.

'Ble rwyt ti wedi'i frifo?'

'Ffêr.'

'Fedri di dynnu dy drainer?'

'Wn i ddim.'

'Tyrd i mi drio.'

Datododd Bethan y careiau a thynnodd yr esgid yn araf ofalus. Roedd ffêr Mari'n chwyddedig ddu a chochni ffyrnig yn dringo i fyny'i choes.

'Oooww!'

Rhoddodd Mari ochenaid boenus.

'Wwww, mae hi'n brifo.'

'Aros imi roi cadach gwlyb arni,' meddai Bethan.

Roedd hi'n cofio iddi hithau droi'i throed unwaith, ac i Mam roi cadach oer arni.

Brysiodd i wasgu cadach o dan y tap dŵr oer a'i osod yn ofalus ar ffêr Mari.

'Yli, aros yn fan'na,' gorchmynnodd Bethan. 'Mi a i i nôl Mrs Morris.'

'Na, dydw i ddim eisio hi.'

Ond roedd Bethan wedi diflannu trwy'r drws cyn i Mari orffen siarad.

Dobiodd ar ddrws cefn y tŷ nesa.

'Mrs Morris! Mrs Morris!'

Agorodd y drws ar unwaith.

'Mari wedi brifo. Syrthio a throi'i ffêr,' eglurodd Bethan yn frysiog.

Daeth cydymdeimlad i wyneb Mrs Morris.

'O diar!' meddai gan gychwyn yn syth wrth sodlau Bethan.

Gwgodd Mari wrth ei gweld.

'Rydw i'n iawn,' meddai'n anniolchgar.

Chymerodd Mrs Morris ddim gronyn o sylw o'i geiriau.

'Tyrd imi weld,' meddai gan blygu i dynnu'r cadach oer am eiliad.

'Mi wnest yn iawn, Bethan,' meddai. 'Mae rhywbeth oer yn dda i anaf fel hwn. Ond mae'n well iti fynd i'r ysbyty, Mari. Helpa fi i'w chodi hi, Bethan.'

Ar ôl iddynt osod Mari yn ofalus mewn cadair freichiau, estynnodd Mrs Morris glustog a stôl fechan, a rhoi troed y claf i orffwys arnynt.

'Mi a i i ffonio'r ambiwlans y funud 'ma. Dal i newid y cadachau oer, Bethan, tra bydda i.'

'Dydw i ddim eisio . . .' cychwynnodd Mari.

Ond roedd Mrs Morris wedi diflannu'n ôl i'w thŷ.

'Does ganddi hi ddim hawl,' meddai Mari rhwng ei dannedd. 'Dydw i ddim yn mynd.'

Taflodd y glustog o'r neilltu a cheisio rhoi ei throed ar y llawr. Ond bu'n rhaid iddi ddisgyn yn ôl.

Newidiodd Bethan y cadach oer a cheisio ei chysuro.

'Mrs Morris sy'n iawn, ysti. Be taset ti wedi torri asgwrn yn dy ffêr?'

Edrych yn flin wnaeth Mari a dweud dim.

Daeth Mrs Morris yn ôl.

'Mi ddaw yr ambiwlans yma rŵan.'

Nid atebodd Mari.

'Well imi ffonio dy dad,' ychwanegodd Mrs Morris. 'Be ydi rhif y gwaith, Mari?'

'Dim ots ganddo fo,' meddai Mari.

Pwysodd yn ôl yn y gadair a'r dagrau araf yn treiglo i lawr ei hwyneb.

'Dydi o'n malio dim.'

'Wrth gwrs ei fod o,' meddai Mrs Morris. 'Y chdi ydi'r un bwysica yn ei fywyd o.'

Trodd Mari ei phen i ffwrdd heb ddweud gair.

'Be ydi o, Mari?' holodd Mrs Morris eto.

'392415,' meddai Mari'n anewyllysgar.

'Reit,' meddai Mrs Morris. 'Fydda i ddim chwinciad. Mi gaiff ein cyfarfod yn yr ysbyty.'

'Meddwl mai hi ydi'r bòs,' meddai Mari rhwng ei dannedd.

Cyrhaeddodd Mrs Morris yn ôl fel yr arafodd yr ambiwlans wrth ddrws y ffrynt.

'Mae dy dad allan ar joban,' meddai. 'Ond maen nhw am drio cael gafael arno fo.'

'Wel! Wel!' meddai'r dyn ambiwlans wrth weld Mari. 'Trio gwneud campau oeddet ti?'

Yn fuan roedd Mari'n eistedd mewn cadair arbennig ac yn cael ei chludo allan i'r ambiwlans.

'Tyrd hefo mi,' meddai wrth Bethan.

'Ia, tyrd, Bethan,' ategodd Mrs Morris. 'Mi fydd Mari'n falch o dy gwmni di.'

Gwgodd Mari arni heb ddweud gair.

Rhoddodd calon Bethan dro sydyn fel y dringodd i mewn ar ôl Mari. Mewn ambiwlans y dygwyd Mam i'r ysbyty? Oedd hi wedi gorwedd ar y gwely y tu mewn a'i chorff yn friwedig boenus tra canai'r seiren uwch ei phen? Ynteu oedd hi wedi . . . marw . . . yn y ddamwain?

Doedd neb wedi dweud, ac roedd ganddi hawl i wybod, doedd?

Ceisiodd wenu ar Mari.

'Fyddwn ni ddim yn hir rŵan,' meddai. 'Gei di blaster caled, tybed?'

Powliodd y dyn ambiwlans gadair Mari i'r adran ddamweiniau. Roedd y lle'n llawn o bobl yn disgwyl yn amyneddgar. Breichiau wedi'u brifo, bysedd wedi'u brifo, coesau wedi'u brifo, a rhwymynnau tros dro ar lawer ohonynt.

Mi fyddwn yma am oriau, meddyliodd Bethan.

Yna cofiodd am Anti Catrin. Efallai y dylai ffonio i ddweud wrthi beth oedd wedi digwydd. Jest rhag ofn iddi fod yn hwyr am ginio. Ond doedd ganddi ddim dimai yn ei phoced. Chafodd hi ddim gan Dad ddoe. Wnaeth o ddim gofyn oedd ganddi arian, ddim ond ffarwelio a neidio i'w gar ac i ffwrdd â fo. A'i gadael hi a Ceren ar ôl. Dyna oedd yn brifo.

'Mari Beynon,' galwodd y nyrs. 'Ffordd hyn.'

Amneidiodd i gyfeiriad y drysau dwbl.

Cododd Mrs Morris a gafael yn y gadair olwyn. Wyddai Bethan ddim beth i'w wneud.

'Tyrd, Bethan,' meddai Mrs Morris. 'Mi fydd 'na le i eistedd trwodd hefyd.'

Dilynodd y gadair olwyn i stafell aros fechan. Fydden nhw ddim yn hir, wedi cael sylw mor fuan.

Amneidiodd y nyrs i gyfeiriad dwy gadair wrth y wal.

'Eisteddwch,' meddai. 'Mi a i â Mari drwodd at y meddyg.'

Eisteddodd Bethan wrth ochr Mrs Morris. Pa bryd y deuai tad Mari tybed? Oedd o ar ei ffordd rŵan, ac yn poeni am yr hyn a ddigwyddodd?

Aeth yr amser heibio.

'Maen nhw'n hir,' sylwodd Mrs Morris. 'Ond fel'na mae hi mewn adran ddamweiniau. Mae'n dda bod yna le fel hyn, yn tydi?'

'Y-y?'

Trodd Mrs Morris i edrych arni.

'Wyt ti'n iawn, Bethan? Ddim yn hapus mewn awyrgylch ysbyty?'

Ysgydwodd Bethan ei phen heb ddweud gair.

'Mi fydd Mari'n iawn, os mai am hynny rwyt ti'n poeni,' meddai Mrs Morris. 'Os ydyn nhw'n llwyddo i drin damweiniau ceir a phethau felly, maen nhw'n siŵr o lwyddo i drin ffêr, yn tydyn?'

'Marw wnaeth Mam,' meddai Bethan mewn llais bychan bach.

'Be?'

Roedd syndod yn llais Mrs Morris, a braw hefyd.

'Marw wnaeth Mam,' meddai Bethan eto.

'O, Bethan bach. Wyddwn i ddim. Pa bryd?' meddai Mrs Morris.

Yn sydyn, roedd ei breichiau am Bethan, a

hithau'n beichio crio ar ei hysgwydd. Roedd ganddi gywilydd, ond eto fedrai hi ddim ei hatal ei hun. Roedd fel petai rhyw lifddor wedi agor yn rhywle, a holl loes y colli a'r troi cefn a'r gadael yn byrlymu o'i thu mewn.

Fe wyddai fod llais Mrs Morris uwch ei phen, ac fe wyddai ei bod hi'n trio'i chysuro hefyd. Ond nid y geiriau oedd yn bwysig. Y breichiau cynnes a'r cydymdeimlad oedd yn cyfri, a'r wybodaeth fod rhywun yn malio digon i'w chofleidio o ddifri. Nid fel Anti Catrin. Yn cofleidio ac yna'n pellhau ar unwaith.

'Rydw i'n iawn rŵan,' meddai Bethan o'r diwedd. 'Sori.'

'Diolch,' meddai wedyn.

Ac yn sydyn, roedd hi'n dweud popeth wrth Mrs Morris. Am y ddamwain a'r angladd, a Dad yn troi ei gefn, a neb yn egluro beth oedd am ddigwydd iddi hi a Ceren.

'Mae colled fel'na yn anodd i bawb,' meddai Mrs Morris. 'Rho di amser i dy dad. Y chi 'ych dwy sy'n bwysig iddo fo rŵan.'

Rhywbeth tebyg ddywedodd Mrs Morris wrth Mari hefyd, 'tê? 'Y chdi sy bwysica yn ei fywyd o.' Weithiau, roedd hi'n credu hynny, ond fedrai hi ddim dro arall. Pam roedd Dad wedi'i gadael hi a Ceren?

Doedd ganddi hi ddim i afael ynddo wedi colli Mam. Dim byd diogel, dim ond bywyd ar chwâl. A doedd neb am egluro beth oedd am ddigwydd. Dad nac Anti Catrin na neb.

Gwenodd yn ddagreuol ar Mrs Morris.

'Well rŵan?' holodd honno fel y daeth y nyrs â Mari'n ôl atynt.

'Rhaid iddi gael Pelydr X,' meddai. 'Y rhieni heb gyrraedd eto?'

Roedd Mari'n edrych yn obeithiol o gwmpas. Yna suddodd ei phen ar ei brest ac ni ddywedodd air.

'Mae Mr Beynon ar ei ffordd,' eglurodd Mrs Morris. 'Byw drws nesa rydw i.'

Estynnodd y nyrs bapur iddi.

'Ewch â hwn hefo chi,' meddai. 'Dilynwch yr arwyddion i'r adran. Wedi cael y prawf, dowch â hi'n ôl yma. Mi gaiff y meddyg air hefo chi wedi gweld y darluniau.'

Ni chododd Mari ei phen fel y gafaelodd Mrs Morris yn y gadair a dechrau ei gwthio ar hyd y coridor.

'Ydi dy ffêr yn dal i frifo?' holodd Bethan wrth ei hochr.

'Na, mi fedrwn i redeg milltir,' meddai Mari'n frathog.

Yna edifarhaodd.

'Sori,' mwngialodd.

Crafangiodd y munudau hirion heibio wrth iddynt ddisgwyl yn yr adran Pelydr X. Roedd Mari'n dawedog, ac wedi trio siarad unwaith neu ddwy, fe ddistawodd Mrs Morris a Bethan hefyd. Disgwyliodd y tair yn ddistaw.

'Mari Beynon!'

Daeth yr alwad eto. Gwthiodd y radiolegydd hi drwodd.

'Fyddwn ni ddim yn hir rŵan,' meddai Mrs Morris yn ddiolchgar.

Edrychodd ar ei wats.

'Diar! Mae 'mhell wedi amser cinio. Wyt ti eisio bwyd, Bethan?'

Wedi amser cinio? Mi fyddai Anti Catrin yn wyllt gacwn. Roedd yn rhaid iddi ffonio ar unwaith.

'Plîs, Mrs Morris. Ga i fenthyg rhywfaint o arian? Eisio ffonio Anti Catrin. Mi fydd hi'n poeni.'

'Wrth gwrs.' Palfalodd Mrs Morris yn ei bag llaw. 'Hanner can ceiniog. Mae 'na fwth ffôn yn ymyl y fynedfa.'

'Diolch.'

Brysiodd Bethan i'w gyfeiriad. Deialodd.

'Anti Catrin? Bethan sy 'ma.'

'Bethan! Ble rwyt ti? Rydw i'n disgwyl yn fan'ma, a dim gair gen ti. Thâl peth fel hyn ddim, Bethan.'

'Yn yr ysbyty . . .'

'Be? Yr ysbyty? Wyt ti wedi brifo? Be sy?'

Dyna syndod! Roedd panig yn llais Anti Catrin. 'Run fath â phetai ots ofnadwy ganddi.

'Mi ddo i yna ar unwaith.'

'Anti Catrin. Arhoswch. Ddim y fi. Mari. Wedi syrthio. Mrs Morris o'r drws nesa a finna wedi dŵad hefo hi.'

'Ac mi rwyt ti yn iawn?'

'Ydw. Ffonio i ddweud y bydda i'n hwyr. Cael Pelydr X mae hi rŵan. Ar ei ffêr. A dydi ei thad ddim wedi cyrraedd.'

Roedd hi'n falch ei bod wedi ffonio. Gwasgodd gynhesrwydd llais Anti Catrin ati'i hun. Roedd hi'n poeni o ddifri amdani, doedd?

Cyfarfu Mari a Mrs Morris hi yn y coridor.

'Dim ond gweld y meddyg eto,' meddai Mrs Morris.

Ddywedodd Mari yr un gair; dim ond ciledrych o dan ei haeliau'n wgus.

'Crac bach i'r asgwrn, ac anaf i'r gewyn,' dyfarnodd y meddyg wedi archwilio'r lluniau. 'Mi rown ni un o'r rhwymynnau tiwb yna iti, Mari. Mi gei faglau, ond dydi wiw iti roi pwysau ar y ffêr 'na. Mi welwn ni di yn y clinig ymhen pythefnos.'

Edrychodd ar Mrs Morris.

'Wnewch chithau ofalu ei bod hi'n bihafio, Mrs Beynon?'

'Mrs Morris, Doctor. Byw drws nesa. Ond mi ofala i amdani.'

Gwgodd Mari fwyfwy.

Gwthiodd Mrs Morris y gadair olwyn tua'r fynedfa. Roedden nhw bron â chyrraedd, pan agorodd y drysau tro yn frysiog.

'Mari! Be ddigwyddodd? Be wyt ti wedi'i wneud?'

Roedd golwg drafferthus ar dad Mari. Roedd sment ar ei ddillad gwaith, ac olion ei draed ar y llawr sglein. Rhwbiodd law ffrwcslyd trwy'i wallt fel y trodd at Mrs Morris.

'Diolch ichi am ddŵad â hi yma.'

Yna trodd at Mari eto.

'Sut wyt ti'n teimlo, Mari?'

'Iawn.'

Roedd llais Mari'n fyglyd gan ddagrau. Rhoddodd ei thad law ar ei hysgwydd am eiliad, cyn troi wedyn at Mrs Morris.

'Be ddywedodd y meddyg?'

'Crac bach i'r asgwrn, ac anafu'r gewyn. Gorffwys a'i throed i fyny am bythefnos, a pheidio â rhoi pwysau ar y droed,' oedd yr ateb.

Gwelodd Mr Beynon Bethan am y tro cyntaf.

'A phwy ydi hon?'

'Bethan. Ffrind Mari.'

'O! Wyddwn i ddim.'

Roedd golwg ansicr ar wyneb Mr Beynon am eiliad.

'Efalla y dylwn i fod wedi cymryd mwy o sylw. Ond mae hi'n anodd . . .'

Ochneidiodd. Yna rhwbiodd law sydyn tros wallt Mari.

'Dy gael di adra gynta, pwt. Ac mi gawn ni weld wedyn, 'tê?'

Eisteddodd Bethan wrth ochr Mari ar y sedd ôl.

'Dydi o ddim wedi 'ngalw fi'n "pwt" ers pan oedd Mam gartre,' sibrydodd Mari'n sydyn. 'Wyt ti'n meddwl ei fod o'n gwella, Bethan?'

Arafodd y car o flaen y tŷ. Cynorthwyodd ei thad hi o'r car ac estyn y baglau.

'Wyt ti am ei mentro hi?'

'Ydw.'

Symudodd yn undroed ansicr am y drws. Estynnodd Mrs Morris glustog fel y suddodd ar y soffa.

'Paned, a thamaid i'w fwyta?' holodd.

Yna petrusodd ac edrych o Mari i'w thad.

'Mi helpa i hynny fedra i. Tasa ond am yr hyn sy wedi digwydd. Wil a Bet yn mynd i ffwrdd fel y gwnaethon nhw. Ond dydw i ddim eisio bod yn niwsans.'

'Rydyn ni'n ddiolchgar iawn,' meddai Mr Beynon. 'Tydyn, Mari?'

'Ydyn,' oedd yr ateb anewyllysgar.

'Wel, rhywbeth fedra i'i wneud,' meddai Mrs Morris. 'Dim ond gofyn.'

Diflannodd am y gegin i lenwi'r tecell.

'Mi a i i helpu,' meddai Mr Beynon.

'Mae hi'n ffeind, tydi?' meddai Bethan.

'Hy!' meddai Mari. 'Bachu'i chyfle, 'tê?'

14.

Estynnodd y dyddiau'n batrwm undonog i Bethan. Codi, chwarae ychydig hefo Ceren, helpu Anti Catrin, mynd i weld Mari, ac yn fwy na dim, disgwyl cardiau post gan ei thad.

'Y fi'n mynd,' meddai Ceren wrth glywed sŵn y blwch post yn y boreau.

Ac fe fyddai'n rhedeg yn fusnes i gyd am y drws.

Mae hi'n sôn llai am Mam, meddyliodd Bethan un bore. Ydi hi wedi anghofio?

Edrychodd ar Ceren fel y gorffennodd ei brecwast. Roedd hi'n bwyta ac yn siarad, ac yn sôn am chwarae hefo Solomon fel petai dim wedi digwydd.

Efallai mai dyna'r ffordd, meddyliodd. Byw bywyd bob dydd yn gyffredin normal. Gwneud y pethau bach ac anghofio'r pethau mawr. Bwytaodd ei grawnfwyd yn araf ystyriol. Doedd hi ddim yn hapus, ond rywsut doedd hi ddim yn anhapus chwaith. Gwag oddi mewn oedd hi. Mewn limbo. Yn disgwyl i Dad ddod yn ôl fory, ac yn poeni beth a ddigwyddai wedyn.

'Rydw i'n mynd at Mari,' meddai wedi helpu gyda'r golchi llestri.

'Ia, dos di,' meddai Anti Catrin. 'Mi fydda i'n dy ddisgwyl di adre erbyn pedwar, cofia.'

Adre! Doedd tŷ Anti Catrin ddim yn 'adre' iddi, nac oedd?

Roedd Mari yn eistedd ar y soffa a'i choes i fyny pan gyrhaeddodd.

'Hiya! Ydi dy ffêr di'n well?' holodd Bethan.

'Ew!' meddai wedyn wrth weld blodau ar y bwrdd bach yn y gornel, ac ôl caboli ar y dodrefn. 'Pwy sy wedi bod wrthi?'

'Y hi,' meddai Mari.

'Hi?'

'Mrs Busnes Morris, 'tê?'

'Ond mae hi'n ffeind.'

'Am wn i.'

'Mari! Rwyt ti'n gwybod ei bod hi. Mae dy dad yn gweithio. Pwy arall allai ofalu amdanat ti?'

'Does dim eisio iddi, nac oes? A does dim rhaid i mi'i licio hi na'i gofal chwaith. Ond mae Dad yn . . .'

'Yn be?'

'Yn meddwl ei bod hi'n angel.'

Dobiodd y glustog yn ffyrnig.

'Daria'r baglau 'ma. Fasa ddim eisio iddi hi ddŵad yma oni bai am y rhain.'

'Fedra i wneud rhywbeth?'

'Na, mae honna wedi gwneud popeth.'

Eisteddodd Bethan heb wybod beth i'w ddweud nesaf. Roedd yn amlwg fod tymer ddrwg ar Mari, fel pob diwrnod ers pan syrthiodd.

'Ydi dy dad yn well?' mentrodd ofyn.

Meddalodd wyneb Mari.

'Weithiau. Mae o'n siarad mwy hefo mi.'

126

Gwgodd drachefn. 'Ond mae o geg yn geg hefo hi drws nesa.'

Disgynnodd distawrwydd rhwng y ddwy.

'Pa bryd mae dy dad yn dŵad yn ôl?' holodd Mari o'r diwedd.

'Fory.'

'Wyt ti'n meddwl y byddi di'n gadael?'

'Siŵr o fod.'

Doedd hi ddim yn siŵr o gwbl. Doedd neb wedi dweud, dyna oedd y drwg. Dim ond 'rhaid trefnu' ac 'mi gawn ni weld' nes roedd hi bron â sgrechian weithiau.

'Biti os ei di.'

'Ia.'

Ond doedd hi ddim yn meddwl hynny chwaith. Er ei bod hi'n dechrau arfer hefo byw gydag Anti Catrin, ac yn licio Mari fel ffrind, adre roedd hi eisio mynd. Petai hi ond yn cael mynd adre, mi fyddai hi'n siŵr o deimlo'n nes at Mam. Gartre roedd ysbryd Mam. Ymysg y pethau cyfarwydd bob dydd. Hances mewn drôr, dillad yn hongian yn y wardrob, a hoff declyn ar y seidbord. Pethau roedd Mam wedi'u dewis am ei bod hi'n eu hoffi. Bwrdd a chadair a charped. Roedd ôl llaw Mam ym mhob un ohonyn nhw.

'Ddoi di'n ôl weithiau?'

'Dof, siŵr.'

Dychwelodd i dŷ Anti Catrin erbyn te. Roedd

Ceren yn eistedd ar y soffa a'r teclyn teledu yn ei dwylo.

'Cartŵn, Bethan,' meddai. 'Tom a Jeri. Dydi Solomon ddim yn gath ddrwg. Solomon yn gath dda.'

'Ydi,' meddai Bethan heb fawr o ddiddordeb.

'Chwarae hefo Solomon bob dydd,' meddai Ceren. 'Am byth!'

Teimlodd Bethan yr oerni yn cerdded ei chorff. Am byth ddywedodd Ceren. Heb sôn dim am fynd yn ôl adre.

Aeth i'r gegin at Anti Catrin.

'Popeth yn iawn?' holodd Anti Catrin gan edrych yn graff arni.

'Ydi.'

Yna yn anewyllysgar bron.

'Mae Ceren yn anghofio.'

'Anghofio dy fam, wyt ti'n 'i feddwl?'

'Ia,' yn ddigalon.

Rhoddodd Anti Catrin ei braich am ei hysgwyddau.

'Dysgu byw mae hi. Ffordd o ymdopi hefo'i cholled. Nid ei bod hi wedi anghofio, Bethan. Mi ddaw pyliau o hiraeth a holi arni eto.'

'Mae gen i ofn anghofio hefyd. Ofn anghofio sut un oedd Mam, sut lais, sut wên. Mae gen i ofn iddi hi ddiflannu am byth!'

'Wnaiff hi ddim. Mae hi'n ddiogel yn dy gof, a fedr neb ddwyn hwnnw oddi arnat ti.'

Gwenodd Anti Catrin arni ond roedd ei llygaid yn llaith.

'Rhaid i tithau ddysgu byw, Bethan. Nid anghofio, ond symud ymlaen. Cam bach bob dydd.'

'Ond rydw i eisio cadw 'ngafael arni, a byth ei gollwng. Dydi hi ddim yma, a finna'i heisio hi.'

'Mae'r cof gen ti. Am byth.'

Tybed a oedd cof yn ddigon i gadw Mam yn fyw? Wyddai hi ddim. Ond roedd cysur yng ngeiriau Anti Catrin. Trodd fel y daeth Ceren i'r gegin. Roedd un o gardiau Dad yn ei llaw.

'Fydd Mam yn anfon cerdyn, Bethan? Cerdyn o dŷ Iesu Grist?'

Na, doedd yr un ohonyn nhw wedi anghofio.

15.

Doedd dim pleser mewn cerdded yn y parc na mynd i'r sièd bellach. Ddim â Mari'n garcharor gartre.

Fe aeth hi yno unwaith neu ddwy i sefyll yn hir a syllu ar y llyn a breuddwydio am oriau yng nghwmni ei mam. Cofiai gychwyn i'r ysgol ar frys gwyllt a Mam yn estyn pethau iddi, gan chwerthin a dwrdio bob yn ail. Cofiai gyrraedd yn ôl wedyn i gynhesrwydd y tŷ a Mam yno'n ei disgwyl. A chofiai benwythnosau o siopio a chrwydro'n deulu, gwyliau yn gymysgedd o hwyl a miri ac anghydweld, a Mam yn galon y cyfan. Roedd Mam yna i ddibynnu arni pryd hynny. Ond byth eto!

Ymwthiodd ei ffordd trwy'r llwyni rhododendron a dringo i lawr y llethr i'r sièd. Crychodd ei thrwyn wrth sawru'r arogl swrth a myglyd braidd a orweddai'n drwm ar bopeth. Breuddwyd oedd y sièd hefyd. Breuddwyd dianc oddi wrth broblemau. Ond fedrai neb wneud hynny. Dim ond mynd â'r problemau hefo nhw.

Brysiodd o'r parc ac anelu am gartref Mari. Efallai y bydden nhw'n mynd i eistedd allan i'r ardd heddiw. Roedd ganddi baced o greision a thuniau Coke i'w mwynhau.

Aeth rownd i'r cefn ac agor y drws.

'Fi sy 'ma, Mari. Sut wyt ti?'

'Wedi cael llond bol. Blino eistedd, blino bwyta, blino darllen. Blino gwrando ar honna drws nesa hefyd.'

'Tyrd i'r ardd i eistedd. Yli, mae gen i greision a Coke.'

Ymaflodd Mari yn ei baglau.

'Llond bol ar y rhain hefyd. *One down, carry one* i bobman.'

Dechreuodd hopian am ddrws y cefn.

Daeth sŵn allwedd yn y drws ffrynt. Arhosodd Mari ar unwaith.

'Dad! Chi sy 'na?'

Troediodd sodlau uchel ar hyd teils y lobi, a daeth dynes ddieithr i Bethan i'r amlwg.

'*Mam*!'

Roedd wyneb Mari'n wên i gyd.

'O *Mam*! 'Dach chi wedi dŵad yn ôl?'

Ysgydwodd y ddynes ei phen.

'Ddim yn ôl, Mari. I dy nôl di i fyw ata i.'

Ymledodd sioc yn gymysg â llawenydd tros wyneb Mari.

'I fyw atoch chi? Ond . . .'

Cwympodd ei hwyneb yn sydyn.

'Beth am Dad?'

'Beth amdano fo?'

Roedd llais ei mam yn oeraidd.

'Wel . . .' cychwynnodd Mari.

Yna caeodd ei cheg yn glep. Roedd dyn yn sefyll y tu ôl i'w mam. Wil Morris! Trodd Mari at Bethan.

'Mi ddo i hefo ti i'r ardd rŵan, Bethan.'

Edrychodd Bethan o un i'r llall. Roedd mam Mari yma, ond eto roedd Mari'n troi ei chefn arni. Teimlai fel crio. Roedd Mari'n cael cynnig ei mam yn ôl, ond châi hi, Bethan, byth gynnig Mam eto.

'Mari . . .' Estynnodd y ddynes ei llaw i afael yn ei braich. 'Gwranda.'

'Dydw i ddim eisio gwrando,' gwaeddodd Mari. 'Dydw i ddim eisio byw hefo chi a *fo*!'

'Does a wnelo dy dad ddim â hyn. Hefo fi y dylet ti fod. Dydi o ddim yn gofalu'n iawn

131

amdanat ti. Mi wyddwn i hynny cyn gynted ag y clywais i dy fod wedi syrthio.'

'Sut clywsoch chi?'

Symudodd ei mam ei hysgwyddau'n ddiflas.

'Dy dad. Pwy arall? Swnian fel babi i gael rhywun yn ôl.'

'Wyddwn i ddim 'i fod o'n gwybod ble i'ch cael chi,' meddai Mari yn guchiog.

Meddalodd wyneb ei mam fel y ceisiodd gofleidio Mari.

'Wyt ti ddim yn credu y baswn i'n troi fy nghefn arnat ti? Fy merch fy hun? Na, roedd dy dad yn gwybod ble i gael gafael arna i.'

Edrychodd Bethan i gyfeiriad y dyn a safai yn nrws y lobi. Roedd o'n pwyso yn erbyn y wal a hanner gwên ar ei wyneb. Teimlai Bethan y casineb yn codi ynddi'n syth. Pa hawl oedd ganddo fo i rwystro mam Mari rhag dŵad yn ôl. Roedd Mari ei hangen hi fel roedd hithau angen Mam.

'Dydw i byth yn dŵad yn ôl at dy dad,' meddai mam Mari. 'Ond rydw i'n fam i ti . . .'

'Ac yn wraig i dad hefyd,' gwaeddodd Mari.

'Am ychydig eto . . .' Roedd y llais yn oeraidd. '. . . ac mae'n well iti fyw hefo Wil a finna. Mi gei gartre hapus.'

'Nes y bydd Wil wedi crwydro eto,' meddai llais tawel o'r drws cefn.

Safai Mrs Morris yno. Llithrodd ei llygaid tros fam Mari ac ymlaen at ei gŵr hithau.

'Nid dyma'r tro cynta iddo fo ffansïo dynes arall, ond hwn fydd y tro cynta i mi wrthod maddau iddo fo. Ys gwn i pa mor faddeugar fyddi di, Bet?'

Roedd amheuaeth ar wyneb mam Mari am eiliad. Yna gwenodd.

'Collwr fuost ti erioed, Lisa.' Trodd at Mari. 'Wel, wyt ti'n dŵad?'

'Na.'

Crogodd y gair yn foel rhyngddynt, cyn i'w mam erfyn eto.

'Ond, Mari!' Roedd ansicrwydd yn ei llais am eiliad.

'Rydw i'n aros hefo Dad.'

'Does dim i'w ddweud felly, nac oes? Ond mae'r cynnig yn aros. Unrhyw dro.'

Caeodd drws y ffrynt yn ddistaw bendant y tu ôl i'r ddau.

Safodd Mari'n fud am eiliadau cyn cwympo'n ôl ar y soffa. Eisteddodd yno'n ansicr.

'Fedrwn i ddim mynd, na fedrwn? Ddim gadael Dad?'

Caledodd ei hwyneb fel y cofiodd am Mrs Morris wrth y drws.

'Eich gŵr chi ddaru. Fo berswadiodd Mam.'

'Efalla.'

Roedd llais Mrs Morris yn dawel fyfyrgar.

'Dydw i ddim o'ch eisio chi. Dydi Dad a fi ddim eisio neb,' haerodd Mari.

Trodd Mrs Morris i adael.

'Wna inna ddim aros felly, Mari,' meddai.
'Ond mi fydda i yna os byddi di fy angen i.'

Rhwbiodd Mari ei llygaid yn ffyrnig.

'A phaid titha â sbio fel het,' sgyrnygodd i
gyfeiriad Bethan. 'Mae'n iawn arnat ti. Dy
Dad a Ceren ac Anti Catrin gen ti.'

Rhwbiodd ei llygaid eto.

'Ond dydi Mam ddim gen i, nac ydi?' meddai
Bethan.

'Doedd dy fam di ddim eisio mynd. Mi roedd
Mam eisio, doedd?'

Cerddodd Bethan yn araf am dŷ Anti Catrin
a geiriau Mari yn ei chlustiau. Na, doedd Mam
ddim eisio mynd fel mam Mari. Ei chipio i
ffwrdd yn y ddamwain gafodd hi. Doedd dim
dewis ganddi.

16.

Fe gyrhaeddodd Dad ddiwedd y prynhawn
hwnnw. Rhedodd Bethan a Ceren allan i'w
gyfarfod.

'Anrheg, Dad?' holodd Ceren. 'Anrheg o
ffwrdd?'

Gwenodd eu tad ychydig. Ond roedd golwg
flinedig arno fel y daeth gyda nhw i'r tŷ.

'Wedi blino, Huw?' holodd Anti Catrin.

'Do.'

Ond fe wyddai Bethan fod adeg penderfynu wedi cyrraedd. Dyna pam yr edrychai Dad mor flinedig. Efallai ei fod o am eu gadael yma hefo Anti Catrin am byth.

Rhwbiodd chwys ei dwylo ar goesau'i jîns. Beth oedd am ddigwydd iddyn nhw? Ond ddywedodd Dad yr un gair. Dim ond eistedd a llymeitian ei de ac ateb Anti Catrin hefo 'Do' ac 'Ia' a 'Naddo' yn drymaidd, fel petai pwysau'r byd ar ei feddwl.

'Chwarae hefo Solomon rŵan,' meddai Ceren gan lithro oddi ar y gadair ac anelu am ddrws y cefn.

Fe gaeodd Dad ac Anti Catrin eu hunain yn y gegin ar ôl te. Eisteddodd Bethan yn y lolfa a'i dwylo'n troi ac aildroi ar ei glin. Roedd hi'n gwybod eu bod yn trafod beth i'w wneud hefo Ceren a hithau. Ond roedd ganddi hithau hawl i drafod y dyfodol hefyd. On'd oedd?

Cododd a cherddodd tua'r drws yn bwrpasol. Roedd murmur y lleisiau'n codi a gostwng tu mewn. Petrusodd ei bysedd ar y dwrn. Fedrai hi wynebu ei thad ac Anti Catrin a derbyn y dyfarniad? Na, fe âi'n ôl i'r lolfa. Trodd. Yna rhewodd yn sydyn fel y clywodd eiriau ei thad.

'Mae'n rhaid imi gael rhywun, Catrin.'

'Rwyt ti'n gwybod fod croeso iddyn nhw aros yma hefo mi.'

'Ond dydi hynny ddim yn deg. Ddim i ti, na Bethan a Ceren, chwaith.'

135

'Wyt ti wedi gofyn i'r Siân 'ma?'

'Naddo. Ond rwy'n siŵr y byddai hi'n fodlon. Mae'n rhaid imi gael rhywun, Catrin.'

Tynhaodd bysedd Bethan am y dwrn. Siân! Pwy oedd honno? A beth oedd ei thad yn ei feddwl wrth sôn am ofyn iddi? Gofyn be?

Deallodd yn sydyn. Roedd o am gael dynes arall yn lle ei mam. Ai dyna beth roedd o am ofyn? Gofyn i ryw Siân ddŵad i fyw atyn nhw? Ei phriodi?

Cododd surni'n don i'w gwddf fel y ffrwydrodd trwy'r drws i wynebu'r ddau.

'Chewch chi ddim. Cartre Mam ydi o.'

Trodd ar ei sawdl a rhuthro am ddrws y ffrynt. Baglodd trwyddo.

'Bethan! Aros! Dwyt ti ddim yn dallt!'

Nid arhosodd i wrando. Carlamodd ymlaen ar hyd y stryd. Fedrai hi ddim credu. Doedd wiw iddi gredu. Ond eto, roedd hi wedi clywed y geiriau. Roedd Dad am gael dynes arall i fyw atyn nhw. Dynes arall i gymryd lle ei mam, i fusnesu a bodio'i phethau hi, ac i *fyw* hefo nhw!

Roedd yn rhaid iddi ddianc. Ymhell. I rywle rhag iddi orfod ailglywed geiriau ei thad. Fe wyddai fod Dad yn rhedeg o'i hôl, ond doedd hi ddim am wrando.

Anelodd ar frys gwyllt am y parc. Rhedodd am y mur rhododendron ac ymwthio trwodd heb boeni a oedd rhywun yn ei gweld ai peidio. Rhedodd, llithrodd, baglodd i lawr y llethr ac at

136

y sièd. Fe'i taflodd ei hun ar y llawr a'r digalondid yn ffrydio trwyddi.

Dim ond newydd farw roedd Mam. Ac roedd
Dad am gael dynes arall i fyw hefo nhw. 'Mae'n
rhaid imi gael rhywun.' Dyna ddywedodd o.
Roedd o am gychwyn bywyd newydd hefo
rhywun arall, 'run fath ag y gwnaeth mam
Mari. Doedd hi byth am fynd adre eto.

Pwysodd ei chefn ar fur y sièd a chuddio'i
phen ar ei phenliniau. Wyddai hi ddim beth i'w
wneud. Ond roedd hi'n gwybod na fedrai hi
groesawu dynes arall yn lle ei mam.

Pwy oedd hi? Rhywun wnaeth Dad ei chyfarfod ar un o'i deithiau darlithio? Neu rywun yn
y coleg busnes? Efallai ei fod o'n caru hefo hi
ers amser. Fel roedd mam Mari wedi bod yn
caru hefo gŵr Mrs Morris!

Daeth sŵn o'r brwgaets y tu allan. Sŵn
rhywun yn anadlu'n drwm wrth ymlwybro a
baglu tua'r sièd.

Gwnaeth Bethan ei hun yn rholyn bychan
bach a'i chefn ar fur y sièd. Fe wyddai mai ei
thad oedd o, ond doedd hi ddim am wrando.

Ymddangosodd ei gysgod yn y sgwaryn
heulwen ar lawr y sièd. Trodd ei chefn arno.

'Bethan!' ochneidiodd.

Wnaeth hi ddim cymryd arni'i glywed. Teimlodd ef yn eistedd wrth ei hochr.

'Bethan!' meddai eto.

Yn sydyn fedrai hi ddim dal rhagor. Ffrwyd-rodd y geiriau oddi ar ei thafod.

'Dydach chi ddim yn ein caru ni. Ceren a fi. Chawson ni ddim mynd 'nôl i'n tŷ ni o *gwbl*. Jest i weld y cartre lle buon ni'n hapus. Rydw i eisio mynd yno. I drio gafael yn yr atgof am Mam rhag ofn imi anghofio. A dydw i ddim eisio'i hanghofio hi. Byth!'

'Wnawn ni byth mo hynny, Bethan.'

'Ond mi rydach *chi*'n anghofio. Mynd i gael dynes arall yn lle Mam. Tŷ Mam ydi o. Pethau Mam ydyn nhw. Teulu Mam ydyn ni.'

'Bethan! Bethan!'

Roedd gwên a thristwch yn gymysgfa ar wyneb ei thad.

'Dynes i *helpu* fydd hi. Rhywun ddaw i mewn i llnau a nôl Ceren o'r ysgol feithrin, a mynd adre i'w chartre ei hun pan ddo inna adre. Tebyg i howscipar!'

'*Howscipar*?'

Gafaelodd ei thad ynddi a'i thynnu ato.

'Ia. Dynes hŷn na fi. Lot hŷn.'

'A fydd hi ddim yn byw hefo ni?'

'Na fydd.'

'Ac mi rydyn ni'n cael mynd adre? Wir?'

'Wir.'

'O Dad! Sori!'

Eisteddodd y ddau yn y sièd a'r agosatrwydd yn tyfu rhyngddynt. Cododd ei thad o'r diwedd a'i thynnu i fyny gydag ef.

139

'Teulu ydyn ni o hyd. Teulu wedi colli rhywun annwyl, ond teulu wnaiff gofio amdani. Bob dydd.'

'Ia.'

Roedd popeth yn glir iddi rŵan. Fedrech chi ddim anghofio colled. Ond roedd yn rhaid ichi ddysgu byw, doedd? Magu croen rhag poen.

Yna cofiodd am Mari.

'Gawn ni ddŵad at Anti Catrin weithiau?'

'Cewch siŵr. Mi ddown ni 'yn tri.'

'Ac mi ga inna weld Mari.'

'Cei.'

Dilynodd Bethan ei thad i fyny'r llethr. Roedd hi a Ceren yn lwcus. Mynd o ganol cariad wnaeth Mam, ond *dewis* mynd wnaeth mam Mari. Ond efallai y gwnâi Mari ddysgu dygymod hefyd. Rhyw ddiwrnod.

Teitlau eraill yng Nghyfres Cled:

Myrddin yr Ail Hilma Lloyd Edwards (Y Lolfa)
Canhwyllau Emily Huws (Gomer)
Modryb Lanaf Lerpwl Meinir Pierce Jones (Gomer)
Pen Cyrliog a Sbectol Sgwâr Gareth F. Williams (Y Lolfa)
Y Sling Emily Huws (Gomer)
'Tisio Bet? Emily Huws (Gomer)
Gwesty'r Llygaid Aflan Ifor Wyn Williams (Hughes)
Cathreulig! M. Potter/Gwenno Hywyn (Gwynedd)
'Tisio Tshipsan? Emily Huws (Gomer)
Nefi Bliwl! C. Sefton/Emily Huws (Gomer)
Tân Gwyllt Pat Neill/Dic Jones (Gomer)
'Tisio Sws? Emily Huws (Gomer)
'Dwisio Dad Emily Huws (Gomer)
'Dwisio Nain Emily Huws (Gomer)
Piwma Tash Emily Huws (Gomer)
Lleuwedd D. Wiseman/Mari Llwyd (Gomer)
Yr Indiad yn y Cwpwrdd L.R. Banks/Euryn Dyfed (Gomer)
Delyth a'r Tai Haf Pat Neill/Dic Jones (Gomer)
Sothach a Sglyfath Angharad Tomos (Y Lolfa)
Madfall ar y Mur Menna Elfyn (Gomer)
Tash Emily Huws (Gomer)
Gags Emily Huws (Gomer)
Jinj Emily Huws (Gomer)
Y Gelyn ar y Trên T. Llew Jones (Gomer)
Dwi'n ♥ 'Sgota Emily Huws (Gomer)
Strach Go-Iawn Emily Huws (Gomer)
Haf y Gwrachod addas. Siân Eleri Jones (Gwynedd)
Craig y Lladron Ioan Kidd (Gomer)
Ydw i'n ♥ Karate Emily Huws (Gomer)
Tic Toc Emily Huws (Gomer)

Simon Raven w̲ ̲ ̲ ̲ ̲ ̲ ̲ ̲ ̲ ̲ ̲ educated
at Charterhous̲ ̲ ̲ ̲ ̲ ̲ ̲ ̲ ̲ ̲ where he
read Classics. ̲ ̲ ̲ ̲ ̲ ̲ ̲ ̲ ̲ ̲ my as a
regular officer i̲ ̲ ̲ ̲ ̲ ̲ ̲ ̲ ̲ ̲ ̲ntry and
saw service in G̲ermany and Kenya where he comm̲anded a
Rifle Company. In 1957 he resigned his commission and
took up book reviewing. His first novel, *The Feathers of
Death*, was published in 1959. Since then he has written
many reviews, general essays, plays for radio and television
as well as the scripts for a number of successful television
series including *Edward and Mrs Simpson* and *Love in a
Cold Climate* plus a host of novels. The highly acclaimed
ALMS FOR OBLIVION sequence is published for the
first time in this Panther edition in chronological order.
The sequence takes its title from a passage in Shakespeare's
Troilus and Cressida, has been referred to as 'a latter-day
Waugh report on another generation of Bright Young
Things', and has been compared favourably with the *romans
fleuves* of Anthony Powell and C. P. Snow. With the
publication in 1984 of *Morning Star* he began a new novel
series under the title THE FIRST-BORN OF EGYPT. It
is a sequel to ALMS FOR OBLIVION. Simon Raven lives
and works in Deal, Kent.

By the same author

Novels

The Feathers of Death
Brother Cain
Doctors Wear Scarlet
The Roses of Picardie
Close of Play
An Inch of Fortune
September Castle

The ALMS FOR OBLIVION sequence,
in chronological order:

Fielding Gray
Sound the Retreat
The Sabre Squadron
The Rich Pay Late
Friends in Low Places
The Judas Boy
Places Where They Sing
Come Like Shadows
Bring Forth the Body
The Survivors

Belles-Lettres

The English Gentleman
Boys Will Be Boys
The Fortunes of Fingel

Plays

Royal Foundation and Other Plays

Autobiography

Shadows on the Grass

SIMON RAVEN

Morning Star

The First-born of Egypt: Volume 1

PANTHER
Granada Publishing

Panther Books
Granada Publishing Ltd
8 Grafton Street, London W1X 3LA

Published by Panther Books 1985

First published in Great Britain by
Muller, Blond & White Limited 1984

ISBN 0-586-06350-1

Made and printed for
William Collins Sons & Co. Ltd, Glasgow

Set in Plantin

IMPRIMÉ EN FRANCE

List of Characters in Order of Appearance

Jean-Marie Guiscard, an antiquarian
Jo-Jo (Josephine) Guiscard, his wife: *née* Pelham
Major Fielding Gray, a novelist
Colonel Ivan Blessington, a stockbroker
Betty Blessington, his wife
Jakki Blessington }   their daughters
Caroline Blessington
Donald Salinger, a retired man of affairs
Max de Freville, a professional gambler and property dealer
Gregory Stern, a publisher
Isobel Stern, his wife: *née* Turbot
Marius Stern, their son
Rosie Stern, their daughter
Peter Morrison, MP, 'Squire of Luffham by Whereham
Ptolemaeos Tunne, an amateur scholar; uncle, through his
    dead sister, to Jo-Jo Guiscard
Sir Thomas Llewyllyn, kt, D. Lit. & Litt. D., Provost of
    Lancaster College Cambridge, father of Lady (Baby)
    Canteloupe, brother-in-law of Isobel Stern being married
    to her sister Patricia
Len, Private Secretary to Provost Llewyllyn
Captain the Most Honourable Marquess Canteloupe of the
    Aestuary of the Severn
Mungo 'Avallon', Bishop of Glastonbury
The Marchioness Canteloupe (Baby): *née* Llewyllyn; niece
    to Isobel Stern, and cousin to Rosie and Marius
Tullius Fielding d'Azincourt Llewyllyn Gregory Jean-Jose-
    phine Maximin Sarum Detterling, called by courtesy
    Baron Sarum of Old Sarum, son and heir to Lord and
    Lady Canteloupe

Daisy, Lord Sarum's nurse

Ivan ('Greco') Barraclough, an anthropologist; Fellow of Lancaster College

Nicos Pandouros, indentured page to Barraclough after the Maniot custom; undergraduate of Lancaster College

Jeremy Morrison, an undergraduate of Lancaster College; younger son of Peter

Carmilla Salinger, an undergraduate of Lancaster College; Donald's adopted daughter

Theodosia Salinger (Thea), an undergraduate of Lancaster College; Carmilla's twin and Donald's adopted daughter

'Mrs' Maisie Malcolm, Proprietress (with Fielding Gray) of Buttock's Hotel

Teresa (Tessa) Malcolm, Maisie's 'niece'

The 'Chamberlain', Peter's manservant at Luffham; formerly manservant to Canteloupe

Nicholas (Nickie) Morrison, Peter's elder son; in hospital with incurable brain damage

Wilfred, the Porter of the Night Gate

Wilfred's Assistant, the Fifth Porter of Lancaster College

Vanessa Salinger, Donald's (now dead) wife: *née* Drew

Titus Spencer-Drew, Vanessa's cousin

A Fireman

An Inspector of Police

Walter ('Wally' or 'Bunter') St George, an assistant master at Oudenarde House

'Glinter' Parkes, Headmaster of Oudenarde House

'Artemis'
'Pontos'   } Conspirators
Shamshuddin

An Official with fake prole accent

Mrs Gurt and Mrs Statch, Servants to Ptolemaeos Tunne

PART ONE
The Order of Baptism

On a morning early in April, in the eighth year of the eighth decade of the Twentieth Century, a number of people set out to attend the christening of the infant son of the Most Honourable Marquess and Marchioness Canteloupe of the Aestuary of the Severn. The service, which would be conducted by the Lord Bishop of Glastonbury, was to take place in the chapel of Lancaster College, Cambridge, of which venerable house Lady Canteloupe's father, Sir Thomas Llewyllyn, Doctor of Letters (*et Cantab et Oxon*), was Provost.

Apart from this connection and the Perpendicular distinction of the chapel, there was little to recommend the venue. Since Lord and Lady Canteloupe lived on the march of Wiltshire and Somerset, a land furnished with beautiful churches in many of which Mungo Avallon (as the Bishop of Glastonbury styled himself) could have officiated by right instead of by the reluctant indulgence of the Dean of Lancaster, a West Country setting would have been a great deal more appropriate. Or again, since the principal guests and the godparents lived for the most part in London, a metropolitan fane would have been at least convenient. Or yet again, there were those who urged that the first son of the Lord Canteloupe of the Aestuary of the Severn should be baptized in the Fishermen's Chapel at Severn-Manche, as had been the custom for the last hundred and fifty years. To the latter contention Lord Canteloupe had replied that, since he had inherited the Marquisate through a very tenuous connection on the distaff side, the direct line was broken and what amounted to a parvenu dynasty had sidled into the title: it would therefore be presumptuous in him,

9

who had been born Detterling, to ape the procedures peculiar to the Sarums (the family name of the previous incumbents); and in any case, His Lordship had added, he proposed to leave the choice of date and place of this affair entirely to his wife, who had had a great deal more to do with producing the infant than he had.

Whereupon and without further ado Baby Canteloupe had declared for Lancaster Chapel, privately believing that this would please her old father the Provost (infidel though he was) and publicly remarking that it would cause gratifying annoyance to the left-wing dons who abounded in the college. That it would also cause annoyance to almost everyone who must attend the christening did not occur to her; nor would she have been one whit deterred if it had.

The two people who had farthest to come to the christening were Monsieur and Madame Jean-Marie Guiscard – all the way from Dieppe, where Jean-Marie, a young antiquarian of promise, was writing a book about a curious episode in the history of the nearby Castle of Arques-la-Bataille. Madame Guiscard, who was English, having been born Jo-Jo Pelham, was very pregnant but very determined to make the expedition to Cambridge.

'Baby Canteloupe was the love of my life,' she had said, soon after the invitation arrived and Jean-Marie began protesting that she was in no state to travel. 'She still is, in a way.' Jean-Marie nodded, accepting the assertion with dignified good nature. 'The love of my life,' repeated Jo-Jo, 'and so I wouldn't miss being there for . . . for all the Queen's Yellow.'

'The Queen's Yellow?'

'The Queen's Gold in the Bank of England.'

10

'But surely, it is no longer your Queen who really – '

'No, darling heart, of course it isn't. Just an expression.'

'Your English expressions. I feel that I shall never learn them until the day I die.'

'You're doing very well,' said Jo-Jo, patting him on the tiny tonsure which had begun to appear at the root of his parting, 'and you will get a lot of useful practice at the christening.'

'But Jo-Jo, oh my darling, I do not wish you to travel across the sea just when – '

' – Look,' said Jo-Jo, banging on her belly with both fists, 'our boy is settled in there by now. It was only at the very beginning that he might have worked loose, before he was big and strong enough to get a grip. He's there now till it's time for me to throw him.'

'Throw?'

'Drop.'

'Drop?'

'Foal, for Christ's sake. And another thing,' she went on, stroking her stomach as if to console its inmate for the drubbing she had just administered, 'when *he* is christened, Baby Canteloupe will be there, wherever "there" may be, even if she's as big as a barge with her next brat . . . though somehow,' she added warily, 'I think that one will be her lot.'

'Oh,' said Jean-Marie speculatively, 'and why do you think that?'

'Let's say . . . she'll find more interesting things to do than breed.'

'And shall you too . . . find more interesting things to do than breed?'

'That very much depends,' said Jo-Jo, 'on how it all turns out the first time. Now, back to Baby Canteloupe. She says her father has invited us both to spend the night after the christening in the Provost's Lodging, along with her and Canty and some of the other guests. It's so long

11

since I spent a night under the same roof as Baby that I ache with wanting it.'

'Darling Jo-Jo,' said Jean-Marie. 'Heart of my heart of my heart – '

' – Funny. Uncle Ptolemaeos used to call me that when I lived in his house in the Fens. He'll be there too. Another reason for going.'

'I was only going to say, my darling, that if you really long to go so much – '

' – Oh, I do – '

' – Then of course we shall go. And indeed I too long to see all your English friends again – '

' – *Our* friends, my Jean-Marie-Jean – '

' – As I have not seen them,' said Jean-Marie, blinking with pleasure, 'since our wedding. All that worries me, despite this so courteous invitation of the Provost, is that you may become tired with the two-way journey.'

'Never. On the way there, I shall be thinking of all those I shall see that I love.'

'And on the way back?'

Jo-Jo looked down from the Castle Cliff, past the sharp grey slate wedge on the roof of St Remy, past the complacent cupola, and on to the eclectic tower of St Jacques. I cannot tell him now, she thought: that must keep. I cannot tell him yet that, though I am very fond of Dieppe, I could no more settle here, or anywhere else in France, than I could settle in Tibet. Before I tell him that, I must let him finish his book. After all, that should not take long now. Then will be the time to say, 'Jean-Marie, I love you and I love your country, but my son must be born and reared in England.' It will be hard, saying this to him, but when the time comes I shall find the strength to say it.

For the time being she merely said:

'I shall always enjoy coming back to Dieppe.'

'But let us drive to Boulogne and take the Hovercraft or the Ferry. That way we shall have less time on the sea.'

'Just as you like,' said Jo-Jo, 'but I am a good sailor, and so' – she touched her belly – 'is he.'

Fielding Gray drove down from London. These days he was beginning to find it rather a strain driving with his one eye, but anything was preferable to travelling by British Rail, the First Class compartments of which were even filthier than the Second. This, he presumed, was due to class hatred on the part of the rebarbative females employed to do the cleaning, one of whom he had once observed while she was deliberately hawking on to the antimacassars. She had a gentle, dreamy look on her face, he remembered, as if she had been taking part in one of the more sentimental rites of the Church, such as the carol service on the Vigil of Christmas or this christening to which he was going, much against his will, today.

Fielding Gray disliked, in ascending order, funerals, memorial services, weddings and christenings; but the obligation to attend this one was quite ungainsayable. He had, for a start, known Baby Canteloupe virtually since the day she was conceived, having been a close friend of her father, Tom (now Sir Thomas) Llewyllyn, in the days of their spunky youth, and for a brief period the lover (though not until some time after Baby was born) of her unfortunate mother, who subsequently went off her head and was now permanently confined. Even if all this hadn't been enough to compel Fielding's attendance, there was also his multiple connection with Lord Canteloupe, with whom he shared an Old School and an Old Regiment. After both Canteloupe (Detterling) and Fielding had left the Army, the former set up as a partner in an adventurous publishing company (Stern & Detterling) which had adopted Fielding out of faith, hope and charity as a would-be novelist and still published him, nearly twenty years later, as an established and passably profitable one . . . a long, eventful and affectionate association which further dictated his presence at this afternoon's ceremony.

All of which was all very well, thought Fielding as he drove through the kind and dowdy little town of Baldock: the fact remained that there was to be, that very afternoon, a very pretty meeting on Ascot Heath, to which he would far sooner be driving . . . and to which indeed he would have been driving, for all the obligations, so far summed, to attend this baptism, had it not been for yet one more consideration, which dwarfed all others of any kind whatever and yet, even as he bowed to it this afternoon, must for ever be shut away and disavowed.

Ivan Blessington, unlike Fielding Gray, had two eyes, one wife and two daughters, Caroline and Jakki, nine and ten. What he had in common with Fielding (apart from having held Her Majesty's Commission in the same regiment many years before and having been in the same house at school during the war) was a similar hankering to be driving, not to Cambridge as he now was (through the narrow and treacherous little town of Royston), but to Ascot Heath.

'Two three-mile 'chases,' he was grumbling to any of his three females who might be listening. 'Last decent meeting over fences until the autumn – and you' (he singled out his wife in the front seat beside him) 'have to make us all come to this bloody christening. It's not as if I'm a godfather or anything – indeed I'm not at all sure why I've been asked.'

'Because you're Deputy Honorary Corporal-Major General of Hamilton's Horse. Lord Canteloupe has invited you

14

as a distinguished former member of his own regiment. I dare say he'll want to send his own son into it – just for a few years, of course, before he settles down to marry and mind his inheritance.'

'Darling Betty,' said Ivan Blessington, 'all that's now left of Hamilton's Horse is one single troop in a collective called the Macclesfield Belt Tank Regiment. As Deputy Honorary Etcetera I propose the Loyal Toast once a year to a party of regimental ghosts in a mouldy side-room of a thing called the Madrasi and Sporting, Public Schools, Commercial Air Pilots and Light Cavalry Club. Detterling, or Canteloupe as he now is, has not been to such a dinner for years, and small wonder. Hamilton's Light Dragoons were devils in their day, with the bravest uniform of any army in Europe: but all that is now over. If Canteloupe wants to put his boy in the Service, he'd best send him into the Royal Electrical and Mechanical Engineers – although even that will by then be called something else even more squalid – that is, if it isn't already.'

Caroline and Jakki set up a gay little clap in the back seat.

'The wonder is,' continued Ivan, waving acknowledgement back to the girls, 'that anything nice is left at all. One of the few nice things that *is* left is National Hunt Racing on Ascot Heath, and so why, I ask you, are we now driving through the most boring countryside in the Kingdom to stand blathering round a bloody font?'

'*You* won't be doing any blathering,' said Caroline: 'the godparents do all that.'

'*We* were christened,' said Jakki, 'and you expected people to come to that. Anyway, they came. I've seen the photos.'

'We had you both done on Sundays – when there wasn't any racing. Even so I had more sense than to bore Detterling with an invitation to such a dismal business, and he might have done the same by me.'

Instead of getting huffy at this disparaging reference to their christenings, the two girls fell into each other's arms with whoops of laughter.

'What I thought was,' said Betty equably, 'that it would be a good chance for the children to see the windows in Lancaster Chapel. To say nothing of the Rubens. The Provost's Lodging is rather famous too. One of the Provosts' wives was decapitated by the Parliament men on the doorstep.'

'Any chance of a replay?'

'You know perfectly well, darling, that Tom Llewyllyn's wife had to be – er – '

' – Chucked in the bin,' said Jakki. 'I'll tell you one good thing, Daddy: Rosie Stern will be there.'

'Rosie Stern? Sounds like a damned Yi – '

' – Rosie Stern is a friend of the girls at Collingham's,' said Betty firmly. 'Her mother, Isobel, is Lady Canteloupe's aunt.'

'Rosie is smashing,' said Caroline.

'Is she?' said Betty. 'I always find her rather a plain little thing.'

'We all love her,' said Jakki, 'but she likes Tessa Malcolm the best.'

Both girls giggled.

'She likes Tessa's you-know-what.'

'Well, what?' said Betty, rather crossly for her.

'Her Rumpel Stiltskin,' said Caroline. 'She's the only girl that's got one.'

'Got what?' said Ivan.

'Tessa Malcolm,' said Betty, 'has a tiny deformity: an almost invisible hump on one shoulder. They are all fascinated by it.'

'Particularly Rosie,' said Jakki. 'I wonder whether Rosie will be the same, now we're in the holidays.'

'She won't be wearing Collingham's School clothes, if that's what you mean, any more than you are.'

'I meant . . . being with her parents and not with all the other girls and the masters and the mistresses. I wonder whether she'll be stuck up . . . in her home clothes.'

'Why should she be stuck up?'

'Her father is a famous publisher,' said Jakki. 'He's rich.'

'And she has a super brother,' said Caroline. 'She showed me a photo of him in his white flannels. He has lovely fair hair. I'm longing to see him properly.'

'Fair hair?' said her father from the front. 'You wouldn't expect anyone called Stern to have fair hair.'

'The mother – Isobel – was a Turbot,' Betty said.

'I still don't think,' said Ivan, 'that any of this offers better value than Ascot Heath.'

'Don't you?' said Betty. 'Fielding Gray will be there, I'm told; and Peter Morrison.'

'Will they now?' said Ivan, and became silent, thinking of a lake in a wood on a summer's afternoon, just after the war.

Donald Salinger took the train to Cambridge from Liverpool Street. He had nearly been deterred from this by the same suspicion of British Rail as had deterred Fielding Gray; but since he no longer drove a car himself he would have been compelled to hire a chauffeur-driven car for the journey, and an innate element of Yorkshire caution made such a proceeding distasteful to him. Since he lived, these days, in the Ritz when he was in London and in the most commodious hotel available when he was elsewhere, this economy was absurd, and the more absurd if one considered the nature of the occasion which he was attending and his own exceedingly poor health. A series of duodenal ulcers during the 1960s, and a radical hiatus inflicted by shock on his neural reflexes in the early 1970s (consequent on the death of his wife, Vanessa), had reduced Donald to a state of physical and nervous debility that rendered his movements and reactions more like those of a man of seventy-five than of one who had only just passed fifty. If ever a man had means and cause to hire a chauffeur-driven car that day, it was Donald Salinger.

But North Country prudence had prevailed, and Donald was now sitting in a Second Class compartment (more likely than the First, he had correctly surmised, to be properly heated) and was wearily gazing out over a waste of yellow mud between Bishop's Stortford and Audley End. Surely, he thought, somewhere round here used to be that particularly charming ground on which Detterling – sorry, Canteloupe – and himself had played for I Zingari against the Gentlemen of Hertfordshire in 1951. Detterling – Canteloupe – had made 102 not out and Donald 45. *Eheu fugaces*. They had played a lot of agreeable cricket together at one time, rather good cricket at that, thought Donald, brightening a little at the thought of having played among men of mettle. From what he had heard, if Detterling, his senior by some ten years, had concentrated properly on the game before the war he might have had a County Cap, for surely a decent regiment like his would have given him special furlough for the first class season. Even just after the war it might not have been too late, for Detterling still cut finer and neater than any man in England; but by then, of course, everything had gone all sour and dreary and there had been no question of a serving officer's getting four months leave to play county cricket – not without some dismal socialist whining about it in the House. And when Detterling had finally left the army – some time around 1950 that must have been – it was to go into the House himself, which precluded any serious cricket apart from the occasional club match like the one they had played

18

in together on that pretty ground near here . . . which had apparently disappeared for ever under the yellow mud, for try as he might, Donald could see no sign of it.

And now here he was, going to the baptism of Detterling's – CANTELOUPE's – first-born son. Since the man was now over sixty, Donald reflected, he had left it a little late to commence propagation. Donald remembered him as being always blatantly indifferent to domestic notions or activities, a bachelor if ever there was; but presumably he had felt that he ought to make an effort after his unexpected accession to his splendid peerage, and so had chosen that succulent little trollop, Tullia (Baby) Llewyllyn, who was even now under twenty unless Donald was badly mistaken, and had managed to do the trick. Well at least, thought Donald, he had positively done it, unlike Donald himself, who conspicuously had not. Not that this was necessarily his own fault: Vanessa's interior had been much meddled with in its day, and she was almost certainly, by the time she got round to Donald, incapable of conception. Just as well, he thought now: God knows what sort of monsters she might have hatched; whereas the twins whom they had adopted as ten-year-olds, though Vanessa herself soon came to hate them, had been ample, wholesome, easy girls, who had survived both Vanessa's detestation and her death with comfortable aplomb.

But how do I feel, thought Donald now, how do I feel about meeting them today? For the twins, Carmilla and Theodosia, were undergraduates of Lancaster College, and had been invited, as Donald's daughters, both to the christening in Lancaster Chapel and the shindig that was to follow in the Provost's Lodging. I ought, he thought, to be looking forward to seeing them, and oh, I am, I am; but I also feel guilty, inferior, ashamed, about all those years I spent away from them in St Bede's Hospital, or rather in the dark night of my soul. Can they forgive me without despising me? But then again, why should they not? Liberal

19

arrangements were made for them by the lawyers (who had been previously instructed, through my foresight, against any such contingency) for their education, maintenance and pleasure. During the few weeks that I have been . . . out . . . they have been attentive without being pointedly so: for example, they both returned to Cambridge half way between the beginning of Term and the beginning of Full Term, i.e. neither scurrying back to the place as soon as it was open to them, nor, on the other hand, lingering officiously with me in London until the last possible moment. In short, they have so far shown gratitude and duty with their customary good sense and moderation, and there is no reason why this should not continue. And yet, thought Donald, and yet: if they should get it into their heads that I want too much from them . . . or that I want nothing at all . . . or that I'm just not worth their trouble in any case . . . or if one or both of them should want some man and should see me as an obstacle, prudish or possessive . . . There are so many things which could turn them indifferent to me or even hostile (the little girls with pigtails who came to me at ten), that I dread meeting them in case this time, or the next, or the one after, something should go, perhaps irrevocably, wrong. It is my joy to see them and my torture: please God, make it be all right today.

Skull-faced Max de Freville, being, unlike Donald, immune from the quirks of Yorkshire parsimony or indeed from any kind of scruple whatever, had no hesitation in hiring a chauffeur-driven Rolls to carry him to the christening. These days, to be sure, he kept just such a vehicle on twenty-four-hour call every year from All Fools' Day to the Autumn Equinox, the period which he was accustomed to spend in London, where he owned a voluminous flat in Piccadilly and was attended by a jaded Venetian with the physique of a sometime gondolier.

Since de Freville's flat was within spitting distance of the Ritz, where he knew very well that Donald Salinger now hung out, since he also knew that Donald had been bidden to the christening, and since, finally, he had been on friendly if never intimate terms with Donald for twenty-five years, one might have supposed that he would have offered Donald a lift. The reason he did not do so was that he was much looking forward to a discussion which he proposed to hold in the back of the Rolls (with the glass partition up) during the journey to and from Cambridge. This discussion was to be with two people: his long dead mistress, and his recently deceased business partner.

There had been a time when he would summon his mistress through her effigy, a half-scale copy of the life-size monument which he had raised to her in the British Cemetery on Corfu; but this had been smashed the previous year in transit between London and Venice, and the copyist who had executed it turned out to have died some months previously. Although arrangements were in train to find another copyist, the search might well be lengthy as the work required was curious; and meanwhile Max found that the best way of bringing Angela to him and retaining her attention was to motor at a steady 50 mph in the back of a partitioned car – a mode of travelling which had been her own favourite during her life, especially towards the end of it, when she had developed a seemingly inexhaustible passion for being driven, day after day and week after week, anywhere between Oslo and Antioch.

Whereas normally Max would conduct his conversations with Angela *tête-à-tête*, on this occasion he would also require Stratis Lykiadopoulos to be present, as his dead friend and partner was knowledgeable about certain topics (fiscal) which might need analysis. Lyki, Max had found

21

during the seven weeks since his death by coronary thrombosis, was easy to summon, his voice, his idioms, his modes of thought and argument being still fresh in Max's mind and hence easy of imitation. For in fact Max did not 'summon' or 'call up' anybody. He simply spoke aloud, in his normal voice, then thought out what Angela or Lyki would probably have replied, and answered for them in their own tones and with their own gestures in so far as he could render them. It was all a matter of memory and mimicry; so small wonder that Angela Tuck (*obiit* 1970) was increasingly difficult to conjure.

Max opened the debate as the Rolls passed Lord's Cricket Ground.

'Tax trouble,' he said aloud. 'Today I am to stand as godfather to the son of my oldest friend. I shall wish to leave most of my money to him, and also to let him have the use of a large sum of it as soon as he comes of age – perhaps sooner. How am I to transfer money to him without paying tax on the transfer?'

'I should have thought you knew all the dodges,' he answered himself in Angela's robust tenor (pitching it, as usual, slightly too low).

'I do,' said Max *in propria persona*. 'Get the money to America or Switzerland, where they do not pry into what one does with one's own capital, and hand it over to him there. Very well; but such money as I have in America or Switzerland I need for my own day-to-day use on the spot.'

'Then send more to one or both of those countries from your store in England,' he suggested to himself in Lykiadopoulos's excellent but slightly Yiddish cast of English. 'England is an easy country out of which to send money and will soon, I think, become even easier.'

'But once again,' said Max as Max, 'what money I have in England I shall need for my own use here.'

'That's right, darling,' he said with Angela's hoarse, ginny chuckle. 'Get your priorities right. Number One

22

first, second and third, and fourth if there's more than sixteen runners.'

'*Sois sériuse*,' Max answered urbanely. 'Since you and Lyki are dead, I have no one to whom I would wish to leave or give money, except this godson and his father, Lord Canteloupe, with whom I was close, almost as close as I was with you, Angela, in the time between our youth and middle-age. Such money as I give to either, I wish to give unhampered by vexatious taxes. To do so I must put money in America or Switzerland. I cannot afford to send money there from England. What then am I to do?'

'Where else have you money which you might send?' he asked himself, giving a long suck at the end of the question, as of Angela soaking up her fifth *apéritif*.

'Here is the trouble,' said Max. 'I have money available both in Greece, i.e. the Corfu Casino and Leisure Investment, and in Italy, from the profits of the Baccarat Bank which we were funding in Venice when Lyki died there. Now then: both countries have currencies which, though weak, are realizable; but in both the export of more than mere chicken feed is absolutely forbidden. So: how am I to get my money out of Greece and Italy . . . where I, of all men, am closely marked and followed in my financial dealings?'

There was a thoughtful silence at the back of the Rolls. Eventually, 'Max, my dear,' said Max in Lykiadopoulos's Hebrew lilt, 'this is one very old problem with which we have all been faced in the past. The answer is childishly simple: either you smuggle it yourself, and risk a huge prison sentence; or you engage others to smuggle it and pay a huge discount.'

'I can't afford the discount,' snapped Max de Freville.

'Getting mean in your old age,' he taunted himself with Angela's late night snarl.

'Yes,' he answered her. 'It hurts my soul to pay others – to pay them through the scrotum – to do what I know I should have the courage and ingenuity to do myself. And now at last I think I have thought of a foolproof scheme which I can operate without being seriously dependent on anybody else. That is why I have asked Lyki to come with us to Cambridge: I want his opinion of my solution.'

'I can't think,' said Max 'Angela in a *blasé* way, 'why you are taking all this trouble. As you say, you have money enough in Switzerland and America for your own needs. As for little Lord Snooty and his Dad, let them have what you can spare as and when you can spare it, and leave the thing at that. They are not exactly deprived.'

'I agree,' said Max, nodding to his gaunt reflection (cropped hair, deep trenches from the corners of his nose to those of his mouth) which was superimposed on a Tudor roadhouse in the window. 'There are, as it happens, stories that Canteloupe has been mildly imprudent with his private means, but Cant-Fun Corporation stands as high in the stately home business as the enterprises that run Woburn or Longleat. So whatever Canteloupe's indiscretions with his pocket money, so to speak, neither Canteloupe himself, nor Tullia, his wife – Baby, as everyone seems to call her – nor Tullia's child, my godson, are ever going to lack the price of a suite at the Connaught. Even so, I should like the child to have something substantial by which to remember me, so that when he is grown he will say . . . oh, how will he put it? . . . "Most chaps of my age," he will say, "want their fathers out of the way so that they can latch on to the loot. But I like my old man, and anyway I've got my own money. Funny old friend of Papa's, it was, a professional gambler, ran a big chemmy game in London in the 'fifties, left Aspinall standing, had his sticky patches but went on and up – he passed me a cool seven figures plus, more than most godfathers come good for." Something like that, I imagine his saying to his chums, and I think I have hit on a way of getting the necessary money out of Greece and Italy and into Switzerland or the United

States, without any risk and without paying any service charge. Now, would you both like to hear about it?'

'Very much indeed, my dear,' said Max in Lykiadopoulos's ghetto voice as the Rolls hummed on towards Hendon.

'Then you shall both hear after the christening,' said Max. 'Talking to you both has tired me. Now I must rest.'

Gregory Stern and Isobel his wife drove from London, Isobel at the wheel, in Isobel's vintage Lagonda. Marius, their twelve-year-old son (just turned) and Rosie (nearly ten) sat in the back and complained of draughts – quite justifiably, as the hood did not fit and was in any case rotten.

'To be beautiful one must suffer a little,' their father told them from the front. 'There will be no more distinguished car than this at today's christening.'

'Should we live to get there,' Rosie said.

'Isn't there a rug in the back somewhere?' Isobel suggested.

'There is,' said Marius. 'It is very damp and covered with a kind of yellow scurf.'

'Never mind,' said Gregory as they whizzed through Swiss Cottage. 'It is not very far to Cambridge.'

'Don't tell silly lies,' said Isobel. 'It is all of fifty miles to Cambridge. They'll just have to put up with it. It'll toughen you both up,' she said, turning back from the wheel to smile at Marius and nearly annihilating a flock of old age pensioners on a zebra crossing. 'They all ought to be dead by now anyway,' she said in reply to Gregory's gentle remonstrance.

Gregory's long face lengthened yet further in disapproval,

although he knew, or hoped he knew, that she did not really mean it.

Blond Marius opened his green eyes wide and laughed. He always enjoyed his mother's jokes, the more savage the better. Black-haired Rosie's mousy little face remained impassive in its frame of thick, dangling tresses.

'A master at school,' said Marius, 'Mr St George the cricket master, says that statistics say that by the year two thousand and fifty half the population will be over seventy.'

'You'll be one of them,' said his father.

'Mr St George says it will be a frightful nuisance for the younger people – having to take care of all the old and pay for them. The burden will be "quite unwarrantable". That's what he said.'

'How old is Mr St George?' said Rosie.

'Oh, pretty old; all the masters are. But not old enough yet to be an "unwarrantable burden". I think he had his thirty-first birthday last summer.'

'All I was thinking,' said Rosie, 'was that everyone gets old and nobody can help it.'

'With certain qualifications, that is a very just remark,' Gregory said.

'What qualifications?' asked Marius.

'Even now, a few people die young or middle-aged. And I have to add,' said Gregory Stern, 'that no one is compelled to live a single second longer than he wants to.'

'Suicide,' said Rosie, 'is a sin.'

'It's not illegal any more,' said Isobel. 'And you don't get buried at the cross-roads with a stake through your heart.'

'It may not be a crime,' said Rosie, 'but it is a sin. A sin against God.'

'Is that what they've been telling you at Collingham's?' asked Isobel.

'No. At school they do not teach us much about sin. Or about God. I read it in a book – a book published by

26

Daddy's firm. Stern & Detterling,' she enunciated with pride.

'Are you going to change it to Stern & Canteloupe?' said Marius, tapping his father on the shoulder. 'That would sound much grander. Or Canteloupe & Stern? That would sound grander still.'

'I think not,' said Gregory with commendable restraint. 'It costs a small fortune to register a change in a company's title.'

'Ikey Mo,' grinned Isobel over the wheel.

Gregory chuckled softly. Although from a social point of view he had totally discarded his Jewish origins, he retained an atavistic sense of the splendours and the squalors of his race, and enjoyed a perverse pleasure whenever Isobel made anti-Semitic jokes, no matter how infantile, at his expense. Frequently, indeed, he encouraged these jokes by aping and exaggerating what he conceived to be low-Jewish modes and mannerisms of speech. But such play-acting must never last long (for perhaps he feared deep down lest the jokes should turn out to reflect a reality) and the conversation in the Lagonda was now steered back to its proper course.

'Tell me, Rosie,' he said, turning towards the back seat, 'in which of our books did you read this? That suicide is a sin against God?'

'*Love's Jest Book*. By Fielding Gray.'

'So my Rosie is reading *Love's Jest Book* already?'

'There are copies all over the house,' said Isobel. 'It was your first big success in fiction, remember? Yours and Fielding's both. We had a party to celebrate, and all the guests were given copies – most of which were left behind. Nice people we knew in those days.'

'I thought it was a sad book,' said Rosie. 'This poor boy killing himself because he thought his friend didn't love him any more.'

27

'But who says that his suicide is a sin against God?' said Gregory. 'I do not remember that.'

'A clergyman at the funeral,' Rosie said. 'He tells them all that evil courses have ended in the prime sin of destroying God's greatest gift.'

'But that clergyman was meant to be wicked and vindictive. I remember him now. You must not accept his judgment, Rosie. Fielding meant you to hate him.'

'Nevertheless,' said Rosie, 'what he said rang true to me.'

'Will Fielding Gray be at the christening?' said Marius. 'I hope so. He gave me a fiver last time we met . . . and rather a funny look with it.'

'He'll be there,' said Isobel, overtaking a hearse. 'He and Baby have been very thick just lately, I hear. Why is this damned thing going so fast? Has the driver no respect for the dead?'

'The coffin is covered with canvas,' said Rosie. 'That means it's empty. They're just taking it somewhere, for somebody. Some body,' she muttered.

'Still no need to carry on as if this were Brooklands.'

'Oh *Mummy*,' said Marius, hating her to let herself down. 'Brooklands was closed years ago.'

'Brands Hatch, then.'

Rosie leaned forward and touched her mother's neck.

'What was that you said, Mummy, about Fielding Gray being thick with Cousin Tullia?'

'Cousin Tullia? Oh, *Baby*, you mean. I shouldn't think anyone's called her Tullia since the day she was born – except you and her father. Well, darling, I only meant that Fielding Gray is a very old friend of their family. He's known Canteloupe since the fall of Jericho – they were both in the same ridiculous regiment of toy soldiers. And come to think of it, he was quite chummy-whummy with Baby's mother, your poor Aunt Patricia.'

'And you think he might now be getting quite chummy-whummy with Cousin Tullia?'

'Mr St George at school,' remarked Marius, 'says that however many women a man may fancy, they are all, *au fond*, the same one. *Au fond*, he said: which means "at bottom".'

Isobel giggled coarsely.

Gregory said, 'It would perhaps be more fitting that Mr St George should confine his instruction to cricket.'

'He's a Classics beak too. He told us *that* bit when we were reading Ovid. What I was trying to say,' said Marius patiently, 'was that anyone who was chummy-whummy with a girl's mother would naturally want to be chummy-whummy with the daughter too. At any rate if Mr St George is right. Because being mother and daughter they'd probably be pretty much the same *au fond*.'

'At bottom,' said Rosie gravely.

'Tell me,' said Gregory, wishing to divert the discussion, 'how did you find Ovid? Which poem were you reading?'

'One of the *Heroides: Oenone*. What Mr St George said was that the principle – that a man always really fancied the same woman, however many he disported himself with – was very neatly illustrated by the behaviour of Paris. First, Paris fancied Oenone; then he awarded the Golden Apple to Venus; and finally he eloped with Helen. Clearly, said Mr St George, he fancied all three of them because all three were the same *au fond* – randy and promiscuous sluts. *His* expression,' said Marius, as his father twitched in preface to rebuke.

'Unfair to Helen,' said Isobel. 'The only person she was unfaithful to was Menelaus, who always seems old enough to have been her grandpa.'

'Lord Canteloupe is old enough to be Cousin Tullia's grandpa,' murmured Rosie.

Before anyone could think of an answer to this, she had

folded her hands between her bare knees, put her head on Marius' shoulder, and fallen asleep.

Peter Morrison, MP, motored to the christening from his manor house at Luffham by Whereham in Norfolk. His journey was rather shorter than that of those who were coming from London and a great deal more attractive; for while the inland landscapes of Norfolk tended to be monotonous, he nevertheless passed such singular man-made features as Castle Dawn and Castle Acre; and later on, when he came into Suffolk, he journeyed through the faerie Breckland down long avenues of pine.

Later still, when he came to Lavenham, he remembered that there was, or had been until recently, a Doctor Barnardo's Home nearby, and he started to think, by loose association, of his dead brother, Alastair. Alastair, the elder, the rightful heir to Luffham, had been killed over thirty years before, while rescuing one of his men from drowning during a desperate embarkment from an enfiladed beach. Rather oddly, the dominant brother during their childhood had been Peter. Though he was three years younger, it was he who invented their games, who devised the rules for their small-cricket matches, who discovered by tactical prying that Nanny (and by extension probably Mummy) had hair just *there*, and who imparted the intelligence to the cringing and weeping Alastair (ah, bitter spring of remorse for many years to come) that when he was dead they would put him in a wooden box and bury him.

Which was what they did. Alastair stepped briefly into his proper and senior role when he became a commissioned

30

officer while Peter was still at school; but almost immediately he had stepped out of it again, into the embrace of black death in the shallows off windy Crete, leaving Peter dominant for ever more. For Alastair the world spared a posthumous VC and a tear or two: to Peter it afforded not only the lands and the house at Luffham but also a brilliant place in his School, Vice-Regal Citation for services rendered during the last days of the Raj, and in time a seat in Parliament and prominent office in the Conservative Government of the early 1970s.

Yet Alastair, he knew, had been the better man. Why did death always take the better man? It had done the same with his two sons. Jeremy, the younger, a plausible but in Peter's eye mediocre youth (not 'genuine' he would have said, had Jeremy been a racehorse) had sailed smoothly through his schooldays and into a fluky Exhibition at Lancaster College; whereas the elder, the shining and striving Nickie, had been blighted, not indeed by death itself, but, far worse, by a living death, which had stolen his wits and sent his shambling carcass to whimper and dribble its years away in the asylum of St Bede.

NOT, thank God, a case of lunacy, thought Peter now, as he drove across Newmarket Heath, which stretched to infinitude under the spare April sun. A physical disease had disordered and then destroyed the cells of Nickie's brain: there was no taint of insanity here. And yet . . . was this in the end of any comfort? He thought of the other inhabitants of St Bede's who were, or had been, personally known to him. Patricia Llewyllyn, Tom Llewyllyn's wife and Baby Canteloupe's mother, had been the victim not of a physical illness but of a mental obsession, which turned on the son whom she had never borne. Patricia (one of the staff had told him while he was on a recent visit to drooling Nickie) passed her time dressed as a Black Nun and doing penance (often with violent self-laceration) for having maimed or murdered (she seemed uncertain which) her imaginary sixteen-year-old son. But at least her position had some basis in reality, for she had indeed most brutally, if unintentionally, injured an adolescent boy while making love to him some years before; and her actions were not altogether without purpose or dignity, as she was repenting of her crime and trying to obtain forgiveness. Who was to say, then, that the mentally diseased Patricia was not, as a human being, preferable to the totally nullified Nickie?

Or take the case of Donald Salinger, who, he understood, had been discharged from St Bede's only a few weeks previously. Donald, as a result of his wife's death, had suffered some kind of extreme nervous shock. His was neither a case of downright insanity, as was Patricia's, nor of radical physiological damage, as was Nickie's: it was somewhere between. A mental or moral shock had been so severe that it had affected the function of certain neural circuits and reflexes to the extent that Donald had been, as it were, arrested in time, permanently imprisoned in the moment at which the initial shock had struck at him, and so doomed to experience and re-experience, time after time and non-stop, the atrocious agony which had just been inflicted on him. Horrible as all this might be, once again it was clear to Peter that Donald, like Patricia, had retained in good measure the *mechanism* for thought and action, however intermittent the current that drove that mechanism might be, however perverse the direction or bizarre the purpose. In Nickie's case, on the other hand, some virus or lurking allergy had destroyed his entire cerebral equipment, leaving only a breathing and barely sentient lump of flesh.

From all of which, thought Peter as he drove past the exorbitant fertility of the Botanical Gardens, it would seem to follow that Patricia and Donald with their mental flaws or inherited taints were far better off than Nickie who had neither. Some kind of life, however distorted, was surely better than none. But in fact, of course, if one looked at the thing absolutely square, the Morrisons (if not Nickie

32

himself) had the abiding comfort that what had happened to Nickie was a medical accident of an exceedingly rare type, against the occurrence of which, in Jeremy or any children he might have, the odds were many millions to one. Patricia's blood relations, by contrast, her sister Isobel and her daughter Baby (to leave aside any question of their children) must be faced by an incessant fear, a fear lest the psychic abnormality, which caused the frenzied Patricia to bite off the ear of a sixteen-year-old boy, had sprung from some hereditary taint that might at any moment make itself manifest in either of them (to say nothing, once more, of those born to them).

At least, thought Peter, as he parked his Mercedes on the College Stones outside the Great Gate of Lancaster, when I see Jeremy here today at this christening, I shall *know* that he is and will remain as sane as I am.

Apart from the guests who lived in Cambridge itself, the person who had the shortest distance to cover to the christening was Ptolemaeos Tunne, who dwelt in the Fens, in a large, lonely and well heated house, some considerable way from the nearest village, which in turn was some considerable way from the nearest town, which was Ely. Although most Englishmen find the East Anglian Fens dreary and unhealthy, Ptolemaeos maintained that proper heating (on which he spent a sizeable fraction of his enormous income) would keep the damp at bay and that the damp, by and large, would keep the world at bay, which was for him a paramount requirement; for Ptolemaeos, though he dearly loved a chosen circle of friends, relatives and servants, hated people in general and *the* people most of all.

There had been a time when his orphaned niece, his favourite of all, Jo-Jo Pelham, had lived with him in his house in the Fens; but now that Jo-Jo was married to Jean-Marie Guiscard, Ptolemaeos lived alone, attended during the day by two old women who came by bus from the village, otherwise self-sufficient and entirely contented in the enjoyment of his comprehensive cellar and even more comprehensive library. At any one moment Ptolemaeos would be conducting scholarly research into several subjects, usually of an obscure if not arcane nature. When his library failed him, his vast wealth (his father had founded, and Ptolemaeos had sold, a manufactory of stool-pans) enabled him to procure books, manuscripts, incunabula and oral information from all over the world. He even maintained, from time to time, teams of agents who looked after his interests or investigations 'in the field' on the frequent occasions when his loathing of the climate or the natives prevented his visiting it in person. On this particular morning in April, however, his lines of research all ran close to home, and his main line the closest: for Ptolemaeos was currently much exercised by that most ancient of philosophic enigmata, the relation which obtains between the human mind or intellect and the physical brain.

And now, as he climbed into his souped-up Mini (which he ran because it was convenient to park and provided him with plenty of beneficent exercise in the exertion and contortion necessary to wheedle his nineteen stone bulk in and out of the thing), Ptolemaeos began to assess progress. The whole matter had started when his friend and contemporary, Ivan (El Greco) Barraclough, a Fellow of Lancaster College, had observed to him at dinner in Hall one night that they were both well over thirty-five, the Psalmist's half-way mark, and that it therefore behoved them, since they were going downhill, so to speak, to consider what they might find at the bottom. Ptolemaeos had answered that they still had a long way to go ('If you watch your weight,' interjected Ivan cattily) and that he knew very well what lay at the bottom – oblivion. Very probably, Greco had agreed: but he had just discovered an authoritative dissertation, by an Edwardian biologist called Sheraton, which seemed to hint at livelier possibilities.

Returning from Lancaster to the Fens next morning, Ptolemaeos had carried with him a copy of *Man on His Being* and against all expectation had been fascinated by it. Sheraton's initial premise had been that the physical actions of a man were governed by a brain which sent instructions to the nerves, sinews and muscles, and co-ordinated these in obedience and harmony. Nothing new in that. His second premise had been that there must be something (mind, soul or intellect) which was superior to the brain and issued instruction to it on any occasion when anything more than mere reflex or mechanical response was required; for while the brain by itself could certainly observe an oncoming motor-car (for example), deduce threat and dictate and organize evasion, it could not take decisions or prescribe action where judgments of strategic, aesthetic or moral value were required. Or again, when there was more than one choice in any given situation, an element of *intellect* was needed to make it. True, the brain by itself could certainly perform feats of memory and calculation, and possibly of logic or reason; but in almost every case in a man's life when decisions of a more than merely instinctive kind were called for, the brain must at some stage refer to, and thereafter be guided by, a higher authority: Mind? Intellect? Soul? Or all three?

Once again, Ptolemaeos had thought, nothing very original in *that*.

But at this stage Sheraton, by continuing to insist on the obvious, had suddenly raised the level of his dissertation to something (in Ptolemaeos' view) near to sublimity. Ordinary cerebral and neural processes, he wrote, were fuelled by electricity generated for the purpose by the body. Up to

35

a point, such electrical processes could be traced and even, in a very general way, recorded. The processes of the soul or the intellect, however, were fuelled by an energy (if energy it were) that was traceable by no instrument and accountable to no system of calculation. Moral or intellectual decision took place (as far as instruments or equations were concerned) *in vacuo*, beyond space and time. How then (and here Sheraton arrived at the climax of his enquiries) did the disembodied mind/soul/intellect communicate its decisions to the *physical* brain, how did it enforce them, and how did it make the nature of its instructions, which originated in a non-spatial and non-dimensional Being, comprehensible to a corporeal and material organism? How did the mind/soul/intellect, possessed of no physical power, set off in the brain the electrical currents necessary to propel the body into activity? In short, how did mind move matter?

Answer this question, wrote Sheraton, and you will have come a long way towards understanding the very essence of Human Being, of the spirit which rules the body and may possibly survive bodily death. If you can once find out by means of what type of impulse or energy the intellect (etc.) activates the physiological mechanisms which are provided to do its bidding, then you may come at the innermost secret of the Universe, or, for that matter, of God Himself.

Very well: but how does one even begin to investigate the means by which the mind communicates with and gives orders to the body? No instrument can record the phenomenon, because no physical energy is involved. The use of physical and detectable energy begins with the *brain*: to observe the power behind the working of *mind* or *soul* is beyond us. Yet we may know, argued Sheraton, what are the lucubrations of a person's mind or soul by the simple method of questioning him. If such a person tells us of his processes of thought and the resultant decision, we shall know at what stage his mind must have communicated that decision to the brain in order that the latter might initiate the required activities of the body. So, said Sheraton: select a person who is intelligent and sensitive, yet undevious; see to it that he is totally confident and relaxed; then apply to him a variety of stimuli – visible, audible, sensual. Observe this person as the stimuli produce their initial bodily response and as the brain refers the problems or questions which are raised up to the intellect or soul. Observe the person again as the soul or intellect issues answers and directions to the brain. Then catechize the person most rigorously about the two crucial phases of the operation, i.e. when brain is in direct contact with the intellect and vice versa. What did he feel at these junctures? Was there any bodily shock or discomfort? Was there any kind of discontinuity or hiatus? Thus and thus, said Sheraton, one may try to penetrate the secret of how physical impulses set up reactions in a non-physical and non-spatial Being, and how these incorporeal reactions in turn spark off fresh physical impulses. The whole secret lies in the process of transition, of the leap from the material world to the immaterial and back: only reveal that process and you reveal all.

So unfashionable, in Sheraton's day, were the concepts in which he was dealing (independent soul and the power of pure spirit, thus at least implying the existence of a supreme spirit or God), so inimical was his interpretation of the mind's control of body to the dominant material determinism of his time, that one would expect him to have been rent in pieces by scientists contemporary with him. But in fact, as Ptolemaeos discovered through subsequent reading, few of Sheraton's colleagues had bothered with the matter at all. He had been ignored rather than refuted or repudiated. And of course, thought Ptolemaeos, it was clear why. His method of investigating the vital transitional phase (how do the impulses pass from brain to intellect and back?) was so naïf and crude that none of his conclusions could be properly formulated, let alone proved. His experiments, if such they could be called, were flabby and disreputable, his deductions therefore invalid. And yet some of his friends, and even some of his enemies, had conceded that Sheraton's *theory* had something to commend it. If only, they had observed, a method *could* indeed be found of analysing the process of communication between the palpable and the impalpable, then a lot of important questions would be answered about both.

Amen to that, thought Ptolemaeos now, as he parked the Mini by the Fellows' Garden Hostel and engaged in the preliminary gyrations necessary to swivel his frame towards the car door. The matter is curious, worth my time and trouble: the problem is to devise a method more precise and subtle than poor old Sheraton's confessional box. What is needed is to arrest the process of communication or instruction at the all important stage of transition. No use just asking people vague questions about what they thought they might have felt: you must have them in your control so tightly that you can stop the process (just as you can stop a film) and conduct a detailed examination of a static frame, as it were, of the brain-to-mind and mind-to-brain passage of thought and/or impulse. Questions of course there must be; but he, Ptolemaeos, would be asking them of people absolutely conditioned, in whom the processes of thought would have been absolutely halted and laid bare for his inspection.

The practical requirements were quite simple, he told himself for the hundredth time as he walked, with a kind of lumbering spriteliness, from the Garden Hostel, over Queen's Road, through the Postern Gate of Lancaster, and up the avenue towards the bridge: comfortable and reassuring surroundings in which those questioned could be soothed and wooed (this much, at any rate, Sheraton had got right); certain drugs, easily procurable by a man of resource, to assist the hypnotic and physiotherapeutic techniques by which he hoped to halt his subjects' chain of thought at the critical stage and lay their mental and cerebral functions open to the most intimate probing; and, of course, the subjects themselves, who should be young men and women or, for preference, children, because these were trusting, ingenuous, malleable and so more easily approachable by his chosen method (*vulnerable*, some might say if they knew the details, but no one was going to know these, only that Ptolemaeos was going to conduct an amusing and harmless variant of the truth game in the interest of epistemological research).

And doubtless, he told himself as he vibrated over the bridge, there will be several potential subjects, specimens of high quality and gentle nurture, of obedient and affectionate disposition, prominently on display at this afternoon's concourse among the expensive progeny of my acquaintance.

While all these people were making their way to the christening, Sir Thomas Llewyllyn, Provost of Lancaster College, was having a last minute discussion of the arrangements with his private secretary, Len.

'Lord and Lady Canteloupe, with the child and its nurse, are safely installed in the Lauderdale Wing,' said the Provost, waving his grey curls at Len, 'where they will be served with a light luncheon before the ceremony.'

'And I've checked on the Shepherd Suite,' said lank-lipped, truffle-cheeked Len, 'which is all ready for Gregory Stern and his family, and on the Benson Room, which will be very suitable for Jo-Jo Guiscard and her husband. What with Jo-Jo being preggers and all, I should think they'll be very grateful to stay overnight. But what I don't understand,' said Len petulantly, 'is why we're putting our fannies about for the Sterns – four of them, Provost, and all they've got to do is go back to London.'

'Canteloupe wants to talk to Gregory about publishing – he doesn't get up to their London office as much as he used to, and he needs to be filled in on recent developments. Tullia wants to talk to her Aunt Isobel about child-rearing. Both Canteloupe and Gregory want to talk to Jean-Marie about that book he's writing, which they will almost certainly publish. And I,' said Tom, 'want to take a long, keen look at the two Stern children, who are said to be something rather special.'

'Where did you hear that?'

'All over the place. Tullia adores Marius, she tells me. He is the idol of his preparatory school, a real "Tell England" juvenile. And from the sound of it Rosie promises to turn out rather like Jessica – a bit ratty just at present but with fine feline prospects.'

'Well, anyway, they've got the Shepherd Suite,' said Len, admiring the impeccable bad taste of his green tubular trousers and lemon brogues. 'One room with a double bed and one with two singles for those prodigious kiddies, and a portrait of Provost Shepherd in the loo, trying to look like Sophocles in a grubby wing-collar. Any other worries?'

'The Bishop of Glastonbury,' said Tom, 'who should arrive very shortly. I'll have to give him lunch. Could you come and help me out?'

'I could,' said Len. 'But isn't there about a platoon of clerics in the college, any one of whom would be more suitable?'

'They're all miffed because he's been invited to officiate. They think it should be the Dean or the Chaplain.'

'They're dead right too. Why are we having this Bishop?'

'He's a very old friend of Canteloupe, who served with him during the war. Mungo Chevenix, he was called then, though now he signs himself Mungo Avallon, special prerogative of the Bishops of Glastonbury. The thing is,' said Tom, 'that in those days he was a tough, hard-drinking, hunting and cricketing parson, just the kind of thing to appeal to Canteloupe . . . who hasn't seen much of him these last years and doesn't understand how much he has changed his tune to further his career. You know the kind of thing they go in for now – Unilateral Nuclear Disarmament just for an *entrée*. Canteloupe was talking of joining us for lunch but I put a stopper on that one (bad luck to meet the priest before the christening, I said) in case they quarrelled before anyone even gets as far as the Chapel. So please, Len, save me from tiffin *tête-à-tête* with Mungo Avallon.'

'Right you be. Before he gets here,' said Len, 'I'd better put you wise about the home team.'

'Home team?'

'Members of the college that are coming. Greco Barraclough, for a start.'

'That's all right. Canteloupe and Tullia know him quite well through Ptoly Tunne – or they wouldn't have asked him.'

'Yes; but Greco insists on bringing Nicos – in attendance. Nicos has not been asked.'

'I really must have a word with El Greco,' said Tom, 'and explain that it is no longer the custom in England to drag one's personal page behind one wherever one goes. But it won't matter today as Canteloupe is sympathetic to that kind of behaviour. Until only just a year or so ago he took his own servant wherever he went – as a matter of course and without warning anyone. Luckily Tullia's got him out of that, but he won't resent Greco's knight and 'squire performance with Nicos.'

'So that's Nicos okay. Now: the Morrison boy, Jeremy.'

'No problems there, surely.'

'He's got debts in the town.'

'I didn't think local tradesmen gave credit to undergraduates any more.'

'They do to the sons of Members of Parliament who own large slices of Norfolk.'

'How much does young Morrison owe?'

'Call it . . . two monkeys.'

'Two monkeys, Len?'

'Two monkeys make a thousand, Provost. Of course it sounds a lot more than it is,' said Len airily. 'You don't get far off the ground these days for a thousand. But I don't think his Daddy is going to be pleased when he hears about it.'

'What about his Mummy?' said Tom. 'Is Helen Morrison coming? We might get it through her.'

'Wake up, Tom. She's dead. Six months ago. Fit as a fart one minute, total cardiac fuck-up the next.'

'Oh yes. You had a tricky job getting me out of the Memorial Service. So, no Helen – which means we'll have to approach Peter for the money direct.'

'No, we won't. Ptoly Tunne will cope.'

'Ptolemaeos? Why should he?'

'Ptolemaeos,' said Len in his immaculate Cambridge drawl, 'has got some new screwball theory about the human soul – about how you can maybe prove it exists and then go on to find what it's made of. The trick is, you trap it just as it's sparking off the brain, see, and by watching how it manages to do that you find out what it is – you hope. So he's getting a little gear together to go into the thing, and he rang me up the other day to say he's going to want all the bright boys and girls he can get to pop under his microscope, and how about my using my influence to drum up a little talent? That's why he's coming today – not so much for the christening as to see how I'm doing and to look about for himself.'

'Damned presumption,' said Tom. 'Using my undergraduates as guinea-pigs.'

'Rubbish,' said Len. 'Twenty-five years ago, the story runs, when Rothschild wanted human spermatozoa for his experiments, the smart lads of Lancaster were queueing up with their milk bottles at the ready – and all Rothschild was paying was a pint of his worst Burgundy and a quick look at a book of naughty pictures. Now, Ptolemaeos is paying money down – like he'll settle dear little Jeremy's two monkeys with the tradesmen, and maybe give him more, if Jeremy will promise to go to Ptoly in the Fens some time in the summer and be a patient boy while Ptoly works the old hocus-pocus on him. It's a good square offer, Tom, and all for the furtherance of knowledge.'

'What's your cut?'

'You forget. These days I'm loaded.'

'You must be getting something.'

'Well . . . perhaps the odd invitation to stay in the Fens when something really succulent is being spread out under Ptoly's prying proboscis. He's very keen to take impressions when the subjects are asleep . . . or under the influence of certain harmless drugs. He'll have his hands full and may need an assistant.'

'For Christ's sake, Len, you don't mean – '

' – No, teacher, I do not. From now on it's all looking and no touching with little Lennie. There's some very nasty new diseases around, in case you hadn't heard, real killers oven-fresh from America, Tom, and they're finding their way into even the most sheltered families. So Lennie is laying down the lance of love, and is going to get all his future kicks from sensuous appreciation – like a pretty pair of legs to see is a pretty pair of legs to see, so let's thank the gods for them and leave the thing at that.'

The front door bell jangled in episcopal summons.

'One last item,' said Len. 'The Salinger girls.'

'Don't tell me *they're* in trouble.'

'Far from it.'

43

'Will Ptolemaeos ask them . . . to help with his investigations?'

'He may, if he likes their cut. They're quite old enough to answer up for themselves, to judge from the way they've just been talking to me.'

'Met your match at last, have you?'

'Pretty well. I was saying to the Salinger girls that since this was a kind of old-fashioned christening with an old-fashioned party to follow, it would be appreciated if just this once they would appear in skirts or dresses. Oh would it? they said. Well, they'd be damned to Hades, they said, if they were going to turn themselves out like a couple of bloody dykes.'

'No, no, no,' said the Marquess Canteloupe. 'We must have the proper words.'

The congregation stirred with pleasurable embarrassment.

'What do you mean, sir?' said the outraged Bishop.

'I mean, my Lord Bishop, that my son is to be baptized in the same words as his father and his father's father. You have just invited the godparents to affirm their allegiance to Christ and to reject evil – '

' – Very properly so – '

' – No, my Lord Bishop. We must have the Devil in all this. They must reject the Devil.'

'Yes,' said Fielding Gray, his one eye glistening and his tiny mouth trembling. 'As one of the infant's godfathers, I am here to renounce the Devil.'

'Yes,' said Jo-Jo Guiscard, looking like a handsome and heavily pregnant boy. 'As godmother I renounce the Devil

44

and all sinful and fleshly desires. Something like that it goes. Not just "evil". Surely you can do better than that.'

'The new form of the service expressly and purposefully excludes – '

' – The new form of the service be damned,' said Lord Canteloupe. 'I will have the proper words.'

'We no longer talk of the Devil in the liturgy,' intoned the Bishop of Glastonbury unctuously, 'nor of fleshly desires.'

'In God's name, why not?'

'It offends modern taste.'

'It don't offend mine.'

'Please settle this quickly,' said Baby Canteloupe. 'Little Tully is getting heavy to hold, and I rather think there's been an accident.'

'You can settle it how you will,' said Mungo Avallon, 'but you will settle it without me.'

He stalked away through the West Door, which had been thrown open for the day in his honour.

'Trendy fool,' said gangling Isobel Stern, who stood with Jo-Jo as second godmother. 'As the child's godparent and great-aunt, I should very much like to know who invited him.'

'Canteloupe,' said Fielding. 'Baby chose the place and Canteloupe chose the priest. He was a temporary chaplain in our regiment during the war. Just before my time. Canteloupe says he once killed six Krauts with his shooting stick. He seems to have deteriorated since.'

'The thing is now,' said skull-faced Max de Freville, who as second godfather stood next to Fielding Gray, 'who is to christen the child?'

'I am,' said Tom Llewyllyn. 'This is Lancaster College Chapel, and I am Provost of Lancaster. So I shall christen him.'

'But Papa,' said Baby Canteloupe, 'you are not in Orders and you don't believe a word of it.'

'I approve of the ceremony. Who shall prevent me from christening my own grandson in my own chapel?'

Nobody, it seemed.

'Very well,' said Tom, nodding his grey wavy head and then turning it towards the godparents. '"I demand therefore: Do you, in the name of this child, renounce the Devil and all his works, the vain pomp and glory of the world, with all covetous desires of the same, and the carnal desires of the flesh, so that you will not follow, nor be led by them?"'

'We renounce them all,' said the godparents with gusto.

'Poor Tully,' whispered Baby. 'But luckily I don't think they quite mean it. Not on their past performance.'

'Give me the child, Tullia.'

Baby handed over her baby.

'There has certainly been an accident,' Tom said, 'so we'll have the old acts as well as the old words.'

He began to strip the infant, dropping its garments on the floor.

'But Papa???'

'It's quite clearly laid down in the Book. "And then, naming the child, if they certify him that the child may well endure it, he shall dip it in the water . . ." You're not going to tell me that a child of yours is too feeble to go through with *that*.'

Tom immersed the baby in the font and vigorously cleansed its posterior. A howl of anger rose up to the vaulting.

'In the Name of the Father, and of the Son, and of the Holy Ghost,' boomed Tom, raising the infant on high and looking it straight in its furious face, 'I here baptize thee: Tullius Fielding d'Azincourt Llewyllyn Gregory Jean-Josephine Maximin Sarum Detterling, henceforth to be called, by courtesy of England, Lord Sarum of Old Sarum. AMEN.'

'I don't think the Bishop would have approved of that last bit,' Baby Canteloupe said.

'I'm surprised your father put it in,' said Jo-Jo Guiscard. 'His socialist principles must be wearing thin.'

'Do you wonder? Just look around.'

Jo-Jo looked around and saw the withdrawing room of the Provost's Lodging. An assortment of faces looked back at her from the walls, variously learned, fatuous, scornful, indolent and sceptical, none of them dispensing compassion. Lowering her sights, Jo-Jo watched elderly and deferential servants while they poured Mumm's 1949 into Venetian glasses of 1710.

'Do you think,' she said to Baby, 'that the vain pomp and glory of the world have corrupted him?'

'No. He simply enjoys and despises them, as he always has. He loves his knighthood, for example, and is hugely amused by it, and holds himself in utter contempt for ever having accepted it.'

Isobel Stern appeared, carrying Tullius.

'Sarum is all decked out again,' she said. 'Nanny and I coped.'

'Bless you both. Do you think "Sarum" is quite right? Rather a heavy spondee, and you can't shorten it any way at all. "Sar" or even "Sarry" would be disastrous. Others may do as they please, but I shall stick to "Tully".'

She took the child, smiled into his eyes, and handed him to the cuffed and collared nurse who was in close attendance.

'You may as well learn now as later, little Tully,' she said, 'that though Mummy loves you, she will dump you whenever convenient.'

The child's face wrinkled. Baby tapped his nose.

'Take him away, Daisy,' she said to the nurse, who, with all her starch, was tender and dimpled. 'He's had his moment for today.'

'Yes, My Lady,' grinned Daisy, and then to Tullius, 'we'll have our fun upstairs, my sweeting.'

'Very ginger, that nurse,' said Baby, as the little Lord departed on Daisy's bosom. '"Hell's Bells and Ginger Women," old Grandfather Turbot used to say when he was trying to be roguish. Why "ginger" women, one wonders?'

But this line of conjecture was to be for ever discontinued as Gregory Stern now led up Marius and Rosie to greet their cousin Baby.

'Rosie darling,' said Baby, bussing her on one cheek, 'we must be careful not to confuse you with Tully's nanny. She's called a flower, too.'

Rosie Stern received this information with indifference, her face sallow and still amid her rich black hair. Baby turned to Marius. 'Oh my darling,' she murmured in his ear, 'how you shine those great green eyes at me. Eyes like the Sons of the Morning, not Marius but Lucifer.'

She caught herself up, wondering whether the occasion had made her hysterical, regretting the bestowal of the beautiful but sinister cognomen. She turned to Jo-Jo for help, but Jo-Jo had slipped away to Jean-Marie on the other side of the room. It was Isobel, quick to recognize her niece's predicament, who came to her rescue.

'Did you ever see William Blake's painting of Lucifer? Not a fallen angel but a pagan god. But of course Blake believed that God was really the Evil Principle and that Satan or Lucifer was the Spirit of True Joy.'

'Very quick, oh Isobel my wife,' said Gregory, deliberately if only very briefly the stage Jew. He looked gently at his poker-faced daughter. 'Let us go into the Provost's Garden, Rosie, and you can tell your ignorant old father the names of all the flowers.'

Rosie nodded, apparently in acquiescence rather than in pleasure, and led him by the elbow through the glass door into the garden. As they went, they passed pregnant Jo-Jo and slender, nimble-faced Jean-Marie, who, with two other men, was trying to comfort his wife for the loss of her figure.

'Who are those two gentlemen with M'sieur and Madame Guiscard?' Rosie asked her father.

'They are of this college,' said Gregory. 'I cannot tell you more.'

Greco Barraclough, the elder of the two men, was in fact a Fellow of the college, an anthropologist of distinction. His undergraduate friend, Nicos Pandouros, his page or esquire as he was sometimes called, was present in that rôle alone, having himself no distinction nor even an individual presence, though ambitious of acquiring both before very long. Meanwhile, he was more or less content to be there merely as the adopted companion of his learned master, although he privately thought that for rich people those around him spoke of very foolish things – almost always of what was past or theoretical, very seldom of what was here and now, the actual and the present, which, with all their money and freedom, they could surely have enjoyed so well.

Now, for instance, 'Your book about that business in the Castle at Arques,' the Greco was saying to Monsieur Guiscard, 'is it yet finished?'

'Not quite,' said Guiscard, and went into a spate of scholarly jargon, of 'sources' and lacunae', all of which were in some way delaying his completion of some dismal tale about a Greek princess who had, it appeared, been held as a hostage in Arques and deceased most wretchedly in 1255. Oh how much better, thought Nicos, if such labours to reconstruct the death of the long dead had been expended in enhancing the lives of those now living. Evidently Madame Guiscard (now there was a live and

49

lusty woman) either felt the same, or took pity on Nicos's palpable boredom, or simply wished to be revenged on the Kyrios for switching the conversation from herself and her pregnancy, for she now deliberately and rather brutally switched it again, to the person of a little girl who was wandering among the flora outside the window hand in hand with a man who (Nicos correctly assumed) was her father.

'That little Rosie Stern,' Jo-Jo said, 'is eclipsed by her brother.'

Since neither Greco nor Nicos knew anything of either, and since Jean-Marie always allowed his wife to be the expert on their English acquaintance, this pronouncement was not contested.

'She is drab,' pursued Jo-Jo, 'whereas Marius is beautiful. She attends a dreary day school in Kensington where she is a figure of mediocrity, while Marius goes to the smartest prep. school in southern England, where everybody from the Headmaster down to the boot boy grovels at his feet.'

'Is he then of such a merit?' asked Jean-Marie, in polite encouragement of a topic for some reason so dear to his wife.

'A natural games-player, brilliant at his work, and as dazzling as a seraph.'

'That is he – across the room with my Lady Canteloupe?' said Nicos.

'Yes. That is he.'

Nicos viewed Marius carefully.

'As you know,' he said at length, 'we Greeks have many legends about boys as fair as that one. Few of these legends conclude happily.'

'I don't know,' said the Greco. 'Ganymede was made cupbearer to the gods – '

' – And Hylas was suffocated by greedy water nymphs, while Hyacinthos was killed in a hideous accident.'

'Anyway,' said Barraclough, 'this boy is not Greek. He is, one infers from his surname, Jewish.'

'No,' said Jo-Jo, revelling in inside knowledge. 'To be properly Jewish, you have to have a Jewish mother. Isobel Stern is not Jewish. So emphatically not Jewish that she wouldn't let Gregory have Marius circumcised, or so the story went at the time.'

'Rightly not,' said Nicos. 'It would have spoiled his beauty.'

'And given him trauma,' said Jean-Marie.

'Rubbish,' said the Greco. 'I was circumcised – most of my generation were in this country – and I have no trauma from it.'

'Neither have I,' said vast Ptolemaeos, who now joined them with scrawny Len. 'Have I, honeypot?' he appealed to Jo-Jo.

'You were shameless and quite heavenly,' said Jo-Jo, 'but I do not discuss past love affairs in front of my *caro* Jean-Marie.'

'I shouldn't at all mind,' said Jean-Marie affably.

'Then you ought to be ashamed of yourself.' Jo-Jo patted her jutting belly. 'How could you say such a thing in front of your own son? You Frogs are meant to be jealous.'

'I perceive,' said Jean-Marie, rather archly, 'that sexual jealousy is despised by those of the English upper class. In this, as in most matters, I applaud them.'

Jo-Jo giggled and patted his hair.

'We were talking,' she said to Len and Ptolemaeos, 'of the Stern children. Poor, Jewy, dingy Rosie – and blissful Marius.'

'Ah,' said Ptolemaeos, 'I apprehend that Rosie has possibilities.' He turned to Len. 'Put her on the list, Len,' he said.

'I don't know whether Gregory – '

' – Put her on the list.'

'Marius too?'

51

'Yes.' Ptolemaeos looked across the room at Marius who was stroking Baby's arm and whispering into her ear. 'But I should prefer them separately.'

'What is this list, you old monster?' Jo-Jo said.

'New experiment, heart of my heart,' said Ptolemaeos. '"*De mente animoque virorum*," as Lucretius has it: to do with the mind and soul of man. There's something about little Rosie which tells me that I may need a long and special session with her. Don't worry,' he said to Len, 'about Isobel and Gregory; they can be there the whole time if they want. But I should prefer Marius not to be there when I'm doing his sister.'

'He'll be away at his school for the next three months,' said Jo-Jo. 'I must say, I find it very odd – your interest in that stringy little stoat, Rosie.'

'Rosie's soul,' said Ptolemaeos, 'may not be as stringy as its envelope.'

'Family gossip has it,' drawled Len, ' – and I hear a lot of it from Tom, who is, after all, Isobel's brother-in-law – family gossip has it that Rosie Stern has a surprising number of loving and loyal friends among girls of her own age and a bit older. Since it cannot be her looks that fetch them, one asks oneself what else it can be.'

'The girls in that family are odd,' said Jo-Jo. 'Every now and then Baby lets something slip about her mother which makes my hair crackle. I gather her grandmother was rather fishy too. Now, there doesn't seem to be much the matter with Baby, as sane a girl as you could meet in a three months' march, but with heredity like that something very peculiar could have rubbed off on her little cousin Rosie.'

'I did *not* say Rosie was peculiar,' said Len. 'I merely reported that she is believed to be much loved by girls of her own age, or to be precise, by girls between nine and fifteen. Why do you deduce oddity from that?'

'Because,' said Jo-Jo, 'you made a point of adding that

since she is not attractive physically there must be something else about her to bring these chums in.'

'And why,' said Greco Barraclough, 'should that something be odd?'

They all considered the question, none of them wishing to be the first to answer.

'I think,' said Ptolemaeos Tunne, who had been watching Gregory and Rosie through the window, 'that that little Rosie is a witch.'

'Oh, Ptoly. Black or white?'

'Potentially either.'

'Why do you think this?'

'The way she walks. She appears, if you notice, to skim the ground, to be walking an inch or so above it . . . I must return to my den in the Fen,' said Ptolemaeos. He shook hands heartily with Jean-Marie, hugged the Greco (for they had been boys together in this very college), smiled at Nicos, kissed Jo-Jo intimately on the throat, and rumbled out like a tank, deferentially attended (as a rich Old Lancastrian should be) by Mr-Private-Secretary-to-the-Provost Len.

'El Greco is not improving,' said Ptolemaeos to Len as they walked round and out of Provost's Court and down towards the river. 'He seems to have got stuck back in Vatheia. He hardly spoke, if you noticed – '

' – He didn't get much chance, what with you and Jo-Jo – '

' – And he puts on ridiculous airs towards that boy, Nicos. I know he adopted him and all that back in the Mani, where such a connection entails definite obligations of trust and obedience, but none of that cuts any corn here. You'd better send Nicos off home to the Peloponnese before the Greco makes bloody fools of both of them.'

'Nicos now has a place in the college as an undergraduate,' said Len.

'Then God help you all,' said Ptolemaeos. 'Now,' he

went on as they crossed the bridge and came into an avenue of elms between two meadows, 'this list of names for my soul-searching experiments. Those two little Blessington girls, yes, if additional material is needed and for making routine confirmations. I do not think the mother will be keen, so we will say nothing at all unless they are wanted later, when we will bounce her into it. The Salinger girls, most definitely – they seemed to take an intelligent interest in the subject. One of them, Carmilla, was quite knowing about it; she'd actually read Sheraton. Rosie Stern, as you know, I desiderate for this purpose; and, though separately, Marius.'

'You are being rather sanguine about those two,' said Len. 'Have you spoken to Gregory himself?'

'No. I want you to take him a message when you go back there. Say that I am preparing a book which he might well care to publish; that I need his help and his children's and that . . . my mother was called "Toeman" before she married. He will understand, I think. Finally,' said Ptolemaeos as they reached the Garden Hostel Car Park, 'I am happy to be able to tell you that Jeremy Morrison has been much relieved by my offer to pay up for him as he was dreading asking his father, who, though rich, is puritanical. Jeremy can now enjoy his term, concentrate on his Preliminary Examination, and look forward, so he says, to joining me in the Fens for a spell during the summer. A well spent afternoon, and thank you for your help . . . my dear Len.'

Ptolemaeos began the grotesque writhing motion which was necessary to introduce him into the Mini.

'I'll be in touch soon,' he puffed to Len. 'Don't forget my message to Gregory Stern. If he makes any objections, tell him that before her marriage my mother was called "Toeman".'

When Len arrived back at the party, Jo-Jo and Jean-Marie were still with Barraclough and Nicos, the three

54

men looking rather stupefied by Jo-Jo's fond peroration about the attractions of Len, who came up behind her.

'He's so deliciously morbid,' Jo-Jo was saying. 'He sort of appals and fascinates one at the same time, like a vampire.'

'Thanks for the compliment, doll,' said Len, 'and in return here's a tip. Don't go near your Uncle Ptoly until you've finally whelped. What he's up to is probably harmless, but he's getting obsessed. He might well come up with some theory about the souls of foetuses – and then suck you and yours into his psychic laundromat for a whirly-birly . . . which is not what you'll be wanting just now, I think.'

'Heavenly Len,' sighed Jo-Jo. 'So understanding.'

Heavenly Len departed to look for Gregory Stern, and Lord Canteloupe came up. Barraclough and Nicos edged away, for though the Greco liked the little he knew of Canteloupe, Nicos mistrusted all aristocrats.

'I want you to meet two old friends of mine,' Canteloupe said to Jo-Jo: 'Peter Morrison and his son, Jeremy. Peter is in Parliament – '

' – I do read the papers, Canty – '

' – And Jeremy is up here at Lancaster.'

'Is that nice?' asked Jo-Jo.

'Lovely.' Jeremy wrinkled his full moon face into a joyous smile, but did not seem disposed to analyse his appreciation.

'Your son,' said Jean-Marie to Morrison, 'was before, perhaps, at one of your famous public schools?'

'The same one as myself.'

'Ah. The English way. And before that?'

'My own preparatory school has gone phut – there's been a lot of that these last ten years – so I sent him to one in Kent, on the Saxon Shore . . . rather well known for its cricket and sound traditional teaching. Oudenarde House, near Sandwich.'

'Ah,' said Jo-Jo. 'That is where Marius Stern goes.'

'So he does,' said Canteloupe. 'I know the Headmaster a bit. Glinter Parkes. Useful slow bowler in his time.'

He looked over his shoulder, apologized, and went to help a venerable waiter with a recalcitrant cork.

'And what else,' said Jo-Jo to Morrison Senior, 'have you to say of Oudenarde House?'

'Why do you want to know?' said Morrison, courteous but reticent, the politician on habitual guard.

'Because Baby Canteloupe is a big thing in my life,' said Jo-Jo, 'and her little cousin, Marius Stern, is a big thing in her life, so naturally I take an interest in his school.'

'It made a fair job of Jeremy here. Taught him not to snivel when things got rough, and that life runs on luck and not on justice.'

'I loved it,' said Jeremy, smiling hugely, but once again he seemed disinclined to proffer analysis.

'Why?' said Jo-Jo. 'Please tell me your exact reasons. I'm anxious to know.'

'Go on,' said Jeremy's father. 'Give Madame Guiscard your reasons.'

'Well.' Jeremy paused lengthily. 'There was a very fat master there,' he deposed, 'called Mr St George. We called him "Bunter". He used to get into terrific tempers and do super conjuring tricks. All the boys loved it.'

I suppose, thought Jo-Jo, that this Peter Morrison, as a Member of Parliament, has some sort of influence here at Lancaster; it is difficult to see, otherwise, how a place was allotted to his son. Aloud she said: 'Conjuring tricks? How amusing. And what about the tempers? Did he hit you?'

'Oh no. He jumped up and down and went frothy at the mouth. I loved it.'

'Did anything happen which you didn't love?'

'Yes,' said Jeremy Morrison. 'There was a matron who asked too many questions. We thought her rather ill bred.'

Jeremy moved across the room towards his friends, the

56

Salinger twins, two great leggy girls with wide bottoms and long horsey faces, who were lounging about in green velvet trousers, which gave the impression of being at once voluminous and yet extremely tightly cut, on either side of their flabby father, Donald.

'Surprising, really, that Canteloupe should have asked me,' Donald was saying, 'since I've been . . . away so much lately. Of course we once played a lot of cricket together; but that was *Consule Planco*.'

'Cricketers have long memories, sir,' said Jeremy; 'and I expect that Canteloupe wanted to get a look at your girls. They're famous in Cambridge, you know.'

'Carmilla and Thea – famous?'

'Yes, sir. Carmilla is the first woman ever to win the Lauderdale Prize, and Theodosia is a real whizz at badminton – a possible for the 'Varsity girls next year. You must have heard?'

Jeremy smiled his enormous rumpled smile, first at Donald, then to the left for Carmilla and to the right for Theodosia. Both girls reciprocated generously; but Donald looked harassed and puzzled.

'Theodosia,' he said, 'with those great feet – Theodosia a . . . a whizz at badminton?'

'It's a question of accuracy, sir. Theodosia is so accurate that she makes her opponents do all the running.'

Donald looked more puzzled than ever. Max de Freville approached, his skull face poking and ferreting just ahead of him, as if in fear of ambush.

'Ah, Donald,' said Max. 'So here are those celebrated girls of yours. Llewyllyn tells me that one of them scooped the Lauderdale . . . whatever that may be.'

'A prize for a substantial essay or dissertation,' said Theodosia, speaking up for her sister, 'on an historical subject chosen by the Chancellor of the University, in this case "The Institution of Knighthood". The prize is open to all resident members of the University,' she said, her voice

57

ringing, 'beneath the degree of Doctor; and Carm here beat the bloody lot.'

'*Brava, brava,*' cried Max, rising to the occasion.

'Why didn't you let me know?' said Donald Salinger.

'You were having one of your bad times, Da,' said Carmilla softly. 'The Staff said it wouldn't get through to you. And later on . . . well, it got forgotten.'

You didn't want to boast, Donald thought: you were afraid you might seem to be crowing over your poor old wreck of a father, just home from the bin. He took one hand of each girl; both clasped warmly back without squeezing.

'Yes,' said Donald. 'One of my bad times. I think they are over now. I think . . . that your mother's spirit has been laid.'

Since this was a proposition to which it was not easy to respond, Jeremy made a tactical turn of subject.

'Did you meet my brother Nicholas in hospital, sir?' he asked. 'Father sent him to the same place you went to.'

'I do not remember. I remember very little . . . of what occurred there.'

'And a good job, Da,' said Theodosia. 'Winter's over, summer's coming. You're with us now.'

'Who are those great hoydens with whom Jeremy is so taken?' Peter Morrison asked Lord Canteloupe, whose group he had just joined (after Jo-Jo and Jean-Marie had left him, bound lover-wise for the garden) in the area of the champagne table.

'The Salinger girls? Donald's adopted daughters. Vanessa, you remember, was too – well, too *dérangée* – to have any.'

'Didn't she die?'

'Drowned. There was something . . . eerie about it. After it happened Donald was very ill for years – in St Bede's.'

'Where I sent Nickie in the end. But of course Nickie is

58

not curable. Donald seems to have emerged in tolerably good order.'

'Let's hope it lasts. They gave him up at one stage.'

'What was it? Guilt of some kind?'

'No,' said one-eyed Fielding Gray, who had been listening rather impatiently. 'There was never any suggestion that Donald was in any way to blame for his wife's death, or that his behaviour towards her was in any way reproachable. Through all their married life he was kindness itself – and incidentally undertook the entire care of the girls, whom Vanessa chose to ignore completely after the first few weeks of their adoption.'

'They seem fond of him.'

'They were not fond of her.'

'What was so eerie about her death?'

'The place, among other things,' said Fielding Gray: 'Green Oxley Laris . . . as it was called in the local chronicles. Poetic name, but situated in one of the most prosaic parts of Kent. Donald and Vanessa had been to the girls' Sports Day at Benenden, for although Vanessa loathed the twins Donald made her go to official school functions for the look of the thing. After the sports were done, they were driving to Sandwich to stay with friends, and they passed a house near Deal called Oxley Court, which Vanessa had once visited as a child. The house was in the middle of a straggling wood, almost a forest by modern standards, Green Oxley Laris it was called. Well, Vanessa said she'd like to look about the place for old time's sake, and of course good-natured Donald – '

– But now good-natured Donald, flanked by his two daughters, was coming to say good-bye to Canteloupe, and the story must be discontinued. Tom Llewyllyn, as honorary joint host on his own ground, arrived to say good-bye to Donald. Fielding Gray moved over to a bulky man of boisterous complexion who was standing on the edge of the group: Ivan Blessington.

'I say,' said Ivan Blessington, 'I should like to hear what happened in that forest.'

'Another time, Ivan. When I'm interrupted the spirit leaves me.'

'I see. Writers' temperament. But you were always a temperamental bugger, weren't you? At school, in the regiment . . .'

'At school, in the regiment . . . our old Hamilton's Horse.' Fielding shook his head slightly, pronouncing the words as if they were a prescribed form of epitaph. 'Listen, Ivan,' he said. 'Your two little girls over there with . . . with your wife . . .'

' – Betty,' said Ivan blandly. 'The girls are Caroline and Jakki.'

'They're at school in Kensington with Rosie Stern?'

'Yes. Collingham's.'

'Well, there's something I want to find out. They must know a girl called Teresa Malcolm, usually Tessa. Rather older than they are – about thirteen.'

'I seem to have been hearing rather a lot about her today. What's *your* interest?'

'She's the niece . . . of a very old friend. Of my landlady, you might say. In London.'

'Tessa Malcolm. What was it all my women were saying in the car? Maimed in some way? She has a hump?'

'Right,' said Fielding. 'A tiny but just noticeable hump. What effect does it produce? Fear? Pity? Disgust?'

'Fascination, or so I gather. And apparently the one who's most fascinated of all is that little Rosie Stern, whom the rest of them seem to worship. Betty says she's a plain little thing, this Rosie, and I had to agree when she was pointed out to me in the chapel just now; but it seems that the other girls simply yearn for her, including my two. But Rosie, they say, has eyes only for this Tessa Malcolm of yours.'

60

'I see,' said Fielding, who was evidently pleased by this information. 'Excuse me, please, Ivan. Regards to Betty.'

Fielding crossed rapidly to the saturnine portrait of Provost the Lord Constable of Reculver Castle, under whom Isobel Stern was standing with Jean-Marie and Jo-Jo (now returned from the garden) and Baby Canteloupe.

'Isobel,' said Fielding, leading into his topic with a question the answer to which he knew very well already. 'How long has your Rosie known Tessa Malcolm?'

'About eighteen months; since she went to Collingham's. Why do you ask?'

'They say Rosie has a very sound taste in her choice of friends.' Fielding paused; careful now, he told himself, for here was the heart of the matter. 'They also say her great friend is Tessa. I wondered . . . why Rosie chose her.'

'I think Tessa chose Rosie, Fielding. Originally at least. Not but what Rosie was happy enough to be chosen.'

'All right. But what is it all based on?'

'What are little girls' pashes ever based on?'

'So this is a "pash"?'

'A pash, a crush, or what you will. Funny. Rosie's so . . . well . . . ordinary.'

'The girls at her school don't think so. And she walks very prettily. Look.'

Rosie joined them, followed by a tearful Marius.

'Where have you been?'

'In the Provost's Garden,' said Rosie. 'Daddy had to go in to talk to some people, and then *he* came.'

'Rosie was mean,' snuffled Marius.

'Mean?'

'Spiteful. She said I'd have a rotten cricket season next term, and not make any runs. She said she'd wish it, and it would happen.'

'She can't make it happen.'

'I can *wish* it,' said Rosie. 'He called my friend Tessa ugly. He said he'd been talking to Jakki and Caroline

61

Blessington, and how pretty and jolly and fresh they were, but that Tessa was just frowsy, like the Bad Fairy with her hump. So that's what I have wished: no runs for Marius this summer.'

Marius slung a right hook at Rosie, but Gregory Stern, coming up behind, cleverly caught the boy's wrist in his hand.

'We don't hit ladies,' he said. 'Not even our sisters. Isobel, my wife, take these two away and teach them their manners.'

Isobel seized the children by their collars and frog-marched them back into the garden.

'Funny,' said Baby. 'I've never known Marius show such ugly temper before. Have you, Gregory?'

'It is a thing of late. At first occasional, now more frequent.'

'*Pubes*?' said Fielding.

'Perhaps. Two or three, a tiny cluster, Isobel reports from the bathroom.'

Len came lolloping up.

'I've been looking for you,' he said to Gregory. 'There's a message from Ptolemaeos Tunne. He's thinking of writing a book.'

'And high time, after all these years in the Fens, cramming himself with learning like a Strasbourg goose. Does he want me and Canteloupe to publish it?'

'Very possibly,' said Len, 'when, of course, it's written. He's got a lot of research to do first.'

'He's making a list,' put in Jo-Jo, mindful of the conversation when Ptolemaeos had come by earlier on. 'He wants to experiment on Rosie and Marius.'

'Over my tomb shall he experiment on Rosie and Marius.'

'It's quite harmless,' drawled Len, 'and could lead to a very important advance in our knowledge of our nature.'

'Could it now? Then let Ptolemaeos Tunne take himself

off to Africa or India, where he may buy all the children he wants and experiment with them as he will.'

'He wants good quality specimens,' said Len. 'Intelligent, well bred and la-di-da-di-da. Not a load of black rubbish. He wants 'em carefully nurtured, you know. Refined.'

'Then let him nurture and refine his own to put under the knife.'

'For Christ's sake, Gregory baby,' said Len. 'Ptoly's experiments will have to do with the soul, with the intellect, with the connections and communications between all that flooty-tooty malarky and your actual physical brain-box in your actual physical bonce. Because if he can prove that there is something which communicates with your brain cells but has no verifiable physical existence of its own, then maybe you got wings after all, baby, a highly revolutionary conception in this day and age of Hire Purchase and Hypermarkets. So what he's doing, he's preparing a new method of finding exactly how the soul (if any) contacts and gives orders to the physical brain. Because once you understand that –'

' – So now he wants to meddle with their brains?'

'Only to ask questions which may reveal how and why the brain responds to the soul,' said Len, judiciously refraining from confusing his audience with detail. 'And of course Ptoly longs for little kids because their intelligence isn't yet fouled up by life and lust and greed and suspicion. He particularly longs for kids like yours because they're so smart and articulate they'll answer up the way he needs, and he'll be able to watch their little souls as the brainwaves wash in – and vice versa.'

'So now he wants to track down their very souls to possess them?'

'No,' said Len with unbreachable patience. 'All he wants, Gregory doll,' he drawled on, once again eschewing tiresome particulars, 'is to ask them some questions and

63

'draw his own conclusions. You and Isobel can be there, breathing right into his shirt collar, the entire time.'

'Tell him that all of us have better things to do.'

'Have you now?' said Len. 'Then in that case I was to give you a second message. I was to tell you that Ptolemaeos's mother, rest her soul, was called "Toeman" before she got married. Just what that will mean to you, I don't know, but that was the message: his old lady's maiden name was "Toeman".'

Gregory began to sweat. He turned from pink to puce to purple, then shut his eyes for a good ten seconds before reopening them, looked at Fielding Gray, at Jo-Jo, at Jean-Marie, at Baby, separately but without, apparently, seeing any of them, then slunk across the Provost's withdrawing room and through the glass door, after Isobel his wife and their offspring, into the Provost's vernal Garden.

After the christening party, Fielding Gray drove back from Cambridge to his London quarters, which were a single room with private bath in Buttock's Hotel in the Cromwell Road.

Fielding had been an *habitué* of this dingy but commodious establishment for nearly twenty years. A close friend of the original and eponymous owner, Mrs Tessie Buttock, he had inherited a half share of the hotel on her death in 1975, the other half having been bequeathed to Tom Llewyllyn, an even earlier *habitué* than Fielding though of late a less constant one. 'To my two favourite boys,' Tessie had written in her holograph will, 'Fielding Gray and Tom Llewyllyn, I give and devise Buttock's Hotel and all that therein is, one half to each, split down the middle, in the hope that they'll have the same rorty times in the dear old place as they did in the dear old days – on this one condition, that they never never sell it to those fucking development sharks, who'll just knock it flat like a ninepin.'

Fielding was averse neither to a little rortiness, in so far as he was still up to it, nor to owning a half share of an exceedingly valuable property, excellent security, if not, in honour, readily disposable. Tom, these days, was averse to both. His experience with his wife, Patricia, had finally sealed him up sexually some years before; and his residual socialist principles (however 'thin', in Jo-Jo's phrase, they might be wearing) made him reluctant to commence *rentier*. On Fielding's suggestion, therefore, Tom had sold his half of the hotel for a modest but fair price (in the circumstances) to one, Maisie Malcolm, not a fucking development shark but another old friend of Fielding's who, having practised her profession in Shepherd Market and later in Artillery Mansions with enthusiasm, flair and commensurate emolument for nearly a generation, now felt the need of peaceful retirement.

'So now you own half of it,' Fielding had said. 'If you manage it, you can take all the profit. All I want is my old room at the back.'

'"And no dragging back, dear,"' said plump, placid Maisie, quoting a favourite precept of the late Mrs Buttock.

'"But if you've got someone nice and clean, duckie,"' said Fielding, also quoting the deceased, '"one of your own sort what won't whip the soap nor the hangers, just you bring 'em in day or night, and the very best of British."'

'Like Mrs Buttock,' Maisie said, 'I shall reserve the right of inspection.'

'I don't think there'll be anyone, Maisie. I really find, nowadays, that as a rule the effort is out of all reasonable ratio to the return. Anyway, I've got you in the next corridor.'

'I've said farewell to all that, love. From now on I'm Mrs

Maisie Malcolm, the church-going widow woman, who runs this hotel as tight as a frigate and educates her niece Tessa in a school fit for little princesses.'

'Point taken. Just old friends, then . . .'

And so it had been agreed.

And now, some two years later, on the evening of the day of little Lord Sarum's baptism in the chapel of Lancaster College, Fielding returned to Buttock's and found the 'widow' Malcolm and the thirteen-year-old Tessa in the foyer-cum-sitting room of the hotel, where they were sitting on the fender in front of an ample spring fire while Tessa read to Maisie from her 'holiday book':

> '"The moon shines bright. In such a night as this
> When the sweet wind did gently kiss the trees
> And they did make no noise – "'

Tessa looked up and smiled as Fielding entered but did not interrupt her reading.

> '"——— In such a night
> Troilus, methinks, mounted the Trojan walls,
> And sighed his soul towards the Grecian tents
> Where Cressid lay that night."'

> '"In such a night,"' said Maisie without text,
> '"Did Thisbe fearfully o'ertrip the dew,
> And saw a lion's shadow ere himself,
> And ran dismayed away."'

> '"In such a night,"' capped Tessa,
> '"Stood Dido with a willow in her hand
> Upon the wild sea-banks, and waft her love
> To come again to Carthage."'

As she finished this speech, Tessa put down the book on the fender and came towards Fielding. He kissed her strong handsome little face, patted the very slight hump on her shoulder, and allowed himself to be led by the hand to the

66

fender, where he was installed between the girl and the woman.

'Not many clients around,' Maisie said. 'Somehow the Yanks and the Wogs don't fancy us much just now. So we were having a bit of a read.'

'You seemed to know your bit by heart.'

'When you've a niece that's being educated,' said Maisie, 'it does no harm to join in. I read all Tessa's set books – and learn the parts I fancy. Then I can say them out loud on walks in the park. Everyone thinks I've a screw loose. Some day they'll send for a van.'

'Please, Auntie Maisie,' said Tessa in a low, husky voice, 'ask Major Gray to tell us about the christening.'

'Ask Major Gray yourself.'

'No. They say at school that it's not for little girls to introduce a subject of conversation. Any new subjects must be broached by their elders.'

'I thought that was only with Royalty,' said Maisie, 'but I dare say there's something to be said for it – like stopping awkward enquiries on tender topics. Very well, my darling, your elder will do the broaching. Major Gray, please tell us about the christening.'

'There was a bit of a rumpus at the start,' said Fielding, and described the scene at the font.

'Good for Tom,' said Maisie. 'But I hope the baby don't get pneumonia.'

'It seemed all right at the party afterwards. Not that it stayed very long.'

'Was Rosie Stern there?' said Tessa, asking the question which (Fielding thought) she had clearly been longing to ask from the beginning, though she had listened without apparent impatience to the tale of the font.

'Does your school allow little girls to ask direct questions?' Fielding enquired.

'Yes. Once the main subject has been started. Was Rosie at the christening?'

67

'Rosie was there.' Shall I say she sent love? he wondered. No: she might thank Rosie when they next met and find out that I'd lied. 'She had a row with Marius. In the Provost's Garden.'

'It's a good thing Marius is going back to his school very soon,' said Tessa serenely. 'She loves him most of the time. But he is sometimes very cruel to her.'

'I rather thought, on this occasion, that Rosie had got the best of it.'

'Good for Rosie.' A clock struck eight. Maisie checked it against her watch, then gave a politely dismissive look at Tessa. Tessa wriggled. 'Can I talk to you while you have your dinner?' she said.

'Not tonight, love,' said Maisie. 'Major Gray and I have got to go through the accounts. Bed, my darling; bath and bed.'

'Yes, Aunt Maisie,' said Tessa, huskily obedient. 'But you'll both come and say good-night?'

'Yes, girl. Now be off.'

Tessa curtsied and vanished. Later that night, when Maisie and Fielding had been up to kiss her good-night and were eating a soundly cooked dinner of nursery food alone in the dining room, Maisie said, 'She can hardly wait for her term to start so's she can see Rosie Stern every day.'

'Hasn't Rosie been loyal during the holidays?'

'Ye-es . . . but she was away in Italy for ten days. Then she had visits to the theatre and other treats to which Tessa wasn't invited – and why should she be, she didn't expect to be, she's far too sensible; but all the same she would like to be with Rosie all the time. When term starts she can be.'

'Not at night. Not at weekends.'

'Even then, later on. Mr and Mrs Stern are going to Israel for a month. It's been arranged that Rosie shall come here while they're away.'

'They'll share a room?'

'I think so. Don't you?'

'Yes. They'll like that. But Tessa mustn't become obsessed.'

'Obsession is in her blood.'

'Ah. Back to the old question. Who got her? Are you never going to own up?'

'When the right time comes, which is not this evening. Those accounts – remember?'

'You've just hinted, Maisie, that Tessa's father was an obsessed man. I myself am in some ways an obsessed man.'

'Many of my clients were in some ways obsessed men. Horny Somerset. That nice sot, Balbo Blakeney – '

' – he came on your list too late. Only eight or nine years ago – '

' – Loopy Canteloupe, rest his rotten soul. Plenty more you never even heard of. I wasn't there exclusively for the use of your lot, you know . . . though I admit I preferred them to most. Your lot had style.'

'Maisie. Do you really know who Tessa's father was?'

'Accounts of Buttock's Hotel,' said Maisie, fishing a school exercise book out of her bag. 'Quarter ending March thirty-one last. Now then – '

' – Maisie. Answer the question.'

'I told you just now, Fielding Gray. You'll know what there is to know, which is rather more than you might think, when the right time comes for you to be told. Just now it's time for the hotel accounts, and very dismal reading they make.'

Fielding looked at the figures without interest or understanding.

'Worst ever,' Maisie prompted him. 'Up till now, we always broke more or less even, a pony or two either way, and I don't mind the odd pony out of my pin money, not these days. But this time, Fielding, there's a minus of nearly two thousand quid. Almost total falling off in custom from late Feb., and not a hint of its picking up though we're well into April. It can't go on, love.'

'We can't sell the place. Old Tessie would haunt us. She was offered huge sums by the property jackals before she died. "You shove off," she used to tell them, "or I'll ask Albert Edward to piss in your boots." Albert Edward was her Sealyham, dead years before, but his ghost kept yapping on.'

'No question of selling, anyhow. This is Tessa's home, and I'm not shunting her about at her time of life.'

She pursed her lips uneasily, as though, for all her apparent determination, she was having awkward second thoughts.

'Could we . . . fine down the staff?' asked Fielding.

'Over my pauper's coffin. They've been dead loyal ever since I came.'

'If you like, I'll start paying for my room.'

'Don't be silly, ducks. We shan't come to that for a bit.'

'But come we shall if things go on like this.'

Fielding surveyed the empty dining room and the huge Victorian dresser by the kitchen exit.

'What, Maisie, has gone wrong? Do you think . . . that we are too old-fashioned – too seedy, perhaps? There is a whiff of Miss Havisham about the place.'

'Miss Havisham? Don't tell me, I've nearly got it . . . *Great Expectations* by Charles Dickens, Tessa's holiday book last summer. Much too old for her, if you ask me.'

'But you take the point?'

'Most certainly not. No cobwebs or rotten wedding cake in here. Everything spick as a Grenadier, and food fit for Chatsworth.'

'Amen to that. Then what's the matter?'

'Tessa. Tessa's the matter.'

'*Tessa*?'

'Young girls . . . sprouting breasts . . . often sprout

something else as well. A familiar spirit. Had you ever heard that?'

'Yes. There is a fascinating painting, by a Norwegian called Münch, of a naked and pubescent girl who is somehow . . . exuding . . . a spirit from her body. An old superstition.'

'Superstition or not, I'm sure that there can be a sort of . . . aura,' said Maisie, 'if nothing more. I think that Tessa is giving off an aura, an aura of adolescence, which is driving the guests away like a funny smell.'

'I haven't noticed it. The aura, I mean.'

'Neither have I. But then we wouldn't. If you live with a smell you never do. Except that you probably get a whiff of it when it first begins, but if it's not too bad you don't bother, and then you get used to it and you don't notice it getting worse. I think that's what's happened with us – and the staff – about Tessa. But of course you can't expect the guests not to notice. It all fits, Fielding. About the middle of March a lot of guests, some of them old friends of the house, started leaving early – sometimes after only one night. There'd be some excuse or other, and they'd be off. And they haven't come back. They must have been putting the word round, because the bookings have nearly dried up altogether. We haven't had more than three guests in Buttock's for the last ten days.'

'But Maisie . . . Tessa is so loving. So innocent. It is quite impossible to connect her with anything evil.'

'I didn't say evil. Something funny – strange. That's enough to keep 'em away.'

'Yet it hasn't bothered you any more than it has me.'

'No. But like I was saying, you sometimes get a quick early sniff of what you don't notice later on. I had an early sniff of this, though at the time it made no impression, or rather it made the wrong one. One afternoon last month, just after the girls' Easter Term was over, Rosie came to spend the day. Dreary and rainy it was, so Tessa and Rosie

71

were kept indoors and went upstairs, to wash their hair, they said. I looked in on them a little later, and there they both were in Tessa's bathroom, bare to the navel, Tessa using the drying machine on Rosie. As she played it on her, she was crooning a little chant, praising Rosie's hair and saying how beautiful it was and how everyone must love it. As for Rosie, she was sitting there glowing, her eyes fixed on Tessa's little new breasts. Well, no harm in that, I thought. She's just wondering when her own will come and whether they'll be the same. So off I went, thinking just that, and it was only hours later that I realized something else, something quite different. I was thinking of the scene again, telling myself how pretty it had been, when I realized, Fielding, that Rosie hadn't just been looking and wondering in an ordinary sort of way, she had been gazing very intently at Tessa's little tits, with a kind of obsessed almost mad look in her eyes, with her lips wet and slightly parted, as though . . . as though – '

' – As though she was wanting to touch? – '

' – No, you dirty bugger. Nothing like that. What she was was amazed, Fielding; perhaps a little appalled as well. *Stupefied.*'

'But she must have seen tits before. Seen Tessa's, come to that. In the changing room at school. Anyway, Maisie, these days they all know all about tits and where they come from. They take 'em as read. They're taught all that kind of thing with their multiplication tables – the only trouble is that they're probably *not* taught the tables.'

'I can only tell you, love, that something about Tessa's tits had knocked Rosie out of the ground for six. I simply couldn't see it myself. To me they were just tits – very pretty too, just beginning to lift, but still nothing more nor less than a thirteen-year-old's tits. But now I've had time to think it over, it occurs to me that whatever it was in Tessa that was so amazing to Rosie might be the thing that's putting off our guests.'

'But Tessa doesn't go round showing off her tits to the guests.'

'They're beginning to show through her school blouse.'

'But they couldn't put anyone *off*, Maisie. If anything they'd bring more people in. Or do you think the wives are getting jealous, and whisking their husbands away?'

'No. Not quite that. I think that the combination of Tessa's little deformity with her new and normal development, the combination *and* the contrast, Fielding, the contrast, I mean, between the natural growth of her breasts and the unnatural growth on her shoulder – I think that this worries people. Disconcerts 'em. In Rosie's case there was stupefaction. In other cases there may be at the very least uneasiness. Enough to keep people away from the hotel.'

'But in your case and mine – nothing.'

'Perhaps we've known her too long to feel like that. Perhaps we're just insensitive.'

'So you don't, after all, think that she's putting out this . . . aura of pubescence you were talking of?'

'But isn't it much the same?' Maisie said. 'It's all to do with that – but in a very special way. She is demonstrating that maimed or abnormal people have the same processes of growth and ripeness as anyone else. Now, in her case the abnormality is so tiny it hardly matters. But it is there; it is just visible; so that she, Tessa, constitutes a visible proof, duckie, in flesh and blood and three dimensions, that the abnormal and the deformed make the same claims on the world and on nature as anyone else and possess the same strength.'

'Added to which,' said Fielding, 'the fact that she is, despite her shoulder, beautiful to look at and already physically desirable introduces a weird element of the erotic into the matter. Or so one may presume. Just as well oneself is immune from it.'

73

'You just stay immune, Fielding Gray. I can't have you fancying my Tessa.'

'I love your Tessa.'

'I know. I only hope others will be as pure in their attentions.'

'I shouldn't worry too much – not for the time being. The whole point of this conversation has been that the total effect which Tessa produces, whatever elements of beauty or attraction she may possess, is to repel people. To judge from your guests' behaviour, that may well be the case . . . though I think your explanation is over-ingenious.'

'Can you think of a better?'

'I shall try, as time goes on.'

'Well, whatever it is, explained or unexplained,' said Maisie rather wanly, 'I hope it doesn't put the paying public off much longer. I don't want to drop another two thousand nicker come next Midsummer Day, and how's yer bloody father.'

'Carmilla?'

'Yes, Jeremy?'

'That was jolly nice. Absolutely super. But why can't we do it properly? You know – go the whole hog.'

'Go the whole hog? Make the beast with two backs, as everyone in Rabelais keeps calling it? I'll tell you why not, darling Jeremy,' Carmilla said, cupping her breasts. 'Because the beast with two backs is too vulnerable. Both literally and metaphorically, it is too inward looking, and therefore unaware of the dangers which threaten it and of the achievements which might otherwise be open to it.'

'In other words, you'd sooner have the Lauderdale Prize than you would me.'

'I have you both.'

'You don't have me. Or not as much of me as you could.'

'No; but quite as much of you as I want. This way I get most of the pleasure and none of the annoyance.'

'Annoyance?'

'Conception.'

'But if you ever did get preggers, of course I'd marry you . . . though these days it would be very easy to get rid of it.'

'Getting rid of it would be a painful and humiliating bore. Being married to you would be an even more painful and humiliating bore.'

'Oh, I say, Carmilla.'

'You'd have old-fashioned ideas about white weddings, even if I was already as big as an airship, and you'd start preaching sermons, the minute the honeymoon ended, about a wife's place being in the home and the nursery.'

'Yes, I suppose I would. My father was pretty strict with my mother about all that. Not that she minded. She managed him from behind the scenes.'

'I thought your father looked absolutely sweet at that christening business this afternoon. Rather like you, only a hundred and fifty years older. So weary. So distinguished with that huge head and those droopy eyelids. I think I should rather like to be his mistress. They say that elderly men are far more considerate.'

'Would you go the whole hog with him?'

'I expect he'd be much too weary for that. No, I'd warm his slippers and make a fuss of him . . . and get him to pay those debts of yours. Though something tells me that would be a long job. What a fool you are, Jeremy.'

'Not such a fool as you might think. Those debts have been settled . . . or will have been within the week.'

'You asked your father? You plucked up the courage to ask him?'

'No. An unsolicited offer from Mr Ptolemaeos Tunne. Len had told him how the land lay – '

' – How did Len know? – '

' – Len knows everything. Len had told Tunne before he introduced me to him; and Tunne looked me up and he looked me down, and then just told me to send him a list of my creditors and the amounts owed – "without omission and without shame", as he put it – and he would settle. Provided, that was, I would agree to come and help with some experiments he's making. Some time later, he said, in the summer.'

'Well, I think you've been much luckier than you deserve. But oh, good, good, good, darling Jeremy. Thea and I are coming for the experiments too. Only he didn't offer us any money.'

'I expect he knew you had a generous father. But you know, I'm not at all sure he'll let us all come at the same time. Len says he's got a huge house, but even so there may be reasons for having us separately.'

'Like what?' frowned Carmilla.

'From what I gather, he's trying to check up on the relation of the human mind and/or soul to the physical body. Perhaps . . . if there were certain combinations of people in the house . . . their minds and/or souls might start inter-reacting – playing tricks.'

'What kind of tricks?' said Carmilla, stretching herself complacently and surveying the length of her ample and magnificent form.

'Well. Twins are always supposed to be very close. If there is to be deep searching of minds and brains, something of yours – some impulse or vibration – might work loose, so to speak, and get mixed up with something of Theodosia's . . . and then, just think what a muddle.'

'Sweet Jeremy, how most improbable. But even if this could happen, any impulse or vibration of mine that worked

76

loose, as you call it, could never do any harm to Theodosia, because she's my sister and I love her.'

'And she loves you. Even so, you might be more different from each other, in certain secret ways, than you know. In which case . . . a mixture might not be a very good thing.'

'And I suppose there could be other mixtures. After all, you and I are very close,' said Carmilla, 'even if we don't make the beast with two backs. How would you like some of my soul-waves getting mixed up with yours?'

'We might both get some very nasty surprises.'

'Well,' said Carmilla in her soft, deep voice, 'we shall just have to let Mr Tunne decide it all for us. Although he's so grotesque to look at, I have confidence in him.'

'Me too,' said Jeremy. 'He has what my father calls "officer-like quality".'

'So *that's* all right. He'll be totally reliable. But wouldn't it be enormous fun, darling Jeremy, if we could all be there together?'

After the christening, Peter Morrison had driven over the Fens from Cambridge and then across the Breckland of East Norfolk and back to his house in Luffham. As usual these days it was empty save for a half-crazed but harmless manservant, who had been Nickie's nurse and companion, until Nickie had finally been put away, and now lingered on in the place from year's end to year's end performing the duties of caretaker and occasional cook-valet.

The water for Peter's bath was hot; suitable clothes for the chilly spring evening had been laid out with taste and care; he was served a delicious four-course dinner in the long, high dining room, seated alone at the head of the table, underneath the Orpen portrait of James Ulster Morrison, of Luffham in the County of Norfolk, Esquire, his father before him. The manservant attended him throughout, unobtrusively serving the dishes or pouring the wine, then retreating to a post on the left of Peter and against the wall, under the Buhler portrait of Peter's dead wife, Helen.

'Everything is in very good trim, Chamberlain,' Peter said.

The Chamberlain (a title on which he himself insisted) bowed profoundly.

'Lord Canteloupe sends his best regards,' Peter continued, 'and says that you'll be welcome to return to him in Wiltshire at any time, should you wish to leave Luffham.'

'My Lord Marquess is very kind, sir, but this has been my place since I came to help Master Nickie.'

'And you are welcome to stay in it as long as you please. But Master Nickie has long since gone and will not come back. I feel it is lonely for you here.'

'Oh no, sir. Master Nickie is still here with me, you see. Everywhere I go in the house or on the estate holds some memory of the time we were together. I talk to him every day.'

'And does he answer you?'

'In his look, sir, if not in words. He knows what has happened and accepts his fate, which says he must be dumb until the last day.'

The Chamberlain crossed to the table, poured some Vichy water, and retired to the wall.

'He knows what he was and why he can no longer be so. He knows why his tongue must be still and his fine brain has been taken from him. He does not resent his misfortune but wishes you all well, his dead mother, and you in Parliament, and his little brother, Master Jeremy, at Cambridge. You saw Master Jeremy today, sir?'

'Yes,' said Peter, thinking morosely of Jeremy as he stood over the sprawling Salinger girls. Well and why not, he said to himself, detecting and checking the onset of the sour jealousy of middle age: his turn now and he's welcome to it. And yet . . . what was it about that air of his, as he stood over those girls, an air at once slightly less than proprietorial and yet rather more so, an air of manipulation, of 'I could an' if I would', an air, as the French said, *pas honnête* – what was it (all of these and yet something else besides) which made him shiver at the memory?

'How is Master Jeremy, sir?' the Chamberlain said. 'Minding his book, I hope.'

'So do I. He has his Preliminary Examination at the end of May.'

'He's not the brilliant boy Master Nickie would have been, but he's shrewd enough . . . if rather slow when it suits him to appear so.'

'Yes. Slow when he chooses to be. By his own choice,' said Peter, disregarding discretion in his mounting unease at the remembered *tableau* of his son and the two sturdy damsels. 'By his own calculated choice,' Peter repeated, 'deliberately withholding any warning. Nickie was not only superbly intelligent, but always candid. I have the impression that Jeremy, having far less intelligence, uses low cunning – and perhaps something worse – to make up.'

Peter and the Chamberlain pondered this awkward characteristic for some seconds. Then, 'Might I ask, sir, if it is your intention to return soon to London?'

'Early next week. To prepare for next session.'

'My Lord Marquess should go more often to the Upper House. He might make a splendid career there. And you yourself, sir, should think of joining him. The title of Esquire is not without honour, but as the master of many acres you should be created Earl or Viscount, secure of descendants through Master Jeremy, who could proceed proudly in Peer's estate through all generations to come.'

The Chamberlain was working up for one of his spells.

Peter did not explain to him that the House of Lords was not a seat of power, nor that the dignities of Earl and Viscount were no longer to be had through creation; he simply assured him that he would reflect on these matters and wished to be left alone with the decanter to do so.

'At what hour will your Lordship breakfast?' enquired the Chamberlain, anticipating the fruits of his advice and backing slowly away down the dining room table.

'At a quarter past eight of the clock.'

'As you command, my Lord Duke. I wish Your Grace good-night.'

The Chamberlain backed through the double door and closed it.

I hope, thought Peter, that he will be undeluded in the morning; but even if he isn't the service will be as good as ever – probably much better if he still thinks that I've been ennobled, in whatever degree. So, he thought, back to London at the beginning of next week, leaving the Chamberlain to roam the house with the phantom of Nickie, to wander through the gardens hand in hand with Nickie's shade (as they had always walked before Nickie went, at last, to St Bede's), to dig and plant and cleanse and scour until the Young 'Squire Morrison (as Peter had been known ever since his father's death in 1950) should come once more to his manor and demesne, to oversee his lands and count the produce of his farms and steadings.

This would not be for some considerable time; for the love of the land, which had been so strong in the dead Alastair and would have lasted his lifetime, had withered in Peter after his thirtieth year. Affairs, influence, contention, intrigue, imbroglio, debate – that was where his pleasure and talent lay. So what should he want as a farmer (for that was all it came down to) on these flat, boring fields? And there would be no company here. Nickie was gone, Jeremy would seldom come, Helen was dead.

'"Sweet Helen, make me immortal with a kiss,"' he

muttered over his port, dredging up the line from *Doctor Faustus,* last read thirty-five years ago for School Certificate English.

Though Helen's kisses had not done that, they had given him confidence and purpose; if Helen approved what he was doing at any time, then he too had always been happy in it. And now there was no Helen to give his actions meaning, on his wide and unwanted estate, his soggy, unloved fields.

But equally there was no Helen to give meaning to his actions in London, actions which were becoming increasingly burdensome and futile. Which being so, when all the factors were finally ranged and assessed, might he not in the end be happier, the 'Young 'Squire Morrison', if he stayed in his own little kingdom with the Chamberlain and his shadowy companion, if he eschewed at last the smoke and sweat and lies of the Forum? He was a tired man, tired beyond his fifty years. He had had his little moment of power, he had held a position as high as he would ever hold. Now that the Government of which he had been part had gone, now that he was in Opposition and likely for many dreary years to continue so, now that his greatest friend and ally, the old Lord Canteloupe, was dead, could he not retire honourably, having done his duty as he saw it, into bucolic peace? But even as he weighed the question, even as he pictured himself with gun and rod and saddle, with book and pen (of course – his memoirs) in the low-ceilinged library, even as he summed the Sabine pleasures that might be his, there appeared to the eye of his heart Chamber and Speaker and Benches and Galleries, and he heard the sounds of battle which he loved so well.

'I've written you a cheque,' said Theodosia Salinger to Jeremy Morrison. 'Fifteen hundred pounds. That's what you need, isn't it?'

'*Thea*,' said Jeremy. 'Well, come in, dear. Don't hang about in the doorway. Tea, coffee, beer or whisky?'

'Nothing, thanks,' said Theodosia, closing the door of Jeremy's set of rooms on Staircase 'T': 'I'm in training.' She walked buoyantly to the window. 'I always like coming to your rooms,' she said. 'Lovely view of the bridge and the river . . . twice as nice under this moon.' She turned back towards Jeremy, who was standing solidly in the middle of the room. 'Here's the cheque,' she said.

'Oh, Thea . . .'

'Don't worry, Jeremy. Da's always given us plenty, or the lawyers when he was away, and today he told us before he left that he was increasing our allowance because he was so pleased with us.' She waved the cheque. 'Take it, Jeremy,' she said. 'But don't, whatever you do, tell Carm. She's very puritanical . . . very *tidy* about money.'

Just for a moment Jeremy thought of telling Theodosia that he had already found the money he needed. He would not, of course, reveal that this was really only £1,000 and that his request to her for £1,500 had merely been a try-on (a sure instinct in these matters having told him that if she were good for the money at all then she would be good for the larger sum): but he could say, in general terms, that he had raised the wind elsewhere, that he was grateful, oh, so grateful, darling Thea, and then gracefully decline to take her cheque. On the other hand, he thought, £1,500 is a gratifying sum (even nowadays); there will be May Week coming up and then the Long Vac. to cater for . . . and quite apart from anything else Theodosia is evidently *enjoying* this. There is a kind of sheen about her, comparable to that which Carmilla has when she is undressing to get on to the bed. But steady the Buffs, he thought to himself (a phrase sometimes used by his father when a pause was needed for tactical reflection): what about Carmilla? Theodosia won't tell Carmilla she's given me this money because obviously she wants it to be her secret and mine (in much the same way, I suppose, as Carmilla always insists that our bouts of hot bananas should be strictly my secret and hers): but something that *could* happen is that Carmilla *could* mention to Thea that I'm being paid to assist Ptolemaeos Tunne, who is to settle all my debts for me, and then Theodosia would think I'm the most frightful shit. How boring, he thought, to have to look one and a half thou in the mouth and say 'no'.

But just as the words of affectionate refusal were rising like bile to his lips, his instinct in these matters told him what to say instead.

'You're very sweet, Thea,' he said, 'and of course it's an enormous relief. But I should tell you that there is a chance that I may be getting the money from elsewhere. Only a chance, mind you, but – '

' – Take this,' she said. 'I want you to have it whatever else happens.'

His instinct had been right, he thought: just suggest to a woman that someone else might be getting in on her act, and there was nothing she wouldn't do to keep the stage to herself.

'I want you to have it,' she went on, 'because I can't . . . can't do the other thing for you. I love you, Jeremy, I really do, I wish I could do everything you'd like. I *want* to do it all. But I have this horrible feeling that if once I give way . . . to all that . . . all strength of body and purpose will leave me, that my badminton will just collapse.'

'But Thea . . . athletes and games players do have sex lives, you know.'

'Of course I know. It's just that with me . . . I have this feeling . . . that if once I should begin to have a sex life, I should very soon cease to have any other.'

'What nonsense.'

He came up behind her, passed both arms round her, and clasped his hands just under her firm, copious breasts.

'Lovely Thea,' he murmured. 'Lovely big Thea.'

She separated his hands, briefly kissed the backs of both of them, then released them.

'Good-night, Jeremy,' she said. 'I'm so happy that I could give you the money.'

So that's all right, thought Jeremy: all 't's crossed and all 'i's dotted; *carte blanche*. And there might even be more later. She loves me, this one, she loves me far more than that ramping sister of hers.

'You're a brick, Thea,' he said.

She raised her right palm towards him, moved it from right to left two or three times, and quietly went out.

Not a bad old day, thought Jeremy, as he helped himself to a generous whisky. Two and a half grand to the good, and the prospect of an interesting visit to Ptolemaeos Tunne, the Savant of the Fenland. A friendly encounter, on the whole, with his father (but did the old man look a bit sour as he left?), friendly enough anyway, on the face of it, to exempt him from making any efforts in that direction for several weeks to come. A nice little bit of exercise with Carmilla, who had squawked memorably in appreciation. But work, he thought crossly: not much of that; must do more. As it happened, there was no danger whatever of Jeremy's failing his Preliminary Examination, as he had been far too well drilled in the Classics at school; but a mediocre result would be rather humiliating, and might lead to his being removed from his agreeable rooms by the river and shoved into some creepy little court with students

84

from places like Brummagem and Hull. Even for the son of a Member of Parliament, who was also an old friend of the Provost, there was little security of privilege these days.

The Blessington family had driven much of the way back from Cambridge to London in contented silence, for they all liked each other's company and were quite capable of enjoying it without supererogatory communication. But eventually, just before Stevenage, Caroline had said: 'What was it like, being an officer in the same regiment as Lord Canteloupe?'

'Being a soldier in the same regiment as Lord Canteloupe,' her mother corrected her mildly. 'Only foreigners and policemen refer to themselves as "officers" in ordinary speech. Your father and Canteloupe were *soldiers*.'

'Well, what was it like?'

'Canteloupe – Detterling, as he was then – sent his papers in not long after I joined. He'd got a safe Conservative seat waiting for him in Parliament. So I didn't see much of him in the army. I saw much more of Fielding Gray.'

'The one-eyed man.'

'He wasn't one-eyed then . . . not till he was blown up in Cyprus. 1958, that would have been.'

'How horrid.'

'Best thing that could have happened to him. It meant that he had to find something else to do, and he found something he did much better than soldiering. He'd never have gone very far or been very happy in the army. Far too cerebral. That bomb didn't come a second too soon for Fielding. I wish one had come my way.'

'Would you have been an author too?' said Jakki.

'Who knows?'

'What nonsense, darling,' said Betty. 'You're far better off as a stockbroker. At least you do an honest job of work. Authors just sit about telling lies for money.'

'Precisely. It sounds the most tremendous fun. Let's have Fielding round to dinner to tell us a few. And while he's about it, he can tell us a true story as well . . . the end of the one he was telling at the party before he was interrupted. I want to hear what happened to the late Mrs Donald Salinger. I knew her when she was still called Vanessa Drew. A grand girl, Vanessa.'

There was a silence while the three females in the car chewed the phrase over mentally. All three apparently decided not to invite elucidation. Some minutes later, 'Can we have dinner downstairs with you,' said Jakki, 'when Mr Gray comes?'

'Major Gray. No. You'll have supper upstairs.'

'Mean,' said Caroline.

'You can ask Rosie Stern.'

'I expect she'll be staying with Tessa. Her parents are going away soon, and she's going to stay in Tessa's Auntie's Hotel.'

'Then ask Tessa too,' said Ivan. 'I've heard so much about her that it's time I met her.'

'I wish we could ask Marius,' sighed Jakki. 'He talked to us at the party. He's the most scrumptious and exciting person that I ever saw.'

'Marius will be back at his school, darling,' said Betty coolly and firmly. 'Rosie and her friend Tessa will be quite enough for one evening. And very convenient,' she said to Ivan, 'if anything ever comes of all this. You realize that Fielding Gray lives in that hotel? He can drive them all over.'

'So *that's* why he was so interested in Tessa . . .'

'Tessa loves Mr Gray,' said Jakki.

'Major Gray. Who told you that?'

86

'Tessa. She and Rosie do *sometimes* talk to the rest of us. She says she wishes he was her Daddy.'

'Well, he isn't. She hasn't got a Daddy, and she hasn't got a Mummy. Only her Auntie Maisie.'

'Poor Tessa.'

'*Not* poor Tessa,' said Caroline. 'Rosie loves her. And Rosie loves Tessa's hump. She strokes it and plays with it in the changing room while we all watch.'

'But you don't all play with it?'

'No. That's only for Rosie.'

'Has Rosie said so?'

'No,' said Jakki, 'but all the same she has made us feel that it is so.'

'How?'

'The only person who might understand that,' said Caroline, 'is that great fat man who was at the party. Toll something.'

'Ptolemaeos Tunne,' said her mother. 'We were introduced. He did not find me interesting but managed to be very civil about it.'

'He found Rosie interesting,' said Caroline. 'I saw him looking at her . . . as if he were wondering which way to cook her.'

'You may not have noticed,' said Betty, 'that he gave you and Jakki precisely the same sort of look while he was being civil to me. It was on the tip of his tongue to ask me about you – though ask me *what* I don't quite know – but at the last moment he thought better of it and went on his way.'

'How insulting,' said Jakki, 'just to be passed over like that. I bet he hasn't passed Rosie over. I bet he's asked Rosie's mother about Rosie whatever he didn't ask you about us.'

'So much the worse for Rosie, I'd say,' Betty Blessington said.

'Rosie had a row with Marius,' said Caroline, 'after he'd

been talking to us. He went into the garden, and I saw what happened through the window. He said something with a nasty look on his face and those green eyes of his going all crooked. Rosie's face didn't change at all, but suddenly that hair of hers seemed to go even blacker than usual, and she touched Marius on the shoulder and said something – and whatever it was, Marius looked furious, furious *and* frightened.'

'Marius tried to hit her when they got inside again,' said Jakki. 'So obviously he wasn't frightened when the grown-ups were there once more.'

'Perhaps he was more frightened than ever. Perhaps he tried to hit her from fear as well as temper.'

'Nice friends you have,' said Ivan briskly, and turned on the wireless. A voice announced that Lover Pie had come first at 50 to 1.

'There you are,' said Ivan. 'If we'd been at Ascot I should have backed that horse. I might even have had a tenner on it. And don't think I'd have forgotten all of you.'

Jakki and Caroline hugged each other in gales of derisive giggles, while Betty in the front seat put her hand very gently on Ivan's knee.

Having left the christening party rather early, Ptolemaeos Tunne had driven home in leisurely fashion. First he paused at Waterbeach and walked down the river to the lock from which he used to fish as a child. Had it been hitting below the belt, he asked himself, to threaten Gregory Stern with the name of 'Toeman'?

It was certainly a mean blow even if legitimate. Gregory was about the grandest and most anglicized Jew (leave aside the occasional Yiddish affectations which he put on largely for Isobel's amusement) in the United Kingdom: he had been an Oppidan Scholar at Eton, he had ridden as Cornet with a squadron of the Tins during his National Service, and he had been President of the Petronian Dining Company while in his last year at the House. He had long since contrived to bury the fact (among others) that his grandfather had been a jobbing tailor in Wapping who had been saved from bankruptcy only by marrying into a family of small but brutally usurious pawnbrokers called 'Toeman'. And now, here was Ptolemaeos (who was not in the least ashamed that one of this appalling tribe had been his mother and had indeed brought his father the tiny capital with which the manufactory of stool-pans had been started) – here was Ptolemaeos reminding Gregory that he knew what he knew and could let a whole lot of other people know it as well, if Gregory made difficulties about the use of his children for the purposes of Ptolemaeos's research.

Yes, a mean blow, thought Ptolemaeos. He struck away from the lock on a path which led to a fen pond. Once he had caught tench here – as had his niece, Jo-Jo Pelham, while she lived with him in his Fenland mansion, before she married Jean-Marie Guiscard. Ptolemaeos looked into the yellow waters. A mean blow, he conceded once again; but not foul and surely necessary. For without this threat, Gregory would have refused him out of hand. Not, of course, that it was yet certain that Gregory would comply, thought Ptolemaeos, as he walked back past the lock and approached the caravan site and public toilets that had now replaced the riverside gardens of his childhood; but he would be very surprised if there were much difficulty made now. Once Gregory had got over the shock of being . . . conscribed . . . he would realize that the project was, after all, a fascinating one and that a very prestigious and profitable book might come of it. What was more, Gregory's wife, Isobel, was known to be interested in studies of this kind, and she would help bring him up to the mark and keep him there.

And on the whole, thought Ptolemaeos, as he drove through the purple mist of the Fenland evening, he would be doing the Sterns as good a turn as they would be doing him. For while his primary motive in taking up the Stern children was to use them as high-class material for his investigations, he was, at the same time, offering a service. He was ready to protect. When he had called little Rosie a witch (he thought) he had been exaggerating, dramatizing, showing himself off as the Amateur Savant; for Rosie, of course, was nothing of the kind. Nevertheless, she was to be regarded with caution. She had a faerie way of walking and (to judge from her demeanour with her father in the Provost's Garden) considerable powers of entrancing (hand in hand with Gregory among the flowers, her face grave and impassive, his face dazed with happiness, as if in some kind of paradisal dream), powers which could do much harm, make much misery if used in the wrong cause.

And what cause, thought Ptolemaeos, as he let himself into the kitchen of his huge, hot and empty house, what sort of cause do I mean by that?

He set about warming up the dishes which the two old women, who came daily from the nearest village, had left for him. The old women were quite skilful cooks, canny in their use of local herbs and Fenland creatures, snails and pike and eels and *écrevisse*; but their cooking lacked the accuracy and style achieved by Jo-Jo in the days when she had been with him, good days that had to end, nor would he see their like again. For no one could replace Jo-Jo in the house, the kitchen, the bed; Jo-Jo now big with boy-child (so she seemed certain) by her chosen husband. Not but what she still loved her uncle Ptolemaeos . . . but that special time had ended for ever, he told himself, as of course it had to end, so do not brood over its loss or you will poison it, remember it briefly now and then and be grateful that you had it, oh be a man, Ptolemaeos, and think of other things.

Of Rosie, then. Her . . . special talents, he had just been telling himself, if used in the wrong cause, might bring about misery and disaster. What sort of cause, he must now ask himself again, could the wrong cause be?

He carried his soup of carp and perch over to the kitchen table and sat down slowly and carefully in a vast armchair of oak.

Rosie, it seemed to him, was a loving child: her plain face, though often apparently impassive, was underlain (as she walked with her father in the Provost's Garden) by care and consideration. So she would not act spitefully or maliciously: but she might act very vigorously to protect or to justify someone whom she loved. Like many good people, she might make a wrathful, vindictive champion. Rosie's message for the world, thought Ptolemaeos as he sipped the muddy brew before him, was 'See that ye love one another'; to which, however, she might well add the rider 'And woe betide you if you don't'. If ever she went into action on the second count, there might well be need of Ptolemaeos the Savant to protect others against her and her against herself. Yes: he had been right to force Gregory to let him into his children's lives, even if in order to do so he had been compelled to conjure the unsavoury spectre of the Jew Tailor of Wapping.

Canteloupe and Baby, Gregory and Isobel with their two children, and Jean-Marie and Jo-Jo Guiscard had been invited to spend the night after the christening in the Provost's Lodging. After dinner Canteloupe walked with

Gregory in the Provost's Garden. For a while they talked of the books which Stern & Detterling would be bringing out that spring, and then of more distant prospects. At length Gregory said: 'As you recommended, I have bought an option on Jean-Marie Guiscard's book, *La Demoiselle d'Arques* – an option, that is, on the English version. I gather, from conversation with Jean-Marie at dinner, that Jo-Jo will translate it for him as soon as he has finished his text in French.'

'Which should be very soon now. I don't think we'll regret it, Gregory. It's an intriguing story.'

'So I gather. Satanic possession of a Greek Princess, or something of the kind, and a scandal about her buried treasure, which was finally unearthed, not so very long ago, by your acquisitive friend, Ptolemaeos Tunne.'

'Purely for the pleasure of the hunt. As Jean-Marie's book will make plain, Ptolemaeos's interest in the affair was solely that of the questing scholar. When he had the treasure in his hand, he gave it back to Greece, whence it originated. There's nothing acquisitive about Ptolemaeos, Gregory: he's got enough of everything already.'

'Then why does he wish to acquire my children?' Gregory said.

'Ah. Children he *is* short of – since his niece Jo-Jo left him to be married. But I'm sure you'll find, as Len has been telling us, that the investigations which Ptoly wants to conduct are *bona fide* and of some importance to philosophy or science or both. *And*, you must remember, you and Isobel are invited to be present the entire time. I dare say, as well, Gregory, that Ptolemaeos might continue to take an interest in them later on . . . which could be – well – beneficial.'

'People who want children in whom to take an interest,' said Gregory, 'should marry and get their own. Marius and Rosie are well provided for already.'

'And yet Len tells me that you'll probably do as Ptolemaeos asks.'

'There is . . . disagreeable pressure. A threat, Canteloupe, which might make me a mockery.'

'Might one ask what this threat is?'

'One might, but one would not be answered. Let me simply say, Canteloupe, that in all our interests, particularly my own, I shall have to do as this confounded Ptolemaeos requests.'

'And who is this, complaining under the moon,' said Isobel Stern, who now approached through the rustling garden with Baby and Sarum (at suck). 'Let Ptolemaeos Tunne test the children as he wishes – and so make for them and for us an ally. An ally, Gregory my husband. A well-wisher. What is the matter with that?'

'The matter is, Isobel my wife, that I do not like interference.'

'I think I should be rather grateful for it in this instance,' said Baby, switching Sarum from left to right. 'There is the interest in what Ptolemaeos is doing, in the questions which he is asking.'

'Fundamental questions,' said Isobel, 'about our whole condition of being.'

'And there is also the fact,' added Baby, 'that Ptolemaeos is an expert on evil.'

'Evil?'

'If there should be any threat to your children,' said Baby carefully, thinking of what she had seen that afternoon in her beloved cousin, 'Ptolemaeos would spot it, by instinct, in the course of his questioning.'

'But why should there be a threat of evil? Why should there be any such threat to children who are correctly fed, securely housed, brought up gently yet with sound discipline by Isobel my wife, and are at present being choicely educated in the finest schools in the land?'

'That's just it,' Baby said. 'You think all these things are guarantees. You are innocent, Gregory: perhaps smug would be a better word. For although you know that there is evil in the world, you think it would never dare to operate at the expense of the distinguished and egregious Gregory Stern or his beautifully kept and educated children. Now, Ptoly Tunne knows different. Ptoly knows that there are no guarantees. You take a good long look around you, and you'll see that he might – he just might – have a point.'

'But surely,' said Gregory, shaken and sentimental, 'there is no necessary reason why anything evil should befall my little Rosie, my gallant Marius?'

'No reason at all,' said Canteloupe, 'and if nothing happens there will be no interference. Ptolemaeos will make these tests of his, draw up his record, and that will be that.'

'But if . . . there should turn out to be anything amiss,' said Baby, remembering the vicious punch which Marius had tried to deliver, and which, as she (and she alone) had been standing at exactly the right angle to appreciate, would have hit Rosie on the nape of the neck had it ever landed, a vulnerable and even mortal spot, '*if*,' Baby said, 'there should ever turn out to be anything at all odd, then Ptolemaeos will be aware and he will watch. He will protect.'

'Protect,' said Isobel. 'A comforting word. Let this Ptolemaeos make his investigations, Gregory my husband, and then protect the children if need be. I for one shall feel the happier for this when we are away in Israel in May and June.'

'There can be nothing to fear in May or June,' said Gregory fiercely. 'Marius will be at Oudenarde House, Rosie will stay with her friend Tessa Malcolm in Buttock's Hotel. What is there to fear?'

'Nothing,' said Isobel wearily, 'except that, to put it in very general terms:

"The world is sick and the Devil is slee;
Timor Mortis Conturbat Me."

Which being the case, Gregory my husband, it is always a consolation to have experts in these matters at and on one's own side.'

'Amen to that,' Baby said, and shifted Sarum back from right to left.

After dinner in the Provost's Lodging, Tom Llewyllyn, seeing that his guests were happy with each other's company, had slunk off to his study for a word or two with Secretarial Len.

'I am worried,' said Tom, 'about those Salinger girls.'

'Why? They've got everything going for them. Carmilla has lifted this dandy prize. Theodosia queens it on the badminton court. What makes it better, Carmilla the swot takes plenty of healthy exercise and Theodosia the gym girl enjoys reading her books. Positively no worries, Tom.'

'They are adopted. Their adoptive mother, who hated them, is dead. Their adoptive father . . . is unbalanced.'

'So the mother's dead, and good riddance, from what I hear. And the father's been in the hatch, but now he's out. They're pleased to see him – good for them – and between them they'll give him the affection and attention he needs, but without spoiling their careers. Whatever he may be, they're steady as rocks, Tom. They've been put through it by their arsehole of a mother, and they've come out safe the other side, and there's nothing going to upset them now.'

'Suppose . . . that Donald became really possessive, really greedy of their time and presence, surely that might trouble them.'

'No. They'd do their sums. Although they intend to do the right thing by him, they'd count the cost,' said Len, 'and if the emotional bills came too high he'd find himself back in the hatch.'

'What about Jeremy Morrison?'

'What about him?'

'You tell me he goes to bed with Carmilla.'

'Yeah. Though she don't let him fuck her. And a bloody good job she don't, at their age. No fucking equals no trouble.'

'Let's hope so. What about Theodosia? Does she mind his carrying on with her sister?'

'She doesn't know. And I'll tell you this, Tom. Theodosia carries a much brighter torch for Jeremy Morrison than Carmilla does. With Carmilla it's just good dirty fun, and now what's for tea? Whereas Theodosia would lie down to be his doormat – but not for any other reason. She's the original Diana – "Queen and Huntress, Chaste and Fair" – and she's going to keep her cherry locked up as tight as the Koh-i-Noor diamond to stay good and fit for her badminton. Meanwhile she worships Jeremy like he was Apollo – and won't let him touch her.'

'Well, no one can complain about *that*,' said the Provost. 'But there must be care, Len. There must not be a scandal.'

'Why should there be one?'

'Donald. I knew him quite well in the old days, before he went into St Bede's. He is very old-fashioned in some ways: chivalrous, reverent of purity. If he finds out about Carmilla, it might . . . it might . . .'

'Send him round the twist again? Back into the hatch?'

'Yes. And there might be quite a lot of unpleasantness before he actually arrived there. Scandal, as I say.'

'Jealousy? Violence?'

'I don't know. Something like what happened when his wife died.'

'*What* happened when his wife died?'

Tom shrugged.

'No one really knows – beyond the fact that she was drowned. Something happened, clearly, something ghastly enough to make him mad.'

'I've always heard there was no question of his being remotely to blame,' said Len, 'in any respect whatever, for his wife's death.'

'So everyone says. Then why should he have been so stricken, immediately after it, that he had to spend several years retired from the world and under intense treatment?'

'Ask me another.'

'Watch that girl and Jeremy, Len. We don't want anything of the kind again.'

'But *what* kind?'

'How should I know? Just tip Master Jeremy the wink that if he must play little Jack Horner with Carmilla Salinger, he'd better make sure that no squeals of excitement waft their way to Donald.'

At about the same time as Tom was conferring with Len, Greco Barraclough was dismissing his esquire, Nicos Pandouros, with final instructions for the next day.

'Come into College and wake me at eight A.M.,' the Greco said. 'Breakfast – bacon, eggs, toast, marmalade and lemon tea – at eight-thirty. Rest of the morning free – for you. Luncheon, one P.M.: Bath Chaps, mashed potatoes, green salad. Two P.M., set out in the Range Rover for Long Melford, where I wish to examine some tombs. Tea in Lavenham. Return five P.M.'

'Need I come to Long Melford? I have work.'

'You have all the morning for that. I may want you to drive, particularly on the way back.'

'Very well, *Kyrie*. Can I take it you will not need me in the evening?'

'You may,' said El Greco with an air of munificence. 'I shall dine at High Table. But you must be ready to attend me to Ivor Winstanley's evening party – drinks after dinner – on Thursday. And now, Nico, you may withdraw.'

Nicos withdrew. He ran down the staircase from Barraclough's set in Sitwell's Buildings, and came out into the Great Court by the south door of the chapel. He decided to walk across the grass. *Kyrios* Barraclough was allowed to walk across the grass: why not Nicos Pandouros? True, Nicos Pandouros was only an undergraduate, and only that by special courtesy of the Provost and by favour of *Kyrios* Barraclough, who furnished him with a purse. True, Nicos Pandouros did not have a commodious set in Sitwell's (sitting room, study, dining room, kitchen, bedroom, guest room, two bathrooms with loos) but a basement bed-sitter in Mill Lane (one shower with loo on second floor). But even so, thought Nicos Pandouros, he was a free man, and if he wanted he could walk upon the grass.

As he did so (unchallenged, though he was clear to see beneath the moon) he thought of two things: of how horribly he was falling behind with his work for the Classical Tripos because of *Kyrios* Barraclough's demands on his time; and of how imperative it was in any case that he should resign from Barraclough's service and set up as his own man. Imperative, perhaps: also traitorous, for the *Kyrios* was his acknowledged and adoptive master and had been for five years; and in any event impossible, for without the *Kyrios* he had no money and no place in Lancaster College – no place anywhere in England. Unless, he thought, he could persuade his patron to be magnanimous – to let him go but continue to pay his stipend. After all, they were no longer in Greece: the strict obligations imposed by Maniot custom on the adopted page or companion did not apply here. In England, he had heard, one had a right both to freedom *and* money: one was morally (or at least socially) entitled to be paid *not* to serve.

Somehow, Nicos did not think that the *Kyrios* Barraclough had quite taken this in. The *Kyrios*, it appeared, thought of Nicos, and treated him, exactly as he had in the old days, in the Mani, in the house with the broken tower. The same services were still required of him, the same friendly and educative patronage accorded. This expedition to the tombs at Long Melford tomorrow would be just like the hundreds (due allowance being made for cultural disparities) on which they had gone to tombs and remnants all over the Peloponnese. But one thing was different: there (thought Nicos as he stepped off the grass and under the Gate Arch) he had been a little orphan lad eager to earn a living and please a kindly master; now (he thought as he emerged through the wicket into King's Parade) he was a grown man who yearned to be independent of a demanding employer and prosper by his own efforts in a land of opportunity.

'Mr Barraclough's young man just gone through,' said Wilfred, the Porter of the Night Gate, as Nicos closed the wicket.

'Too big for his boots, if you ask me,' said Wilfred's colleague. 'He came here as a kind of valet or manservant, and in no time at all he's an undergraduate of the college – without a single "A" Level to his name.'

'The Provost of this college,' said Wilfred, 'is sovereign within its walls. He can give judgment upon whatever felony may come under his notice; he can expel or *admit* whomever he may wish.'

'I dare say. But there must have been some wheedling.'

'Very likely. If you were a poor Greek boy, you might get up to a bit of wheedling.'

'Poor Greek boy, indeed. An undergraduate of this college while I'm only Fifth Porter.'

'Fate,' said Wilfred placidly. '"The wind bloweth as it

99

listeth." It may blow you half a million through Littlewoods tomorrow. Meanwhile, as Assistant Porter of the Night Gate, you'd better set out on your rounds and give thanks for a beautiful moon.'

'Interesting old day,' said Jean-Marie Guiscard, as he helped Jo-Jo lie down on the bed in the Benson Room, whither, being exhausted by the events of the day, she had wished to retire immediately after dinner. 'Demned amusing scene in the chapel.'

'I must say, darling,' said Jo-Jo, 'your English idiom has been improved by this short visit more than I should have thought possible. "Demned", indeed. Straight out of Buchan or the Baroness Orczy. At this rate you'll be able to translate the *Demoiselle* into English all by yourself.'

'Thank you, *chérie*,' preened Jean-Marie. 'And what about my accent?'

'I'm afraid, Jean-Marie-Jean, that your accent rather lets you down. Anyone would know you for a froggy.'

'Oh,' said Jean-Marie, dejected. Then, remembering his manners, 'Care for a drink, old girl? I could pop down and fetch you one.'

'That would be nice. I fancy a Bloody Mary. I know it's peculiar after dinner, but that's what I fancy.'

When Jean-Marie came back with Jo-Jo's Bloody Mary, he said, 'You are quite right about my accent. And the only way to improve it is to live in England. I know we must come to live here sooner or later, although you have very sweetly tried to adapt yourself to France, because England is the country you love. Shall we come . . . say . . . after I have finished *La Demoiselle*?'

100

'Darling Jean-Marie. Yes: when you have finished *La Demoiselle*.'

'My first draft in manuscript should be done in about a month. We will come then. You are sure that you would not wish to come sooner? It is, as they say, your money.'

'Don't think of that. You'll be making plenty yourself as soon as "La Dem" comes out. The thing is, my Jean-Marie-Jean, shall you be happy in England?'

'Happy with you. Shall we live near your Uncle Ptoly? I like his style, you know.'

'Not near Ptoly, my precious. Those Fens are poison for babies. Besides, although most people at dinner seemed to think his new researches are going to be so marvellous, I don't quite trust them. They *could* just have funny effects on any foetuses or pregnant ladies who happened to get mixed up with them. Or so Len warned me.'

'But at dinner Len was the most vociferous in their praise.'

'Quite rightly. It's a fascinating affair. But Len, who knows a thing or two in this area, has certain reservations, which he conveyed to me, on behalf of our unborn son. Ptoly can be very persuasive, you see, and if he persuaded me to start answering questions . . . in what, I suspect, will be very imaginative circumstances . . . something or other might get upset or come unstuck.'

'So we shall not live near Uncle Ptoly. Perhaps near Lady Canteloupe?' said Jean-Marie.

'Yes. Near Baby. In the West Country. Possibly even *with* her for a little while. They've got plenty of room, and I'll need her to talk to while I'm stuck with Alexandre in my belly.'

'Why are you so keen to call him Alexandre?'

'Not for the soldier. For Paris of Troy; his other name was Alexander.'

'Paris was of ill fame – was the most frightful bounder,'

Jean-Marie corrected himself. 'He was a liar and a cheat and a funk.'

'Paris had Helen,' said Jo-Jo. 'The most beautiful and fascinating woman in all the legends of the world.'

'Little good it did either of them.'

'Except that even now, three thousand years later, hearts beat and eyes glisten whenever their names are mentioned.'

'Alexandre, then. But suppose, just suppose, that the child turns out to be a girl?'

'Then the child will be exposed in the customary Greek manner. I'm not going to spend years of my life buggered up with some whingeing little female.'

'No, of course not. Exposure is the answer,' said Jean-Marie, playing up to his wife's joke. 'Very sensible people, the ancient Greeks. Exposure. Ha! Ha!'

'No laughing matter these days, I'm afraid. Very difficult to manage without being noticed – too many busybodies about,' Jo-Jo said. 'We might have to go abroad, to Greece itself perhaps. Parts of the Taygetus range are still pretty remote. Greco Barraclough might have some useful advice.'

Jean-Marie nodded thoughtfully, then went to answer a knock at the door. Baby Canteloupe came in, carrying Lord Sarum of Old Sarum.

'I have brought Tullius,' she said, 'to say good-night to Alexandre.'

'Ah, so you have already heard the child's name,' said Jean-Marie, pleased. He was about to add that they would have to think again if the child were a girl, but something about the remembered tone of the jokes which Jo-Jo had made on the subject just before Baby's arrival decided him to keep silence.

Baby lowered Tullius until he was sprawled on Jo-Jo's belly. Jo-Jo drew her breath in sharply and clasped him there. Very quietly, Jean-Marie left the room.

Max lost no time, on his way home, in summoning his confidants.

'It was a fine bawling boy,' he told them as the Rolls sailed through Trumpington. 'I shall leave him a fortune if I perish for it.'

'First things first,' he admonished himself in the voice which Angela used to use when being nannyish. 'In order to leave the boy a fortune you must first bring back your loot, from Greece and Italy, intact. Well, no doubt it can be done, Maxie; but how?'

'Yes,' Max repeated in Lykiadopoulos's throaty monosyllables. 'How?'

'Hotels,' he answered them. 'Use existing assets in Greece and Italy to buy hotels in Corfu, say, where I already have some, and in Sicily. The essential thing is that whenever possible bookings must be paid for in advance in countries where currencies are hard and free-moving, and where there are no busybody laws about what one does with one's own money; the most reliable of such countries being the US and Switzerland. Such payments will simply be left in those countries, while the hotels themselves will be run from my surplus funds in the appropriate local currency. Thus huge pools of hard currency will soon accumulate in countries from which they may be drained at will, or where they may be banked in Sarum's name or his father's without interference or penalty.'

'Too simple, darling,' he told himself in Angela's ginny rasp. 'Hundreds of people have thought of that gimmick and dropped it. The countries in which you will own these hotels – grotty Greece and grimy Italy – will *demand* that hard-currency payments made overseas shall be sent to them at the outset.'

'Yes,' he said in Lykiadopoulos's snidest style of mockery. 'Those Wops and Grecos will buzz about like flies after shit.'

'Indeed,' Max told them, 'and they shall have a lot of shit, enough for them to batten on happily and indefinitely. But meanwhile, let us say, four or five payments in any hundred, possibly quite inconspicuous ones, will be left in the US or wherever. The Wops and Grecos, gorged with dollars, made fatuous by incompetence and satiety, will not detect those. And those, in the eighteen years I have until Sarum comes of age, will add up to the million and more which I would wish to leave him.'

'A question,' from 'Lykiadopoulos'. 'How much will a million – or more – then be worth?'

'A question,' from 'Angela'. 'What makes you think that you're going to live long enough to supervise all this?'

'I can only hope to leave matters in the best possible order,' said Max to his interlocutors, 'when I do die.'

'Well, it could work, darling,' granted Max's Angela-at-midnight voice, 'and at least it will provide you with an innocent and amusing occupation until the whistle blows.'

Donald Salinger had taken a train back to London after the christening and had then dined alone in the Ritz, as he usually did these days. He looked forward to the girls' vacation, as then they could all three dine together, though he rather thought (to judge from occasional signs of impatience during the previous vacation) that they might prefer somewhere less formal. A bistro, perhaps. Vanessa had always liked bistros. Not that Vanessa had been their real mother, or even very dutiful as an adoptive one, but somehow there seemed to be a connection. After all, Vanessa had always *been there* with them all; however hostile a presence, she was part of the family, and just towards the end she had shown signs of relenting. 'Those girls are coming on well,' Vanessa had said as they drove away from Benenden that Saturday afternoon after the School Sports. 'I'll try to be more attentive from now on.'

This had made Donald happy, and he became happier still as they journeyed on towards Sandwich, because Vanessa, for the first time in many years, was jolly and loving and prattling – *dulce ridentem Lalagen amabo* (he remembered from his favourite Horace) *dulce loquentem* – just as she used to be when they were first married and lived in Cheyne Row.

'Oh, Donald,' she said soon after they had turned along the coast road. 'We are coming to Oxley Court. Please let's stop. I went there one summer as a child. It was one of the happiest times I've ever had.'

The road veered away from the cliffs and dipped downhill, into thick woodland. At the bottom of the dip, on their right, was the entrance to an ill-kempt drive which wound steeply up through the crowded oak trees.

'The house is up there,' Vanessa had said. 'We'll park just here first and go and see the chapel.'

Donald parked the BMW under a bank near the mouth of the drive.

'It was during the war,' Vanessa said, taking his hand and dragging him up the bank and into the trees. 'I had to get special permission to come because the area was officially closed except to permanent residents and the Forces. Luckily my uncle, the one who owned all this, was a retired Colonel of Marines, and he'd gone back to the Colours during the war, to help them in their barracks down the road in Deal, so he was able to fix it for me to come. The thing was, he wanted a holiday friend for his son. The mother had just died, and the Colonel was busy in his barracks, and he wanted someone to play with his only boy, his only child, who was my cousin. Do you remember the war, Donald? No one had much time for children in the holidays, they had to make their own fun if they could. Titus and I certainly had to make ours.'

They came into a clearing in which sat a broken chapel with a broken arch, spikes eating like rotten teeth from the circumference into the sagging tympanum.

'We used to come here often,' Vanessa said, 'Green Oxley Laris, they call it. Lar is the Latin for ghost, did you know? It's supposed to be haunted by the ghost of an Abbess who came from a convent near Dover to keep tryst with the Knight of the Manor . . . for there was a fortified Manor House in the trees at the top of the hill, though it has long since and many times been replaced. The Knight went on a Crusade in penance for having loved the Abbess, who should have known no lover but Christ, and after he had gone she used to come here and pray for him, pray that her gilded Knight might return safe and as beautiful as ever . . . until at last she died, when she was quite an old woman, having learned just towards the end that he had been killed in a tournament in Sicily on his way to the Holy Land, far from home and yet far from Jerusalem, only a few months after they had said farewell; so that these many years, while she had been praying for her lovely Knight in armour, she should have been praying for his soul in Purgatory. We used to come here often, Titus and I, hoping to see the poor ghost. But we never did.'

Vanessa passed under the lintel, over which presided a crooked Christ in Judgment, canopied by the carious arch.

'Uncle came with us sometimes, on Saturdays or Sundays. He used to change out of his uniform into a tweed suit with a cricketing tie – one of the ones you wear, yellow, black and orange – '

' – The I Zingari,' Donald had said.

' – The I Zingari. Uncle said he would like to be buried here, but this would not be permitted, as the ground was no longer hallowed, and anyhow the health authorities, who were just beginning to be important, back then in 1942, would make officious difficulties. So he said he would like a slab put on the wall – and here, yes, here it is,' she cried, clapping her hands: '"To Robert Vespasian Spencer-Drew,"' she read, '"of Oxley Court in the County of Kent, Esquire; *obiit* 24/x/59; true husband, loving father, loyal soldier, merry cricketer. Placed here, in memory of all the happy summers, by Titus, his son." Oh,' said Vanessa, 'the happy summer that I was here. Why, I wonder, was there only one? Why did I never come again till now? Something to do with the war, I suppose: people were always being moved on and disappointed and forbidden and put off.'

'But nothing can take away *that* summer,' Donald had said.

'No, no, nothing can take that away. When we were bored with waiting for the ghost who never came we would walk up the hill to one of our special places, a bank at the edge of the trees, looking over the fields that lay towards the cliff-tops and the sea. We were forbidden to go beyond the edge of the trees,' Vanessa had said, 'because the fields and the cliff-tops were crowded with gun emplacements and hangars for barrage balloons and huts for the men. Grown-up business: the war. So we sat in a special place and watched that bit of the war. But all through that summer nothing seemed to happen . . . as we sat there, Titus and I, or went to other special places in the garden or the orchard or inside the house itself – for even during that summer some days were wet.

'Come on,' she said to Donald, 'I shall take you to our special place at the edge of the trees. Someone told me that the gun emplacements and the hangars are still there on the cliff.'

It is at this stage that what Donald remembered (sitting over his *Riz de Veau* in the Ritz) started to differ from the official version of what had happened, from the version which had always been put out, the version which Fielding Gray would have told at the christening party, had he not, to the chagrin of Ivan Blessington, been interrupted in the telling. For what Fielding would have said was that during Donald's and Vanessa's walk through the forest Vanessa trod on the wooden lid of a forgotten well; that the lid, concealed and rotted by the decaying leafage of several decades, instantly gave way, precipitating Vanessa down an eighty foot shaft, at the bottom of which, having been knocked unconscious by the fall, she sagged down into a few feet of water and died of drowning within a matter of minutes. That is what Fielding would have said at the party. But what Donald remembered was this:

As they walked through the trees, Vanessa and he, they met a man in a tweed suit and a yellow, black and orange I Zingari tie. At first Vanessa had thought this was her uncle (for so she remembered him when he was off duty on his estate during the war) and although she showed no signs of fear she told him that he ought not to be there, since the tablet in the chapel said that he had died on 24/x/59. But the man said he was the Colonel's son, Vanessa's old playmate, Titus, and greeted her with warmth. 'What splendid luck,' he said. It appeared that though the house and the land were now sold to another, he, Titus, still came down from London at weekends sometimes, to look and to remember. Now they could look and remember together.

So they all three continued towards 'the special place' on the bank at the edge of the woods; and they looked out over the fields, towards the cliff-tops and the sea; and there indeed were the ruins of the gun emplacements and the hangars and the Nissen huts, any nearer to which they had been forbidden, as children, to approach.

'Quiet as ever,' Titus had said. 'Nothing much ever happened, even during the war. Just the occasional trumpet call, bidding them rise, dine or sleep. The only activity I remember clearly is the movement of water-lorries. For some reason they had no running water, and it used to come in tanks or drums on lorries every day. Rather a waste of effort, we used to think,' he said to Donald, 'as there was an abundant well very close, if only they had known it, just inside the wood. We never thought of telling them, of course: it would have been like talking to the inhabitants of another planet, and besides, we were forbidden to go beyond the bank.'

'The well was about ten yards over there,' Vanessa had said. 'Behind Donald and just by that big thingummy bush.'

'Rubbish,' said Titus in friendly correction. 'It was by the foot of that beech.'

'By that bush,' said Vanessa. She walked towards the thingummy bush, while Titus's eyes glittered and quizzed.

'Here,' she said, scraping at the leaves with her left foot. She brought the right foot up beside it to give herself better purchase. There was a small, phutting noise, and Vanessa disappeared into the ground while Titus still quizzed. After some seconds, Vanessa began to scream. At first the noise was muffled, but when Titus and Donald came to stand at the well-head it rose to them clear and shrill.

'God has punished her,' Titus said, 'for the wrong she did me.'

'I thought you were friends,' said Donald. 'Such dear friends. We must do something. Police, ambulance.'

'Two little innocents, you thought? Having an idyllic summer?'

'So it seemed from what she said.'

'I was seventeen. She was ten. Too young, my father said, but he could think of no one else in the family to

109

come and stay with us. And it had to be family, otherwise there would be no permit to enter a military zone. So there came that summer my little cousin of ten. Older than she looked.'

'This screaming. We must go for help.'

'There is none. That well is many yards deep. By the time they come and get her out, she will be dead.'

'The house? A telephone?'

'Very well. I will guide you there.'

'No. You go and telephone,' said Donald. 'I must stay here.'

'As you please. But understand this. God has punished her. She was vile, mocking, cruel – all that summer. She was strong for her age, quick, intelligent. I was thin; thin but also flabby, brittle-boned; undernourished on wartime food at school; backward too. So she was the first up every tree, looking down and sneering. "Come on, weedy old spindle-shanks," she used to call, sneering again as I scrabbled desperately and fell. And this although she knew I loved her, loved her so dearly, would have done anything for her, would have lain down and died . . . She knew this, and what was her response? "Come on, old sossle-legs, old scabby spots." Jeering, humiliating, heartless contempt.

'And when it was wet she would sit down happily with a book and sneer again because I couldn't settle and somehow she had sensed that I couldn't really read properly. I was dyslectic, you see, no one knew about that then, if you were dyslectic they just thought you were an imbecile – and somehow she knew this and used to taunt me with it . . . before going back to her own book and being utterly content for all the long hours of rain which for me held only boredom and misery. On one such afternoon I went away from her . . . to be private . . . but she followed me and found me out and danced about the house making up a song about it, and then she blackmailed me for all my money, saying she would tell my father when he came

110

home. *That* was our innocent summer. By the end of it my love for her, my pure devoted love, had turned to everlasting hate. Even many years later, when I had grown properly and become a happy man, thanks to the love and care of my father after the war was done, even then I hated her still and wanted her to be tortured as I had been.

'And now . . . God has punished her. Very well. I shall go to the house. But I know there is no telephone. It is a shell. Nobody lives there. The man who bought the place lives in a bungalow in the village and comes by daily to farm the land. But I shall go, if only to look at the places where she taunted and humiliated and blackmailed me, and to give thanks. Later, I may find a public telephone, or a bus to take me to Dover or Deal. So if you are patient, at some time help will come.'

As Titus walked away through the trees, Vanessa had stopped screaming. Unconscious, thought Donald: or dead?

'Dead or alive,' said the Section Leader of the Fire Brigade, as the evening gathered some hours later, 'there's no getting her up out of there. I'm sorry, Mister, very sorry, believe me. But it's narrow, that shaft, and very, very deep. The sides are falling in, they might collapse altogether at any moment if further disturbed. If we did put a man down, there's no saying we'd ever get him out again, let alone get 'em both up.'

'What is down there?'

'Who knows, Mister? It used to be a well, they say – no one's known or cared for many years now, because no one comes here any more. Come to that, Mister, what were *you* doing here?'

'Walking with my wife and . . . and an old friend, who raised the alarm. What do you think is at the bottom?'

'Earth. Rock, perhaps. Maybe a little water. She must . . . sorry, Mister . . . she must have hit the bottom a real whack, water or no. She stopped screaming some hours ago, you say? Then let's thank God she's gone, even if

111

there's no saying just how. Here's the ambulance men. There'll be nothing for them. And here's the police . . . I was just telling the gentleman, Inspector, there's no putting anyone down *there* or fetching anyone out. Luckily the poor lady's gone . . .'

But then a thin wailing, as of an exhausted banshee, came up out of the well: *de profundis*. It showed no sign of strengthening or weakening: it just went on. 'Sorry, Mister . . .' 'I'm afraid, Mr – er – Salinger . . . that I shall have to ask a few questions as to the circumstances.' On and on. 'Sorry, Mister . . .'

'. . .Yes, we know Mr Titus Spencer-Drew. Family used to own the estate; much respected in these parts at one time. No doubt Mr Spencer-Drew will bear you out, Mr Salinger. I have his London address. Despite – er – altered times, he's still a patron of the Dover Police Cricket Club, as his father was. So there'll be no difficulty *there* . . .' The wailing: a kind of low keening: Vanessa keening for her own death. 'Sorry, Mister.' 'I'm afraid, Mr Salinger, that I must absolutely agree with the Section Leader. It is painful for you, I know. It is distasteful . . . and irregular . . . from the point of view of the police. But she will simply have to stay there, now and – er – later. Have you looked at that shaft? Even as we stand here, it is *disintegrating*. It has been suddenly uncovered, you see, after many years of being sealed.' 'Sorry, Mister.' Keening, that keening; it's really quite melodious. And then, for Donald, the dark.

But now, thought Donald in the Ritz, now after many months I have come back from the dark. The keening has stopped; the well has been sealed again; the due offices of the Church have been sung and spoken in the forest; Vanessa sleeps in peace in Green Oxley Laris. I have turned from the dead to the living, to my two fine daughters, Carmilla the Scholar and Theodosia the Athlete, daughters, not of my flesh indeed, but of my heart.

PART TWO
Gifts for the Guests

And of the gifts that lie in the treasure
chamber within my house, I will give thee
that which is fairest and costliest of all.

HOMER: *Odyssey XV: 11 113/4:*
Menelaus to Telemachus

When Tessa Malcolm and Rosie Stern came home from school in the evenings, they usually found that Tessa's Aunt Maisie and her friend, Major Fielding Gray, were waiting for them in the foyer, sitting on the fender in front of the fireplace. Since May was half spent the grate was empty now, though the foyer of Buttock's Hotel was a gloomy place, summer or no, without a fire. And so indeed Major Gray was saying to Aunt Maisie as the children arrived back on this particular evening – the evening of the day on which Tessa had won the Recitation Prize. Eager as they were to announce the good news, they were compelled to listen without interruption to their elders' conversation on the ethics of having fires in May, since the precept of Collingham's forbade them to introduce the topic of school activities, or of anything else, until they were invited to do so. And so, while Tessa and Rosie quivered under the burden of their undischarged intelligence, Maisie said to Fielding, 'A fire in the merrie month of May! Whatever next?'

Whereupon Fielding muttered something about taking economy too far, and added (while the girls were removing their school hats and pretending not to listen) that the deliberate infliction of discomfort was not the way to bring back guests to the hotel.

'*Pas devant*,' said Maisie haughtily, giving him a nudge. Then, as Tessa and Rosie approached once more, she put on the face which she always put on when about to enquire into the day's doings at Collingham's, and said, 'Two letters for you, Rosie love, by the second post, one with a funny foreign stamp and one postmarked Sandwich.'

She handed them over.

Clearly, thought Rosie, no one was going to ask what had happened at school until she had gratified Mrs Malcolm's evident and glutinous curiosity about what was in her letters. So she gave a little side-smile at Tessa, which meant, 'Hang on, darling, hang on, it'll be all the nicer when they *do* get round to asking,' and started to open the envelope with the funny stamp. Inside was a picture postcard with a message on the reverse. '"Boring postcards they have here,"' she read out. '"This one is typical."'

She turned it over and showed everyone the picture, which was of the new cubic Lecture Block at the Proto-Polytechnic at Joppa.

'"They take themselves so seriously,"' she went on reading aloud, '"that no one's allowed to have any fun or make any jokes, or not about Israel at any rate. They very much like your father's Jewish imitations because they think he is behaving quite sincerely and naturally and they take it as an enormous compliment that a distinguished Jew from England should carry on so like themselves. Since your father is so kind and likes to give pleasure, he has taken to doing his imitations all day long. I do hope no harm comes of it: my Nanny used to say that if you made a face or got up to silly actions and then the wind suddenly changed, you were stuck with your face or your actions for ever."'

'There must be another card,' said Rosie. 'The first one's run out.' She fished in the envelope. 'Here we are. Two more.'

She showed them all a picture of a man in a scruffy frock coat and a huge round black hat, who was banging his head against a wall.

'Lawks,' said Maisie. 'He reminds me of a client I once had who liked to – '

– She checked herself and nodded magisterially at Rosie to proceed.

'We never had anyone in the hotel who looked like that,' Tessa protested.

'Don't contradict,' said Maisie formidably, 'or I'll send you to bed.' She nodded again at Rosie.

'"This is where they all come and blubber,"' Rosie read, '"if they lose a few shekels or ducats or whatever on the Jerusalem Stock Market. Luckily I've dissuaded your father from carrying his act *that* far. We went to Sodom yesterday (not at all what I'd been hoping for) and we're going to the Sea of Galilee tomorrow. If I see anyone walking on it, I'll let you know. After that we've got a long series of business calls for your father in Haifa and Tel Aviv. I do hope he won't agree to buy too many of their dismal and self-righteous books, about how God gave this country exclusively to his own chosen people, or how it was the Romans and not them that did the crucifixion. Then home via Cyprus, Crete and Athens. I'll ring you up at Buttock's when I know the date – this side of the solstice, at any rate. Love to you all in the Cromwell Road, and a smacking kiss for that delicious old monster, Fielding Gray, from your doting Mama, Isobel."'

'Very grown-up way of writing to you, dear,' said Maisie. 'Are all her letters like that?'

'Yes,' said Rosie, and looked rather as if she wished they weren't. She went to Fielding and kissed his flaring pink cheek. 'There's Mama's kiss,' she said. 'What does she mean by "this side of the solstice"?'

'Before June 22,' Fielding said, 'the midsummer solstice when the sun is at its highest. There is also a winter solstice when – '

' – They'll tell her about that at Collingham's,' said Maisie, her dewlaps twitching with impatience and curiosity.

Now, thought Tessa, that'll surely remind her to ask what happened there today.

117

'What I want to know,' said Maisie (now, now, she'll surely ask), 'is what happened to your other letter?'

'It's from Marius,' said Rosie dourly. 'I've put it away to read later.'

Maisie opened her mouth and then, at a look from Fielding, shut it again.

'You've both been asked to supper,' Fielding said, 'by the Blessington girls. Colonel and Mrs Blessington have asked me to dine the Saturday after next, and they said how nice it would be if I could bring you too for nursery supper upstairs. All in favour? Maisie? Are you happy to let 'em out for the evening?'

Maisie nodded abruptly and waddled out, muttering something about the roast for dinner. Fielding looked after her and got up to follow.

'She didn't like it,' said Tessa to Rosie, 'when he stopped her asking to see your other letter. She loves looking at other people's letters.'

'All women do.'

'Let's look at it now they've gone.'

Rosie lifted her dress and drew the letter out from the leg of her knickers.

'Marius hasn't made any runs,' she said bleakly, a minute or two later. 'He's blaming me.'

'Why?'

'That wish. You remember – I told you weeks ago. That wish I made at the christening at Cambridge, that he shouldn't make any runs this summer.'

'I remember. You made it after he said something horrid about me. That wish rather served him right.'

'Yes. But it was only a temper wish. Marius seems to think I've got some kind of power to make it work.'

'Perhaps you have. Little raven-haired Rosie.'

Tessa put a hand on the crown of Rosie's head and began stroking her hair back and down over her neck.

'If you can make me love you so much,' Tessa said,

'perhaps you also have the power to put a spell on Marius's cricket.'

'I shouldn't use it even if I had it. Although Marius was so beastly that afternoon, I wouldn't really want to harm him – and you of all people wouldn't want me to. I only meant to upset him for a little while, as a punishment.'

'What shall you do now?'

'I'll write and tell him it was only a temper wish to annoy him, and that of course I can't make it work, and don't want it to work. I shall send him both our loves and wish him loads of luck with his batting.'

'I don't think he's going to believe you.'

'Why on earth not? Why shouldn't he?'

'Well, we'll see. Touch me. Please.'

Rosie began to rub the little lump on Tessa's right shoulder blade, but stopped and moved away from her as Maisie came in, smiling all over her face. Fielding Gray came in behind her. Neither he nor Maisie seemed to have noticed what the girls had been doing as they came in, so amused and pleased were they at some private joke.

'Major Gray's been on about the old days,' Maisie burbled. 'Such a sauce-box. Now tell me, I knew there was something I meant to ask: did anything exciting happen at Collingham's today?'

'Tessa won the Recitation Prize,' said Rosie, 'with the first hundred lines from Lord Tennyson's *Morte d'Arthur*.'

'You never told me you were going in for a prize,' said Maisie, taking two uncertain steps backward and sitting down rather heavily on the fender.

'I kept it as a secret,' said Tessa, 'so that it would be a sort of present if I won.'

'What is the prize?' asked Fielding.

'A book token for one pound and fifty pence,' said Tessa.

She looked towards her Aunt Maisie, who was rocking to and fro on the fender, happily weeping.

'I must learn that poem,' Maisie said. 'Lord Tennyson's "Morte d'Aaaaarthuuuurrr – "' She went off into a fresh bout of sobbing, while the two girls sat down on either side of her, and held her hands, and cried for company.

At one end of the library in Ptolemaeos Tunne's house in the Fens was a large semi-circular alcove, dominated by a chubby and snub-nosed bust of Socrates and lined with an eclectic collection of philosophical volumes. By moving Socrates and his pedestal a few yards back Ptolemaeos was able to make room in the alcove for the installation of the two pieces of equipment which he would need for his investigations.

The first item was a marble sarcophagus. The outer surfaces of this had been carved in low relief, by a Roman of the 2nd century AD, with the resurrection of Christ at the top end, with Hermes as marshal of the dead at the bottom end, with the rape of Ganymede on one side and the penitence of the Magdalene on the other. The inner space of the coffin had been smoothed, polished and blocked in the corners by an English craftsman of the 20th century AD, so that it would do very well as a bath, to assist it in which office taps and plugs had been fitted ready for connection with the household water system.

The second item of equipment was a tape recorder, about the size of a chest of drawers, highly sensitive to vocal tone and embodying a computer which could discern, record and number all particulars of accent and idiom.

The plumber who came to connect the sarcophagus thought the notion exquisitely funny. 'Now yer can read all these books in yer bath, 'squire,' he said, 'and when yer finished yer can be carried off in it.'

The man who delivered and installed the tape recorder, on the other hand, was clearly very resentful that any individual citizen should have enough money to buy such a piece of equipment, which in his stated opinion would have been appropriately employed only in the public service and in somehow 'bringing welfare to folks in distress'. Eager to avoid any further exposition of sanctimonious cliché, yet uncertain how to get rid of the man without making even greater bad feeling, Ptolemaeos decided to try to justify himself.

'All this is to do with an investigation I am making,' he said, 'into the nature of the human soul and its relation to the body. Are you, now, of any particular religion? Are you interested in the human soul?'

'No,' said the man. 'Religion was what they used to keep us down, wasn't it? A place for the soul in heaven – *that* was the bribe they used to make us stay in our place on earth. We've seen through all that now.' He examined a lead low down on one side of the tape recorder, then straightened up and looked at Ptolemaeos. Ptolemaeos, expecting a self-righteous scowl at the least and possibly a retributive blow with the man's spanner, was relieved to be treated to an ingratiating smile.

'I think you'll find everything in order, sir,' the man said, his free palm twitching its way towards Ptolemaeos. So that's all I have to do to keep him happy, thought Ptolemaeos. I should have known. It's just as easy as that.

'Thank you very much for your help, old chap,' he said, and passed the man a twenty-pound note.

'Nice to talk to such an understanding gentleman,' said the man, noting the size of the note, and fingering it, with a technique almost sexual, into his breast pocket. 'Just one little matter, sir: you should be very careful not to touch that red button unless you wish to wipe the tape.'

'Very kind of you to remind me, and thank you for the tip,' said Ptolemaeos. 'My two good ladies in the kitchen will provide you with anything you might fancy by way of refreshment before you leave. Pray forgive me if I don't join you. I have work.'

'Very nice too,' said the man, looking sneerily round the library as if to say, 'Call *this* work?', and clumped out.

So now he's annoyed again, thought Ptolemaeos: it didn't take long for the effect of that twenty pounds to wear off. Perhaps he expected another twenty for that warning about the red button. Or perhaps he was offended at being sent off to the kitchen. They're so touchy nowadays. If I can eat in the kitchen, why can't he? And I suppose I ought to have found out his beastly surname and called him 'Mister' whatever it is. The lower they are, the more they insist on 'Mister'. I suppose they regard it as promotion. What was it that man said about being bribed to stay in their places on earth? 'A place for the soul in heaven' – how did it go? – 'that was the bribe they used to make us stay in our place on earth. We've seen through all that now.' Precisely: you can't keep us down any longer: we're all *Mister* now – and don't think that rubbish about the immortal soul is going to wash any pots. Very typical, thought Ptolemaeos, not only of the man's class but also, in the latter respect at least, of his entire generation.

For of course, thought Ptolemaeos, no one believes in the soul any more. Who was that clergyman – when he last dined with Ivan Barraclough in Lancaster – who more or less dismissed the whole concept? 'Personal survival after death?' this reverend gentleman had said, when questioned by Ptolemaeos about modern doctrine in the matter. 'Personal survival of the soul?' he had repeated with patronizing contempt. 'Well, I dare say we'll be pushing up the daisies when we're dead, and in that sense may be said to survive, but candidly there are more urgent issues to think about – race relations, the Third World . . .' Even the Church of England was no longer concerned with the soul. As for philosophers and scientists, they had regarded the topic as thoroughly disreputable since long before Sheraton did his work or wrote his book; and by the time he did, belief in the soul had been so far discredited that few or none even troubled to listen.

Nor, he thought, will anyone listen to me. A rich amateur, researching in a dead area – no one, except, perhaps, a few friends, will know or want to know. But I don't care a rap about that, thought Ptolemaeos; for if I can establish something to my own satisfaction, then I shall know what I shall know, and never mind the rest of them. How, I am asking, does the physical brain communicate with the impalpable mind? If I can arrest and examine that process, then who shall deny to me that I may come at the secret of the human soul, and so perhaps at proof of its immortality and therefore of my own?

'I must say, darling,' said Jo-Jo Guiscard to Baby Canteloupe, 'this is very soothing for a girl in my condition.'

Jo-Jo was lying on a hung and canopied couch, which Baby, seated on a canvas chair nearby, was gently swinging with one foot. They were in the Rose Garden of the Canteloupe home in Wiltshire; only a few yards away were all the monstrous appurtenances of 'Cant-Fun', the Space-Zoo-cum-Time-Circus-cum-Feely-Theatre-cum-Four-D-Galaxy Trail, the whole hideous conglomerate by which the House of Canteloupe and its fortunes were splendidly maintained; but all of this was totally concealed by banks and trees and hedgerows so cleverly arranged that they shut out the clangour of Cant-Fun along with any sight of it. Jo-Jo and Baby might have been in the heart of Eden before the Snake.

'So soothing,' said Jo-Jo. 'Would you like to read those lines again?'

> '"As the last apple hangs,"' read Baby,
> '"High on the topmost bough,
> As the last apple hangs
> Which the pluckers forgot somehow –
> Forgot it not, nay, but got it not,
> For no one could have it till now – "'

– Baby broke off. 'Here's Canty,' she said, 'with that Messenger look on his face. How now, my Lord,' she said, making a queenly gesture of welcome from her chair, 'and what's the news with you?'

'The good news,' said Canteloupe, 'is that Jean-Marie is now happily settled in the Second Nursery, typing out his manuscript. A marvellous place to work, he says: he loves the view of the lake – trippers and all.'

'In Dieppe,' Jo-Jo said, 'he used to work looking out on the sea-front – trippers and all. He used to say it was a marvellous melancholy feeling, as the evening came, to watch them slowly disappear, minute by minute; or, as the autumn passed, to watch them grow gradually fewer, day by day. That's what he'll be thinking about your lake: how elegiac it will be to watch the trippers as they dwindle in September, in October, until the last tripper is left lingering with the last leaf – but I fear we must be gone well before then. Alexandre is due at the equinox. By that time we must have our own establishment.'

'Stay, darling,' said Baby. 'There will be plenty of time to think about your own establishment later. What with Alexandre, and what with translating Jean-Marie's book when he's typed it, you will have more than enough to think of. Stay with me and Canty, and have Alexandre here.'

'Yes,' said Canteloupe. 'Stay.'

'Money,' said Jo-Jo breathlessly. 'I shall give you lots of

money to pay for the housekeeping and so on. Although my mother didn't get as much as Uncle Ptoly from Grandpa's lavatory pans, she did very nicely, thank you. And it all came to me, you know . . . when that accident happened. And all my father's. And what my brothers would have had. All of it. So I shall give you lots of money,' she cried, 'lots and lots and lots of – '

' – Calm down, darling,' said Baby, going to Jo-Jo and putting both arms round her neck. 'We'll drain you dry and cheat you rotten, if that'll make you any happier. So long as you'll stay. So that's more good news,' she said to her husband, 'before you spout the bad.'

'Who said there was any bad?'

'It's fretting away at the back of your eyes.'

'Well, yes,' said Canteloupe. 'Marius Stern,' he said. 'Gregory asked me to stand *in loco parentis* to Rosie and Marius while Isobel and he were away. And of course he told Maisie Malcolm, with whom Rosie is staying, and he told Marius's Headmaster at Oudenarde House, my old chum "Glinter" Parkes.'

'"A useful slow bowler in his time"?' said Jo-Jo, remembering the discussion of Oudenarde House at the christening.

'That's the chap. Well, this morning I had a letter from Glinter. He says that Marius is having a rotten cricket season, and is making no effort at his work, and is going round the place scowling like Beelzebub.'

'Your phrase or – er – Glinter's?' asked Baby.

'Glinter's. He was an ordinand at one time, though he didn't stay the course, and he's always had a taste for biblical and theological reference.'

'They all go through phases, these little boys,' said Jo-Jo. 'It was just like that with my brothers. Snarling round the house for days on end – and then suddenly something nice would happen and it would be Alleluia time. All

Marius needs is to hit one six, and he'll be a little Greek god again.'

'Hermes,' said Canteloupe.

'Hermes?'

'The Messenger, you may remember. Also the Pimp and the Thief.'

'Canty . . . what are you saying?'

'That apart from everything else, and apart from a suspected but unproven instance of bullying, Marius has been nicking.'

'Nicking what, for Christ's sake?'

'Anything. Fountain pens, toothpaste, tennis balls, other boys' tuck. Nothing serious yet, thank God, and Glinter has managed to pass it off as a joke – "Marius Stern playing at being Raffles, ha, ha, ha. Raffles was a cricketer too, did you chaps know? Palairet, get the book from the library, and I'll read us all a chapter." That kind of thing, I imagine – I can just hear him at it. Sometimes I think that Glinter should have stayed at the wicket and become an ordained priest after all. Full of pastoral care and concern – and as shrewd as a pawnee with it. He'd have been a bishop long ago.'

'And we could have had him to christen Tullius instead of that other wretch,' Baby said.

'Mungo's all right. It's that wife of his makes him go in for these fads. During the war, before he had a bloody wife – but where was I?'

'Marius Stern,' said Baby, and bit her lip, thinking of her fallen Lucifer.

'As I was saying, Glinter Parkes has more or less tidied things up. For now. But if it gets any worse, or if it should turn out that Marius *has* been bullying . . .'

'Not proven, you said – the bullying.'

'But not disproven. Scottish verdict.'

'I wonder,' Baby said, 'if there was anything in that

126

threat of Rosie's? Do you remember? At Tully's christening. Marius accused Rosie of wishing him to make no runs. And she admitted it. He'd said something beastly about her friend, Tessa Malcom, and so, she said, she'd wished no runs for Marius this season.'

'But that,' said Jo-Jo, 'has to be nonsense.'

'Of course. But if Marius believes in it, if he believes she has some power over him, it might poison his morale. The fewer runs he made the more he'd believe it, and the more he believed it – '

' – I think,' said Canteloupe, 'that it's early days yet for anyone to get knotted up. So I've written a line to Glinter, and told him to keep in touch, and promised that we'd all come running out of the Park if he really has to ring the bell.'

'Green eyes, those green eyes,' Baby said.

'Quite,' said Canteloupe. And then, 'Well, you girls get on with your poetry reading. I've got the Directors' Board of Cant-Fun. Toodle-ooh,' he said, and moved off at Officers' Informal Pace (for Mounted Officers Wearing Spurs but Presently Unmounted).

'Something has gone very wrong with Marius,' said Baby to Jo-Jo when they were alone. She renewed the swinging of Jo-Jo's couch with her foot. 'I felt it at the christening. We must find out what, follow the thing up. Both for love of Marius – and for our own instruction, darling Jo-Jo. Young mothers must know what can go amiss and why.'

'You sound very clinical all of a sudden.'

'One has to be. It's a clinical age. I wish Isobel were here; I could follow it far more closely through her. *Directly*, you see; at first hand. As it is, we've got to rely on Canty, who's got to rely on this Glinter man, who's probably got to rely, for the most part, on underpaid assistant masters or nasty, sneaking boys . . .'

'Fielding Gray, the novelist,' said Jo-Jo.

Baby started nervously, then steadied herself.

'I thought you hardly knew him,' Baby said.

'I don't. But I saw him at the christening. A friendly type called Blessington told me who he was, and said he was now part-owner of that tumble-down hotel on the Cromwell Road – Busker's? Bosom's? – '

' – Buttock's – '

' – Buttock's. The place where Rosie went to stay because she's a friend of the manageress's niece. So if you know Fielding Gray well enough, you can come at Marius through him and Rosie's friend and Rosie.'

'Same trouble as before,' said Baby peevishly. 'Too many links in the chain.'

'Why,' said Jo-Jo, 'did you nearly take off like a rocket when I mentioned his name just now?'

'Whose name?'

'Fielding Gray's.'

'Is there room on that swing for me to lie with you and Alexandre?'

'Yes.'

'Then listen,' said Baby as she stretched herself by Jo-Jo and turned in towards her. 'Now then: would you not say that heredity must play a part in all this? In determining the character and actions of Marius, of my little Tully, and soon of your Alexandre?'

'Yes. But no one seems to know how big a part.'

'At any rate, *a* part.'

Baby put one foot to the ground, set the swing swinging, and drew up her leg like a sailor putting off from shore.

'Heredity,' said Baby. 'Canteloupe could not get a child. We agreed that we would decide together who should lie with me and get our son.'

Jo-Jo was silent. She passed one hand between Baby's belly and her own. Then she kissed Baby, first on the left eye, then on the right, and lay still.

'It must be, we said, a friend of Canteloupe's and a friend of mine. He must be someone whom I found

128

attractive, because Canteloupe wished me to enjoy what must be done – what must probably be done several times. "You can have a few jollies, girl," he said. "Skindles and places like that. No good behaving as if you were taking a nasty medicine. The more fun you have, so they say, the bonnier and blither the baby." We also wanted someone clever. Someone handsome. Someone with accomplishments. Fielding Gray.'

'But . . . so old.'

'I did not want some silly, blundering boy. Anyway the only young man I know whom I ever found attractive became a monk – some years ago, near Venice. Of all the people I knew only two fitted the bill – and one was my father.'

'But Fielding Gray . . . handsome?'

'He'd been beautiful before he'd been disfigured. I had Canteloupe's word for that: spectacular, Canteloupe said. And there were pictures . . .'

'Attractive?'

'Yes. Louche. Like my mother – who also found him attractive – I have a liking for the louche. I'm louche myself. Always have been. I remembered ogling Fielding, rubbing myself up against him, when I was a tiny child. Oh yes. It had to be Fielding Gray.'

'And Canteloupe agreed?'

'Delighted. Fielding, you see, was one of the old gang.'

The couch stopped swinging. Starched ginger Daisy appeared, wheeling Sarum of Old Sarum in a pram. The little boat which had borne Baby and Jo-Jo alone together over the ocean had come back to a familiar haven.

'Will you be feeding His Lordship here, My Lady, or shall I be taking him upstairs?'

A breeze of evening blew across the Rose Garden.

Jean-Marie Guiscard appeared.

'My typewriter riband has twisted again,' he said. 'Jo-Jo, please come and mend it.'

129

'Time to go in,' Baby said.

'Never mind. We have all summer.'

'Hush, my darling. The gods may be listening. They deprecate presumption in their creatures.'

At Oudenarde House it was time for Preparation. Members of the privileged VIth Form, among whom was Marius Stern, did their Preparation in the VIth Form Study, under the genial supervision of Mr Walter ('Wally' or 'Bunter') St George. The convention was that the first half hour of the period set aside for prep. should be spent by all in actually doing it, but that after that any boy who had finished his work should be free to ask Mr St George questions which related to 'General Knowledge'. The almost inevitable result, foreseen with relish both by master and pupils, was an informed session of gossip, comprehensive in *esprit* though governed by certain polite conventions of idiom.

This evening, 'Please sir, I've been reading *The Persian Boy*,' said scrofulous Roseworm ma., 'on your recommendation.'

'Suck up, suck up,' giggled pretty little tow-haired Pitts, and pursed his lips like a rose-bud.

'You said, sir,' continued Roseworm, 'that we would get a vivid idea from this book of Alexander's expeditions, but that we weren't to pay much attention to a character called Bagoas.'

'So of course Wormwood has been thinking of nothing else,' said Marius grouchily.

'And talking of nothing else,' said blithe Palairet, smiling at Wally St George as if every foot of his huge circumference gave him (Palairet) more pleasure than the foot before. 'He says that early in the book something was *done* to Bagoas which made him a eunuch, but that Bagoas was still able to get pleasure when he met Alexander later on.'

'The point being, sir,' said Roseworm, 'that you told us that people were castrated and turned into eunuchs like Bagoas just so that they shouldn't get any pleasure and could safely be left in charge of all the women. But if Bagoas could get pleasure with Alexander, he couldn't have been a proper eunuch.'

'Bagoas was lucky,' said Wally. 'Sometimes they took the whole lot off, do you see, sometimes just the testicles. Sometimes they only *disconnected* the testicles. Now, what comes out of the testicles, the semen, you see, makes babies: but testicles or no testicles *other* things come out of *other* glands to help the semen on its way, and it is the emission or ejaculation of *all* these things that makes men feel pleasure. So obviously, even if there isn't any semen to be emitted there could still be a lot of pleasure from the emission of everything else. Perhaps that is what happened to Bagoas.'

'But surely,' Roseworm ground on, 'if he could get pleasure from doing it they wouldn't have wanted him in with the women – and he *was* in with the women, sir – because even if he couldn't make them have babies they wouldn't have wanted him to do it with them at all.'

'The ladies might,' snickered Pitts.

'But not the Court Chamberlain or whoever was responsible. Surely, sir, they would have ensured that all the glands which might give pleasure were removed from Bagoas and not just the testicles.'

'Perhaps the chap who did the operation on Bagoas didn't take away as much as he was meant to,' mused Palairet. 'Perhaps he was too decent.'

'They do say it has a lot to do with the blood vessels,' said Walter.

'Or wanting to pee,' grated Marius. 'Disgusting, that's all.'

'Tee-hee,' commented Pitts, and pouted.

'My old pater,' beamed Palairet, 'says just to take it all as it comes.'

'Tee-hee,' commented Pitts again.

'A wise man, your pater,' said Wally.

'What I want to know,' said Roseworm, savaging a ripe pimple with a dirty finger nail, 'is exactly what Bagoas and Alexander *did*.'

'Always leave something for next time,' said Walter as he rolled towards the door. 'Hands and hair, please, gentlemen. Prayers in five minutes, do you see.'

Jeremy Morrison was dining at Luffham. In his father's absence, he occupied the chair at the head of the table, under the Orpen portrait of his grandfather. The Chamberlain was in waiting.

'An unexpected pleasure, Master Jeremy, to see you here. Did you tell your father you were coming?'

'I wrote him a note yesterday,' said Jeremy, 'saying that I wished to spend a night here *en passant*.'

'Had you sent me too such a note,' said the Chamberlain, 'you might have eaten a better dinner.'

'Thank you, Chamberlain, the dinner is very well as it is.'

'That is not quite what I meant, sir.'

'I know very well what you meant, Chamberlain.' Jeremy grinned up at the man, who was standing to attention, in the fashion proper to a soldier who is addressing his superior officer, under the portrait of Jeremy's dead mother. 'I'm very sorry, truly I am. The whole thing was decided on the spur of the moment. I meant to write to you, only I'd run out of stamps and would have missed the last post. I could have rung up, but somehow I never seemed to be anywhere near a telephone and when I did see a box the thing had been smashed up. Please don't be cross.'

'I'm not cross, Master Jeremy: only hurt. There's the telephone now.'

'I didn't hear anything.'

'You need a trained ear, sir, to hear it from this room.'

Jeremy rose swiftly to his feet, but the Chamberlain was out of the door before him.

'If it's for me – ' Jeremy called.

The Chamberlain bowed sternly from the door. Jeremy sat down heavily. He had given Carmilla and Theodosia the number in case they found out his examination results while he was away from Cambridge. The results were not due to be published until the following day, but often they were 'leaked' by kindly Tutors who in the know. Carmilla and Theodosia would be just the kind of people to detect such a leak, so this could be it.

Please, God, make it a First. I know it's only Prelims, but please make it a First. He told himself to pull himself together, that it was childish to care so much about the results of a mere exam, that he didn't really care, no, he didn't – *but what was taking the Chamberlain so long?* Carm or Thea would ask to speak to him straight away. Perhaps it wasn't Carm or Thea but something quite different. Oh, all right, God: then *let* it be something quite different.

The Chamberlain reappeared.

'A person styling himself the Provost's Secretary is on the telephone for you, Master Jeremy . . .'

'. . . Hullo, hullo . . . *Len*.'

'You in some kind of nut-house, boy? The guy that answered said that he was Chamberlain to the Household to the Hereditary Esquire of Luffham, and would I kindly address him by that title or not at all.'

'Old family servant. A bit funny up top.'

133

'Well, I got news for you, baby,' drawled Len. 'Carm told me where you were, and I would have let her do the telephoning, only there's a little appendix to this news that's best delivered by me personally.'

Oh God: don't say I've made a flop of it and they're taking away my room by the river.

'First off. You got a Two-One in your Prelims. No problem there. A First would have been much better but a Two-One's pretty well okay for an Exhibitioner in his first year – especially when there's a sweetener.'

'A sweetener?'

'Yep. When the examination results go up outside the Senate House tomorrow, there'll be a little notice alongside them saying that Jeremy Ulster Morrison has won the Kilmarnock Prize for a poem in Latin hexameters. Which is worth a small gold medal and a cheque for fifty.'

'Sweet Jesus Christ, Len, I'd almost forgotten I'd entered for the bloody thing.'

'Well, you just remember now, baby, and get ready to answer a few questions . . . because here comes that appendix I mentioned. A copy of your Prize Poem was sent, by courtesy, to the Provost, who showed it, by courtesy, to me . . . who showed it, by courtesy, to my old chum Ivor Winstanley, as Senior Latinist in Lancaster.'

'And was he impressed?'

'Very impressed, Jeremy babe, by the taste and skill which you showed in lifting lines from other people's work. Six lines from Calverley's Latin version of Milton's *Lycidas*, three lots of between two and seven lines from Milton's *Epitaph on Damon*, and a heap of nice fat phrases from some other cunt, who shoved into Latin *The Complete Works of Thomas Gray*. Any comment?'

'It's all in the game, Len. Anyone who writes Latin verses is always fishing useful phrases out of Ovid, Virgil, Horace – '

' – Yes, so I was told,' said Len, in what was now a

Cambridge super-drawl. 'Ovid, Virgil, Horace, it's fair play to steal from that lot because everyone knows *their* stuff, and so the judges can take cognizance of how much of it has been used and make allowance accordingly. But except for a few old-fashioned numbers like Winstanley, *not* many people have read Milton's *Epitaph on Damon,* still less Calverley's collections of Latin versions, and no one at all has opened Pringle's Latinization of Gray since the day it was published by Heffer in 1882. So you do see, baby boy, that it looks as if you've been a bit sneaky. At least half your fucking poem was written by all these other pricks.'

'What's going to happen?'

'Nothing. I've persuaded Winstanley to see it as a joke. He says that the judges are obviously such ignorant turds that they'll never find out. For Christ's sake, darling, what would you expect in the Space Age? The Latin Verse scene is Deadsville; it's no longer even set seriously for the Tripos. So there's just this one prize left; so the Faculty lets a pair of downtrodden and heavily married junior arseholes judge the thing at half a guinea a go, and they're not going to take time off from washing nappies in order to hunt for pilferage even if they were capable of spotting it, they're just going to take a quick sniff at the entries and pick out the one that smells best – not difficult in this case, as yours was the only one. And if they *should* ever find out they've been conned, they're going to keep as quiet as little pink mice about it for fear of losing face, should they have any. So you've got nothing to worry about, sweetheart. Congratters.'

'Congratters on what? You don't seem to regard it as a very laudable achievement.'

'It'll look pretty enough in the score book, lovie. Kilmarnock Gold Medallist – it'll more than make up for your not getting a First. So that's all the news, doll, and now it's paying time.'

'Paying for what?'

'This expensive telephone call on the college, and my good offices with Ivor Winstanley. First a question to be answered. You're not running off, are you? I mean, this vanishing into the wilds of Norfolk bit: you're not going to cut loose for the vacation and welsh on Ptoly Tunne?'

'No, Len, I promise,' said Jeremy. 'I am here at home for one night . . . to settle some personal affairs. This I shall do tomorrow morning, after which I shall return to Cambridge for the College Ball and to await Mr Tunne's summons.'

'Good. It'll come any minute now. He's decided to ask Carmilla and Theodosia at the same time as you.'

'Oh, goodie-goodie.'

'Now you listen to me, boy. *No goodie-goodies* is strictly the message. Here is the second instalment you pay me for being on your side today. *No games of conkers with Carmilla*, not at Ptoly's place: otherwise Theodosia might find out and get upset . . . and upset a lot of other people, including her Daddy. It's one thing your having Carmilla in the College where your squeals of passion get swamped in the general hullabaloo of the whole damn cat-house. But Ptoly's pad, though very big, is also very quiet, and the least little tweak of a bedspring carries half way to Peterborough. So no fol-de-rol in the Fenlands. Right?'

'If you say so, Len.'

'I do say so, lover boy, and here's one smacking good-night kiss for our gorgeous new Gold Medallist.'

The personal affairs which had brought Jeremy to Norfolk did not detain him at Luffham but took him a few miles overland to Broughton Staithe, on the coast. Here, as Jeremy had discovered by telephoning Stern & Detterling,

Fielding Gray was spending a few days out of London at his house by the sea marshes at the end of the golf course.

Jeremy parked his Morris 1000 (an eighteenth birthday present from his mother) at the inland end of a sandy track and walked toward the sea. After a while he came to the golf course, turned right as instructed in the village, and walked down a fairway towards a high platform green which evidently marked the turning point of the course, for beyond it lay only sharp-grassed sand dunes which descended into a country of criss-cross ditches, tall thick reeds, and occasional meadows of the colour and apparent texture of moss.

Just before Jeremy reached the platform green, he saw, on his right, what must be Fielding's house, a structure of black pine, two storeys high, with a steep roof of green slate. Coming out of this affair, by a glass door which led on to a verandah, was Fielding Gray himself, reading a folded newspaper and looking cross. Uncertain quite how to proceed, Jeremy waved from the fairway and called, 'Ahoy there!' At this Fielding looked up, looked even crosser and then rather thoughtful, and finally beckoned Jeremy, with his whole arm, to approach his precinct. This entailed walking through a lot of very dewy rough, towards a small gate in the wired fence which lined the bottom of Fielding's unkempt garden. For his part, Fielding threw down the paper, descended some sagging wooden steps from the verandah, walked down a path which proceeded, with some diffidence, through waist-high feather grasses, and met Jeremy at the gate.

'Good morning, sir,' said Jeremy in his politest voice.

'Good morning to you, sir,' Fielding said. 'Don't tell me, it's coming. You were pointed out to me at Lancaster in April . . . Peter Morrison's younger son, called . . .'

'. . . Jeremy.'

'Jeremy. Well, Jeremy Morrison, and what can I do for you, in my way?'

'Tell me the secret of eternal life.'

'Rather a strong order. "If there were dreams to sell, What would you buy? Some cost a passing bell, Some a light sigh . . ." Enough of this nonsense. I am now going for a walk. You may accompany me if you wish, and on condition you talk sense. Very well; you may begin.'

As Fielding led the way through the dewy rough and across the fairway, and thence along a ridge towards some low sand dunes (beyond which was visible the slowly stirring Wash), Jeremy said: 'I saw you at the christening, and at the party afterwards. I knew who you were, of course, because my father had spoken of you and I have seen photos of you in the *Sunday Times*. And a friend of mine, called Theodosia Salinger, said your book on Conrad was very perceptive – perverse but perceptive, Theodosia said.'

'Nice to hear. We aim to please.'

'Well, when I saw you in the flesh, I thought, the thing about him, to judge from the look on his face, is that he's a free man.'

'Aren't we all, in this country?'

'No. We have nagging parents, clinging girl-friends, demanding colleges, scolding bank managers, and, in some cases such as my own, a heritage which will be forced upon us and which we very much wish to avoid.'

'And so you can, along with the rest of it. Take a cheap flight to India, remove all your clothes, and sit in the street with a begging bowl over your private parts. It's called renouncing the world. Though whether you will actually feel more *free* as a result I am inclined to doubt.'

They passed a crumbling mass of cement, twisted about with chains of rusted iron.

'Gun emplacements,' said Fielding Gray. 'Left over from the 1939 War.'

'I love ruins,' said Jeremy. 'All ruins. Oh for Hubert

138

Robert or a Joseph Vernet to paint these. Just about their scale.'

Fielding too loved the ruined gun emplacements, among which he walked for hours whenever he was at Broughton. Wittingly or not, Jeremy had said the right thing.

'To revert,' Fielding said. 'When you saw me at Lancaster, you thought: there is a man who is free – who, that is to say, does *not* have nagging parents, clinging girl-friends, demanding colleges, scolding bank managers (I trust I have the list right), or heritages which will be forced upon him?'

'Yes. A man who has got out of all that – but *not* by taking to the street as a beggar. A man who has somehow rid himself of the annoyances and strictures of the world and yet continues hugely to enjoy its amenity. A man who has it both ways.'

'And this you regard as the secret of eternal life?'

'That was an exaggeration, of course. But I do regard it as a very neat trick to be going on with.'

They passed a gun emplacement with a yawning mouth.

'Hubert Robert would have put a peasant whore in there,' said Jeremy, 'trying to drum up our custom as we passed.'

'I hope she would have cleaned away those turds,' said Fielding, feeling quite light-hearted at the compliments which Jeremy was paying him. 'So what you've come to find out is how one has one's cake and eats it?'

'That's about it. Mind you, I don't mind a bit of hard work. Rewards which one has earned are far the sweetest. What I want to do without is all the social *impedimenta*.'

'Clinging girl-friends and the rest?'

'Right. My own girl-friends are all right at the moment. But what does one do if they do start clinging? That was the sort of question, I thought at the christening, to which you'd know the answer.'

'And so I do,' said Fielding Gray, 'though I don't think it will have much appeal for you. It is very largely a matter of patience and common sense. You rid yourself of incommodious parents by waiting until they are dead. You avoid having possessive girl-friends by going only to whores. You satisfy your demanding college by doing the work which it very reasonably requires of you. And you anticipate the scolding of bank managers by ensuring that there should always be ample or at least adequate funds in your account.'

'Oh,' said Jeremy. 'It doesn't sound much like freedom to me.'

'Because by freedom you mean anarchy . . . If your kind of freedom obtained, there would be no pleasure to be had from the world because there would be no rules and no framework, and therefore no security in which to enjoy that pleasure. There must be rules – and there must be *rule*. The secret which you seek, Jeremy Morrison, lies in learning to accept both rules and rule with equanimity, and in training yourself to obey them with the least possible inconvenience.'

'Ah. Now you seem to be saying something.'

'You think so? Although I use the anodyne phrase "with the least possible inconvenience", I assure you that that usually means "with very considerable inconvenience". How else should it be? Does one remove importunate tax-gatherers by waving a wand? Or avoid obligations just by gliding away from them?'

'I must say, you looked to me – and you still look – as if you might know a stroke or two in that line.'

'If I do, they have all come from very long and painful practice. I've only one thing to tell you, Jeremy: you've just got to sit it out with the rest of us. But the good news is that if you use your eyes, ears and wits while sitting it out, instead of snivelling about injustice or fatuously chasing up blind alleys in the hope of finding short cuts – if you just sit still and let the thing go on and watch the way of it – then you have an excellent chance of coming, at least temporarily, to moderate terms with reality, which is the nearest that any of us ever comes to freedom.'

'All right. But this inheritance of mine, Luffham by Whereham. How do I get out of that?'

'Why should you want to get out of it? It's a fine estate. I spent a very happy week there with your father when we were boys just a little younger than you are now. I was much struck by everything he showed me.'

'I don't want to spend my life as a farmer. My old man's sick of it, I know, and I rather think he's getting ready to turn it over to me – to save himself the bother of supervising it and keep all his time and energy for politicking in Westminster.'

'Just sit quiet, as I said, and *let the thing go on.*'

For some time they had been walking by the sea. Now Fielding turned inland, through the dunes and back towards the golf course.

'The place is entailed on me,' said Jeremy. 'In case of Nickie's continuing to be mad – and he will continue to be mad – the place is entailed on me as second son, and no amount of sitting quiet will get me out of it.'

'Precisely. The place is entailed on you; you can't refuse it. Accept that as given. Then tell yourself that even so nobody can object if you adopt a profession of your liking, as your father has done. Tell yourself that revenue from the estate will in any case be considerable, that this will enable you to follow your chosen career with integrity and discrimination, and that there are worse landlords than absentee landlords, provided the latter make conscientious arrangements.'

'But,' said Jeremy, 'they'll all expect me *to be there* when it comes to me. The Chamberlain, the tenants –'

' – The Chamberlain?'

' – Old servant going gaga who likes to be called that. He came to us from Canteloupe years ago, having been *his* soldier servant since the Indian Mutiny. The Chamberlain

141

and all of them, they'll think I'm letting them down if I do what you suggest. They're not very happy about the way my father goes on, but at least his excuse for being away so much is the House of Commons, which makes it just all right. But if I became a barrister or a diplomat or a globe-trotting novelist like you – don't you see, sir, the excuse just wouldn't be strong enough and they'd think I'd betrayed them.'

'A soldier? They'd have to pass that.'

'Not in peace time. Or not for more than a very few years at most.'

'Pity. Your father was a good soldier.'

'I'm not sure that I'd be. Anyway, it just isn't on. Sooner or later, sir, I'm doomed either to take over at Luffham or to be considered a deserter by my people.'

'Then the thing is quite clear,' said Fielding. 'You must go to Luffham when you are called and take with you a copy of Descartes.'

'Descartes? Cartesian co-ordinates and all that? What's he got to do with it?'

'Descartes was a philosopher as well as a mathematician. He taught that happiness lies in not wanting what we cannot have and in making ourselves desire what we can or must have.'

'A strong order – to use your own expression.'

'Yes. But this of course would be the real freedom. I spoke just now of coming "to moderate terms with reality". That may serve, but it's only second best, you know. Do what Descartes recommends, and you have beaten reality at its own game. Dante made rather the same point from a different angle: "In His will is our peace."'

'Now you have surprised me, Major Gray.'

They squelched through the rough to Fielding's gate.

'I must drive to London, Jeremy. I must go to a dinner party given by a man called Blessington – another old friend of your father, by the way. I could give you – I should be very happy to give you – a lift back to Luffham, or to Cambridge if you go there. In fact I'd be most grateful if you could drive my car for me that far. Driving tires me these days.'

'I'm afraid I have my own car with me, sir. We're not meant to keep them at Cambridge, but I've got a tame garage man in the Milton Road.'

'Ah. It would have been pleasant to go together.'

'We still can, sir. If you'd like to leave your car here and come back by train, when you come, I'll happily drive you to London and then double back to Cambridge.'

'You are a good, kind boy, Jeremy Morrison. But I must have my own car with me, as I'm taking some young friends to dine in it.'

'Surely – a taxi?'

'And also taking them for a run in the country on Sunday. But I hope we shall meet again soon, Jeremy.'

'I hope so, sir.'

'Say "Fielding".'

'Fielding.'

'Go well to Cambridge, Jeremy.'

'Go well to London, Fielding, and with God thereafter.'

'Ah,' said Fielding, as the tears of pleasure rose to his eye. 'You have learned how to take leave in the proper fashion.'

'My father taught me. He himself learned from an Indian, he told me, an Indian officer under whom he served as a cadet. Captain Gilzai Khan, the man was called. A prince in his country, my father told me, with manners to match. Go well now, Fielding Gray . . .'

'So that's how it was?' said Ivan Blessington when Fielding Gray had concluded his narrative – the official and orthodox version – of Vanessa Salinger's death. 'Pretty gruesome affair. Thank goodness she was knocked unconscious as soon as she hit the bottom. They were quite sure of that?'

'So I have always heard.'

'I mean, people can fall a very long way and still be conscious at the end of it. I remember a nasty accident on a summer training scheme. A newly joined cornet fell over a cliff. A good two hundred feet. There were chaps at the bottom who'd already gone down the way you were meant to go down – on a rope – including a pretty dim officer called Piers Bungay – '

' – I had him in my squadron as a subaltern for a time – '

' – Well, by now he was a captain. Hadn't a clue what to do. The cornet, whose thigh bones had been driven up through his pelvis but who could still talk and think, explained to Piers that he must improvise a stretcher, from rope if there was nothing else, and send a man along the shore to telephone for an ambulance and tell it where to meet the stretcher party. But all Piers could do was to repeat, over and over again, "It's too bad, old chap; but why couldn't you come down the proper way?" At length a junior non-commissioned officer took over – too late. Not that they could have saved the poor fellow anyhow, but you see what I'm getting at? If Vanessa had still been conscious, like that cornet, when she was at the bottom of that well . . .'

'. . . Horrid,' said Betty Blessington. 'But as it was . . . I don't quite see why her husband was so affected by it all.

144

A nasty shock, yes, but not enough to send a man into an asylum for several years.'

'I don't know,' said Fielding. 'You're walking through a wood and your wife just disappears into the earth . . . it must have been – well – rather bizarre. Somehow we expect people to fall over cliffs from time to time, but to fall down a concealed well . . .'

'. . . *Not* a kosher thing to happen,' said Ivan. 'Definitely unfair. And of course he was always obsessed with her. She led him every kind of dance, and she was rotten to those girls, but still he persisted in adoring her.'

'You said the other day,' said Betty, 'that she was a "grand girl".'

'When a chap says that,' said Ivan, 'all he means is that you've only got to whistle and her knickers fall off.'

'A very good thing Margaret Cartenay couldn't come – if you're going to talk like that,' Betty said. 'I thought we should have a fourth,' she explained to Fielding, 'and I asked an old friend of mine who's recently been divorced and needs cheering up. But she rang up this morning to say that she had summer 'flu – whatever that may be.'

'She's always got something wrong with her,' said Ivan. 'Dismal bitch. Either her tubes have got twisted or her tits are growing inwards or she's sprouting a clitoris in her navel – '

' – Really Ivan – '

' – A real health freak and as prim as a post with it. I thank God on bended knee that she couldn't come,' said Ivan, pouring himself a very full glass of wine, 'and so would Fielding, if he knew what he'd been spared.'

'Nevertheless, we owe Major Gray an apology for not inviting anyone to meet him.'

'There's no one I should have wanted to see,' said Fielding, 'except for a few that are dead.'

'I think it was a mean thing to do,' said Caroline at nursery supper upstairs, 'to wish no runs for Marius.'

'He had been very nasty about Tessa,' Rosie Stern said. 'And he tried to hit me. But it isn't true, what he thinks. He thinks . . . that I have some kind of power . . . to back up my wish. Of course I haven't. Nor the will. It was all just a bit of spite – one bit of spite in return for another. Whatever's gone wrong with Marius's batting, it's nothing to do with me.'

'Have you told him this?'

'Yes. I wrote to him at once, the same evening I heard from him.'

'But the trouble is,' said Tessa in her husky little voice, 'that he still isn't getting any runs. He rang Rosie up yesterday. Do you suppose that if you've wished a thing hard enough . . . even if it was only spite . . . that thing can actually happen?'

'No,' said Jakki. 'None of this wishing has anything to do with it. He's just out of form. It happens quite often.' She hunched her shoulders and perused an imaginary newspaper. 'I see P. W. Bum of Northants has laid another egg,' she mimicked her father. 'Wretched fellow's having a bad patch.'

'But Marius doesn't know he's having a bad patch,' said Rosie. 'He still thinks it's me.'

'But you said you wrote straight away to say it wasn't.'

'Oh yes. And told him when he rang up yesterday.'

'Then he *must* know,' said Jakki, 'that he's having a bad patch.'

Rosie still seemed unconvinced.

'The thing about Rosie's brother,' said Tessa, 'is that he

146

thinks he's too marvellous to run in and out of form like ordinary people. If he does badly, something or somebody else has got to be to blame.'

'Then the only way you can convince him that it's nothing to do with you,' said Jakki, fetching a bowl of tinned peaches from the top of the toy chest, 'is to swear by something you both hold sacred.'

'Marius doesn't hold anything sacred,' said Tessa, 'except himself.'

'Then by something which he knows Rosie holds sacred.'

'My friendship for Tessa . . ?'

'No,' said Tessa. 'He doesn't like your friendship for me. He doesn't trust me.'

'Nevertheless, if he knew I hold it sacred . . .'

'I don't think he'd understand that.'

'I know what,' said Jakki. 'Swear by your mother's honour. By the honour of your mother who is also his. We all have to hold that sacred.'

Rosie looked very doubtful and frowned heavily. But, 'All right,' she said at length. 'Why not?'

'I suppose they dug her out in the end,' said Ivan.

They were back on Vanessa Salinger.

'I suppose so. I never really went into that,' Fielding said.

'I'll leave you to your port,' said Betty.

'No. Stay with us, old girl.'

'I'm sick of the sound,' said Betty, 'of that bloody Salinger woman.'

She rose and walked out with long strides.

'It takes a woman,' said Ivan, 'to be jealous of a corpse.'

'Did you ever have it off with Vanessa?'

'No. Just a quick feel in the loo at somebody's party.'

'What on earth were you doing in the loo together?'

'She'd invited me in there with her. She said she wanted to watch a man peeing. Typical Vanessa.'

'Did you oblige?'

'Oh yes. Though I suddenly got such a horn that it went all over the wall.'

'What happened then?'

'Someone knocked on the door and said he was desperate. Vanessa wanted to stay there and take no notice, but I thought that was too tough on the poor chappie and bad manners to hog the loo at a party. So out we went – straight into the arms of that old queen Jonathan Gamp, who started clacking like a peacock.'

'This was before she married Donald, or after?'

'Oh, long before, back in the late forties. I think that once she married him she settled down a bit. Not altogether, perhaps, but at least she gave up going to the loo with people in public. Where she really behaved badly, or so everyone always said, was over those girls. She agreed with Donald to adopt them, and then treated them like dirt.'

'They seem to have turned out all right,' Fielding said.

'I heard something about them the other day. It seems that Tom Llewyllyn told Baby who told Canteloupe who told me – at the Regimental Dinner last week, first time he's attended for years, you'd better start coming too – *anyway*, according to Canteloupe according to Baby according to Tom, those two Salinger girls are going to be experimented on by that fat fellow who was at the christening, Ptolemaeos Tunne.'

'*Experimented on?*'

'Well . . . questioned in a special field. I suppose it's all quite harmless really, an investigation into the way the mind links up with the brain, that sort of thing . . . but there is just one aspect of it which is causing minor worry.'

'The questions may turn rather too personal . . . even offensive?'

'No. He can be trusted not to offend. He has an easy way with the young – according to his niece, who gives him a first-rate chitty for looking after her when she was orphaned.'

'Does she now?' Fielding remembered the way (observed by him from across the room) in which Ptolemaeos had kissed Jo-Jo good-bye at the christening. 'Perhaps he has the gift of being offensive without offending,' Fielding said. 'That always gets the best chitties of all.'

'Perhaps. But on the face of it the bother – if there is a bother – is about a man called Sheraton, who wrote a book, oh, well before the First World War, called *Man on His Being* – *the* book, apparently, that set Ptolemaeos Tunne off on his present line of research. It's all to do with the working of the brain cells, and how these communicate with some kind of higher faculty which Sheraton took to be non-bodily mind, or perhaps the soul. No one seemed much impressed at the time, and shortly after the publication of his book Sheraton faded off the scene. Now, Provost Llewyllyn's secretary, an inquisitive bugger called Len something, thought it might be interesting to find out what happened to Sheraton, and by digging around in forgotten memoirs and so forth, he discovered that for a year or two after his book was published Sheraton had continued with his research, and had then suddenly taken to drink – having previously been a total abstainer – and was dead within a twelve-month.'

'Disappointment at neglect of his work?'

'No. There were *some* circles in which his book had been praised, and there were signs that several influential people were beginning to take notice, if only adverse. In the end the whole matter was dropped (not without relief, one gathers) as soon as Sheraton was dead: but the point is that his death was *not* caused by slight or neglect. All the signs

149

are . . . that as he went on with his research . . . he found out something which he didn't at all care for. So little, indeed, did he care for it that he shut up shop forthwith and took to the bottle.'

'This Sheraton – did he want to believe in the non-bodily mind or the soul?'

'Very much, apparently.'

'Well, perhaps he discovered that neither was there, that all his work had been the pursuit of a Will-o'-the-wisp, an *ignis fatuus.*'

'Perhaps he discovered just that. But perhaps he discovered something else . . . something *about* the mind or the soul . . . and *this* was what sent him on the booze.'

'Something nasty, you think?'

'If I'm right, whatever it was made him drink his way into his box in less than a year. Pretty fast going.'

'And so now they're afraid that Ptolemaeos Tunne might make the same discovery as Sheraton did – '

' – Whatever that might have been – '

' – And that he too might end up under a heap of gin bottles. I doubt it, Ivan. A very tough number, from the look of him. He'd face down the Devil.'

'But the people whom Tunne is going to catechize might be . . . more vulnerable . . . than he is.'

'So,' said Fielding, 'the worry is lest these investigations should lead to some psychic Grand Guignol which may prove too much for the participants.'

'Right.'

'Well, wherever they may lead, my money's on Ptolemaeos Tunne to hack his way out and come safe home.'

'And the Salinger girls? And anyone else Tunne uses? That's what worries Llewyllyn, you see.'

'Tom's a rationalist. He knows there's only one end the investigation can come to: the brain is the mind is the soul is the end of the whole matter. *That* won't worry the Salinger girls, or anybody else these days.'

'Perhaps Tom's not so sure in his old age. Or perhaps he thinks that even if that is the end of the whole matter, the journey there could nevertheless be . . . rather devious . . . if the pilot is Ptolemaeos Tunne.'

'Jakki,' said Caroline, after they were in bed and their mother had turned the light out, 'I don't think Rosie was too pleased with your idea.'

'What idea?'

'That she should swear to Marius she has no power to spoil his cricket *on their mother's honour*.'

'She's got to swear on *something* that will convince him. And she seemed to accept my suggestion. "Why not?" she said.'

'She still didn't like it.'

'Do you think,' said Jakki, 'that she thinks . . . that her mother *isn't* honourable?'

'I don't know what to think. I only know that for some reason she didn't like the idea. Perhaps she's got something . . . about her mother . . . on her mind.'

'Her mother's away.'

'Rosie could still have something to do with her . . . something not nice . . . on her mind.'

'Well, I've done my best,' said Jakki, 'and I dare say she'll have a go. She said she would. And that's really all that can be done for now.'

'But what is going to happen,' said dogged Caroline, 'if Marius just goes on and on doing badly?'

'I don't know,' said her sister miserably.

'Do you suppose Rosie could try wishing that he *should* make runs?'

'But she herself thinks – knows – that these wishes have no power and have nothing to do with it at all.'

'So she says. But Marius thinks otherwise. So if she told him she had wished that he *should* – '

' – It might not work and then we'd all be in a bigger mess than ever.'

Jakki sat up in bed and switched on her bedside light (intended for emergencies only).

'Marius has just been silly,' Jakki said, 'and the best we can hope for is that he will now stop. But you know what I think? I think that he really blames Tessa. After all, it was because of Tessa that Rosie made her wish in the first place. And Tessa herself said that Marius didn't trust her. I think that *he* thinks that Tessa is really behind it all and that Rosie is only her agent.'

'Why are you saying this?' said Caroline. 'Why should you know anything at all about what Marius thinks about Tessa or about anything else? You haven't seen him since that christening.'

'Do you remember what we talked about at the christening? You and me and Marius?'

'Not really. I was too busy looking at him.'

'Me, too. But I do remember that one of us – me, I think – mentioned Tessa's name. And when I did, Marius's face sort of sagged. For a moment he almost looked ugly – if that were possible. I think he's *afraid* of Tessa.'

'Then it's no good *Rosie* swearing she's not spoiled his cricket – not if it's Tessa he really blames?'

'I just don't know, Caro. It's all so silly, such nonsense, all so hopelessly *mixed up* that I just don't know how it can stop. But please God,' she breathed. 'Oh, please God, somehow or other let Marius make lots of lovely runs at his cricket.'

In Marius's dormitory the conversation turned on stamp collecting.

'My mother has written to me from Israel,' Marius said. 'The stamp's up for swaps.'

'Why don't you want it yourself?' said Roseworm.

'I think it's ugly. My mother says everything in Israel is ugly, except the Roman remains. Ugly deserts, ugly houses, she says, and a beastly swarm of boring, fanatical, ugly Jews all over the place.'

'Surely you are a Jew, Stern,' said Palairet in a firm, decent voice.

'No. My father is Jewish but not my mother.'

'Then you are half-Jewish,' said Palairet reasonably.

'No. To be a Jew you have to have a Jewish mother.'

'But if your father is a Jew,' said Palairet, persistent in the cause of truth, 'you must be, to some extent, Jewish.'

'I am *not* a Jew.'

'The best way to tell,' tittered wavy little Pitts, 'is to have a careful look and see whether he's elephant or acorn.'

'Yes,' said Roseworm. 'Mind you, it's not certain. Some people who aren't Jews are acorn.'

'But no one who is a Jew is elephant,' said Palairet ponderously.

'Come to think of it,' said Pitts, 'I've never seen Stern's. You see most people's, in the showers or somewhere, but somehow I've never seen Stern's.'

'Nor have I,' said Roseworm. 'What have you been hiding from us, Stern? Come on – let's have a look.'

'Don't be disgusting,' said Marius, glowing red in the dusk.

153

'Come on, Sternibug,' said Pitts, beginning to get out of bed. 'Just for me. Get it ready and I'll be right over.'

'Keep away from me, you yellow little piece of sossel.'

The vernacular was common among them; the tone of a malignity beyond their experience. Pitts, already out of bed, hesitated, then saved face by putting on his slippers and announcing that he had only been pretending and was really off to the shack.

'I don't think you need get so baity,' said Palairet to Marius. 'You never used to be like this, Stern. I've hardly heard you say anything friendly since the term began.'

'I was being perfectly friendly tonight. Offering to swap a stamp.'

'An ugly stamp.'

'There'll be nicer ones later. My mother and father will be in Cyprus soon, then Greece.'

'I've got a set celebrating Cyprus's independence,' Roseworm said.

Pitts came back from the shack.

'Wally's prowling about,' he said.

'It's after nine-thirty,' said Palairet. 'Time to stop talking. Good-night, you chaps.' Then softly to Marius in the next bed. 'Good-night, Stern. I know you didn't mean to be ratty. I expect it's a dreadful worry, having your parents so far away for so long.'

'They're often away. It isn't that.'

'Then what?'

'Oh – M.Y.O.B.,' said Marius, savage in his misery.

'You're sure it's all right to leave Da?' said Theodosia to Carmilla as they walked in St James's Park from the lake towards The Mall.

'Yes. We've been here several days and we shan't be gone for long. He likes us to come and go, Thea. He wouldn't want us to feel chained.'

'So that's all right. What do you suppose Mr Tunne is actually going to do to us?'

'Ask questions to reveal the way our minds work.'

'There must be more to it,' said Theodosia, 'than that.'

'Special questions, to distinguish between the mechanical responses of the brain and the thinking process of the mind. How the one sort of function sets off the other.'

The girls stood to attention in The Mall as the banner of the Blues went by.

'Was that a mechanical response or a thinking process?' enquired Theodosia as the blazing helms receded. 'If you ask me, it'll take more than Mr Tunne to tell the two apart. I think the whole thing's just an excuse to . . . handle people's personalities.'

'As a substitute for handling their persons? Len says it's all right.'

'I'm sure it is. It'll probably be very interesting. Nevertheless, I suspect that Ptolemaeos Tunne hasn't been entirely candid about his motives.'

'Perhaps he isn't too clear about them himself. Anyway, Jeremy will be there too,' Carmilla said, 'so it'll be fun.'

'Amen to that.'

As the days grew warmer and then hotter, Baby and Jo-Jo retreated from the Rose Garden and into a copse of lady-birch, called the 'Wilderness', which had a small pool at its centre fed by a stream from the lake. The copse stood alone in the middle of a meadow, half way between the house and the lake, on ground securely fenced off from trippers and just in view of the window at which Jean-Marie was typing out *La Demoiselle d'Arques*. Although he could not see them beneath the branches, it gave him great pleasure, Jean-Marie said, to think of them there. But neither he nor Canteloupe nor any of the servants (except for Daisy the nurse when bound thither with Sarum) ever intruded on what was understood by all to be a private place; and it was therefore with considerable surprise that Baby looked up from the backgammon board one morning to see Canteloupe advancing grimly through the undergrowth.

'Sorry, girls,' he said, 'but there's been some really shocking news and you'd better hear it.'

'Couldn't it have kept till lunch?' said Baby sourly.

'No. I shan't be here at luncheon. I've got to go to Kent: to Oudenarde House.'

'Marius?'

'Marius. He's half killed one of the other boys.'

'CANTY.'

'I mean it, darling. Apparently some of them were teasing him about his cricket. His top score for the season is seven, and his average is one-point-three-recurring. That was the great joke, Glinter said on the telephone. They all started chanting, "One-point-three-*recurring* . . . one-point-three-*recurring* . . ." About the fourth time round Marius took a back-hander at one of them and hit him in the throat.'

'Just temper,' said Jo-Jo. 'What little boys call a bait. Rage but no malice.'

'Yes, that's it,' Baby said, looking away from Jo-Jo and Canteloupe, remembering the punch at the christening.

'Let's hope so. Apparently the cricket master, fellow called Walter St George, arrived on the scene to stop the row but too late to stop Marius. I'll be hearing his account later. But in any case,' Canteloupe went on, 'Glinter can't keep Marius. The boy he hit bloody near died. They had to force a tube down his throat to keep it open.'

'You mean . . . *Marius will be expelled*?'

'Until the end of this term, at any rate. Provided his victim gets better, and provided Glinter can fudge things a bit when the dust has settled, and provided none of the parents object, he might be allowed back in the autumn . . . *if* we can convince him that Marius won't do it again. But that's the autumn. I've got to go and fetch him now.'

'Fetch him?'

'See to it all somehow. I got hold of Fielding Gray in London and persuaded him to join me down in Sandwich.'

'Why Fielding?' said Baby, flinching slightly.

'*One* place Marius might go to would be that hotel where his sister Rosie is staying. That's the obvious answer at first sight. In which case, quite a lot would depend on Fielding, who's the man of the household, so to speak.'

'Surely,' said Jo-Jo, 'Gregory and Isobel will have to be sent for. It's their job to cope with it all.'

'Marius must go somewhere until they get back.'

'Only a matter of hours by air.'

'That's just it,' said Canteloupe in a grating voice. 'I can't find them. According to the schedule which Gregory gave me, they should have been in the Hotel Ariadne in Heracleion for the last four days, having flown to Crete from Nicosia. So I rang the Ariadne. They hadn't arrived. Then I rang their hotel in Nicosia. They'd left there absolutely at the moment planned and driven off in a taxi towards the airport. So then I rang the Ariadne again. Had they perhaps given warning that they'd be late for some reason? No they hadn't, there was neither sight nor sign of them after four whole days, and could the Manager have my name and address, as I seemed to be connected with them, so that he could send me the bill for settlement. Bloody Greeks, I ask you.'

'Then you must check with the airports,' said Baby.

'What 'plane if any did they take from Nicosia? Did they actually arrive in Crete?'

'Darling heart,' said Canteloupe in a voice that had now turned brittle, 'I have been doing that for the last hour. Have you ever tried dealing with Greek airports? Greek *provincial* airports? No one knows anything but no one will admit to ignorance. All that any official will tell you is that *he* is far too important to be concerned with passenger lists. And it does not help,' said Canteloupe, 'that they disappeared several days ago.'

'So,' said Baby, 'what are we to do with Marius for what may be an indefinite period?'

'I never expected anything like this when I took on the *locum parentis*,' grumbled Canteloupe. 'That self-effacing little Rosie and blue-eyed cherub – '

' – Green-eyed – '

' – Just a manner of speaking. Anyway, I didn't expect it.'

'And now you've got it. Only two places Marius can go: London, with that Malcolm woman in Buttock's Hotel, or here.'

'Somehow,' said Canteloupe, 'I don't think Mrs Malcolm will fancy him much, just now, as company for her niece – or, come to that, for Rosie.'

'And I don't think,' said Baby, 'that I will fancy him as company for Tully.'

'Or, come to that,' said Jo-Jo, 'for Alexandre.'

'Good point, well taken. Anyhow,' said Canteloupe, 'I'll try it on with Fielding about Buttock's. Or Glinter may think of something.'

'Like keeping him after all?'

'Not if I go down on my bare knees,' said Canteloupe. '*That* was made very plain.'

158

At roughly the same time as Canteloupe was crossly telephoning the airport at Nicosia in his efforts to find Isobel and Gregory, Jeremy Morrison was walking on the lawn at the end of Ptolemaeos Tunne's garden.

On the other side of the hedge a raised path marched away between marshland on the left and the dank, rank earth of ploughed but fallow fields on the right. But on Jeremy's side of the hedge the sun shone on the short, dry grass, and a little summerhouse nestled under a beech tree. Finding the sun, even so early in the morning, uncomfortably hot, Jeremy turned into the summerhouse, sat down on a deck chair, lit a cigarette, and started to do his sums.

Item: his debts to tradesmen in Cambridge were paid; and if he set aside enough to meet his college account for the previous term, he still had well over £1,200 in hand, thanks to the generosity of Theodosia.

Item: on July 1 his quarterly allowance of £750 would be paid into his account with his bankers, Messrs Coutts.

Item: presumably the University Chest would soon disgorge the £50 which came with the Kilmarnock Gold Medal.

Comment so far: situation highly satisfactory. The summer could be spent in agreeable places (details later) where he would put in a little easy and dignified reading in preparation for Part One of the Classical Tripos next year, and would also peruse a variety of literary and philosophical works in English, French, and Italian (the two latter tongues in translation), a suitable list of which he would obtain from Ptolemaeos Tunne. How agreeable it was, he reflected, to be a proper undergraduate at leisure to cultivate his faculties rather than a grotty student who must spend his vacation clearing up lopped limbs and excreta in a public hospital. Then he recalled a remark of Len's, to the effect that the gods were apt to punish self-congratulation of this nature but would probably forgive it if tastefully toadied. 'Thank you,' he said, 'Zeus and all you other immortal gods, for offering me so pleasing a prospect.'

Having settled his money, he selected the next topic for calculation, which was how long he should seek to stay here in the Fens. Ptolemaeos had stated no limits either way: presumably the thing to do was to hang about as long as he felt he was being useful and did not become bored . . . or until Ptolemaeos gave him a hint to be off. On the whole Jeremy was in no hurry to be off. His quarters were comfortable, the wines superb, the food eccentric but amusing (though he'd been a bit doubtful about the slugs at dinner last night), and Carmilla and Theodosia (to say nothing of Ptolemaeos) were as ever excellent company. For the time being Ptolemaeos was experimenting only with the girls (he was in session with Theodosia at that very moment); his own turn would come later. Well, so be it. He didn't think he wanted to be left behind for long after the girls had gone, but he wasn't prepared to take too stiff a line even about that. Just sit quietly and let the thing go on, as Fielding Gray had advised him in another context.

This reflection brought him to the week's Starred Question: what was he to do about Fielding Gray? When he had visited him in Broughton Staithe, he had been genuinely anxious to hear what Fielding had to say about his problems because he was genuinely convinced that Fielding would come up with something worth listening to (as on the whole he had). But the visit had also been one of reconnaissance. From the time he had first set eyes on Fielding (in Lancaster Chapel, as Fielding snarled at the Bishop about the form of service) Jeremy had felt that he had some part to play in his own life, that he could be (to put the matter bluntly) of use. He could provide worldly information of the kind which Jeremy's father, though well qualified to dispense, rather priggishly chose to withhold; he might assist with funds if fresh crises arose; he might encourage Jeremy, should his career take a literary turn (and why should it not?), with literary advice and privileged introductions; last, and not perhaps least, it seemed to Jeremy that in a rather ponderous way (call it 'mature' to be polite) Fielding was very tolerable company. It also seemed he found Jeremy to be so too. So: what was to be done about Fielding Gray?

Thinking it over, Jeremy decided that Fielding was a potential asset rather than a present one. He had no particular need of him for the time being. Best keep him on ice. Fielding would be all the better disposed if he did not take advantage of the good impression, which he had evidently made, to wish himself on to Fielding (for whatever purpose) immediately. Let Fielding understand that he, Jeremy, had other fish to fry.

Appendical Question: what should Jeremy do if at any stage Fielding should show signs of becoming 'keen'? To judge from the gossip that Jeremy had heard of Fielding, this was most unlikely, these days, but not, if one considered past performance, absolutely impossible. And then again, as Jeremy had found often enough, his large round face and large round limbs were attractive to middle-aged men of a sentimental type; and Fielding was incontestably middle-aged and sentimental. Well, thought Jeremy, as to that, it must all depend on what the general state of play might be when and if it happened, and on how much was required of him. He could draw up a more precise tariff later. For the second time that morning he found himself remembering Fielding's own advice: just sit quiet and let the thing go on. You really couldn't do better than that, Jeremy thought, especially on a warm, drowsy morning in

161

the Fens, with the cicadas (or whatever they might be) chirruping huskily from the marshes.

He took from his pocket the first volume of Scott-Moncrieff's translation of *Remembrance of Things Past*. 'You better take a dekko at Proust, laddie,' Len had said some weeks before. 'The French themselves think he's lousy, but for some reason the mandarins are looped on him in England.'

'"For a long time I used to go to bed early,"' Jeremy read aloud. '"Sometimes, when I had put out my candle, my eyes would close so quickly that I had not even time to say to myself, 'I'm falling asleep.'"' In such a way did Jeremy's eyes close now, lulled by the prose and the cicadas, so that when Carmilla came to find him half an hour later, his nose and mouth were gently bubbling from the depths of his deck chair.

Since Canteloupe had gone to Sandwich, Baby had decreed a picnic. Jean-Marie had been allowed, just this once, into the copse of lady-birch, while Sarum and his nurse had also been invited. But as soon as the cold lobster had been eaten, Jean-Marie had shown almost insulting eagerness to return to his typewriter and Sarum had started to make a boring row about what Daisy the nurse opined was a new tooth.

'What a relief they've all gone,' Baby said to Jo-Jo. And then, picking her back teeth with her right forefinger, 'I don't at all like the sound of all this about Marius. Something or other has turned him really vicious.'

'Murderous.'

'Of course,' said Baby, 'he has bad blood through Isobel. So do I, through my own mother. *Their* mother was a pathological bolter, among other things, and their father, my grandfather Turbot, was pretty odd too – at any rate towards the end. I wish I knew how much heredity had to do with it all. One of the reasons why Canty and I chose Fielding Gray to father Tullius was that although Fielding himself was a bit out of the ordinary his background and ancestry – in so far as he had any – were as humdrum as they could be.'

'There's always something tucked away in a drawer or a cupboard somewhere,' said Jo-Jo.

'So Fielding once said. In his own case, he told me, his father was a sadistic brute and his mother a bloodsucker – humdrum and boring as they might be on the face of it. That was when I was trying to persuade him. He was very difficult, you know: I felt quite hurt. He started off by saying he was impotent. Then he said he didn't approve of deceit; if Canty couldn't get his own heir he shouldn't have one. Then he said that morally it would be paedophilia: he'd known me since I was in nappies and even before. Then he said it would be tantamount to incest, as he'd once had an affair with my mother – who had taken me to Broughton Staithe for the sea air one summer while Poppa was busy or away, and found Fielding living in a house by the golf course there. Apparently she used to leave me in our bed-and-breakfast joint (she was far too mean, my mother, to go to a proper hotel) between nine o'clock in the evening and ten, when the miserable place was locked up for the night, and go cantering off down the fairways for a rattling short-timer with Fielding. Oh, come on, I said to him, what difference does that make now? And surely, I said, it would be jolly interesting to compare my assets and performance with my mother's. This obviously excited him, but he pretended to be cross. He wanted nothing to do with it, he said. It was all sheer laziness, of course. Even that bit about my mother hadn't made him keen enough to risk trouble and inconvenience. He'd got to the point where he just couldn't be bothered. You know what I had to do in the end?'

'I'm dying to . . .'

'I had to get Canty to remind him of their old regimental motto, "*Res Unius, Res Omnium*", which means that they're all meant to help each other out. So at last he agreed. But then things got even more difficult, because it turned out that he was up to just about everything except actually fucking. I'm not saying it wasn't good fun; he knew a lot of amusing and erudite tricks; but it wasn't, you see, to the point.'

'Couldn't you have done – you know – artificial insemination?'

'No. Canty wouldn't have it. He wanted the thing done the proper way, he said, just as he wanted the proper words at the christening later. Anyway, no one must know, and some busybody might have found out – if we'd turned up at the Institute or whatever with a jug of Fielding's stuff and said it was Canty's. You know how *knowing* all those matrons and people are. So . . . somehow I had to coax Fielding into getting it up. The trouble was that though he wasn't in the least impotent (he was indeed copious), he found it almost impossible to get his thing what the French call *dur*. Properly *dur*, I mean. It was one of those long flappy jobs which kind of skid off the target the whole time. And all the drink he would keep having didn't help.'

'Where was all this going on?' Jo-Jo enquired.

'That was another problem. In the end we couldn't go anywhere close at hand because one of us or both might be recognized. Canty and I get photographed quite a lot, you know – Cant-Fun and all that. And Fielding's face is quite well known in certain circles – once seen never forgotten. So no lovely jollies at Skindles or the Connaught. Canty suggested a beastly French town called St-Étienne, but Fielding and I drew the line at that. So eventually we settled for St Tropez out of season. No one would know us there and then, and French hotels don't make you show passports these days. So there we were, as I told you, doing all kinds of sporty things, except the one thing we were there to do. I tell you, darling, I was getting desperate – and I was terrified that Fielding might get bored or tired and dry up on me. Then one afternoon I had an inspiration. I remembered that even in his "*Noli me tangere*" days, before Canty persuaded him to take the job on, he'd always started breathing rather heavily when my mother came up in the conversation. So: "Tell me," I said, on this particular afternoon in St Tropez, "what kind of noise did my mother make when she was coming?" And that did it. That question, coming from me, really did the trick. Or rather, only just did the trick: because Fielding's *dur*-ness only lasted just long enough to get him stabled. But once I had him there I held on to him for dear life, and since, as I say, he had a copious flow, the job was done, and luckily it took, the very first and one and only time, and now we've got little Tullius to prove it.'

'Suppose that Tully grew up to look like Fielding?'

'But that's just the point, isn't it, darling?' Baby said. 'It's one of the things which Canty and I thought of. No one can remember, any more, what Fielding really looked like. Since 1958 he's been like he is now – a surgical repair job. Tully could be the dead spit of Fielding, as Fielding should be, but nobody would know.'

'There must be photos of the young Fielding.'

'Precious few. His mother and father weren't the kind that kept a scrap-book. And people aren't going to go hunting up old school and regimental groups . . . which by this time, anyway, are very hard to find. Even if they do – well, it's years yet before Tully can start to look like Fielding in the House Team or Captain Gray in the Squadron Sabre Pair. And even when and if he does, nobody can prove a bloody thing.'

165

'So in fullness of time Canteloupe will succeed Canteloupe, and no one the wiser?'

'Except you and me and Fielding and Canty. No worries *there*, darling. But worry there must be. Like Marius, Tully has a bad inheritance on the female side. Even if, as we hope, his father's ancestry is fairly normal, that's still one off par for a start. There are so many dangers, darling Jo-Jo . . . like whatever it is and whencesoever it comes, inherited or not, that has Marius in thrall. We must find out what it is, you and I, the new mother and the mother to be. In order to guard our own, we must find out what devil or curse, what sickenss or spell, has come to haunt my green-eyed Lucifer.'

While Theodosia went behind a screen to put on a two-piece bathing suit, Ptolemaeos ran the taps and filled the sarcophagus with water that was slightly hotter than lukewarm. He then played back brief passages on the tape recorder, to remind himself what had passed just before the recess. When Theodosia emerged, abundant in form but by no means to surfeit, and climbed into the water, he handed her two rubber bathing rings. She put her two feet through the first, one after the other, and adjusted it in the region of her knees; she put the second round her shoulders; then lay back and floated in the enormous bath.

'Comfy?' said Ptolemaeos.

Theodosia smiled and nodded. Ptolemaeos placed a rubber cushion behind her head, so that it could rest conveniently on the ledge of the coffin.

'This morning I just asked questions,' said Ptolemaeos. 'This afternoon I am going to give you an encouraging little drink . . . and then make suggestions.'

He passed Theodosia a glass full of misty liquid. She reached for it hesitantly, her arm slightly impeded by the upper ring. When she held the glass in her hand, she said, 'What sort of drink?'

'A harmless and soothing potation, made from Fenland herbs gathered by the two ladies who clean and cook for me.'

'Witchcraft?'

'Folk medicine.'

Theodosia drank.

'And what sort of suggestion?' she said.

'This morning I was concerned to establish biographical facts. You answered me from your memory, which is operated mechanically by banks of cells in the physical brain. I am now going to remind you of some of those facts, thus calling the memory cells into operation again, and then ask you for intellectual or moral comment on those facts. What I am trying to do is to come at the process by which the function of memory, which is physical, activates or stimulates the function of judgment, which is of the mind or soul, non-corporeal.'

'Serve away,' Theodosia said.

'Very well. Some of the topics will necessarily be disagreeable or mournful, as is this one. The death of your mother. Repeat what you were told of this.'

'She fell down a well in a forest, was knocked unconscious by the fall, and immediately drowned in the water at the bottom. The well was so deep and dangerous that they never got her body out.'

'Facts. Now to approach a little nearer to judgment. Apart from any sorrow which you might have felt – '

' – Precious little. She was a B-One-T-C-H – '

' – And apart from any pleasure or relief, you must have considered the circumstances of your mother's death to be distinctly odd?'

'A weird accident. But not unique.'

'Was there anything about these circumstances to justify your father's extreme reaction? I mean the fact that he had a nervous or mental breakdown of colossal dimensions.'

'No. That he should have been upset was natural enough. He loved her, though God knows why. But he was in no sense guilty, or responsible for what happened. They were in the forest at her suggestion. I have never understood why he collapsed so utterly.'

'So far we are still only *approaching* the processes of real judgment. I have asked you for a calculation which has been performed by the physical brain assisted by the memory. Now, I am going to ask for a deduction, which will still be within the province of memory and mechanical cerebral function. Granted the facts of your mother's death as you were told them do not explain the length and severity of your father's breakdown, what do you deduce from this?'

'That we were not told the full truth.'

'Good. Now for real judgment. Of what kind, Theodosia, of what quality would this untold truth have to have been to justify your father's extreme reaction? We are on the threshold, Theodosia, between the physical brain and the mind or soul that must now pronounce on a question of personality and morals. Let your memory and the deductions made by your brain prompt this question to your intellect: what more would be required to explain and excuse your father's collapse?'

Ptolemaeos looked into Theodosia's eyes. Hers, she found, could not avoid his. Nor could they close, though she felt quite drowsy – drowsy and indifferent to the whole affair, yet somehow sickeningly clear in her mind (soul? intellect?) about the implications of it all. But if her judgment was clear, she found it almost impossible to find the words that would express it.

'I must have time,' she said, 'to formulate my answer.'

'That's my girl. Of course you must. The soul must

communicate very long and carefully with the brain, to stimulate it to devise and deliver the words in which alone the brain can interpret the soul's judgments. You feel this, Theodosia? You feel that something inside you yet something alien to your physical being is trying to communicate with and speak through that being?'

'I can't be sure of that. I know that this judgment can be told only with great difficulty. My father's agony' . . . a long pause, after which the words seemed to delve themselves out of her . . . 'can have been caused only by horror at the suffering of someone he loved' . . . a second pause of perhaps thirty seconds . . . 'suffering infinitely greater and more terrible than the suffering to which Mother was exposed in the version they gave us. I am trying to conceive the reality of such suffering, the reality of both of their suffering. I can get as far as understanding that it must have been far more complicated and hideous than anything we were told, but any effort to make myself grasp its absolute essence makes me feel physically sick, rather as one feels if one tries to grasp the essence of an infinite universe.'

'Have you ever asked your father about it?'

'No point,' she said in a voice now natural and definitely glib. 'No point at all. First he was too ill; and now he's well it would be insane to bring it all up again.'

'Ah,' said Ptolemaeos. 'I fear you have fallen from grace. You are now back on a purely cerebral level, making a snap practical decision. Do you feel the difference between the slick remark you have just made, on the one hand, and your spiritual striving to grasp the essence of your mother's – and father's – suffering on the other.'

'Yes,' said Theodosia, 'I feel it. And though you may think it frivolous of me, I prefer to be on the snap practical level every time. The other thing takes too much out of a girl.'

'Yes. A girl's soul, when consulted, is apt to be rather demanding,' Ptolemaeos said.

'"He alle was a Cock that so did crow,"' Carmilla read aloud, '"That Godde's Will be laid on High and Low."'

Carmilla and Jeremy were in Bishop Alcock's Chantry in Ely Cathedral. Jeremy was examining a screen of very complicated tracery, while Carmilla was deciphering the tablet that bore the Bishop's epitaph.

'"Come High, come Low, and grovel in the Dust:
Where Alcock He has gone, so too Thou must."'

'Do you know,' said Jeremy, 'I think I've heard enough of that.'

'Patience,' said Carmilla. 'There's some splendid stuff to come:

"Anon the Worm will creep across thy Groin
Where once proud Horn did with thy Leman join:
Anon the Maggot tunnels in thy Brain,
Where then canst search for Word or Wit in vain.
Anon the Blow-fly hums within thy Bowell – "'

' – Darling,' said Jeremy, 'come and look at this tracery.' Carmilla came, answering a well-known note in his voice. 'I wonder,' he said, 'how Ptoly Tunne is getting on, tunnelling in Theodosia's brain.'

'We shall hear this evening.'

'The trouble with that house is that proud Horn gets no scope. One feels too nervous.'

'I know. Oh, Jeremy. Suppose someone came in.'

'We're safe behind this screen. It's so elaborate it's absolutely opaque.'

'Someone else might come behind it.'

'Then there'd be three coming behind it,' Jeremy said.

'They were all standing round him,' said Walter St George, his plump yet square face streaming with sweat, his Old Harrovian tie vibrating on his barrel belly. 'All standing round him chanting this refrain, do you see, "One-point-three-re*curr*ing, one-point-three-re*curr*ing . . ." Stern's average, you see.'

'What an odious crew,' said Fielding Gray.

'My dear Fielding,' said Glinter Parkes, stooping to his right as he walked and pushing his face down and round in front of Fielding's, 'you know as well as I do – for we both saw notable instances when at school which I shall not trouble to enumerate – that when pride has taken a tumble the vultures and the ravens gather.' He shifted his half-moon glasses by twitching a muscle on the bridge of his nose. The celebrated 'glint' flashed straight into Fielding's one eye. 'Small boys,' he said, 'indeed all of us, have a strong vulture-cum-raven component in their nature. In taunting Marius Stern, they were simply obeying an instinct.'

'Original sin, Glinter?'

'Just about,' said Glinter. 'As a Headmaster, I see a lot of it.'

'Can we have less moral speculation,' said Canteloupe, 'and more fact. Mr St George here is trying to tell us what happened.'

'As I came up,' said Walter, 'I could see that Stern was crying. Snivelling, rather. He was also selecting. He was

171

shifting his gaze, assessing his tormentors for position, range and angle. He was getting ready to make a stroke.'

'How could you tell?' said Canteloupe.

'Because he had the same look on his face as he has when he follows the ball in a fives court . . . working out pitch and bounce, calculating the precise moment at which to strike.

'"Stop this horrible noise," I called. They all looked at me, the chant dying but not dead. Those with their backs to me began to turn, Palairet among them, you see. Palairet tried to look over his left shoulder, leaving the right side of his throat exposed and stretched. Stern saw his chance – an unexpectedly good one – and took it. He made his right hand into a wedge and swung it backhand – as hard as he could, do you see – into the wretched Palairet's throat.'

'Luckily,' said Glinter Parkes, 'Walter then remembered a ghastly incident which had taken place on the cricket ground – at another school, I'm happy to say – some years ago. A boy was hit on the throat by a fast ball. The throat closed up completely as a result of the blow and the boy died of asphyxiation almost before anyone could turn round. So when this thing happened yesterday, Walter sent the other boys to tell me to ring up a doctor and himself took Palairet straight to the school labs, where he found one of those narrow rubber tubes and inserted it down Palairet's throat to keep the passage open. If he hadn't done this . . . well, according to the doctor Marius would by now be on a charge of murder.'

'Manslaughter at worst,' said Fielding. 'Temper killing.'

'Murder,' said Walter St George mildly. 'This wasn't just a matter of temper, you see. Stern deliberately selected Palairet, you see, very unfair of him because it seemed to me that Palairet was trying to stop the others, but evidently Stern didn't know this or didn't care, because it was clearly Palairet whom he had selected, and he was calculating how to do him the maximum damage, you see, and then, when the chance came, struck . . . with malignance, not rage but malignance, all over his face. And it wasn't just a healthy punch on the nose; it was a backhanded wedge-blow. A potential killer.'

'Would Marius have known that?' said Canteloupe.

'No need to drag up all these hypotheses,' said Glinter Parkes. 'Palairet, thanks be to God, is alive and will soon be tolerably well.'

Glinter turned his face briefly and almost casually up to Heaven in a well bred gesture of acknowledgment for services rendered. It was almost, thought Fielding, as if he were tipping the Almighty or offering Him a good reference. No wonder he had been urged to leave his seminary, twenty-five years ago, without being ordained: quite apart from his marked strain of worldly pessimism (surely proscribed in clerical circles ever since the death of Dean Inge), he gave the impression that he could not take God altogether seriously; the whole notion, his eyes hinted from behind his tilted and flashing half-moon glasses, was just that much too silly, though it would do very well to keep children and servants in order.

'May one ask,' said Fielding, 'what was happening to Marius during all this telephoning and tube-inserting?'

'We will all sit down here,' said Glinter blandly.

He led them off the playing field round which they had been strolling and up a green bank. At its top was a wooden bench which looked down the other side of the bank and on to a narrow canal where ducks were gliding and willows weeping.

JEREMY ULSTER MORRISON

was carved along the back of the bench:

1966 to 1971

'So you got a leaving present out of Peter Morrison when

Jeremy left,' said Fielding to Glinter, pointing to the inscription.

'No,' said Glinter. 'Jeremy paid for it himself. As you see, it is new. He had it delivered just the other day, with a message for myself about some windfall he'd just had (no details supplied) and a request that it should be placed up here. He had always enjoyed, he said, looking down at the canal from this bank. It reminded him of some lines from Ausonius about the reflection of trees in the River Moselle. Since he could hardly have read Ausonius while he was a boy here,' said Glinter, 'I think he must have his memories muddled.'

'Wrong,' said Walter St George. 'He was always a great one for short cuts was Jeremy, you see, and he reckoned that one way of saving himself excessive reading was to go to anthologies, thus getting the flavour of all the important poets without the stodge. One of the anthologies he borrowed from me was Helen Waddell's *Mediaeval Latin Verse* – rather precocious but I saw no harm in it – and one of the first poems there is an extract of four lines from a poem of Ausonius about the River Moselle, an extract describing the reflection of trees in its waters either at dawn or dusk – I forget which, do you see. So on the strength of four lines, Master Jeremy has posed to you as one conversant with the works of an obscure if delectable Latin poet, a typical piece of deceit. But a nice gesture all the same,' said Walter sitting down on it. 'A thoroughly agreeable boy, Jeremy, for all his little games. He always enjoyed my conjuring tricks.'

'Not altogether a wholesome influence,' said Glinter Parkes, 'but what can one do? If they feel their oats they're bound to spill them.'

'Peter never spilled his,' Fielding said. 'Or not at school.'

'So I remember,' said Glinter glumly. 'He was a by-word of purity.'

'Though I did hear,' pursued Fielding, 'that there was trouble with a half-caste tart in India a little later.'

Canteloupe chuckled.

'He came out of that one with flying colours,' he said. 'Or to be more precise, with a Viceroy's Citation.'

'A Viceroy's Citation for shagging a half-breed?'

'No time for the full story just now,'* said Canteloupe. 'Let us simply say that he had political talent even then. What we want to know,' he said to Walter St George, 'is the answer to Major Gray's question about Marius Stern. What was happening to Marius while the Headmaster here was telephoning and you were stuffing tubes down Master Palairet's throat?'

'He came with us to the labs,' Walter St George said, 'apparently penitent. He kept telling Palairet that he'd be all right because his sister Rosie would make a spell. But then he seemed doubtful about that, and started muttering about how Rosie listened too much to somebody called Tessa. It was really Tessa's fault that Stern hadn't made any runs, he said; and it was Tessa that had made him hit Palairet. He said it was this Tessa that had shown him, during the holidays, how to make his hand into a wedge and hit people in the throat. And a lot more, besides. I was desperate to get that tube down Palairet's throat, so I didn't pay too much attention. Anyway, by the time we reached the labs Marius was just babbling. But I did gather that Tessa had taught him other ways of hitting foul, and had also shown him "some secrets". What those were, God knows, because then I told him to shut up and got on with my job – not a very amusing one, because even when I'd managed to introduce the tube there were further hideous complications about the position of Palairet's head and how to make sure he didn't swallow the damn thing completely, and so forth, you see. But pretty soon Parkes appeared

* *Sound the Retreat* by Simon Raven (Panther Books, 1974)

with Matron, who took over (rather huffily, I thought, as though I'd been poaching on her ground) until the doctor turned up and told me to fall out for a stiffish drink.'

'And then?' said Canteloupe to Parkes.

'And then,' said Parkes, 'Palairet was treated in Deal Hospital and returned here, where he is presently in the Sanitorium but won't be for very much longer. Wally's tube saved the day.'

Wally shook his head in modest dismissal of this particular achievement but slapped one thigh in genial affirmation of his general excellence.

'And Marius?'

'Spent the night in a special room in the San., heavily doped.'

'But he'd already shown how sorry he was.'

'His mode of apology,' said Glinter Parkes, glancing at Walter St George, 'had been rather unbalanced. All that stuff about his sister and this girl called Tessa.'

'That can't be true,' said Fielding, stern and loyal, 'about Tessa . . . about her being so spiteful.'

'None of that concerns me,' said Glinter, who now put on a severity to match Fielding's. 'All that concerns me is to hand over Marius Stern to Canteloupe here, who has assumed responsibility for him in the absence of his parents. We have him ready and waiting.'

'What the hell can I do with him?' said Canteloupe. 'What can anybody do with him?'

'My dear Canteloupe, a man with your wealth and connections can surely arrange something. As I told you on the telephone, I might be able to take him back in the autumn – with a lot of fixing and fudging. But for now, for now, Canteloupe, he must go.'

'All the boys are frightened, do you see,' said Walter St George. 'So am I. That look on his face when it happened, do you see. Just for a moment it was as if Satan had got inside him.'

'Are you suggesting I should summon an exorcist?' Canteloupe said.

'No,' said Glinter. 'Merely his parents.'

'I've told you. I can't find them.'

'And I've told you, Canteloupe, I can't keep him here an hour longer, or I'll have a mob of parents in the place stringing me up from the school clock. Be good fellows, you and Fielding, and take him away with you.'

'Easily done; but what then?'

'*Res Unius, Res Omnium,*' said Fielding to Canteloupe. 'I have an idea. Clearly you don't want him down in Wiltshire, in the state he's in, with Sarum and that pregnant chum of Baby's. Nor can he come to Buttock's after what St George heard him say about Tessa.'

'But you don't think it's true, so you say – what he said about Tessa.'

'Whether it is true is not the point,' said Fielding rather uneasily. 'The point is that if he's been saying things like that about her, then he must not be allowed anywhere near her – '

' – Or near any other children,' said Walter St George unctuously.

'So no Wiltshire for Marius,' said Fielding, giving St George a look to indicate that assistant masters should speak when spoken to, 'and no Buttock's. But we're not quite snookered: there's a screw shot we can play off the cush.'

When Ptolemaeos released her, Theodosia decided to take the Volkswagen which she shared with Carmilla during the vacations and drive to Cambridge to look at Lancaster College Chapel. Though a member of the college, she had never been inside the chapel (thinking that such matters had nothing to do with her) until the afternoon of Sarum's christening, when she had perceived it to be of a beauty that made one shed tears and give thanks to the God (if any) within it. Since then she had walked in it often, and today, she thought, she would pay it a special visit in order to thank the God (if any) within it for the brilliant First Class which Carmilla had achieved in Part One of her History Tripos and for the modest but entirely acceptable Second which had accrued to herself. She would also look up at Jeremy's window from the little green court by the river. He wouldn't be there, of course, because he had gone to Ely in his Morris 1000 with Carmilla, but it would be nice to look up at the window, and feel one's way through it, and pretend to be inside.

But when she came to the main road at the border of Ptolemaeos's Fenland kingdom, she told herself not to be silly. Cambridge would be full of tourists at this season, and so would Lancaster Chapel. Quite possibly they would have allotted Jeremy's room to someone who was attending some idiotic conference; and if this somebody saw her looking up, he might come down, and that would be embarrassing. No. She would go to Ely, which was much nearer, instead, and hope to find Carmilla and Jeremy. Then they could all three have tea together in one of those Tudor Pantry places, if there were any left these days. Tourists there would be in Ely too, of course, but not as many as in Cambridge, since people still thought of Ely, in a vague way, as an island, and were therefore often deterred from attempting to get there.

'"Merrilie sang the Monks of Ely,"' Theodosia quoted to herself, taking the right-hand turn for that ancient palatinate, '"When Cnut King rowed thereby."' An island. Beloved Jeremy and Carmilla (with luck) with whom to have a cream tea (goodie, goodie, just this once, training or no). Where should she look? In the cathedral first: then, if she missed her sister and Jeremy, she would at least not have wasted her journey.

'"Merrrilie sang the Monks of Ely,"' she crooned to an improvised variation of Holst's 'Music of the Planets',

> '"When Cnut King rowed thereby.
> Row, my knyghtes, near the shore,
> That we may hearen these Monks sing."'

Canteloupe, Fielding and Marius walked along the shore of Sandwich Bay. The tide was very low and the beach seemed to stretch away to the horizon. Although the wet sand, lower down, would have been fine and firm to walk on, Canteloupe made them stay on the dry, yellow, powdery sand above the tide-line, being worried (as he admitted) lest the damp should spoil the polish on his brogues.

'So I'm not going back?' Marius said.

'No.'

'I didn't mean to hit Palairet so hard. Anyway I don't think he'll mind all that much. He isn't one to bear a grudge. He was quite friendly afterwards – before they took him off to the hospital.'

'They might well have been taking him to the morgue,' Canteloupe said.

'Morgue?'

'They don't know words like that any more,' Fielding told Canteloupe. 'Anything to do with death is taboo at school these days.'

'But people die at schools, just as they do anywhere else.'

'They did when you and I were boys. Not now. The

179

authorities see to that. Just as no one's allowed by the Greeks to die on Delos, so they take damn good care no one dies in a school. Death would be contamination. These days it's the great unmentionable – ten times worse than pederasty. That's why Glinter's being so firm. He's had a narrow escape and he's nervous.'

'Are you two saying,' said Marius, 'that Pally might have died?'

'Yes. Why do you think Mr St George put that tube down his throat?'

'I thought he was going to do one of his conjuring tricks, to cheer Pally up till the doctor came.'

'Why do you think they sent for the doctor?'

'They send for him every time you cut your knee,' said Marius. 'They panic about anything.'

'You see?' said Fielding to Canteloupe. 'They don't take the smallest risk.'

'Who showed you how to hit someone like that?' asked Canteloupe.

'Rosie's friend, Tessa Malcolm. She said it would be a very good way of defending myself against bigger boys.'

'Was Palairet bigger?'

'No. I was upset. They were all baiting me.'

'Mr St George says Palairet was trying to stop them, or so he thought.'

'Mr St George didn't get there till the very end, and anyway I couldn't see any difference between Palairet and the rest. I just told you – they were all baiting me.'

'Because you hadn't made any runs?'

'Yes. It's been horrible. Rosie started it, in a way, but it's Tessa's fault really.'

'You have simply,' said Canteloupe, 'been having a bad patch.'

'No. I've never had one before. I tell you Rosie started it.'

'A bad patch,' insisted Canteloupe. 'I had them. Major

Gray had them. Hammond, Sutcliffe and W. G. Grace had them. Why should you be exempt?'

'Who was Sutcliffe?'

'Ask Mr St George,' said Fielding. 'He seems to know everything.'

'How can I, if I'm not going back? It's a rotten shame, because I know that *now* I shall begin to get runs again – or should do if I was allowed to play.'

'Why now?' said Canteloupe.

'Because Rosie's lifted the spell at last. Should I call you "My Lord"?'

'No. "Canteloupe", as one gentleman to another. I have already told you,' said Canteloupe, 'that it's nothing to do with a spell. It's a bad patch.'

'Tell us about this spell,' said Fielding to Marius. 'Why has Rosie lifted it?'

'Because Tessa has let her. Should I call you "sir"?'

'If you need a vocative, it will serve as well as another. Why has Tessa let Rosie lift the spell? Go back to the beginning.'

'Rosie wished no runs for me, sir, at Lord – at Canteloupe's christening party.'

'Sarum's christening party,' Canteloupe said.

'In the Provost's Garden. It worked. I wrote to her from school and asked her to stop her wish. She wrote back and said the wish didn't have any power anyway. It was just temper. But I knew different. And I still didn't get any runs.'

'A bad patch,' repeated Canteloupe wearily.

'No. Rosie's wish. Her spell. With Tessa behind it all, somehow. So then I rang Rosie up at Buttock's Hotel – '

' – YOU RANG HER UP?' said Canteloupe, horrified.

'These days,' explained Fielding, 'children at school are allowed to telephone to their connections.'

'I'm damned if I'll have Sarum telephoning to anybody when he goes to school. What's the point of packing them off at huge expense if they're allowed to pester you by telephone?'

'Ask me another,' Fielding said; and then to Marius, 'What did Rosie say when you rang up?'

'She pretended to be very upset and repeated that her wish couldn't possibly have stopped me making runs. But of course I still knew that she and Tessa were really at the bottom of it.'

'So your telephone call had no immediate result?'

'But it did a day or two later. Rosie did something very peculiar. She wrote to me and swore . . . on our mother's honour . . . that she had no power to spoil my cricket. I must believe her, she said. And of course when she swore an oath like that I had to. And in a way I do. But I think . . . that what she was really swearing . . . was *not* that she had no power but that with Tessa's agreement they had stopped using it.'

'But where could either of them have got the power to cast such a spell?' Fielding asked.

Marius was silent.

'Do you think,' said Fielding, desperate for some kind of clue to Marius's mental state, 'do you think . . . that it has anything to do with Tessa's hump? They all make quite a to-do about it.'

'Just because she's the only one who's got one. Just a silly piece of gristle. None of this has anything to do with Tessa's stupid hump.'

'Then with what?'

Marius turned down his mouth.

'But in any case at all,' said Canteloupe, 'you believe that *now* you would get runs.'

'If I was allowed to play in the next match. Or if there'd been a match after Rosie swore and before . . . before this business happened with poor Pally.'

'So to sum up so far,' Fielding said: 'Rosie says she has no power over your cricket; this she has absolutely sworn;

but what you believe is that Tessa and Rosie between them somehow have this power, yet have now decided to lift the spell – too late, as it turns out, for you to get the benefit.'

'That's about it, sir.'

'But for heaven's sake, boy. You *must* tell us in what you believe this power of theirs to consist. Don't just sulk when I ask you. You're too intelligent and grown-up for that. You must *explain*.'

'Tessa,' said Marius reluctantly, 'is changing. We all change when we're about twelve or thirteen. Tessa is changing and so am I. That day she taught me how to make those special punches – '

' – Where had *she* learned about them?' said Canteloupe.

' – One thing at a time,' said Fielding crossly, rather as if it were he and not Canteloupe who had been appointed as Marius's temporary guardian. But Canteloupe nodded equably and said, 'Right you be. Where were we?'

'The day Tessa taught Marius those special punches. Well . . ?' Fielding said, turning back to Marius.

'Rosie and I were spending the day at Buttock's because Mummy and Daddy had to go out of London. Not long before Sarum's christening it was. Mummy had asked Mrs Malcolm to take Rosie to the dentist to have her brace altered. So Tessa and I went to the National Gallery, and she showed me a picture of Venus and Cupid. Cupid was kissing Venus in a funny way, with his tongue, and sort of mussing one of her breasts about. "But that's his mother," I said. "You're not allowed to do that with your mother." "They're both gods," said Tessa, "so they're allowed to do whatever they want."'

Marius paused in his narrative. Line abreast, the three of them scrunched along in the dry sand, Marius in the middle.

'Then we went back to Buttock's,' Marius resumed, after a clear minute. 'Rosie and Mrs Malcolm were still out. Tessa said . . . would I like to kiss her like that, like

Cupid in the picture, just once. So I said, no, it was silly. And she said I wouldn't think so when I grew up. So I said I'd grown up already, or almost, and I did think so. And Tessa said, so had she, grown up I mean, and it was a bond. She wanted to make . . . a kind of conspiracy about it. Even leaving out Rosie. "Rosie can join in when *she* grows up," Tessa said. "If I show you something special, will you kiss me like I asked?" This made me inquisitive, and so I said, yes. Then she showed me how to make my hand flat and hard, and how to hit people like I hit Palairet. And she showed me how to hit someone on the back of the neck – it starts like an ordinary hook which we do at boxing – '

' – You still have boxing?' Fielding interrupted. 'I thought they'd given it up at every school in England.'

'Not at ours,' said Marius proudly. 'Mr Parkes says we may need to defend ourselves. At all the other schools round here they learn judo, but Mr Parkes says that's rubbish.'

'Go on about this hook,' said Canteloupe.

'Tessa taught me a new sort of hook which ends at the back of the neck. And how to hit someone – you know – *there*. And how to do it with my knee. Then she said it was time for me to keep my part of the bargain. Time to kiss her. But I couldn't. Her mouth had come open and looked all slobbery. It was all so silly and messy. "Don't be shy, Marius," she said. "I shan't hurt you. I shan't do anything horrid to you. But just for a minute let's pretend we're Venus and Cupid. A goddess and a god." And suddenly I knew what would happen to me if she came any closer, it's happened to me in dreams,' Marius blurted, 'I knew what would happen, the feeling had started, and I didn't want her to be upset or angry or disgusted, and she'd be bound to know as she'd come so close; anyway I always make a noise when it happens, I can't help it, and so I ran away and locked myself in the loo . . . until Rosie came back with Mrs Malcolm.'

'Did Tessa try to persuade you to come out?'

'No. She ignored me. When I did come out, she gave me a kind of hurt look . . . but not just hurt, insulted, yes, as if she'd been bitterly insulted, as if she'd shown me a toy or a book or a picture which she was really proud of, and I'd just laughed at it. And I think that's why, later on, she made me and Rosie quarrel at the christening. Because she felt so insulted. I think she *willed* me to quarrel with Rosie, and she willed Rosie to make her wish, and then wouldn't let Rosie unwish it, not for a long time, and by then it was too late. Too late to stop me being baited about my average, too late to stop me hitting poor Pally like that, and now I'm being sent away – just when I would have made some runs at last. If only she'd let me make them earlier, I'd never have been teased like that, I'd never have hit Pally, I'd have stayed at Oudenarde – oh dear, oh dear, oh dear,' Marius said, and sat down in the sand.

'So you think,' mused Canteloupe, 'that Tessa willed all this to happen because you wouldn't give her the kiss you'd promised?'

'But you know, Canteloupe, I'd have gone through with it if it hadn't been for . . . what I told you. I'd promised Tessa, and she'd showed me the punches and things, I'd have kissed her on the mouth, however slobbery it was – only that feeling had started and I didn't want to annoy her.'

'Perhaps she wouldn't have minded,' Canteloupe said.

'Well, I should. I'd have had nasty damp trousers, like wetting myself, and it might even have shown.'

'Marius,' said Fielding, 'I've known Tessa a long time, and I'm a very old friend of her – aunt's. Whatever may have happened that afternoon, she's a kind, loving girl, and she would never have done you harm. About your cricket or anything else.'

'But she did. It must have been her. I tell you, she willed me and Rosie to quarrel, she willed Rosie to – '

' – So you've already said, but *how*? How, Marius? What . . . what kind of power did she have to do these things? Nothing to do with her hump you said, and of course it wasn't. Then *what*?'

'Growing up, sir, as I said. Some girls have power, Mr St George once told us, just because they're growing up. It was that power which made me . . . have the feeling. Tessa was close but not all that close, not close enough to be rubbing against me or anything. But there was a kind of invisible cushion, between me and her, filling the gap. A warm soft cushion, nuzzling up to my legs and stomach, to my – '

'But it wasn't always warm and soft,' said Canteloupe, 'because later it turned to hate and wouldn't let you make runs. Or rather, that's what you say you think.'

'Do you think Tessa controls this power,' Fielding asked, 'or does it act independently of her?'

'It comes from her. Sometimes it acts through Rosie, as they're very close; but in the end it comes from Tessa. So whatever it does must be wished by her.'

There was a pause. I should refute him there, thought Fielding, as the notion may be a source of dangerous confusion for the future. The *non sequitur* is too plausible to be easily disentangled; yet I must certainly try. He was opening his mouth to do so when –

' – Where did she learn those punches she taught you?' Canteloupe said. 'How to make your hand into a wedge and hit backhand?'

'That at least can be explained,' said Fielding, with an air of one who grasps the nettle. 'I taught her. As Glinter Parkes might put it, I thought that one day she might need to defend herself. So I taught her some of those dirty tricks which army instructors were still teaching us just after the war. Her aunt was present when I taught her. She, too,

186

thought it was a good idea. But we both made Tessa promise that she would use such methods only if she had to, and that on no account would she show them to anyone else.'

'Which is just what she did. And now Master Palairet has the full benefit of your instruction,' said Canteloupe. 'I feel . . . that you owe everyone something in all this. You have, in a sense, corrupted the young. So. Did I hear you say earlier that you had some idea of what might be done with Marius? That might make some amends.'

'I don't think one is responsible for the ill use people make of good lessons,' said Fielding. 'Certainly not if one's pupils have been thoroughly cautioned and sworn to discretion, as was the case between me and Tessa. Nor,' he said, looking down at the rumpled heap of grey flannel on the sand, 'do I think that Tessa herself is necessarily responsible for what this power of hers – if indeed she has it – may do to those around her. It is something, if it exists, which comes out of her without her wishing it.'

But neither Canteloupe nor Marius was disposed to accept Fielding's moral or metaphysic.

'All adult men know,' said Canteloupe, 'that if you stir the water the ripples spread to the banks of the pool – would spread to infinity if permitted. If you give lessons you start ripples.'

'If Tessa knows this power is coming out of her,' said Marius for his part, 'she should keep away from people, to stop it messing them about.'

'All right,' said Fielding. 'I see I must appeal to a higher court. This idea I've thought of, for Marius's immediate future, will involve doing exactly that.'

'Exactly what? Plain speaking, please.'

'Clearly Marius cannot join Tessa and Rosie at Buttock's, and clearly he should not come to you in Wiltshire – much as Baby loves him. But you, in your condition of vicarious parenthood, have got to arrange something for him. You say I owe a debt to everyone in all this. Very well: I shall at once discharge it and repudiate it by an appeal to a higher court.'

'Fielding. What, this minute, do we do?'

'We drive to London. We dine at my club. Marius looks just old enough to be admitted. Then we make a telephone call to the judge of my court, who will be in better conceit with himself and the world after dinner.'

As Theodosia crossed the Cathedral Close at Ely, she saw Carmilla and Jeremy, who were walking very slowly away with their backs to her, in the rough direction of a street which led to the town centre.

Hey,' called Theodosia, starting to run. 'Hey, you two. It's me. Thea.'

Carmilla and Jeremy halted sloppily, turned inward towards each other and then wearily through another ninety degrees towards Theodosia. They looked dazed and interrogative, as if they had not quite taken her in. Then Carmilla side-stepped, so that she stood absolutely flush with Jeremy and as if she were determined that no one should be able to see between them.

Theodosia changed her run to a walk and her walk to an amble. For Theodosia knew what Carmilla's gesture meant, and she needed time before confronting her sister and Jeremy. Love, that was what was portended by this closing of ranks (so to speak) against herself, Theodosia, the intruder. Why had she not seen before? How blind and selfish of her. It was plain for all to see: love; a daze of love. How marvellous for Carmilla. And . . . and for Jeremy. Love. Romantic love. Pure love. Look at the bewildered and lost look on their faces: innocents abroad,

188

not knowing what had hit them or what (as yet) to do about it. They must be left together – without her, without the potential intruder – to find out.

'I came to tell you both,' she said. 'I've decided to go back to London, to Da. I think perhaps he's been alone a bit too long. But you'll be needing the car, Carm, it's just over there and here's the key, so you drive it back to Mr Tunne's, and I'll take a train from Ely station. Never mind my stuff, I've plenty in London, you can bring what's at Mr Tunne's when you come – but don't for God's sake hurry. I only made up my mind on the way here, you see, so I didn't pack. Good-bye, darlings, see you soon.'

Theodosia looked around, as calmly as she could, and saw a British Railways signpost.

'Good-bye, darlings,' she said again. 'Have a lovely. Oh, have a beaut.'

She started off at a long lollop towards the BR sign, trying not to cry in case Jeremy or Carmilla should see her and it should spoil their afternoon.

Fielding's club in London was called the Thackeray. Although the quality of both the membership and the cuisine was indifferent, the situation was central and the architecture was agreeably eccentric. After dinner this evening, Fielding, Canteloupe and Marius drank coffee and other things on a first floor balcony, sitting under a portrait of Robert Browning and looking down on a cloister done in pastiche Romanesque.

'I think,' said Canteloupe, 'that that was the nastiest food I have eaten since the war.'

'Hear, hear,' said Marius, who had been much heartened by two glasses of La Tâche.

189

'You weren't alive during the war,' said Fielding, 'and it is held to be bad manners to criticize food which you have eaten at someone else's expense.'

'Canteloupe criticized it.'

'Only as a permissible preface,' said Canteloupe, 'to praising the drink. This port has been very tolerably kept, the wines at dinner were irreproachable, and it is not often in London that one can procure St Galmier water, which is available here. Now then, Fielding; this scheme of yours for taking Marius off my hands – '

' – Do you mind so much having me on them? I am sometimes considered,' said Marius slyly, 'to be rather an engaging *parti*.'

'Who taught you that word? Mr St George?'

'No. Roseworm ma. (Roseworm is not an engaging *parti*.) Lady Canteloupe would love to have me around, as Gray was saying this afternoon. She likes my green eyes.'

'*Major Gray*, to you.'

'Why? If Canteloupe is Canteloupe to me, Gray is Gray. Why can't I stay with you in Wiltshire?'

'Because Lady Canteloupe is too busy just now to take proper care of you.'

'Why is Baby so busy?'

'*Lady Canteloupe* has a friend staying who takes up all the time she can spare from looking after Sarum.'

'Sarum has a nurse,' said Marius. 'A very pretty girl called Daisy. I quite fancy Daisy.'

'Do you?' said Canteloupe. 'Well, there is one more excellent reason for not having you down in Wiltshire. Come on,' he said to Fielding. 'Out with it.'

'Ptolemaeos Tunne,' Fielding said.

'Mummy would approve,' said Marius coolly. 'She has spoken of him with interest. Daddy hates him.'

'But he has given his permission for you to go there,' said Fielding. 'So Isobel told me before they left,' he said to Canteloupe.

'In principle, yes. Gregory has very reluctantly given his permission for both Marius and Rosie to be used in Ptolemaeos's investigations . . . but his intention was to be present himself when it happened.'

'But that is not an absolute condition?' said Fielding. 'You, as Marius's guardian *pro tem.*, can give permission for Marius to go there by himself?'

'I don't know. You see, Gregory was put under very heavy pressure to allow the children to be used at all.'

'I don't like this word "used"' Marius said.

'Very well,' said Fielding. 'You will not be used; you will assist.'

'There was heavy pressure,' repeated Canteloupe. 'I don't know exactly what form it took, but I gather it was some kind of social blackmail. But however that may be, Gregory clearly understood that Ptoly had clearly consented to Gregory's being present while Marius and Rosie were being u – I mean, while the experiments were going forward.'

'But Gregory's presence was never a *sine qua non* – '

' – Mr St George says that *sine qua non* is both a sloppy and an affected expression – '

' – And anyway Gregory was just being a silly old hen. Now he's gone and got lost, so we don't need to consult him. He's not here when wanted, and you, as surrogate, can do just as you think fit.'

'I knew my father was a silly old hen,' said Marius, 'but I did not know he'd gone and got lost. Is Mummy all right?'

'They're both all right,' said Canteloupe. 'It's just that the arrangements about their hotels have been changed and people are being stupid about messages.'

'Oh,' said Marius, who looked in part relieved by this assurance and in part peeved that he was being deprived of further drama. 'Anyway, I'm not at all sure I want to go to

Mr Tunne. He looked . . . like the Ogre at the top of the beanstalk.'

'He doesn't eat little boys,' said Fielding, 'however pert they may be, and he is exceedingly rich. It is always prudent to oblige the rich.'

'Daddy is rich.'

'Not as rich as Mr Tunne.'

'Is Mr Tunne richer than Canteloupe?'

'He has more control over his money,' said Canteloupe. 'Most of mine is tied up.'

'But has he actually more?'

'In liquid cash, yes.'

'Well . . . would I be able to play cricket there?'

'If you're polite to Mr Tunne,' said Fielding smoothly, 'he'll probably arrange for a net to be put up on the lawn.'

'But who'd bowl at me? I can't see the Ogre getting his arm over.'

'What would you say . . . to an Old Boy of Oudenarde House?'

'You're joking. Who?'

'Yes, who?' said Canteloupe.

'A young friend of mine, down from Cambridge for the vacation. Jeremy Morrison. He's there.'

For some reason this intelligence put Marius into a state of almost uncontrollable excitement.

'The one with the enormous face? Who was at the christening?'

'The same.'

Marius clapped his hands with a bang that boomed round the balcony.

'Super, super,' he cried. 'I longed and longed to talk to him, but he was with those girls.'

'I think they'll be there too.'

Marius's face fell. Then, 'Never mind,' he said. 'If we're all *staying* there, there'll be plenty of time for me to talk to him, won't there?'

'What do you want to talk to Jeremy about?'

'I don't know. I . . . just want to be with him, I suppose.'

'Well then,' said Canteloupe, 'that seems to be settled. Everybody's happy – '

' – You haven't,' Marius reminded him, 'asked the Ogre what he thinks.'

'I'll telephone,' said Canteloupe to Fielding, 'if you'll find out the number.'

This was easier said than done. Ptolemaeos was extra-directory. So Fielding rang up Tom Llewyllyn, who, Canteloupe thought, might know the number, and got Len.

'What do you want him for?' said Len shamelessly.

Fielding explained.

'Gregory will do pieces of coke when he gets back and finds out,' said Len. 'But technically it's okay – though you may find that Ptoly's mansion is *complet* for the moment.'

But when Canteloupe reached Ptolemaeos through the number which Len gave to Fielding, Ptolemaeos was quite delighted with the suggestion.

'Only thing is,' he said, 'what a pity it's not Rosie. I find her the more interesting. But then this is a good chance of having Marius without her, which is the way I want it, *and* of having him without Gregory breathing down my neck like a bellows. Mind you, Isobel would have been all right, a nice inquisitive lady, *and* she could have taken care of his dear little knickers and things. But I'll happily settle for Marius *tout seul*. Most convenient, as it happens, as one of my guinea-pigs has just walked out on me.'

'Not Jeremy Morrison? Marius yearns for him.'

'Does he now? How interesting. It's that face, I think. Marius must want to hold it, as other children might want to hold the moon – or even a schoolroom globe or a basket ball. It's the idea of clasping something large and *round* . . . yes, Jeremy's here all right. It's one of the Salinger girls that went – pity, as I was just getting into her, so to speak. But her departure does mean there's plenty of room and plenty of time for Marius – in fact I think I'll start on him straight away, before Gregory has any chance to come and interfere. One thing: I'll want a full account of all this fracas at his school when you drop him here. When shall you bring him?'

'NOW,' said Canteloupe.

'Any time before three A.M.,' said Ptolemaeos affably. 'See that he has a good thick jersey with him. These Fens can be treacherous to those who aren't used to them.'

'He has his First Eleven sweater,' said Canteloupe, 'and his entire school trunk.'

'I hope you didn't come back on my account,' said Donald Salinger to Theodosia in the restaurant of the Ritz.

'No, Da,' said Theodosia, sipping her gazpacho and with her free hand gripping very tightly on her silk-trousered thigh. 'I was bored. I was looking forward to seeing you, of course, but I came away when I did because I was bored.'

I was fascinated, she thought, fascinated by those investigations. And so happy with the two people I love the best. Why did God (if any) suddenly make me the Intruder?

'How's Carmilla?'

'Oh, so happy.' Should she tell her father about Carmilla's new attachment – or rather, the new nature of her attachment – to Jeremy? No. Carmilla must tell her father, when she thought proper, herself.

'Oh, so happy?'

Her father had detected an abnormal note in the phrase. How careless of her.

'You know, having a good time. Mr Tunne is a very interesting man, Da.'

'Then why were you bored?'

Tricky return. Nasty length. Watch it.

'I wasn't much use to him,' she lied, clutching her flesh through the silk, 'and I was fed up with the Fens. Not a single human being to be seen for miles on end.'

'And very nice too, I should have thought. Carmilla isn't bored?'

'Not yet. She's always liked Jeremy Morrison.'

'Morrison? What's he got to do with it?'

'He was there too. I wrote and told you.'

'I wonder,' said Donald, 'if he's the shit his father is?'

'*Shit*, Da?'

'Sorry. Not a word to use in front of one of my own girls.' He leant over the table and very lightly touched her shoulder, at once asking and assuming her forgiveness for his lapse in courtesy. 'Crook? No, too heavy a word. Hypocrite? No: close but still inexact. Cheat? No, he always obeyed the rules, did Peter. The thing was, he somehow contrived to use them in the spirit in which they were not intended. He used them to make traps for people.'

Traps. God (if any) send that Peter's son, Jeremy, was not making a trap for Carmilla. After all, Da was rich – money rich. Jeremy would sooner have money than the land which he was destined to have. But then two could play at that game. Perhaps Carm was trapping Jeremy, longing to be Lady of the Manor, head bitch in that part of Norfolk. For a moment Theodosia was seized by a frenzy of jealousy and suspicion of both of them. If only it had been *she* that Jeremy wanted. But he *did* want her. For sex anyway. Perhaps if she had done those things he wanted she might have been the one standing there flush with Jeremy in the Cathedral Close. Had he . . . done those things with Carmilla? Had Carmilla lain down and made him free of her splendid loins? Oh, stop, stop, stop. This was Love and she must love them both the more for it, not besmirch it with evil and prurient imaginings.

'What traps did Mr Morrison make?' she forced herself to ask.

'He was an expert at what chess players call the Fork. He was always contriving to threaten two of his opponent's pieces with one of his own, so that whichever piece his opponent moved he was bound to lose the other.'

'But that's quite legitimate, Da. That's what you're meant to do at chess, if you can. Get your opponent's pieces in a Fork.'

'Oh yes. But are you meant to do it in life, Thea? With people?'

The Fork. Jeremy had made them both love him. He was threatening both pieces. Suddenly, seeing Carmilla and herself as standing mitred and trousered on separate squares of a huge chess board, with Jeremy as a snorting country Knight, clumping towards them over the board on a muddy Norfolk roan, she started to giggle.

'Is it so funny, Thea? To set traps for people in life?'

'I was thinking of something else, Da. I was thinking, would you like to take me to Lord's tomorrow? And there's a play I'd like to see in the evening, a revival of Christopher Fry, *The Lady's Not for Burning*. Would you like to take me?'

'I don't see that either cricket at Lord's or the revival of Mr Fry's play are matters to giggle about. Neither do I see why you've left your sister behind in Cambridgeshire. Twins are meant to be together.'

'No, Da. Not all the time, not when they grow up. If they stay too close . . . someone might trap them in a Fork.'

'Someone called Morrison?'

'No, Da,' she answered, almost simultaneously with his question. 'He's just a nice, silly boy.' When he wants to be, she thought. 'We like him. He's fun to be with. Only after seeing him all the year at Cambridge, I got bored.'

'Your sister didn't.'

'It would have been bad manners – if both of us had left suddenly. And what about Mr Tunne's experiments?'

'What about them?'

'Well, he's trying to find out how the human brain works – and whether there's a soul as well. He must have someone to help him.'

'He's got young Morrison to help him.'

'He needs girls as well. All sorts.'

'If it's a soul he's looking for, you'd better have stayed yourself and sent your sister back to London.'

'Don't be silly, Da. Either we all have a soul, or none of us has.'

'I shouldn't be too sure of that.'

'Anyway, I was the one that got bored. Will you take me to Lord's tomorrow? It's Middlesex versus Lancs, second day. You can introduce me into the Warner Stand, and go off to the Pavilion yourself.'

'I'll sit in the Warner with you, girl, and be the proudest man in the realm.'

Canteloupe and Fielding, having dropped Marius, his school trunk, and an oral history of his recent adventures on Ptolemaeos in the midnight Fens, drove back to London, where Fielding spent the night at Buttock's Hotel and Canteloupe at the Ritz. It had been agreed that Fielding, as the expert on Tessa, should be available to help Ptolemaeos with Marius at any time, and to this end he proposed to spend the next few days at his house in

Broughton Staithe, which was hardly an hour's drive from Ptolemaeos's establishment.

'I have to work anyway,' Fielding told Canteloupe on the way back to London, 'and better Broughton than Buttock's for that. What shall you do now?'

'Go back to Wiltshire in the morning,' Canteloupe said, 'and try to track down Gregory and Isobel. They can't just have vanished.'

But by tea time the following day, after Canteloupe had put in several solid hours on the telephone, it began to look as if they had done just that.

The Manager of the Sterns' hotel in Cyprus said, no, they had not returned there, and he could only repeat that he had last seen them when they were setting out in a taxi for Nicosia Airport five days previously.

The Manager of the hotel for which they had reservations in Heracleion stated that they had still not arrived, and repeated his request to Canteloupe to send money on account of their dishonoured booking.

The Immigration Authorities at Heracleion Airport said that they had had time to check their files since Canteloupe's last enquiry, and that they had no record of Mr and Mrs Stern's arrival in Crete.

The Emigration Authorities at Nicosia Airport said that they too had been busy with their files. No holder of a British passport in the name of Stern had flown out of the airport for the last month. They had called for and with great difficulty procured from Olympic Airways the flight lists of the day in question, and there were indeed First Class bookings for Mr and Mrs Gregory Stern on the 1315 hours flight from Nicosia to Heracleion; but the desk personnel of Olympic at Nicosia stated that no one had appeared to claim those bookings – which of course confirmed their own (the Emigration Authorities') assertion that no such persons had flown out of Nicosia.

Then they must have left the bloody place some other

way, thought Canteloupe. Or still be there, for that matter, though not in their previous hotel.

This he rang up again, and asked the Manager if he could make enquiries of the taxi driver who had driven the Sterns to Nicosia Airport.

While Canteloupe was waiting for the Manager to ring back, Glinter Parkes rang up from Sandwich to say that Roseworm Major's stamp album, which contained (according to Roseworm) a priceless issue in honour of Cypriot Independence, had totally disappeared and that there was pretty good reason to suppose it had been exported in Marius's school trunk. Marius had produced a stamp album for Matron to pack, and Matron had naturally assumed it was his; but now she remembered that it answered very closely to the description which was being broadcast of Roseworm's, etc., etc., etc.

While Canteloupe was digesting this item, the Manager of the Sterns' hotel in Nicosia rang back to say that the Sterns' taxi driver, a man well known to the Manager and indifferent honest by local standards, reported that the Sterns had paid him off outside the main entrance to the airport buildings. He had summoned a porter to carry their luggage to the Olympic Airways desk, and had driven away while the porter (a man unknown to him, though he often dropped passengers at the airport) was loading the luggage on to his trolley.

So somewhere between the main entrance and the Olympic desk, thought Canteloupe, they vanished – which was to say, they changed direction. Not Gregory's kind of behaviour – though it could appeal to Isobel. Why? Whither? With whom? Or compelled by whom? Oh, for Christ's sake. All he could do was to report the matter to the Cypriot police and await the results of their enquiries. In order to find out the number, he had to ring up the hotel Manager in Nicosia yet once more – only to discover that the man had had the great good sense to report the whole affair to the Cypriot police himself.

Canteloupe then rang up Ptolemaeos Tunne (having prudently recorded the number which Len had given Fielding the previous night) and reported Glinter's suspicions about Roseworm Major's stamp album. 'He's been doing quite a lot of bagging lately,' he added, 'or so they say.'

Ptolemaeos said he would consult Carmilla Salinger, who had been put in charge of Marius's school trunk and its contents. Ten minutes later Ptolemaeos rang back to say that Carmilla had discovered in the trunk a stamp album which bore the name of Roseworm and did indeed contain a tatty and tattered issue in celebration of Cypriot Independence. Marius was busy playing small cricket with Jeremy, and so Carmilla had simply driven to the nearest village and by this time would already have posted the album to Glinter at Oudenarde House. How Marius would react when he discovered it had gone remained to be seen.

Canteloupe then rang up Glinter to tell him of the album's presence among Marius's effects and of its prompt despatch to Sandwich. Glinter, for his part, undertook to manage its 'discovery' somewhere in the school grounds without implicating Marius . . . who, he felt, should now enjoy amnesty until he was 'sorted out'.

Duty now required that Canteloupe should render a full account of everything that had passed to Baby and Jo-Jo; but he remembered that they were in their private grove of lady-birch, forbidden to all men save the infant Sarum of Old Sarum, and he decided, not without relief, to postpone their briefing until dinner.

'You must see, my dear, that this sort of thing is very difficult for others to live with,' said Ptolemaeos Tunne.

'Yes, sir,' said Marius; 'but they shouldn't have baited me like that.'

From the far end of the library the afternoon sun streamed down a colonnade of fluted pillars and fell just short of the alcove which contained Socrates and the sarcophagus. Marius, dressed in bathing trunks, sat barefoot on the bottom rung of the library steps, conversing with Ptolemaeos and drinking a glass of homemade lemonade, which contained Fenland herbs conducive to candour.

'No, they should not have baited you,' Ptolemaeos conceded. 'And you should not have lowered yourself to their level . . . to beneath their level.'

'I lost my temper, sir.'

'Evidently. Tell me: Rosie's friend Tessa taught you to hit people like that?'

'Yes.'

'And you think – or so Lord Canteloupe and Major Gray told me last night – that Tessa taught you because she wanted you to hit someone and disgrace yourself?'

'Yes.'

'But Major Gray says that Tessa is incapable of such malice.'

'He does not understand the new thing that is growing out of her.'

'On the contrary. He is well aware that girls of Tessa's age often . . . put out . . . some new thing of this kind.'

'But he does not *understand* it, sir. He did not feel the way it came up to me, the way it suddenly excited me, until I nearly did . . . what I do in my dreams.'

'What makes you do it in your dreams?'

'Almost anything. I dream of dogs jumping up at me or Nanny smacking me, or ragging with the boys at school. Or rather, these are the things it used to be. But since Tessa nearly made me do it that time in Buttock's it has always been her in my sleep. Her . . . and whatever is coming out of her. Something warm which comes out of her. Something which Rosie knows about too.'

'Ah.'

'But Tessa is meaning it to hurt me, sir. She makes me . . . do it . . . in my sleep, and that weakens me, and so I can't make runs.'

'You do it in your sleep because your body wants to do it, *needs* to do it, Marius. It cannot weaken you or stop you making runs. It is a sign that you are growing up to be a strong healthy man.'

'But it has stopped since Rosie finally swore that she had nothing to do with it – by which she really meant that she had lifted the spell. That is why I should have made runs again if only they had let me stay. As long as Rosie kept up the spell – as long as Tessa made her keep it up – Tessa was able to drain my strength in my sleep. Now she has stopped I should have been strong enough to make runs.'

'Rubbish. Wet dreams are entirely normal at your age and could do you no harm at all.'

'If they're normal, why have they stopped? Why have they stopped only since Rosie unwished her wish?'

'Of course they stop from time to time. They'll start again when they're ready. But they have nothing to do with Tessa or Rosie, or with your not making runs.'

'It wasn't only . . . that. When Tessa came into my dreams . . . with that something else growing out of her, it seemed to me that she wanted to steal something. Making it come wasn't enough. She wanted something else out of me. Or the warm thing that came with her did.'

'You mean . . . the thing that is growing out of her?'

'Yes. It sort of flows out of her, sir. Flows out of her and then makes a kind of soft cushion all round her. And when it came with her in my dreams, it wanted something out of me. Not just my cream.'

'Marius . . . climb into that bath. Put those rings round you and float . . .'

'. . . It feels good in here. Warm and soft.'

'Close your eyes. Pretend you are back with Tessa in Buttock's that day she wanted you to kiss her. You felt something was flowing from her as you came close and you nearly pumped cream because it felt so nice.'

'Rather like being in here, only a thousand times nicer.'

'But you turned away and didn't let go because you didn't want to make your trousers uncomfortable or to embarrass Tessa. So now, here you are, turning away – '

– Ptolemaeos stretched an arm towards the tape recorder, adjusted it slightly to allow for the timbre of Marius's transitional voice, and then –

' – Tell me, Marius. What did Tessa say?'

'Nothing. I ran from the room.'

'Very well. But you knew, Marius, that she wanted something.'

'She wanted to be kissed. Like a sloppy girl, that's all. But I was afraid I was going to make cream, because of the cushion coming out of her.'

'Was that the *only* reason, Marius? Didn't something . . . something about Tessa . . . or about what was flowing out of her . . . make you feel frightened?'

There was a long silence.

'Take your time, Marius,' said Ptolemaeos in a low, gentle voice. 'Take your time. Sleep. Such questions can be very troubling. You will answer much better and much more easily if you sleep.'

Marius's eyes closed.

'So,' said Ptolemaeos, 'something about Tessa, or what was coming out of her, made you feel frightened.'

203

'Yes,' said Marius, in a small, dreamy voice.

'Well, why were you frightened?'

'I was frightened because of what it wanted.'

'It?'

'What was coming out of Tessa.'

'Marius . . . what did It want?'

'Me. It wanted to leave Tessa and come to me. Tessa wanted this too. Both Tessa and It were somehow telling me, though she never opened her mouth. And then, later, It told me the same thing in my dreams. It sucked my cream and then told me that It wanted something more.'

'Your blood?'

'No. Not my blood. Me.' There was a rasping in Marius's throat. Then, 'IT WANTS TO BE ME.'

'But you say it has stopped coming. You say that since Rosie was allowed by Tessa (on *your* version) to unwish her wish, Tessa . . . and It . . . have stopped coming into your dreams.'

'It will not stop for long. When It has grown enough, It will be able to free itself from Tessa. At the moment It can only go where Tessa goes, and she and Rosie, whatever their reason, have stopped It coming to me. But they cannot stop It for long, and *Tessa does not want to stop It*, even if she could. She wants It to be free of her, and It wants to be free of her, and then It and Tessa want It to come to me. Nothing can stop this for much longer.'

'Couldn't Rosie?'

'I don't think so. When It has grown, It will be too strong for Rosie, even if It obeys her now.'

'But listen, Marius. Lord Canteloupe and Major Gray told me, last night, that you had told them that all spells had been lifted.'

'That was what I thought last night.'

'But this afternoon . . . less than twenty-four hours later, you think completely differently. You think all these things you have just been telling me.'

204

'I *know* all these things I have just been telling you.'

'You didn't last night, when you arrived here, but you do now?'

Marius, eyes still closed, inclined his head forward from the fitted pillow.

'When did you start to know?'

'Today. When I woke up. I tried to brush it away while I was playing cricket with Jeremy, but it is no good. I know.'

'But how do you know?'

'I just know.'

'Is it anything to do with this place, with anything or anyone here?'

'No . . . At least I don't think so. I just knew, even while I was enjoying myself with Jeremy, that neither Tessa nor Rosie can stop It . . . even if they should want to – for very much longer.'

'Stop It from what?'

'Getting free of Tessa and coming to me.'

'To do what?'

'To invade me. To occupy me.'

'Your body? Your brain?'

'ME. What makes me Marius Stern and none other. That is what It wants. My being. My soul.'

'Marius, who has told you this?'

'*It* has told me this.'

'That was in your dreams, which have stopped. Who has told you this since you have been here? When you woke up this morning?'

'I told you. I just knew.'

'I am giving you the lie, Marius. For your sake, I am giving you the lie direct. You did not "just know". Somebody or something told you. *Who or what?*'

For answer came a long howl, which gradually and despairingly faded into little more than a sigh.

After a while Marius slept deeper, snoring heavily. He

205

feels that he has a soul, thought Ptolemaeos: 'My being,' he said, 'my soul.' Entirely relaxed, utterly at ease in the physical sense, he had consulted his memory and this, if Sheraton were right, had referred the resultant problems to his soul. How? Ptolemaeos was no nearer to knowing that; but what he did know was that Marius's soul, appealed to by his memory, had spoken clearly back through the mouth of Marius of its much troubled and beleaguered state. Never mind that the threat of which it spoke did not exist, that it was impossible that his sister or her friend should harbour any such intentions or capacities: to Marius the threat was real (why?) and it was a threat to his being, to his soul, 'what makes me Marius Stern and none other'. Now, thought Ptolemaeos, there must be a strong presumption that if, speaking from his inner self, in total relaxation and without any motive to mislead, he distinguished between body-or-brain and being-or-soul, then the distinction was valid and a soul indeed he had.

So: beyond any doubt, Ptolemaeos told himself, Marius thinks, feels from the gut (as it were) that he has a soul; and why should this not be so? Meanwhile, however, there is a more immediate problem: if I am to save him from this threat (for even if only imagined it is real to him and therefore as maleficent as if it were true), if I am to save him from the effects of believing (whether truly or falsely) that there is a power which wishes to devour his being, then I must find out who or what told him that this is so. The threat had been lifted, he said just now: the voice which used to pronounce it in his dreams had ceased: then, when he awoke here this morning, somebody or something told him (that howl of despair proves this despite his insistence that 'he just knew'), somebody or something told him, made him certain, that the threat was back, was more imminent than ever before, that he was bound, very soon, to be engulfed. Who told him? How? Why here and why now?

PART THREE
The Pastime of Leviathan

Man goeth forth to his work, and to
his labour: until the evening.
O Lord, how manifold are Thy works:
in wisdom hast Thou made them all; the
earth is full of Thy riches.
So is the great and wide sea also:
wherein are things creeping innumerable,
both small and great beasts.
There go the ships, and there is that
Leviathan: whom Thou hast made to take
his pastime therein.

Psalm 104; vv 23–26

'You see, my dear,' said Max de Freville to the imagined figure of Lykiadopoulos, 'the principle is very simple. I accept sterling money for block bookings in my hotels in Corfu and Sicily and Volos, and I keep the money accepted right here, under my nose, in the St James's Street Branch of Lloyds Bank. An ever increasing pool of money for my little godson, Sarum of Old Sarum. Mind you, before I give it to him, it is better I should send it to Switzerland or America, where no one fusses about a gift tax; but such transfers, from here, are getting easier every day. And for that matter, a lot of my bookings are now made in Switzerland or America and the money banked there on the spot.'

'Yes,' replied Max to himself in dead Lyki's Yiddish lilt, 'you have explained the principle to me before; and of course you have plenty of funds in Greece or Italy to run your hotels in local money, and without drawing on the hard currencies which you hoard elsewhere. But sooner or later the Bank of Hellas is going to ask you what has become of the sterling or dollars or whatever which you have received for reservations, and then to demand that you bring them at once to Greece.'

'They can demand nothing of me,' said Max *in propria persona*, 'while I am sitting here with you, Lyki – '

' – Or rather with my ghost – '

' – While I am sitting here having luncheon in my London club.'

'But they can always sequester your hotels and other property in Greece (or Italy), and even attach your own person when you arrive there on your annual visit.'

'Anyway,' said Max, whacking the table, 'they have as

209

yet made no demands whatever. I shall anticipate any such action on their part by sending *some* sterling, etcetera, to Athens and Rome before they even begin to ask for it. That should keep them happy.'

'Not for long. Not when they realize the tiny ratio of the hard monies which you will have sent to those which you will actually have received.'

'The accounts will disguise this. They will make it appear that much of the sterling received, for example, has been spent on administration and advertisement here in London.'

'Why are you so obsessed,' said Lykiadopoulos as played by Max, 'with giving this rich little boy more money?'

'I have told you,' said Max. 'I wish him to have something by which to remember me as his godfather.'

The waiter came to remove Max's plate, which was pretty well cleaned off, and Lyki's, which was untouched.

'I'm afraid your friend does not like our food,' said the waiter to Max urbanely.

'He is Greek,' said Max, 'and therefore a man of uncertain tastes. Let us try him with one of the club's puddings.'

'Very well, sir,' said the waiter; and to Lykiadopoulos's chair: 'We have apple pie today, sir, fruit jelly, or fresh forest strawberries.'

'Bring me this apple pie,' said Max in Lyki's plummiest tones, which he had, when alive, reserved for the discussion of culinary or sexual delicacies. 'I hear the English make a very good thing of this apple pie. And for myself,' said Max in his own voice, 'I shall try the forest strawberries.'

Isobel Stern sat by a closed window and looked through the glass along the length of a long, bare re-entrant, down which a narrow stream curved like a scimitar right-handed into the sea. Where the stream met the sea was a small bay; round the shore of this were scattered clumps of cypress, these partially concealing small, stone, windowless buildings where the fishermen from the hamlet, in which Isobel now sat, kept dinghies and fishing tackle.

In one of these small stone buildings among the cypresses (so she had been told) Gregory was imprisoned. She need not, they said, worry about his health, as he was taken out to sit or walk in the open air for long periods twice a day. She was looking down the re-entrant now in hope of seeing him during one such period; but in the days since she had been brought here she had never once seen him.

Soon it would be time for herself to be taken out into the fresh air. A young woman in a short black dress (well above the knee it hung, a very odd garment indeed) would accompany her along a cart track, past the three houses of yellow brick and of recent date which constituted the central and major portion of the hamlet, and then down a very narrow path with high banks to a pool under a waterfall. There they would sit on two smooth rocks until it was time, perhaps an hour later, for Isobel to be taken back through the yellow hamlet to her room in the house on the edge of it.

The first afternoon, she had tried to run away and had been knocked unconscious by the woman in the short black dress, who had run after her, seized her collar in her left hand and jabbed her in the solar plexus with her right.

A few days later she had asked (in Italian, the only

language she had in common with the woman, though it did not come easily to either of them) whether she might swim in the pool under the waterfall. The woman had disallowed her request, politely but firmly, on two grounds: first, she said, there were dangerous undercurrents in the pool, which might sweep Isobel out of it and on down the stream to another waterfall, where she would be battered to death; and secondly, the woman had deposed, Isobel had no costume for this activity, and must therefore swim, if swim she did, naked, which would be indecent. Since the first reason was quite strong enough to deter any sane person, Isobel wondered why the young woman had bothered to add the second, and had conjectured that there were elements here both of puritanism and of prurience.

The young woman was very handsome and rather stocky. She reminded Isobel of Jo-Jo Guiscard. Although Isobel had never been sexually attracted to other women, she thought that she would enjoy wrestling with this one (particularly in the water, were swimming allowed) as if they had both been boys. Or perhaps it would be pleasant to massage her, or be massaged by her, as though they were athletes after exercise in the gymnasium. Isobel had once feigned a pain in the neck and asked the young woman to rub it for her. She had met with a brisk and even indignant refusal. Isobel, opining that indignation was more promising, in this context, than indifference, had determined to renew her suggestions after a brief interval.

There were, however, problems of far greater scope and urgency than that of how to make physical approaches to the young woman in the black dress. By Isobel's calculations it was now six days since she and Gregory had been . . . deflected at Nicosia Airport. A well spoken and presentable, if jowlly, young man in a dark suit and dark tie had greeted them while they were on their way to the Olympic desk. They were, he enquired in English, were they not, Mr and Mrs Gregory Stern, First Class passengers to Heracleion? Yes, they were. Well, there had been some slight difficulty about their booking; he was very sorry for the inconvenience, but would they kindly accompany him to his office? Of course they would. The young man had nodded to their porter (in confirmation rather than command, as Isobel had realized later) and the whole party, the jowlly young man, Isobel and Gregory, their porter and seven pieces of luggage, had proceeded down the hall towards a door marked

ΕΞΟΔΟΣ

'Rum,' Isobel had remarked to Gregory, '"Exodos" means the way out.'

'Perhaps his office is in another building,' Gregory had sensibly rejoindered.

It was indeed. In another building, in another country: here in this house, in this hamlet in the re-entrant, whither they had been carried, blindfold, by car, then by helicopter, then by motor launch for many hours, then finally by car once more. Isobel had not been told where they were, or why, or what was wanted of them. All she knew was that Gregory had been taken (or so the jowlly young man had said) to live in one of the stone huts in the cypresses by the shore; that she herself was in the charge of a clean, decorous, elderly woman, who lived in the same house and was perhaps the jowlly young man's mother; and that every afternoon the young woman with the short black dress (a daughter of the house? a widow? both?) came to take her for the same walk, to the pool under the waterfall. She was allowed the freedom of her luggage and her books (thank God she had packed the *Iliad* and a complete Milton) and had been told that Gregory enjoyed similar privileges (privileges?), being allowed ample artificial light by which to read (let her be assured of that) when he was not indeed out in the open. For the rest, she was sufficiently and sometimes daintily fed, mostly on creatures of the sea, interesting vegetables and rather pungent cheeses (no eggs).

213

Although she could not communicate with the old lady of the house (who spoke no tongue known to her ears or even vaguely recognizable to them) she could convey her questions and requests in English to the jowlly young man (Pontos, he had told her to call him) or in flimsy Italian to the young woman, whom she had nicknamed and addressed as 'Artemis', apparently to the young woman's rather haughty approval.

All in all, she thought, she had nothing of any substance to complain of in her style of life; but this might not be the case with Gregory (whatever Pontos's reassurances on the subject) and in any case the situation, in the broader sense, was not readily tolerable. Mercifully, both Gregory's business interests and their two children would be in the best possible hands – Canteloupe's – but really, thought Isobel, fuck hanging about round here for ever. On the other hand, there was clearly nothing to be done, as she wanted no more knock-out punches in the solar plexus; presumably they would, sooner or later, be missed, and enquiries then set in train; and meanwhile one had better sit tight and – what was that favourite phrase of Fielding's out of Trollope? – 'just let the thing go on'. So that's it, girl, she admonished herself: just keep your knickers clean (not difficult, as the old lady was an exquisite laundress) and make the best of things as they come.

The door was unlocked from the outside and brusquely opened.

'Ciao, Artemisa mia.'

'Buon giorno, signora. You will now come for our walk.'

'It will much please me to walk with you.'

For the first time, Isobel noticed with a tiny *frisson*, Artemis had discarded her thick black stockings and was wearing silk knee-socks of Oxford blue, which ended, rather oddly, half way up her kneecaps. She had very round and appealing knees; and above them the beginning of strong, spare thighs. If she would only hurt her knee, thought Isobel, how gladly I should bathe it and kiss it better. Aloud she said, 'Let us go then, *cara*.'

'Let us go, *egregia signora*.'

On the second morning after Marius had arrived at Ptolemaeos Tunne's house in the Fens, Carmilla Salinger drove him into Cambridge to buy some shirts and pyjamas, both of which were in very thin supply in his school trunk.

'Matron's just thoroughly slack,' Marius explained. 'She loses half your kit and forgets to send the rest to the laundry.'

'Yes,' said Carmilla, and saw her chance. 'So slack that she didn't notice Roseworm's name on that stamp album when you brought it to her to pack. Though she did remember the album later, when Roseworm complained that it had been stolen.'

'He gave it to me,' Marius said.

'That's not his story.' Carmilla parked clumsily and crookedly near the Postern Gate of Lancaster Collge, leaving the offside front tyre slewed out on to Queen's Road. 'I've sent it back,' she said.

'Then you shouldn't have done. He gave it to me. We did a deal.'

'Oh?'

'Roseworm is the ugliest and smelliest boy in the school. But he knows things. He does experiments. He promised to give me his stamp album if I let him do an experiment with me.'

They walked up the avenue from the Postern Gate of Lancaster towards the bridge. Quietly and naturally Marius slipped his hand into Carmilla's, as though she had been an elder sister or cousin. The dull day brightened for Carmilla, who longed to stoop and hug him.

'What sort of experiment?' she said carefully.

'I had to let him suck blood from a small cut in my finger. And I had to give little bits of myself, a piece of loose skin, and some of the hairs from my legs. I do have hairs on my legs,' said Marius defensively. 'Only very tiny fair ones, but I've got them, and I had to give some to Roseworm, with – one or two other things – and he made a kind of paste and ate it on his bread and butter at tea. He said that in this way he would become more like me, that he'd start being good at cricket and not be so smelly and ugly.'

'No prize for guessing what happened?'

'Of course he stayed as ugly and smelly as ever. Worse, because that paste he ate made his breath stink for days. No amount of Gibbs SR was any help . . .'

'Not very flattering to you – since that paste was made of your ingredients.'

'There's the chapel where we all went to christen Sarum,' said Marius.

'Would you like to go in again now? I don't know whether you noticed the windows last time you were there, but they're something rather special.'

'Let's go in.' He held her hand a little tighter. 'So that's why Roseworm said I stole his album,' he said. 'The experiment didn't work, and he knew I was in disgrace, so he played a mean, dirty trick to get it back.'

They turned left, in front of the courteous yet commanding 18th century façade of Sitwell's Building, and walked toward the south door of the chapel.

'But Lord Canteloupe says they think you have stolen other things,' said Carmilla.

Marius giggled.

'People give me presents because they're keen on me,' he said. 'Then, when their parents or someone ask them what they've done with the things, they're afraid of looking silly and say I stole them. One boy said he'd give me ten pounds if I'd let him touch me.'

'Touch you?'

'You know. There.'

'And did you?'

'No. I said it would have to be twenty-five pounds for a single second. What Mummy calls a pony. And of course he hadn't got it.'

'I'm rather surprised he had ten.'

'Some of the boys' parents are very rich and showy-off. They take piles of notes out and hand them round when they're saying good-bye after *exeats* or things like that. He was furious when I wouldn't let him do it for ten and spread some story that I'd tried to bully him into giving the money to me.'

A notice outside the chapel said:

CONFERENCE IN PROGRESS: NO TOURISTS

They walked past the notice. A fake proletarian voice said:

'Can't you read?'

'I am an undergraduate of Lancaster College,' said Carmilla, 'and I shall enter my own chapel as and when I wish.'

'The college has hired the chapel to us for our conference. Young Christians against the Bomb, and Americans out of San Salvador. You can't come in.'

The young man who had spoken barred their passage and jutted his beard. The next thing Marius knew was that the young man was flat on his back, and that he and Carmilla were stepping over the body and into the chapel.

'I *say*, Carmilla,' Marius said.

'Bloody nerve, trying to keep a girl out of her own college chapel.'

But now Marius hung back.

'Carmilla, Carmilla, I can't go in.'

'Nonsense, sweetheart, what are you saying?'

'I CAN'T GO IN. IT HURTS.'

'Just hold my hand tight and walk slowly forward.'

'No.'

Marius howled and fell on the floor of the porch, next to the fake prole. His body jerked and plunged. Saliva whipped out from the corners of his mouth and round his cheeks. Carmilla stooped to soothe him and was struck painfully by Marius's kneecap in her stomach.

'And what's all this?' said a quiet, jolly voice.

Looking up, Carmilla saw Wilfred the Porter.

'Oh, Wilfred,' she said stupidly. 'I thought you were always on the Night Gate.'

'Change of schedule, Miss Carmilla, for the Long Vacation.' He put his hand on Marius's forehead.

'Peace,' he said.

Marius lay still.

'Useful trick, that,' said Wilfred. 'I learned it in India, during the war. Not everyone can do it. In fact no one can do it unless he means what he says, which almost nobody does.' He smiled at Carmilla. 'Who's the young gentleman?' he asked, as he loosened Marius's collar.

'Marius Stern. Son of an old friend of the Provost.'

'So that's all right then. In two minutes he'll be as trim as walking out order. Take him somewhere for a warm drink, Miss Carmilla, and leave me to cope with this rubbish.'

He pointed at the man with the beard, who had begun to stir.

'Best be on your way before he wakes up and makes trouble, Miss. I didn't see what happened, it goes without saying, but if he complains of you someone might have to pay attention, see, as I'm afraid there's no doubt about it – his lot have hired the chapel fair and square. Shouldn't be allowed of course, but there it is. So on your feet, Master

Marius, and off you both go before beaver boy here recognizes you and starts shouting the odds.'

Carmilla and Marius, once more hand in hand, walked briskly to the Main Gate.

'How do you feel?' she said, as they came into King's Parade.

'A bit muzzy but pretty well all right,' Marius said. 'What on earth happened?'

'Never mind, my darling,' said Carmilla. 'It's over now.'

'Jeremy.'

'What about him?'

'He will still be there when we get back?'

'Of course he will,' said Carmilla, feeling rather hurt.

'Epilepsy?' said Ptolemaeos Tunne. 'But there is no former history of it. An isolated epileptic fit?'

Ptolemaeos, Carmilla and Jeremy were sitting in deck chairs in the summerhouse at the bottom of Ptolemaeos's garden. A bottle of Cognac was on the ground between them all; the cicadas hummed and grated through the close, starless night. Marius, feeling (he said) very tired, had gone to bed.

'Isolated . . . if there are no more,' Jeremy said.

'Epileptics often suffer from kleptomania,' Ptolemaeos pursued. 'If Marius turned out to be a congenital epileptic, that could explain the thefts at his school.'

'He has already explained them,' Carmilla said. She told the two men of her conversation with Marius while she had walked with him through Lancaster.

'You beleive him?' Jeremy said.

'I do. I also believe that this – incident – in the chapel porch this morning was nothing to do with epilepsy. Some

219

kind of violent physical allergy was set off in him as we were about to cross the threshold of the chapel.'

'What could have caused it?'

'Memory?' said Carmilla. 'The last time he went to Lancaster Chapel was on the same day that Rosie, according to his story, first put a jinx on him in the Provost's Garden.'

'He told me yesterday,' said Ptolemaeos, 'that the adolescent Tessa Malcolm is putting out some kind of emanation which not only excites him sexually but is planning . . . to detach itself from Tessa, with her encouragement, and take him over instead. It was this efflux or emanation, he said, that came to him at nights as a succubus and gave him wet dreams, thus draining him of the strength he needed for his cricket.' Ptolemaeos paused and poured himself two thirds of a glass of cognac. 'Up till now,' Ptolemaeos continued, 'his sister Rosie has been able to control this emanation through her influence with Tessa. But according to Marius, he knew, on the first morning he woke up here, that is yesterday, that Rosie had almost lost control, and that the emanation would shortly be free of Tessa and greedy for himself, wishing to absorb his whole being, "whatever," as he put it,' "makes me Marius Stern and none other."'

'You connect this with this morning's affair?' said Jeremy.

'I am trying to. I particularly want to discover why he is so certain that . . . It . . . is now coming close and what is the source of his information. This he refuses to tell me. All I know is that when questioned yesterday (after being given a mildly laced drink to loosen his tongue) he gave the impression that he was contemplating the whole subject, not in superficial and cerebral terms of mere deduction and calculation, but with the deepest spiritual concern of his inmost soul or being. The effort which he had to make to express the sense of his very soul through the crude media of brain and speech was obvious and very affecting. The trouble was that when I asked him the all-important question, "Who or what has told you that It is now so close?", and when I pressed the question for all it was worth, the implications of my enquiry were apparently so distressing to him that all correspondence between his soul and his brain, and so between his soul and me, totally ceased.'

'But the correspondence – between his soul and his brain, I mean – will surely have been renewed since then?' Jeremy said.

'Almost certainly. One theory must be that such correspondence led, in the given circumstances, to a protest, caused by the evil influence of It over Marius's mental or psychic being, against his going on to holy ground this morning.'

'But a few minutes before,' said Carmilla, 'he seemed to welcome the idea of going into the chapel. It was only as he was actually about to enter it, from the south porch, that he was struck down.'

'What better moment for a protest against God,' said Ptolemaeos, 'than on the very threshold of His House?'

'Surely a protest so fundamental could not have been so swiftly and easily defused merely by a kind college porter . . . even if he is an old India hand?'

'There can be no simple answer,' said Ptolemaeos somewhat jejunely, 'if indeed we find any answer at all.'

'What's the plan of campaign?' Jeremy asked.

'Observation, what else? More enquiries intended to elucidate the nature of the link between brain and soul, in the hope that these investigations may tell us something of the soul's – *his* soul's – particular condition or situation.'

'No one else?'

'Not for the time being. Later on, perhaps, I may experiment on you, Jeremy, if you establish friendship with Marius, and, I think, on one or both of the Blessington children, as measures of normality.'

'Rosie Stern?'

'Not until I am satisfied that there is no more to be had from Marius, and he can be sent away.'

'You forget,' said Jeremy, 'there is nowhere to send him . . . until his parents return.'

'They must be back fairly soon,' said Carmilla.

'Have you heard anything on the subject from Canteloupe today?' said Jeremy to Ptolemaeos.

'Not a word.'

'There you are,' said Jeremy. 'That must mean they're still unaccounted for.'

'Jeremy.' Marius stood in front of them, wearing the pale green pyjamas which Carmilla had bought for him at Ryder & Amies in King's Parade. 'Jeremy,' said Marius. He beckoned and moved away up the lawn. 'Please, Jeremy,' the small voice drifted back through the night, almost drowned by the cicadas.

When Fielding Gray told Maisie Malcolm (before he left London for Broughton Staithe) of Marius's expulsion from Oudenarde House and of the incident which had caused it, Maisie was much exercised about what version of the affair should be put up to Rosie and Tessa. 'They mustn't think they are in any way to blame,' Maisie kept saying.

'But they could well be to blame,' Fielding said. 'Whether they meant to or not, between the pair of them they got Marius into such a state of randiness and paranoia that something was bound to snap.'

'That boy's rotten. I've always thought so. Besides, you might say he started it all by saying nasty things to Rosie about my Tessa.'

'Or that Tessa started it all by teaching him how to fight dirty and then asking for a kiss.'

'Or that *you* started it all,' said Maisie. 'By teaching Tessa those horrid ways of hitting people in the first place.'

'You agreed that she should be instructed. You took a great interest in it all. You were present at all the lessons.'

'Perhaps because I wasn't quite sure what she was going to be taught,' said Maisie with a mean edge.

'Let's not be silly, my dear. Let us decide what to tell Rosie and Tessa about Marius.'

In the end they told them neither lies nor truth. Marius had been wickedly teased at school, they said (not mentioning what he had been teased about, though it was clear from Rosie's expression that she at least had immediately guessed); in consequence he had lost his temper, and had hit one of his tormentors so hard that the doctor had been summoned (neither the nature of the injury nor the style of its infliction being specified). It was thought to be as well that he should stay away from Oudenarde for the time being –

' – Then he can come here,' Rosie said, while Tessa nodded vigorously in support –

– And Lord Canteloupe, as his temporary guardian, having decided that he needed fresh air, peaceful surroundings, and as much cricket as could be had in the circumstances, had sent him to Ptolemaeos Tunne's house near Cambridge.

At this intelligence both Rosie and Tessa looked, if only for a split second, very angry, particularly Tessa.

'Rosie has told me about Mr Ptolemaeos Tunne,' she said. 'Mr Ptolemaeos Tunne will *pry*.'

'What if he does?' said Fielding easily.

'He may find things out.'

'Why should *you* mind?' said Maisie.

Neither of the girls answered. Fielding watched them closely while Rosie sent her friend a glance of reassurance, as who would say, 'Hold your tongue and leave it all to me.'

Rosie Stern told Jakki Blessington the story of Marius's dismissal, while Tessa Malcolm told Caroline. This they did in Kensington Gardens, where the girls of Collingham's went to play rounders, in an interval between the innings.

'So you both relented too late,' said Caroline.

'It was just bad luck,' said Tessa serenely, 'that everything happened in the wrong order. *We* weren't to know that the other boys would tease Marius and make him lose his temper.'

'You should never have interfered in the first place.'

'We didn't. Rosie told him what he deserved for his nasty behaviour – to make no runs, she said, and that was what she wished. But she had no power actually to interfere and make it happen.'

'She should never have said anything so spiteful and unkind.'

'Marius said horrid things for no reason. *He* was the first to be spiteful and unkind,' said Tessa. She turned away from Caroline, giving, as she did so, a shrug of the shoulder which momentarily emphasized her irregularity.

Jakki, by contrast, was not concerned to analyse the rights and wrongs of it all; she was quite simply and deeply distressed that Marius should have let himself down so horribly and must now, as she conceived, be wracked with misery and remorse.

'I don't think it's quite so bad as you think,' Rosie told her. 'From his point of view . . . he'll have quite a nice time with Mr Tunne. And there's someone there to play cricket with him – that moon-faced young man at the christening, do you remember, the son of the MP.'

'Oh Marius,' said Jakki, in a low, strained voice.

'Mr Tunne,' said Rosie, 'thinks he's terribly clever at finding things out. He'll try to find out about Marius. Then he'll send Marius away and try to find out about me.'

'Will he succeed?'

'In the end, I expect. But none of it will be anything like what he thinks.'

'Daddy says Mr Tunne is trying to find out if we really have souls,' Jakki said.

'If we were meant to know for certain, we'd know already,' Rosie said. Her long black hair glistened as the sun came out. 'Had you heard that my parents have got lost? Everyone keeps saying it's only a muddle about hotel bookings, but if it was only that sort of a muddle, they'd have cleared it up by now.'

'You don't seem very upset.'

'No. You see my parents, although occasionally very silly, are really good, kind people. So they will be all right. "The souls of the righteous,"' quoted Rosie unsententiously, '"are in the hand of God, and there shall no torment touch them."'

'Where did you learn that? It's not the sort of thing they tell us at Collingham's.'

'I read it in a book, by Mrs Malcolm's friend with the broken face. Fielding Gray. One of the characters, an army officer quotes it – '

' – A soldier,' corrected Jakki. 'Only foreigners and policemen call themselves officers in ordinary speech.'

'He's not calling himself an officer. *I'm* calling him one. It's important you should know he is one, as he's addressing his men after a battle. And in his speech he says this quotation about the souls of the righteous, though he doesn't say where it comes from.'

'But you just said we can't be sure whether we have souls or not.'

'If we do, then the souls of the righteous will be protected. If we don't, then nothing really matters at all, if you'd like to think of it carefully,' Rosie said.

Isobel Stern was sleeping in the house in the hamlet in the re-entrant.

First, Gregory came to her, flying up from the stone hut among the cypresses by the sea.

'They do not want money,' Gregory said. 'What they want is quite simple, something with which I could easily furnish them, but this I may not do.'

'Why may you not?' said Isobel in her dream.

'Because it would destroy my honour . . . my honour as a Jew.'

Gregory sank back towards the sea.

Next, Rosie came, walking up the re-entrant, almost skimming up it so light were her steps, and joined Isobel and Artemis by the pool under the waterfall.

'Enjoy yourself here with this lady,' said Rosie pointing at Artemis. 'Do not hurry home on my account.'

Before Isobel could decide whether or not there had been an element of irony or sarcasm in this remark, Rosie was no longer there. Baby Canteloupe's gay and rather raucous laughter sounded among the trees. Isobel looked eagerly for her niece, but Baby did not come to her.

Instead, Fielding Gray came.

'They are trying to say it is Tessa's fault,' he said, 'and indeed there is a plausible case, if Marius can be believed, to be made out against her; but I am certain in my heart that Tessa is too pure, too kind, too loving to wish anyone ill.'

Before Isobel could enquire what they were trying to say was Tessa's fault or what Marius had to do with it, Fielding too had vanished.

Artemis came near to Isobel and sat on a rock opposite her.

'So you like my knee,' Artemis said, and presented it, bare above her dark blue hose, for Isobel to kiss it. Artemis's toes began to play in Isobel's groin, under her dress. Isobel awoke to find that she was masturbating, agreeably and effectively it seemed, for the first time since she had ceased to be a virgin.

'I'm missing my good old Jew boy,' Isobel thought, and made herself desist.

'Please, Jeremy,' said Marius.

Jeremy and Marius stood on the lawn together, just out of earshot of Carmilla and Ptolemaeos, who were still sitting in the summerhouse. Marius was bare-footed; his new pale green pyjamas had begun to slip and were bunched up round his ankles.

'But it would get me into terrible trouble,' said Jeremy.

'No, it wouldn't. It's Mr Tunne's house and Mr Tunne would understand. We're not going to do anything, Jeremy. I just want you there with me. To protect me.'

'Protect you against what?'

'The thing that's coming for me. Coming from Tessa.'

'But if this is true, which I cannot believe, Marius – but if it is true, how could I protect you?'

'I don't quite know. I just feel that as long as you are there I'll safe. Please, Jeremy. It's a big enough bed, the one in my room, and very comfortable. We shan't be in each other's way.'

Jeremy looked at the slender pale green figure and wanted, in much the same way (had he known it) as Carmilla had wanted that morning in the avenue, to bend down and hug it.

'You'll get cold,' he said. 'Go to my room. It will look better. I'll come later.'

'Soon.'

'As soon as I can.'

'I shan't be able to sleep until you come. I shan't be safe.'

'As soon as I can, Marius.'

Marius trailed away up the lawn. Jeremy returned to the summerhouse.

'Well?' Carmilla said.

'He's frightened. Or says he is. But he thinks I can protect him.'

'How?'

'By . . . sleeping in the same bed.'

'If anyone sleeps with Marius,' said Carmilla, 'it should be me.'

'But it is Jeremy whom he has asked,' said Ptolemaeos Tunne.

'He made it quite clear,' said Jeremy, 'that he wanted nothing but my company.'

'Do whatever he asks,' said Ptolemaeos.

Carmilla handed some keys to Jeremy.

'The keys of Marius's trunk,' she said. She rose and lumbered away up the lawn.

'Oh, Christ,' said Jeremy. 'Women.'

'Do whatever he asks,' said Ptolemaeos, 'on condition that he tells you *how* he learned, on his first morning here, that . . . whatever it is . . . is coming to possess him.'

'And Carmilla?'

'I'll deal with her,' Ptolemaeos said.

'Plans for the Long Vacation,' said Greco Barraclough to Nicos Pandouros in Barraclough's drawing room in Sitwell's Building. 'Ireland for July; brief visits to my old friend Ptolemaeos Tunne in the Fens before we leave for Ireland and when we come back; the Pyrenees in August; Greece in September.'

'Can I make my own plans . . . just for August, *Kyrie*?'

'I shall need you to share the driving.'

'But, *Kyrie* – '

' – Hear me, Nico. You have just obtained an extremely bad result in your examination. I have had a lot of trouble persuading the Provost to keep you on as an undergraduate of this college next year. The very least you can do, by way of gratitude, is to fall in with my arrangements without making a fuss.'

'It is not that I am not grateful, *Kyrie*; but that I do . . . sometimes . . . long to be, just for a little while, free.'

'When we are in Greece, you may go, by yourself, to visit your friends in Areopolis.'

'Thank you, *Kyrie*.'

'They will doubtless remind you of the duties owed by boys in your situation to the patrons who adopt them.'

'They are good Maniots, *Kyrie*, and will speak with authority of the customs of the Mani. But even there things are beginning to change. And elsewhere . . . here in Cambridge . . . no one can understand why I am at your beck. They laugh at me when I say, "No, I cannot come with you this evening, I must go with the *Kyrios* Barraclough." *Kyrie*, one reason why I did so badly in the examinations was that I had constantly to interrupt my

229

studies to do your bidding. You must, please, make me more free.'

'Before you seek to sever our connection, Nico, you had better ask the advice of your friends in Areopolis when you visit them this autumn. Although things may be, as you assert, changing there, I think I know what their answer will be.'

'I am not seeking to sever our connection, *Kyrie*. Merely to make it less constricting.'

'You have caught the English disease. "Give me money that I may not work for it." Do you remember the first day you came to me at Vatheia, Nico? And what you then promised?'

'To be your man, *Kyrie*, until I was twenty-five years of age.'

'You have served me well, Nico; and I have served you well. Do not be discontented.'

Nicos took Barraclough's right hand, turned it palm upward, and stooped to kiss it. But even as he did so he heard again the contemptuous laughter of his companions of earlier that evening, the clipped, spiteful laughter which had followed him when he left, as he told them, to have a drink with Mr Barraclough, but in fact, as they knew, to wait upon his master.

Baby Canteloupe and Jo-Jo Guiscard walked hand in hand through their private grove to the little pool at its centre. It reflected a misty and gibbous moon but no stars nor planets.

'Canty is flapping,' said Baby. 'He cannot find Auntie Isobel or Uncle Gregory. Nor can the Cypriot police. Nor can I, with my little eye.'

A creature of the night squealed in agony, not many feet away.

'Would you expect to?' said Jo-Jo. 'I mean, I thought all that stopped when you were carrying Sarum.'

'Yes. But there have been occasional twinges of vision since his birth. And I have always been close to Isobel, so in this case I might have expected a quick glimpse or a message. It's good news, I suppose, that I haven't had any. It means that Isobel is not unduly troubled by whatever is happening.'

'Could it mean that she was dead?'

'No. Then there would be a different kind of silence. If you knock on a door,' said Baby, 'and there is no answer but someone is really there, you can feel it. The silence is somehow alive. If no one is there, the silence is blank . . . absolute and dead. Between Isobel and me, just now, there is the first kind of silence.'

'If they don't come back for some time, what will happen to Marius?'

'I suppose he'll just stay with your Uncle Ptoly Tunne. Ptoly telephoned while you were with the doctor this afternoon. Sent you oceans of lust – his phrase. He said that Marius liked it there, thought he's in rather a nervous state. But that's not Ptoly's fault.'

'He'll put Marius right, if anyone can.'

'Green eyes,' said Baby. 'My little Lucifer. Sometimes I long to kiss him like this,' she said, and kissed Jo-Jo fiercely on the lips, 'and like this, and like this,' she said, as she lowered her lips to Jo-Jo's throat and then her breast. 'Oh, what fun we used to have, Jo. Do you ever miss it?'

'Yes. But I think . . . that that time has gone by.'

'So do I. What a pity. I'd better get back and feed that little brute Sarum.'

'I thought you were always going to call him "Tully".'

'So I was. But there is something about him, Jo, something about the look in his eye – something not altogether agreeable – which makes me think Sarum is more appropriate.'

'Sarum of Old Sarum. A dead city on a hillside.'

Rather carefully, Baby detached herself. 'Come along, we mustn't keep His little Lordship waiting. I want you to watch, Jo. It makes my milk come easier.'

Ptolemaeos Tunne waited by Carmilla's Volkswagen until she came out into the drive carrying her suitcase and two grips full of all the kit which Theodosia had left behind.

'I can't offer to help you with those,' said Ptolemaeos, 'as my doctor says I've more than enough of my own weight to carry. I'm sorry you're going off so suddenly. And in the dead of night at that.'

'I'm sorry too. But it's just as well . . . Thea was upset by what she saw – or thought she saw – when she met Jeremy and me in Ely. She thought she saw newly budding young love, and that she'd be in the way. It's time I went to her and set her right.'

'So what did she see?'

'The end result of a really savage little bout of lust. Behind the screen in Bishop Alcock's Chantry. We hadn't had it for some days, Jeremy and I, and both of us took off like jump-jets. I dare say the unusual surroundings had something to do with it.'

'You'll forgive my curiosity – as you yourself have introduced the topic – but did you actually copulate in Bishop Alcock's Chantry?'

'Jeremy and I don't copulate. We do something less radical.'

'But none the less effective, on your account. So what Theodosia must have done was to mistake exhaustion for a haze of love?'

'Right. And now I'm going back to London to tell her just that. Except that I'm going to fib about the cause of the exhaustion. I'm going to say we'd quarrelled horribly but then we'd made it up. I don't want Thea to know that Jeremy and I have sex . . . in however qualified a form. It might bother her. It would definitely bother Da.'

'But surely, my dear Carmilla . . . you're not leaving us so suddenly simply in order to go to London and tell lies to your sister . . . lies which you could easily have told on the telephone?'

'No. I'm going because that little Marius is going to make fools of us all . . . of anyone that stays around here, that is. He nearly made a fool of me this morning. Infatuated with him, I was. And now Jeremy is too. And don't think you're necessarily immune. Anyway, I'm going before anything worse happens to me.'

'And because you're jealous that he has expressed a preference for Jeremy?'

'Very likely. All ways round, the sooner I go, Mr Tunne, the better for all of us.'

'My friends call me "Ptolemaeos", or more usually "Ptoly".'

'I don't think I am your friend, Mr Tunne. Why are you encouraging Jeremy to get into bed with that little boy?'

'So that he can find out what I need to know: who, or what, made Marius believe, on his first morning here, that some kind of emanation or efflux from Tessa Malcolm was now about to come and take over his whole being. The crucial point is, you see, that this emanation had been known to him for some time before: it used to make him have wet dreams, he says, and had also threatened to possess him. But then, after certain assurances from his sister Rosie, the emanation had ceased to trouble him, until, that is, he arrived here. On his very first morning here he suddenly knew that the threat of the emanation was now about to be renewed, and this time it would . . . swallow him up . . . finally and completely. Now, Carmilla, if I am to do anything for Marius, I must know what made him believe this. He won't tell me. He hasn't told you.'

'I haven't asked him.'

'And do you think he'd tell you if you did?'

'No,' said Carmilla with off-hand candour. 'He quite likes me, but from where he stands women, except perhaps for his mother, are not for confidences. They abuse them, he would think. He's probably right.'

'Well then. That only leaves one person whom he might tell. Jeremy. People in the same bed, however innocent their occupancy, are apt to become very close to each other in every sense.'

'I just don't think it right. I think you're asking for real trouble. Jeremy gets RANDY, Mr Tunne. He goes hard if I just say a rude word. In that Cathedral he would *not* be stopped.'

'Did you seriously try to stop him?'

'No. I get randy too. But I shan't be in bed with Marius, shall I? I think the whole idea is dangerous and rather sick. But don't worry. I shan't blab about it. I don't want to harm Jeremy, you see. And now I'll be off . . . and leave you happy bachelors to get on with your schoolboy games.'

'We shall be the poorer without a female presence,' said Ptolemaeos.

'You know what then? I'd send for that novelist character, Fielding Gray. He's a man, which you all prefer, but half of him thinks like a woman. He'll supply you with a female presence – or enough of one. Also, he'll help you keep Jeremy in order, if necessary. Jeremy is very keen on standing well . . . from what he's been telling me these last days . . . with Mr Fielding Gray.'

'Major Fielding Gray, I understand. Why should Jeremy need keeping in order?'

'I told you. That little green-eyed monster makes people over-excited. He is an agent of what the Greeks called "αψ".'

'Ātē. Infatuation. You have already used the word in this connection.'

'I know. But it's not quite strong enough. "Infatuation" is matinée stuff. Ātē is what made Tereus rape his sister-in-law and Procne serve him up his own kids as a savoury stew for luncheon. Ātē is what got into Paphaë when she spread herself for the bull, and into Dido when she threw herself on to the bonfire. You've got Ātē right here in this house, Ātē with green eyes and blond hair, as pretty as Ganymede, only what he's dishing out isn't wine or nectar but micky-finns with a base of hemlock. So the best of Fenland luck, Mr Tunne, and don't say I didn't warn you.'

The bed in Jeremy Morrison's room was a Jacobean four-poster which had been bought by Ptolemaeos at a local bankruptcy sale. The bathroom (*en suite*) had a marble bath mounted on porphyry lion's claws. The loo at the far end of the bathroom was crowned by a circular seat of mahogany, on which, when Jeremy arrived upstairs (having taken Ptolemaeos at his word and left him to negotiate with Carmilla), he found that Marius was sitting and reading an old copy of *Boys Own Christmas Annual*.

'Super stories in here,' announced Marius through the open door when Jeremy came into the bedroom. 'It was on the table with the loo paper. Three kinds of that, I see. We only have two in our house.'

'Don't you shut the door in your house, when you're doing what you're doing?'

'Daddy does. Mummy doesn't. She just sits there talking to anyone who happens to pass.'

'What about Rosie?'

'Rosie's so careful that no one even knows when she's going.'

As Jeremy went to close the door between the bedroom and the bathroom, he noticed that Marius's green pyjama trousers were on the floor under his feet and that his legs, flecked with a very light down, were slightly thinner than they should have been were the child's proportions to be perfect. Although this detracted from his beauty, it added greatly, in some inexplicable way, to his appeal. For Christ's sake, Jeremy told himself: you'll be looking at his little dick next.

'Don't shut the door,' said Marius. 'I haven't made a smell and I want you to talk to me.'

'How long are you going to be in there? I want to clean my teeth.'

'Then come in and clean them. I shan't look if you have to take them out. Daddy has to take his out.'

'I've still got my own, thank you very much.'

'So has Mummy. The teeth on her side of the family have always been very strong, she says. Rosie told me that Mummy's sister – the one we're not meant to talk about, Baby Canteloupe's mother – once bit somebody's ear off.'

'How did Rosie find that out?'

'Fielding Gray told Mrs Malcolm, and Rosie overheard while she was hiding behind the sofa.'

'You have made a smell.'

'Only a very small one, and I've finished now.'

Marius climbed off the mahogany ring, pulled the rope, turned on both taps of the bath, and stuck his bare bum over the edge of the marble.

'The Arab way,' he explained to Jeremy. 'Only Arabs have to use stones as they haven't got any water.'

'Thhrrrussp,' said Jeremy through the toothpaste.

'What's that?'

'The Arabs use only one hand, the one they don't eat with.'

'I use both to save time.'

Marius dried himself on Jeremy's bath towel and put on his pale green trousers.

'I'm going to bed now,' he said. 'Which side shall I leave for you?'

'The one next to the window.'

'Good. You can stop anything which might try to come through it,' said Marius in a matter-of-fact voice.

Can he really believe that he's threatened, thought Jeremy, or is he just playing some game? If the former, threatened by what? If the latter, why?

'JEREMY, JEREMY, COME NOW.'

Len was having his eighth final nightcap with Sir Tom Llewyllyn in the Provost's Lodging at Lancaster.

'Item,' said Len: 'Theodosia Salinger has already left Ptolemaeos's house.'

'Do we know why?'

'No details. Ptoly just said on the telephone that it was all quite peaceful. Sudden but peaceful.'

'Why did he tell you about it?'

'People like telling me things, Provost. I'm a good listener and it helps them put their thoughts in order. Item: Marius Stern has arrived there. It seems that the little beauty has been sacked from his school for violence, and that there's nowhere else for him to go until his parents come home. Ptolemaeos says they've got lost somewhere in the Levant and meanwhile he's really going to work on Marius.'

'With what in view?'

'Marius is what they call disturbed. What Ptoly wants to know about him is to what extent this is due to some neural or cerebral malfunction, and to what extent it is or could be due to some flaw in the non-corporeal soul or intellect – always assuming that Marius has one.'

'Ptolemaeos,' said Sir Thomas, 'is one huge bag of gas. He has no qualification to investigate such matters, still less to experiment with children.'

'He has Gregory's permission. That's why Canteloupe sent Marius there. Ptoly also has Gregory's permission to go to work on Rosie . . . but that he won't do, he says, until Marius is out of the house.'

'Dear God,' said Tom. 'What on earth are they all thinking of, giving that fat fraud their children to play with?'

'Gregory is thinking that Ptoly knows something very unflattering about his recent ancestors and that to ensure Ptoly's discretion he'd better be obliging. Isobel is thinking that Ptoly, fraud or no, gasbag or no, tends to get results. Canteloupe is thinking that he doesn't want Marius in Wiltshire bashing up Baby's new baby, and that he'd better not be sent to Buttock's where he might start bashing up Rosie or her chum, Tessa. It seems, incidentally, that Marius has been on his best behaviour at Ptoly's because he adores Jeremy Morrison, who is also there. So one way and the other, Provost, we have to admit that the reasons behind the scheme are sound and that so far it has been a success.'

'It seems to me that they are all taking advantage of Gregory's absence to save themselves inconvenience and to exploit his child.'

'Gregory's not just absent, Tom. He's absent without

leave. AWOL. Once you go AWOL you deserve everything you get.'

'We don't know that it's his fault.'

'Makes no difference, darling. AWOL is AWOL, at any rate till you get back and explain yourself, and until you do that you – and yours – are up to the ears in shit.'

Gregory Stern awoke to see the little night-light above the crucifix. The stone hut in which he was lodging was also a chapel, they had told him. They were sorry that there were no windows: but during the day, when he wasn't outside, they would leave the door open.

Gregory looked towards the door. No crack of light was yet visible beneath it. Would it were day (Shakespeare, *Henry V*, he thought; the Eve of Agincourt). Yes, would it were day: for this day the man whom they called Shamshuddin was to come; and at last there might be an end of the weary negotiation, a compromise which would not offend honour.

'I'm sorry,' said Marius to Jeremy. 'I'm afraid I was only trying to draw attention to myself. I did see something move on the lawn, but of course it was only my own shadow, thrown through the window by our lights.'

'If we're to spend the night together,' said Jeremy, as Marius flopped on to the bed and then rolled over to the side away from the window, 'there must be discipline. No more squealing.'

'I promise, Jeremy. Please don't be cross.'

Jeremy took his pyjamas and went into the bathroom to change into them. When he came back, carrying his clothes, Marius said: 'You needn't have been so shy. If you go on fussing about closing doors and not undressing in front of me, I shall think you're a silly old prude.'

'Don't be festive.'

'Festive?'

'The word we used at my school for cheeky.'

'At Oudenarde we say "poppy".'

'I know. I was at Oudenarde too.'

'But you prefer the word they used at your public school? Festive.'

'There's not a lot in it, I suppose.'

'I expect I'll go to Eton, like Daddy. I wonder what they call it there?'

'Whatever they call it there, we'll have no more of it here. Lights out.'

Jeremy turned off the central light at the switch by the door. He walked round the end of the bed and over to the window, then climbed into the bed and turned off the light on his side.

'Now turn off yours,' he said.

Marius obeyed.

Since I have been up here, thought Jeremy, he has shown no real fear (if we discount the little exhibition which was apparently put on 'to draw attention to myself'), no apprehension of effluxes or soul-swallowing succubi. He is calm. He is funny. He is trusting. He is enchanting.

'Everything will be all right,' said Marius, 'if you will only link the little finger of your hand that is nearest to me with the little finger of my hand that is nearest to you.'

'Why should you want me to do that?'

'Because it is what my mother sometimes does when she knows I'm worried. It's just to let me feel that she's there.'

'I'm not your mother, Marius.'

'I shall be all right if I feel that you're there, and I shan't feel it, properly, unless we link our little fingers.'

'All right. Why not? There you are, Marius.'

As he linked his finger with that of Marius, he felt peace, or rather a total lack of care, creep over his entire being. He could lie there for ever, he felt, as if floating just beneath a warm sea or swathed in cotton wool. Marius (whatever his personal disturbances might or might not be) had a soothing, an almost anaesthetizing touch: it was as though an anodyne current were flowing out of the boy and numbing all his, Jeremy's, limbs; no, not numbing, but rendering them unaware of pain, strain or even movement, yet at the same time enabling them to perform all their functions (had they been called upon to do so) swiftly, precisely and without the faintest effort. Pull yourself together, thought Jeremy, before you disappear into a haze of euphoria; do what Ptolemaeos commanded you.

'We can stay like this, Marius,' said Jeremy, 'on one condition.'

'Ummmm,' said Marius, as if nearly asleep.

'Listen, boy. You must answer me a question: who or what told you, on the morning you first came here, that something which you called "It" was very soon coming to possess you? Some kind of emanation projected by Rosie's friend, Tessa – or so you told Mr Tunne – and you *knew*, that first morning here, that It was coming nearer and nearer . . . and would soon devour you. Who told you this, Marius? How did you come to know – or to think that you knew?'

'Mr Tunne kept asking me that.'

'He wants to understand, Marius. If he understands that, he may be able to help you.'

'What's the use of bothering with that? I shall be all right, Jeremy, as long as you're here.'

'I can't stay with you for ever.'

'Then I shall have to hope,' said Marius in a small,

troubled voice, 'that It will get bored with waiting before you leave me . . . that It will go away and look for someone else whom Tessa knows. One of those Blessington girls, perhaps, though I hope not them, because they're so jolly nice.'

'Answer my question, Marius. How did you *know*, on that first morning, that It, that something, was coming for you?'

'You won't believe me. Nor would Mr Tunne have believed me if I'd told him.'

'Try me.'

Silence.

'Listen, Marius,' said Jeremy. 'I like you, can't you feel that, can't you feel it coming through? I like you so much, and there *must* be truth between friends.'

'Very well, Jeremy,' said Marius in an oddly remote voice. 'On that first morning I woke up very early, about six o'clock, and I went to my window to see where I was and what it was like. My window, like yours, looks down the lawn to the summerhouse . . . Standing at the door of the summerhouse, looking away over the Fens, was the figure of a girl dressed in that uniform they wear at Collingham's. Then the girl turned to face the house and I could see that it was Tessa. Only of course it couldn't have been, because everyone said she was in London – where else? – Oh dear, Jeremy. Must I go on?'

'Truth between friends.'

'Well, there was Tessa, or what seemed to be Tessa, looking up at the house . . . and then suddenly it was as if her face, just her face, came hurtling towards my window, which was closed except for a small ventilator at the top. The face had become huge and it took up all the window, Jeremy, mouthing and snarling at me, showing its teeth, gnashing them, kind of clawing with them at the window. Then, very reluctantly, it began to move away from the window; then faster, as though something had got hold of

242

it and was compelling it to go back . . . to Tessa's figure, which waved at me in a sort of cruel, sarcastic way, and then moved nearer the Fens and melted into the morning mist and wasn't there any more.'

'Sweet Jesus, sweetheart,' said Jeremy, unconsciously imitating Len.

'But you see what had happened? In some form or other, Tessa had come here to haunt me. Then . . . whatever it is that flows out of her to do me harm . . . broke away and came as far as the window; but it couldn't quite get through, it couldn't launch away from her altogether, either because it wasn't yet strong enough to detach itself from Tessa, or because Rosie's order, that it was to leave me alone, was still just powerful enough to stop it. But obviously that isn't going to be so for long. Those teeth . . . clawing at the window glass . . . And that,' concluded Marius, 'is how I knew that it would very soon come to take me.'

'Marius. Why is it that you think I can protect you?'

'For one thing, because when I'm with you I think of you . . . of pleasing you, Jeremy . . . and so I don't think of It so much. Thinking of It, remembering It, talking of It, brings it nearer. That's why I didn't want to tell Mr Tunne, or even you, because just my telling makes It stronger. The other thing is, Jeremy . . . that I know you wouldn't let any harm come to me. You wouldn't let any harm come to anyone if you could help it, and least of all to me. Because it *is* coming through to me, Jeremy, what you said just now, about how you like me, oh so much, you said. I think Carmilla began to like me in the same way, then stopped when I fainted in the chapel porch. Anyway, she was only a girl and she would have been no good.'

'She's a grand girl,' Jeremy said.

'But whatever is coming out of Tessa could get past her, because IT is a woman too. It would know how to deceive and slip past another woman, by making her jealous or something, so that she looked another way. But it won't get past you . . . unless you stop liking me.'

'I'll do my best, Marius,' said Jeremy, almost primly. 'And now we must go to sleep. Mr Tunne will be anxious to discuss all this early tomorrow.'

Baby Canteloupe was playing backgammon with Jo-Jo by the pool in the centre of their copse.

'Gammoned again,' said Baby. 'You really are in luck. How much do I owe you?'

'Thirty-two times five quid for that last game. Which makes one thousand and one hundred in all.'

'I'll write you a cheque. Canty's given me quite a lot of money, you know.'

'I don't need it,' said Jo-Jo.

'I know. Neither of us does. Isn't that nice? But all the same,' said Baby, 'you should have it. Gaming debts must be paid by the likes of us, or else everyone will start thinking he can welsh whenever he chooses.'

'All right. You write me a cheque. And now I've got news. This morning I rang Uncle Ptoly and asked him straight out about Marius.'

'Why didn't you tell me before? Then we could have discussed it instead of my losing my arsehole at backgammon.'

'I had to decide whether or not to tell you. What Uncle Ptoly had to say was really rather frightening.'

'I'd have heard sooner or later. Marius *is* my cousin.'

'Precisely. If you think about it carefully, that makes the news . . . by implication . . . a lot more frightful. So frightful that I wasn't sure I wanted to be the one to tell you.'

'But now you've decided you will, so stop faffing about, girl, and spill the beanies.'

'Ptoly says that as far as he can make out Marius is suffering from one of three things. Either he is actually being haunted by some spirit which comes from Tessa Malcolm, a spirit which has hitherto been compèred, as it were, by his sister Rosie, but is now getting out of control.'

'Big red balls,' said Baby, with strained voice and strained face.

'I'm just passing on what Ptoly said. OR, he said, Marius is the victim of psychic hallucinations so powerful that they amount to lunacy. OR he is an inventive and an utterly malicious little liar, with considerable talent as an actor. It seems that he staged a kind of fit at the door of Lancaster Chapel, intending people to draw the inference that he was already so far "possessed" that he could not enter holy places.'

'This fit could have been genuine,' Baby said.

'In which case, either Marius is really being haunted; or he is being deluded into thinking he is, deluded so strongly that he must, in crude terms, be mad; or he has suddenly become epileptic, or something not far off it.'

'I see,' said Baby. 'We conclude that my cousin is either possessed, insane, squalidly ill, or criminally vicious.'

'About to be possessed would be more accurate on the first count.'

'Suppose,' said Baby, 'that it *is* all delusion. People have had visions before and not been called mad. William Blake.'

'He had happy and wholesome visions as well as disagreeable ones. Marius's are quite fiendish. Example: a giant face – Tessa Malcolm's – trying to gnaw its way through his bedroom window.'

'Is there no light in all this darkness?'

'Yes. Jeremy Morrison. He was there for Ptoly's soul-searching experiments, quite a piece of luck, as it turns out that he can to some extent reassure Marius. Marius has a hero-worship thing about him.'

'It seems pretty messy to me.'

'And to Ptoly. He's going to call in Fielding Gray.'

'Why?'

'He wasn't very clear about that. I gather Fielding is a good influence on Jeremy, who may be needing a little. And then again he has insights from time to time . . .'

'And where does all this leave you and me?'

'I suggest that we both think very carefully about it and discuss it further when we have digested it. We might then decide what action, if any, we should be taking ourselves.'

'About Marius?'

'He is in other hands. About Sarum and Alexandre.' Jo-Jo patted her deliciously convex belly. 'Tell you what: to give you a chance to get your money back, let's play for ten quid a point instead of five.'

'Twenty?' said Baby.

'Done.'

Fielding Gray and Ptolemaeos Tunne stood over the sarcophagus in the alcove in Ptolemaeos's library. In the sarcophagus was water to a depth of three and a half feet and in the water was Marius, dressed in his school bathing trunks, borne up by rubber rings, and fast asleep.

'Apparently,' said Ptolemaeos, 'he and Jeremy passed an absolutely untroubled night. In the morning, while they were still in bed, Jeremy asked Marius to tell him in full, for a second time, how he had first come to *know* that he was going to be taken over by this evil spirit which he says emanates from Tessa.'

'Have you summoned me here from Broughton Staithe,

where I had a lot of work to do, Tunne, to tell me rubbish like this?'

Ptolemaeos sighed.

'You did volunteer to come if needed, so now hear me out. Marius then repeated the story he had told Jeremy the night before: that on his first morning here he looked out of his bedroom window and saw Tessa Malcolm at the end of the lawn. Her face then flew up to the window, grotesquely enlarged, and tried to chew through the window with its teeth. Before very long, however, it was called off, by some agency or authority unknown, possibly Rosie's. But Marius opined to Jeremy that this agency had considerable difficulty over the task, and would soon be incapable of exerting control.'

'The boy's barking mad – or a pathological liar. If you knew Tessa Malcolm – '

' – Point taken. And now,' said Ptolemaeos, 'I have mixed him a draught which, as you see, has put him into a deep sleep. It will also predispose him – though it will not compel him, nothing can do that – to tell the truth, or what he thinks to be the truth. I intend to ask him a series of questions, and I've asked you here to bear witness to, and to comment upon, his answers.'

'What about Jeremy? Shouldn't he be here?'

'No. Marius might sense his presence and be reluctant to abandon the story he told him even though he knew this to be lies. Besides, Jeremy wanted to go into Cambridge for something. He's looking forward to seeing you later, he says.'

Playing it cool, thought Fielding; well, and why not?

'While I am asking these questions,' said Ptolemaeos, 'I shall also be observing any effect they may seem to have on the relation between the boy's physical brain and his non-corporeal psyche.'

'How can you do that?'

'I can ask questions of him which reveal the distinction

which he himself makes between the processes of nerves and tissue, on the one hand, and what he calls his real *being*. Or again, his whole tone and idiom is different when what he is saying is said at the dictates of a higher and independent soul or intellect rather than at those of the physical brain. It is a question of energy. The brain works by electricity, the soul or intellect is powered by no form of energy which we can trace. When, therefore, this disembodied intellect wishes to convey something through physical channels to the outside world, it has to find some means of setting the brain's electric impulses into motion. It has to transmit its ideas back to the brain so that the brain may transfer them into words which the speech mechanism can articulate. The process of transformation – from intellectual ideas into mere words, which are the currency of the cerebrum – gives a strained quality to the speech and phrasing, as if the speaker knows that he can never do justice in ordinary, common words to the ideal processes and concepts of intellect and soul.'

'There could be a dozen other explanations of this strain in speech and phrasing.'

'Agreed. But if the speaker himself, in a state of total physical relaxation and therefore maxiumum mental awareness, avers that his soul or being is different from the rest of him – as this boy appears to have done when questioned by me the other day – there must be at least a possibility that this is true and that he *has* a disembodied mind or soul.'

'But whatever this may be,' said Fielding, 'and on whatever sort of power it operates, it clearly depends on the body to send it signals in the first place; otherwise it would simply be a blank.'

'I must beg to differ. It could be receiving signals of a different kind from a different source. It could be working independently on its own terms even though no signals or requests were passed on to it by the body. But of course the body *does* pass it signals quite often, and the nature of this process is as interesting as that of the reverse. How does the physical energy of the material brain influence or communicate with the non-corporeal? Does it cause the same kind of strain as when the non-corporeal is trying to communicate back with the physical brain? And so on and so forth.'

'We'll go into that later,' said Fielding. 'Let's have these questions.'

Ptolemaeos adjusted the tape recorder. Then: 'Marius,' he said, 'did you really see Tessa Malcolm in the garden that morning, your first morning here? Did you really see her by the summerhouse, as you described it to Jeremy?'

Marius stirred inside the rubber rings but did not articulate.

'Defensive, you see,' said Ptolemaeos. 'Did her face,' he said in confidential tones to Marius, 'her gigantic face, really detach itself and appear at your window?'

Marius grunted, then said in a slurred but oddly formal voice, 'I have said what I have said.'

'Most unsatisfactory,' said Ptolemaeos. 'The indication is that Marius, having told the same story twice already, requires us to take it or leave it.'

'I thought that draught you gave him elicited truth.'

'But not necessarily the whole truth. It effectively prevents his telling a direct and outright lie. That would be a more accurate account of its function.'

'But it does not prevent prevarication?'

'I'm getting nowhere,' Ptolemaeos admitted, 'but I'll have one more shot at it. Why,' he said, staring down into the sarcophagus, 'do you think Jeremy can save you from what threatens you?'

After a prolonged gurgle, 'Mummy,' snorted Marius. 'Oh, come back, my Mummy. Kind Jeremy: Mummy kinder. Mummy lost.'

Silence.

'The suggestion seems to be,' said Ptolemaeos at last, 'that Jeremy resembles Marius's mother in some unspecified and far from obvious respect. Not a well spent afternoon, I fear. We'd better leave him here to sleep it off. He'd have to be carried anywhere else, and my doctor has forbidden me to carry things.'

'I'll carry him, if you like. To be frank,' said Fielding Gray, 'it will be a pleasure. What a little beauty it is.'

Quite a heavy little beauty, whose limp unco-operative body gave Fielding a lot of trouble. Eventually, however, he managed to drag him by the armpits through the rubber rings and out of the sarcophagus, and lug him (fireman's lift) to a sofa at the other end of the library.

'Quite far enough,' he said. 'It looks so easy in films, but the human body – even a small one like this – weighs like lead. The last time I did that was when I was a recruit in training . . . Perhaps we ought to dry him.'

Ptolemaeos passed Fielding a towel which had been draped over a bust of Hooker. Fielding dried Marius from the feet up to the crutch and from the shoulders down to the navel. Then he lifted the boy's ankles with one hand, slipped his trunks off over his feet with the other, turned him on one side on the sofa, and began to dry his groin and buttocks.

'Good chance to confirm something I once heard,' he said to Ptolemaeos. He pointed to Marius's penis, plump and snug in its tiny nest of blond hairs and pink scrotum. 'Uncircumcised, you perceive. Gregory the Jew could not prevail against Isobel the Athenian.'

'So that's the state of play at Ptoly Tunne's,' said Jeremy to Len, as they paced the back lawn of Lancaster College. 'Marius telling me I remind him of Mummy and plonking himself in my bed, and Carmilla going off in a bate and leaving me to be Matron. What is a chap to do?'

'Find out whether Marius is shamming,' said Len, 'or whether he really believes what he's saying.'

'That's Ptoly's pitch. And another thing, Len. Fielding Gray's coming. He'll be there by now.'

'So what's with that, duckie?'

'I've got plans for Fielding. Like how he might help me if I want to be an author. He may not think much of me if he finds I'm going to bed with a boy of twelve. He might even get jealous.'

'Is that going to continue?'

'Marius wants it and Ptoly says he must have it. Whatever is or is not the matter, it's helping to keep Marius stable, Ptoly says.'

'Then Ptoly will explain all that to Major Gray, who will not think the worse of you.'

'Ptoly explained it all to Carmilla, who took off in a tantrum.'

'Just as well. Thea will need her help in London. The old man's playing up.'

'What's up with him?'

'His wife again. Not the manner of her death,' said Len, as they reached the far wall and turned to walk back towards the Provost's Lodging, 'which used to be the trouble, or so Thea tells me, but something which happened before they were married . . . something which he never

251

heard about till just the other day. Thea was pretty discreet
about it when she rang me up – '

' – Good old Len the Confessional Box – '

' – Len the fucking dustbin. Used condoms and banana
skins, like I'm a sort of walking disposal unit for all the
shit in the college. Anyway, it seems (Theodosia speaking)
that Fielding Gray went to dinner some time back with a
number called Ivan Blessington (he was here with his wife
and brats for Sarum's christening), and that Blessington's
wife, Betty, "accidentally overheard" Blessington tell Fielding some juicy tale over the port, about what Vanessa
Drew, later Salinger, did at some party with him, Ivan
Blessington, in their hot messy youth, before either of
them was married. So Mrs Blessington, whether in sorrow,
anger, prurience or hysteria, passes this tale on – '

' – What *had* they done at this party?'

' – Thea wasn't telling. But whatever it was, Mrs
Blessington passes on the story during a hen session with a
chum called Margaret Cartenay, and in no time at all it's
been overheard by the floral decorations at the Ritz (so to
speak), and goes whizzing upstairs and along the corridors
and into Donald's suite. What's eating him, Thea says, is
that he never heard this particular bit before. Soon after
his marriage there'd been a nasty spot of bother and she'd
made a clean breast of everything that had ever, ever
happened in order to clear the air, if you'll pardon my
metaphors. But it seems that this bit about Ivan Blessington
got left out, and so Donald, who thought he knew everything about her, is wondering how many other bits got left
out, and so on and so forth. Which reminds me, how are
you getting on with Proust?'

'End of sentence two.'

'Persevere. He's a terrible nag but he knew a thing or
two. Where was I?'

'Donald Salinger.'

'Ah, yes. So now he's lost his grip of Vanessa's past, if

you see what I mean, and this is sending him dotty all over again, though not at all in the same way as before. What he wants now, Thea said, is to find a way of punishing Vanessa *in the past*, of somehow recreating the whole situation, just as it was all those years ago, and humiliating or chastising Vanessa as she then existed.'

'What a bizarre notion.'

'So I dare say Theodosia will be glad of her sister's help at the old home in the Ritz. As for your problem, sweetheart,' said Len, as they turned again under the windows of the Provost's Lodging, 'all you have to do is listen politely to your elders and keep your opinions and your hands to yourself.'

'Be quiet and let the thing go on?'

'That's about it. Remember, Ptoly's paid out a lot of cash on your behalf, and there's more where it came from. You know what a clerihew is?'

'No, Len.'

'Before your time, I suppose. Or sheer fucking ignorance. Anyway, here's what a clerihew is:

> Fielding Gray
> Is well enough in his way;
> But when it comes to mon
> Take Tunne.'

All day long Gregory Stern had been arguing with Shamshuddin. As they walked along the beach by the many-sounding sea (followed by Shamshuddin's guard and the man Pontos who had diverted Isobel and Gregory from the airport at Nicosia) Shamshuddin explained what his terms were, first for reuniting Gregory with Isobel, and secondly for restoring them both to their own world.

'But I am a Jew,' Gregory kept saying.

'That is why I have chosen you. It will come so much more effectively from a Jew – and from a publishing house owned by a Jew.'

'But what you are asking me to do,' said Gregory, 'would wipe out my honour as a Jew.'

'You have never been very fussy in the past.'

'But this . . . this business which you propose. It is not like eating bacon or making anti-Jewish jokes or even being ashamed of the low Jews from which one has sprung and trying to conceal them. What you propose is an absolute betrayal of my own kind. No Jew, Shamshuddin, no man of any creed or race whatever, can betray his own kind without betraying, and in the end destroying, himself.'

'It is only the Israelis who will be affected.'

'The distinction is not admissible. Besides, I have just come from Israel, where I have eaten their salt.'

'Which should have been our salt. I think you had better return to your celibate quarters, Mr Stern, and think some more. By the way, I have news for you: your son in England is in very bad trouble.'

'Oh, Marius, Marius. He is ill?'

'Perhaps.'

'I must go to him.'

'You will go to your quarters.'

'Then send my wife to him.'

'She will stay in her quarters.'

'At least tell me more of Marius.'

'There is only one thing certain as yet: he has had to be removed from his school.'

'From Oudenarde House? But he was so happy there. Marius, Marius . . . Does Isobel my wife know of this?'

'She will be told this evening, Mr Stern. Now, back to your shrine.'

When Jeremy returned to Ptolemaeos's house in the Fens, he found that a new strategy had been decided on. Fielding Gray, who was to have stayed for some days, would now interrupt his visit and leave the next morning for London and Buttock's Hotel.

'It's blindingly obious, now we've actually thought of it,' Ptolemaeos said. 'Here we are, trying to elicit some sort of account from Marius and wondering hopelessly whether what he says is true, when all the time we've been neglecting the supposed source of all the trouble. Let's hear what *Tessa Malcolm* has to say about the spells and emanations she is accused of directing at Marius.'

'Where is Marius?' Jeremy asked.

'Still asleep in the library . . . after a draught I gave him. Quite harmless, but I'd better go and see how he's getting on.'

'Can I come?' said Jeremy. 'He . . . he might like it if I were there when he woke up.'

'You stay with me,' said Fielding Gray. 'I've got something to say to you. We'll go for a walk, across this dismal fen.'

When they had left Ptolemaeos's garden, they walked along a dyke, which appeared to divide an infinity of yellow sludge from another infinity of yellow sludge. After a while, Fielding Gray said:

'I'm on Tessa Malcolm's side, you know.'

'I didn't think it was a question of sides.'

'I mean . . . that I think she is innocent. I've known her for some time. While she is quite capable of making mischief should she feel like it, she could not be deliberately persecuting Marius in the hideous manner he has described.'

'But she could, surely, be the unwilling or unwitting vehicle for some power or spirit that is tormenting him. They say that adolescent girls often have their ghostly familiars.'

'You are a child, Jeremy, of the second half of the 20th century. Can you possibly believe that anything of the kind described by Marius is actually happening to him?'

'I don't know what to believe. I do know that I find him enchanting. When he asks me to help him, to protect him, he makes my heart ache with love.'

'That's honest. It also helps me to say what I wish to you. You must not be misled by your fondness of Marius into accepting his falsehoods as facts.'

'A fair comment. And while we are on the subject, Fielding, you must not be misled by your fondness of Tessa Malcolm into accepting her version as necessarily the true one.'

Fielding accepted this in silence and with apparent equanimity. A pool fringed by tall reeds appeared in the yellow sludge to their left. A path took them down to it from the dyke.

'I've never seen Tessa Malcolm,' said Jeremy. 'What's she like?'

'She has something of the same . . . allure . . . as Marius. That she is very slightly misshapen only adds to it. But unlike Marius, she is, as I believe, innocent, truthful and loving.'

'That is the second time you have used the word "innocent".'

'It is her paramount quality.'

'Define.'

'Harmless. Guileless. Without malice or violence. In the affair of Marius, not guilty.'

'And why are you so keen that I should know this?'

'Because, Jeremy, if you should so far champion the cause of Marius as to impugn the innocence of Tessa Malcolm, I should be displeased.'

'I champion no causes, Fielding. I am merely doing what Mr Tunne tells me because he has paid amply for my obedience. For the rest, the facts will sooner or later be ascertained for what they are, and neither my affection for Marius nor your belief in Tessa will alter them in the slightest. How are you going to proceed with her when you reach London?'

'I shall ask for her account of her relation with Marius. As Ptolemaeos will have told you, he accuses her of trying to corrupt or at least to kiss him. That, he says, was the start of it all. Everything that has happened followed on from his refusal to respond to her advances and the contemptuous language which he subsequently used of her before his sister, Rosie. So I shall go back to the beginning of it all, Jeremy, and see what I find there.'

'With an open mind, Fielding?'

'Yes.'

'But convinced of Tessa's innocence?'

'Convinced of the innocence of her intentions.'

He is not honest, thought Jeremy. There is some motive, undisclosed, that will impel him, whatever the evidence, to make out and declare a verdict of 'Not Guilty' on Tessa Malcolm. He is blustering and he is equivocating. 'I shall be displeased,' he says: he is trying to stand on age and rank: he is almost petulant. Is he, after all, the patron from whom I would seek advancement, the wise man whom I would hear and follow? No longer the latter, perhaps; still the former.

He is not compliant, thought Fielding. If he finds for Marius, he will say so, however I, his recently chosen Mentor, may judge the case or desire others to judge it. Something in this business has already made him tougher, more mature than the callow boy who came to Broughton Staithe only the other day.

Without another word, the two men turned, walked up on to the dyke, and back to the house of Ptolemaeos Tunne.

For the first time, Artemis came to Isobel in the evening, not to take her out for exercise, but to talk with her. Artemis was not wearing black; she was wearing a green kaftan, embroidered with two gold serpents which writhed up either flank and eyed each other ferociously across her bosom.

Slowly and carefully, in clear pidgin Italian, Artemis told Isobel that news had come from associates of Pontos and Shamshuddin in England that her son had been expelled from his school, that he was suspected of being mentally unbalanced to a dangerous degree, and that she and her husband would be released to take care of him only when Gregory had met the demands of Shamshuddin.

'What are these demands?' Isobel asked.

Artemis told her.

'Very well,' said Isobel. 'I shall try to persuade him.'

'Thank you.'

'On one condition. A private one. Between you and me.'

'What would you wish?' Artemis said.

'To see your knees.'

Artemis lifted her kaftan to show her knees. Her legs were bare above and below them. Isobel stooped swiftly and kissed the hollow behind the right knee, letting her tongue play lightly on the sinews. She felt Artemis shiver from ankle to femur. Very slightly the left leg eased away from the right. Isobel rose. Artemis still stood with her kaftan lifted.

I could kneel again, Isobel thought; in front of her this time. I could kneel to my gaoler and beg her for the favours which she is now begging me to beg for, so that she may disdainfully bestow them. Thus I could become a means of pleasure to my beloved wardress, while at the same time seeking my own pleasure, as is appropriate to a captive, in giving service and duty as the humble (but loyal and loving) slave. But here is the rub: to me she would be the loved one; to her I should be the mere instrument to satisfy the lust that after many days of quiet attention and insinuation I have succeeded in arousing. Lust? Less even than lust: curiosity.

So nothing can happen. If I am to make free of these young, tight, damp loins, it must be as the wise and beloved comforter, the adored mother/mistress, not as a kind of flesh and blood vibrator.

'"O Queen and Huntress, Chaste and Fair,"' murmured Isobel. 'O Artemis, my Artemisa, if only you could see me, not with the eyes of a captor that counts the captured and casually takes note which of them may be fit for sexual use, but with the eyes of your namesake as she gathered her companions about her, then we could play with each other in our pool as Diana and her maidens played with each other in theirs. But then I should become Diana, the leader and the ministrant and the instructress, I should be Artemis, and you would be my pupil, my page girl, my maiden 'squire. Such a change in our status is not possible: it is not fitting.' Isobel shook her head; then spoke sharply, 'When shall I see my husband to talk to him?'

'Very soon.' Artemis let her kaftan fall. 'Shamshuddin or Pontos will send for you, *egregia signora*, to go down to the sea.'

When Fielding arrived at Buttock's Hotel, he found a cheerful bustle which had certainly been lacking when he had last been there two days previously.

'Things are looking up, dear,' Maisie said. 'That smell, or whatever it might have been that was putting people off – it must have gone.'

'Have you personally noticed any difference?'

'Can't say I have, but then I never really noticed whatever it was in the first place. I *have* noticed a difference in the two girls. For a long time after Rosie came they were very quiet and sly. Now they're full of beans and laughter, romping and ramping all over the place.'

'Hasn't the disappearance of her parents upset Rosie at all?'

'She might have forgotten their existence for all she seems to care.'

'Is that healthy or unhealthy?'

'Better take a look at her,' said Maisie, 'and judge for yourself.'

'I shall. I don't understand,' Fielding said, 'how the news . . . that what we once called the "aura" has disappeared . . . has got about so quickly. Forty-eight hours ago this hotel was dead. Now the whole place is rocking with new arrivals.'

'Perhaps people have an instinct for these things?'

'On the spot, I dare say. Surely not over a distance?'

'You must always be going into things,' Maisie said. 'Carping and nit-picking and grinding on and on about the where and the when and the who and the how. Why can't you just accept and be happy? The curse has vanished and the old place is on the up.'

'I have a logical mind, Maisie. I like things to be explained. There's rather a lot to be explained just now. Shall you mind if I ask Rosie and Tessa some questions . . . some very awkward questions?'

'What about?'

'What's happening to Marius Stern.'

'They're so happy, Fielding. Why do you have to bother them with all that?'

'Marius says that it's all Tessa's fault. Though I don't believe that, others may. I want to clear her, Maisie. I am eager for her honour.'

Maisie came close to him and fondled his neck.

'Silly old thing. You think she may be yours, don't you now?' Maisie said.

'Whose is she?'

'Soon, Fielding. Not now. I can't somehow bring myself. But if you manage to convince everyone that my Tessa has nothing to do with all this trouble about Marius, then I'll tell you sometime, sometime soon perhaps, because you'll deserve to know.'

'I'd better see them . . . after they've finished their homework. This evening anyhow. Something has to be done about Marius, Maisie, and whatever it is there's no time to be lost.'

Since Carmilla had returned to London, the main topic between herself and her sister had been the evident mental deterioration in their father.

'He was pretty well all right,' Theodosia kept saying, 'until he heard this story of mother and Colonel Blessington (not that he was a Colonel then) misbehaving in the loo at a party. What rankled was that she hadn't told him herself.'

'I bet there were a lot things she didn't tell him.'

'But Da thinks that once at least she told him everything. Never mind that their marriage started to go from bad to worse to downright intolerable very soon after. Da's great consolation was that *at just one time*, soon after they were married, he was in mother's total confidence and knew the lot. Now it turns out that he didn't, not even then.'

'How did he come to hear the story?'

'Max de Freville. He heard it at his club from a man who'd heard it at some party, etc., etc. The thread goes right back to a Mrs Cartenay, who had it from Colonel Blessington's wife.'

'How malicious of Max de Freville to tell Da,' Carmilla said.

'I'm afraid Da asked for it. He started pouring ice-cold water on some scheme Max has for converting foreign assets into sterling without letting the foreigners know. Da said he had never heard of anything so cretinous, and that Max must be going senile – had indeed begun to go senile ever since he took on that woman, Angela Tuck, God knows how many years ago now. So Max came back with a savage riposte about Da starting to be senile from the minute he'd married mother, which was even longer ago, and served up the Blessington anecdote for good measure.'

'So. What then?'

'Da has got up some crazy idea that he can punish mother by going back into the past and humiliating her there.'

'Sweet J.C.'

'Precisely.'

'Has Da done anything yet?'

'He's been down to Green Oxley Laris, where he sat right by that place where mother died for eight hours on end. He hired a car to go there, and the chauffeur told me. When I asked Da what he'd been doing there, he said he was trying to get close enough to mother to entice her back into their past with him.'

'What *could* he mean?'

'God knows. All *I* know is that I'm glad to have you back to help,' said Theodosia. 'Kind of you to guess I might need it. It must have been a wrench, leaving Jeremy.'

'Fuck Jeremy.'

'But I thought – '

' – You were wrong, darling. Jeremy never meant anything to me except as an agreeable playmate, and now he's not even that. He's obsessed with that little Marius Stern. He even sleeps in the same bed with him.'

'???'

'To be absolutely fair, I think not. But I didn't wait to find out.'

'But surely, Mr Tunne – '

' – Mr Tunne encourages it. Mind you, it hadn't yet happened when I left, but it was just about to, and Mr Tunne – "My friends call me Ptoly"' – she gave a greasy imitation of Ptolemaeos's rich, pleasant bass – 'Mr Tunne said it would be therapeutic. And of course Jeremy will do everything Mr Tunne tells him to, whether he wants to or not, because he's being paid to be there.'

'Being paid?'

'Has been paid, I should say, though more may be on offer. Mr Tunne settled his debts last term.'

'Oh,' said Theodosia, and blinked. 'I settled them too.'

Carmilla grinned ferociously.

'I was in love with him, you see,' said Theodosia.

'What a couple of clowns we are. You're an even bigger one than I am. My only consolation is that I never let him shag me.'

'But you did other things?'

'And very nice too. I wasn't going to tell you, but after this business of the money there's an end of Jeremy

263

Morrison for good, and I don't mind your knowing. But for Christ's sake don't let on to Da.'

'I think,' said Theodosia, 'that I still love him in a way. And I wish, oh how I wish, that I'd been able to do the things he asked *me* to do with him. It would have been something to remember him by.'

'Not all that much, and nothing to be proud of. We've other and fatter worries now,' said Carmilla, 'than Jeremy Morrison. For a start, I think that Da will be better out of England. We can both spare a couple of months, till the end of August at any rate. Where shall we take him?'

'Somewhere he didn't go with mother.'

'Easy. She was always griping because he never would take her to California. She wanted to go to movie-land and stay at the Beverly Hills Hotel. For some reason he never would go – kept muttering about dope. So first we convince him that we're in no danger from dope – that's for American perverts, we'll tell him, he'll swallow that all right – and then we imply, without saying so straight out, that by taking us where he never would take mother, despite her yearning to go there, he is, in a sense, punishing her back in her past.'

'Clever Carm. When do we start pushing this idea?'

'Now.'

'And if he says "no"?' said Theodosia. 'If he wants to go on hanging about Green Oxley Laris?'

'Then,' said Carmilla, with a rather jagged edge to her voice, 'we have to think of something else.'

Fielding Gray took mugs of chocolate to Rosie and Tessa, who were lying in twin beds, holding hands between the beds and chattering like monkeys.

'Thank you, Major Gray,' they both said, heartily and not demurely, as he handed them their drinks.

'Question time, ladies,' he said, and sat himself on the stool by the dressing table, with his back to the looking glass.

'Marius?' said Rosie.

'Marius. We'll begin at the beginning. Tessa showed him how to hit people who made themselves a nuisance in the same way I'd shown her. Then she asked for a kiss in payment. Right, Tessa?'

'He'd promised. I'd asked Rosie if she minded before she went off to the dentist with Auntie Maisie, and she said, no, of course she didn't, so I did a deal with Marius. He welshed.'

'You know why, Tessa?' Fielding said.

'Yes. He was embarrassed. Afraid.'

'Afraid of what?'

'Of . . . going too far without meaning to.'

'How far did *you* mean to go?'

'I just wanted to kiss him, Rosie's brother, as I'd have kissed my own, if only I'd had one.'

'That's what I thought,' said Fielding.

'Anything else,' said Rosie, 'was in Marius's mind.'

Her hand squeezed Tessa's.

'But then,' said Fielding, 'you, Rosie, made a wish against him. On the day of Lord Sarum's christening. Marius said something nasty about Tessa and her – her – '

' – Her rumpel hump,' said Rosie lightly.

' – And you said, in your anger, that you wished that he would make no runs this season.'

'Yes. He was unkind and he deserved it. My wish was only a wish – how could it be any more, Major Gray? – but I hoped, *then*, that it would make Marius lose confidence in his batting. Apparently it did.'

'At any rate, he didn't make any runs and so he appealed to you. And you wrote back to say that it couldn't be anything to do with you, you'd only spoken in temper. But even after you'd told him this, he still didn't make runs, and he appealed to you again, this time by telephone; so then, after you'd thought about it, you wrote and swore to him, by something holy – '

' – By our mother's honour – '

' – That it was nothing to do with you. And now he believed you. He still believed you had the power to stop him making runs – '

' – Which I never had – '

' – But at least he was satisfied that you weren't using it any longer. Is that an accurate account of the sequence of events so far?'

'Yes,' said Tessa, replying for Rosie.

'But you swore to him too late,' said Fielding.

'Not if he'd behaved himself properly and kept his temper. There was going to be a match in a few days,' said Rosie, 'and if he'd kept his temper he'd still have been there, and he could have shown them all he was back in form by making hundreds of runs.'

'That's what he said. Why did he lose his temper so easily?'

'Because he's very quick to lose it these days,' said Tessa in her husky voice. 'Besides, I expect he was nervous. If, after all, he still didn't make runs in the next match, then he'd know it was his fault, always had been his fault, and not mine or Rosie's. He'd have found it very difficult to bear that.'

All this was too plausible to be gainsaid. Fielding was on the point of abandoning his interrogation altogether, of giving the girls total quittance (though perhaps mildly admonishing them that they should not make ill-natured wishes even if others spoke rudely of them) when it occurred to him that he should, in all fairness to Marius, make some reference to his claim that he had been haunted, and see whether this drew any response.

266

'Marius thinks,' he said carefully, 'that you two used some power to prevent him from making runs, to weaken him, he said; and he further thinks, although he knows the wish is now cancelled, that this same power is getting beyond your control and is pursuing him.'

'And what does he think this power is?' said Rosie.

'He thinks it is something that comes out of Tessa.'

'What sort of power? Which bit of Tessa? Her rumpel?'

'No. He doesn't care anything about that. He thinks it's a power which comes out of her whole being – a power to threaten him.'

'Something horrible?' said Rosie.

'Yes. Something that wants to possess and destroy him altogether.'

Very gently, Tessa put her mug down on the table between the beds. She took a handkerchief from under her pillow, held it in front of her face and below her eyes like a yashmak, and started to secrete slow, heavy tears.

'How *could* Marius think anything so foul?' said Rosie.

She got out of her own bed, sat down on Tessa's and started to kiss the tears away.

'I *love* Marius,' said Tessa between gulps and snivels. 'Or I do when he's kind to me and my Rosie.'

'But that's the whole point,' said Fielding. 'He was very *unkind* to you and Rosie, and well he knows it. He realizes that one way and another he bitterly offended you both – '

' – Not so much that we'd send some dreadful thing to possess him.'

'Perhaps not. But enough, he thinks, for you to send it to harass him and stop his making runs. And now, he says, this thing, this spirit, this succubus, this whatever it is, has got beyond your control. It is going to leave Tessa altogether, and since it has developed a taste for Marius during the last few weeks it is going to come and possess *him*.'

'Such rubbish,' said Rosie, in a school-mistressy way.

'That is what he thinks, Rosie, or what he says he thinks. I am here to ask you two your opinion of all this.'

'He is making it all up,' said Rosie, 'to make himself seem interesting.'

'You have never – either of you – given him any reason to suppose that anything of this kind could happen?'

'Certainly not. I have told him all along that we have no powers whatever, over his cricket or anything else. And that,' said Rosie, 'is the end of that.'

She patted Tessa, who was now quite calm, on her afflicted shoulder, and went back to her own bed. She was wearing pyjamas with long shorts instead of trousers, and the effect was to make her legs look short, skinny and bandy. Poor, plain Rosie, Fielding thought; then he looked at her black hair, as it settled round her head, and thought again.

'The trouble is,' he said, 'that that is *not* the end of that. Marius apparently *believes* all this that I have been telling you.'

'Poor Marius,' said Tessa gruffly and meekly. 'He must have something wrong with him.'

'We are wondering about that.'

'What does Mr Tunne say?' said Rosie.

'He is very puzzled.'

'You say that Marius does not think he has been possessed quite yet,' said Tessa, 'only that he is going to be. What will happen when he thinks that he has been?'

'A very pertinent question, my darling. Fortunately it appears that Marius thinks he is safe, at least for the time being, if he can be with Jeremy Morrison.'

'That round-faced young man at the christening,' said Rosie.

'Yes.'

'Does Marius think,' said Tessa in a taut voice, 'that this power, this suck-thing – '

' – Succubus – '

268

' – Is part of me or just lives in me?'

'That is none too clear. I should say that he thinks that it somehow grew out of you – which was not your fault – and that you discovered how to use it for your own purposes and later did so – which *was* your fault. It is now about to leave you, or perhaps has left you already, and then it will no longer obey you.'

'So I can't be to blame if it now possesses him.'

'Perhaps not. But it was you and Rosie that sent it to him in the first place, so you are to blame for introducing it to him. And he does not think that you, Tessa, would now try to stop it even if you could.'

'Unkind, unkind,' mewed Tessa.

'Does he think that *I* would try to stop it if I could?' said Rosie.

'Probably, yes.'

'Then tell him,' said Rosie, 'that we can stop it, between us, and we will. He has no need to rely on Jeremy Morrison. We shall see to it that no harm comes to him.'

Rosie and Tessa exchanged a long, placid look.

'And tell him,' said Tessa, 'that he has misjudged me. Tell him that this succ . . . this spirit has not yet quite left me, that I shall be very relieved when it does, but that I shall do my utmost to see that it does not come to him. It is unkind of him to think otherwise, and he has been unkind in many other ways: but all this, tell him, is forgiven . . . provided that he promises, from now on, to love me and my Rosie as we love him.'

'Humour him,' Rosie said. 'It is quite easy. All we have to do is to pretend to believe him, when he says he is being threatened by demons, and then pretend to be protecting him. If, as I believe, he is making it all up, he will have to drop it when you give him our messages.'

'And if, as may be,' said Tessa, 'he is ill in his mind, surely he must be cured when we tell him the danger is over.'

269

'But if he is ill, he will soon imagine new dangers,' Rosie said.

'And if he is lying,' said Tessa, 'he will soon think of new lies to gain attention.'

'But at least for this time,' said both girls in disquieting unison, 'let him now be silenced or solaced.'

'Amen,' said Fielding Gray.

'Of course they said that,' said Marius to Fielding when he returned to the Fens the following afternoon. 'Rosie is trying to cheer me up by pretending she can help when she can't, and Tessa is just trying to put me off my guard. And then they'll both be jealous of Jeremy, so that's why they say I don't need him. I need him more than ever, especially in the night.'

'Impasse,' said Ptolemaeos to Fielding later that evening, after Jeremy and Marius had gone to bed. 'He's got us where he wants us. Blackmail. "Let me have Jeremy on my terms, or watch out for trouble".'

'Jeremy doesn't seem to mind. Very much the reverse.'

'It can't go on for ever,' Ptolemaeos said.

'Until his parents get back?'

Ptolemaeos was silent. At length, 'How are you getting on with your soul-searching?' Fielding enquired.

'I am beginning to see why Sheraton was so put out.'

'Why?'

'The whole thing resolves itself into a very nasty little joke.'

'You mean . . . in the case of Marius?'

'Yes. And in every other case. Marius just happens to be a more than usually dramatic and colourful example.'

'Of what, Ptolemaeos?'

'The vicious circle.'

'Expand.'

'I'll explain in full when I'm certain. I'll have to run round in a few more vicious circles before I can be absolutely sure it's the only route . . . but I shall be very surprised if I come across any other.'

As the morning was wet, Baby and Jo-Jo were sitting in what Baby called her 'study', a light-hearted library-cum-boudoir with a card table on which to write notes or play backgammon.

'This is a good chance to catch up on my social life,' Baby said. 'Item one: telephone Sarum's godfather, Max de Freville, and invite him to come for dinner and the night and a second inspection of Sarum. Item two: ditto for the other godfather, Fielding Gray.'

'Let us hope they'll be pleased with what they see. Sarum . . . has come on a lot since the christening.'

'That's as may be. What we are really doing is making an excuse to get Fielding here to tell us all about Marius. Hot news, first hand from the Fens. Can you remember your Uncle Ptoly's number?'

Jo-Jo remembered it. Then, 'Hadn't you better ask Canteloupe first?' she said.

Canteloupe came in.

'Nice to be able to come and talk to you without violating

your sacred grove,' he said. 'I'm getting a bit fed up with all that.'

'Then you're very unfair. *You* have places to retreat to where women can't follow you – that club of yours for a start. Why shouldn't we?'

'They've let women into all my clubs except one.'

'Precisely,' said Baby. 'You still have one woman-free club. And Jo and I have one man-free grove.'

'I have to go all the way to London to get the benefit.'

'And we depend on fine weather to get the benefit. Do stop *grizzling*, Canty. I'm just going to ring up your old chum, Fielding Gray, to ask him for the night so that he can have another look at Sarum.'

'No man has a better right,' said Canteloupe urbanely.

'I'm also inviting the other godfather, Max de Freville.'

'They say poor Max is going potty. He belongs to one of my clubs – not the woman-free one – where he often has lunch or dinner. It seems he pretends to be entertaining that dead girl-friend of his, Angela Tuck, or else his late business chum, Lykiadopoulos. Sometimes both. He orders meals for them, he talks to them, then he imitates them talking back. The staff have played up splendidly, but some of the members are complaining.'

'How mean,' said Jo-Jo. 'Why?'

'They say the whole thing is done so vividly that they are beginning to see talking corpses at Max's table.'

'Well, I hope he won't ask the Tuck woman or Lykiado-poulos to accompany him down here,' said Baby.

'Never on your life. His manners are much too good. He'd never dream of bringing uninvited people with him.'

'Thank God some fellows still know how to behave,' said Baby, 'even if they are going nutty.'

She picked up the receiver of the telephone and dialled the number which Jo-Jo had given her for Ptolemaeos.

Ptolemaeos's telephone was answered by Marius.

'Hullo, Baby darling,' Marius said. 'Has Canteloupe found Mummy and Daddy yet?'

'No. But you're not to worry. It's only some silly mistake.'

'I do hope Mummy's all right. Ahhhh. There's Jeremy,' said Marius in a voice that throbbed down the wire, 'coming up the lawn. Would you like to speak to him when he gets inside?'

'Not really. I hardly know him. Can I speak to Major Gray?'

'Jeremy's my friend. I sometimes think I shouldn't mind if Mummy and Daddy disappeared for ever, if only I could be with Jeremy instead.'

'Mummy and Daddy will be back very soon. Be a darling, Marius, and fetch Major Gray.'

'Righty. Bye-bye, Baby doll. Consider yourself kissed. Slap on those juicy lips of yours.'

Marius made a sploshing noise. A clatter. Silence.

'Marius has got very forward,' Baby told Jo-Jo and Canteloupe, 'yet at the same time he's utterly infantile. He's got a head over heels nursery crush on Jeremy Morrison . . . Yes, Fielding dear. Canty and I want you to come down for the night very soon and give a blessing to your godson.' She named a day and Fielding agreed it. 'Good,' said Baby. 'We shall want to know everything that's happening with you. Quick trailer now, please, to whet our curiosity.'

'Someone is telling whopping great fibs,' said Fielding, 'and that's the nub of it.'

'Marius?'

'He's the odds on favourite.'

Although Artemis had promised Isobel that she would be summoned to her husband very soon, in the event several days passed before she was taken down to the seashore. Isobel deduced that this delay was to give them both time to brood and agonize over Marius, thus making her the more urgent to persuade Gragory when she saw him and Gregory the softer to comply.

When at last she was taken to meet him, Gregory and she were allowed to walk on the beach, followed at a respectful but constant distance by Pontos.

'He's still wearing the same suit and tie,' Isobel said. 'Ridiculous, here by the sea.'

'I expect it's a kind of uniform which goes with the job.'

'Where are we, Gregory my husband? Who are these people?'

'I suspect that we are on an island off the Dalmatian coast. There is one called Memlinc Rosa that is famous for these kind of stone huts or shrines. As for our captors, Isobel my wife, they are enemies of Israel. They wish me to write a memoir of our recent tour of Israel . . . a memoir in which I shall mock and revile everything that is being thought or planned or done there. I must also discount totally, with arguments and facts which these people, our captors, will themselves supply, the Israeli claim to hold their territory as of right, and protest against everything they have done in defence of it. I must denounce them as hateful and half-crazed fanatics, just sane enough to be criminal, compare them to creeping spiders who cover with their poisonous slime the country which belongs to others and strangle in their murderous web all those who question their rule. I must parody their manners and customs and religion until these become absurd, vicious, obscene . . . Such a book, our captors believe, will come very powerfully from a Jew who controls an established imprint of international repute. As you will realize, I cannot do what they ask.'

'Do it. I shall help you. I have already mocked the Israelis in letters and postcards to Marius and Rosie, and now we shall mock them more. They are cruel and greedy and overweening. They have no right and never had a right to impose themselves on a country from which they were expelled, because of their incompetence, self-righteousness and avarice, over two thousand years ago. *Anything* we shall agree to say, provided we may return to our children who need us.'

'Isobel. I was kept apart from you so that I should pine and weaken and do their bidding. My wife would make me resolute against them, they thought. My wife would fortify my conscience with steel. Little did they know.'

'But they were right. I should have kept you resolute. Obey your conscience, Gregory my husband, I should have said: let your conscience be as rock. That is what I should have said – until there came this news of Marius, upon which your conscience simply ceased to concern me. They know this, and now they have asked me to persuade you, and in return . . . for a small favour . . . I have agreed.'

'A favour?'

'A kiss. A special kiss, which I was allowed to bestow. But in truth that made no difference, Gregory. When I heard what I heard of Marius, I wanted only one thing in all the world – our release; and I was prepared to do anything, with or without that kiss, to win it. Your conscience is now nothing to me; and as for my own, I can settle it with one little question: what are these people to us? Hebrews, Israelis, Judaeans, what are they to us? Let us say what we are asked to say in order to gain our freedom.'

'It will be treachery. Betrayal of trust.'

'It will be pretty much the truth as many men see it.'

'I cannot undermine the position of my own people in Israel. I cannot mock and betray my hosts.'

They came to a place where the river, having reached the end of the re-entrant, flowed into the sea. There were rocks and scrub on either bank of the little estuary, and on the far bank a small herd of goats, whose collar-bells jingled in the silent afternoon.

'Gregory. Gregory my husband. I have dreamed. This trouble of Marius's, of which we have been told, though not yet all of it . . . I know it has something to do with Rosie's friend, Tessa Malcolm. If it continues, and if I do not get back to restrain Marius, then Marius will talk evil of Tessa and seek to harm her. If Rosie's brother harms the friend of Rosie's heart, it will sicken Rosie, perhaps to death. These wretched Jews – which of us cares enough for them to desert Marius and Rosie when they have need of us? Do what these people, these Arabs, these Palestinians –'

' – Sympathizers with the Palestinian cause –'

' – Whoever they are, do what they ask. That the Arabs, the Palestinians, are scum need not concern us, for the Jews are no better. So do what these people ask – or at least say you will – and let us go home to our children.'

'What are you saying, Isobel?'

'I am saying that only those whom we love can count for us. We cannot take the world's woes on our shoulders, still less can we be troubled with the imbecile quarrels of squalid aliens. Aliens, Gregory, that is what these Jews and Arabs are to us, aliens of no account to you or me by comparison with our friends and our children.'

Gregory fidgeted, fingers flying from button to button of his jacket, in uneasy, tremulous distaste.

'I know what you will say now,' said Isobel rounding on him. 'You will say you are a Jew by ancestry. But you are

no more a Jew than I am a Jute or a Viking (though both
must be among my ancestors); you have no more to do
with Israel than I have with Denmark or Norseland. When
did your ancestors leave Israel, Gregory? When Herod
ruled, or Solomon? At the Dispersion, or with the Cap-
tivity? What is this wretched country or its people to do
with you? You are an Englishman. Let those that want
Israel fight for it, these so-called Jews and these so-called
Arabs, these Semites both, let *them* prate and lie and kill
each other if they wish,' she bawled, 'and let us leave them
to it, and go home to care for our own.'

The night that Max de Freville and Fielding Gray stayed
with the Canteloupes in Wiltshire, dinner was served in the
King Edward VII Room, the one in which HRH (as he
still was at the time of the incident) had goosed the reigning
Marchioness under the table.

'Your Royal Highness is pleased to make very free with
me,' the Marchioness (according to family legend) had
frigidly observed.

'Your Ladyship is welcome to payment in kind.'

'Very good, Sir. I shall accept your offer.

Whereupon she had helped herself to a grope of the
royal thighs comparable in scope to that which had been
executed upon her own and savagely pinched the end of
the royal peego.

'How beastly,' said Max de Freville (on Baby's right at
the bottom of the table) as Baby concluded the story.

'There is a picture of the lady over the fireplace,' said
Canteloupe.

They all looked at a full length portrait of a robust and
sardonic lady in hunting kit.

'She once rode astride for a bet,' said Canteloupe, 'and was summoned by the Queen to receive a personal rebuke.'

'She sounds rather ripping,' said Jean-Marie Guiscard. 'Why did she have to be so cruel to poor Bertie's tassel?'

'Raging Sapphist,' said Canteloupe, 'though she didn't find out till she was forty. When she did, she went through every female in the household, including a seventeen-year-old niece who was staying as a companion to her daughters.'

'At least she let *them* off?'

'They both suffered hideously from scrofula.'

'Nice ancestors you have,' said Max.

'Not really ancestors. They were only distant cousins of ours, you must remember. The thing came to me sideways. I am a Detterling and not a Sarum.'

'How *is* Sarum?'

'He . . . I suppose . . . counts as a Detterling too.'

'And a Llewyllyn,' said Baby. 'He's coming along very fast. You'll see him in the morning.'

Was there, Fielding wondered, just a hint of uneasiness here? Was there that in her voice which suggested that Max and he had been invited in order to give reassurance rather than congratulation? Best change the subject, at any rate.

'Ptolemaeos Tunne,' he said to Canteloupe, 'wants Rosie down in the Fens.'

'The devil he does. I thought he didn't want her there with Marius.'

'Nor did he. But now he's reached a dead end. A dead end, I suspect, to his whole scheme of research, and certainly a dead end in his attempts to help Marius. He says his only hope now is to open the whole thing up; and find out who's lying.'

'Couldn't it be Tessa?' said Baby hopefully. 'Why doesn't he get her down there?'

'Because even if her aunt would let her go, she'd disturb or even terrify Marius. Or so he says. Anyway, Ptolemaeos reckons he can draw an accurate bead on Tessa simply by questioning Rosie. Far less embarrassing.'

'What is all this?' said Max de Freville.

'Sorry, Max,' said Canteloupe and outlined the story for him.

'Sounds just your line,' said Max sourly to Fielding. 'You know how he hocus-pocused my Angela?'* he muttered to Canteloupe.

'At her own request. You agreed to forgive and forget a long time ago,' Fielding said.

'So I have done, more or less. I still say that this business of Master Marius sounds just your beastly sort of *bunderbust.*'

'I am only the messenger boy,' said Fielding. 'I am to request Canteloupe, as Rosie's temporary guardian, to give his permission for her to go to Ptolemaeos. I am then to proceed to Ivan Blessington and ask for the assistance of his daughter Jakki.'

'Why Jakki?'

'Because she is a nice, normal little girl whom Marius likes and who (Rosie let slip a while ago to me and her aunt) adores Marius. And because it was after Marius had talked with Jakki and her sister Caroline at Sarum's christening that he compared them with Tessa to the latter's violent disfavour and thus provoked Rosie into making the wish that has set off this whole sequence of misadventure.'

'And so,' said Jo-Jo, 'Uncle Ptoly proposes to stage some kind of re-enactment of what happened at the christening? Or at later stages? To pull the trouble out by the roots, as it were?'

'Something of the kind, I dare say. Though nothing so formal as a re-enactment.'

'Well then . . . a re-appraisal, or series of re-appraisals?'

* *Come Like Shadows* by Simon Raven (Panther Books, 1975)

said Canteloupe. 'Beginning with when Rosie made this wish of hers in the Provost's Garden.'

'What we have to remember,' said Fielding, 'is that that incident, though extremely colourful and important, was the beginning only of the *public* drama. The plot goes sneaking back to some while before.'

'Any chance of a seat in the stalls?' Baby said. 'Ptoly's re-appraisals, even if not formally staged, have a way of being highly theatrical.'

'He'll invite whomever he wants in his own good time,' said Fielding, jealous of his own position of privilege. 'The only people he's asked for to date are Jakki and Rosie. So,' he said, turning to Canteloupe, 'have I your permission to take Rosie down to the Fens on, say, the day after tomorrow?'

Canteloupe considered.

'Will you swear to me,' he said, 'by the memory of our regiment which is now no more, that you think Ptolemaeos's intentions are honourable, and that they may lead to good?'

'Need we be quite so pompous, Canteloupe? Gegory has said the children may go and I gather Ptolemaeos could make things rather sticky for him in some areas if he is disobliged in the matter.'

'Nevertheless will you swear to what I have asked you?'

'Ptolemaeos's intentions are certainly honourable, Canteloupe. But the region in which he is operating is notoriously treacherous.'

'I said, "May lead to good". We cannot hope for certainties. What was it that Meredith said about that?'

'That people who want to bet on dead certs end up with dud tips,' Baby said. 'Or that was about the size of it.'

'"O what a dusty answer gets the soul,"' quoted Jo-Jo, '"When hot for certainties in this our world."'

'Brava,' said Max.

'Well, Fielding?' said Canteloupe.

'The region . . . is not propitious . . . as I have already said.' Fielding thought of green-eyed Marius as he walked lithely away to bed, turning to smile at Jeremy who lumbered after him. 'Nevertheless, and provided this is strictly understood, I will swear by the memory of our regiment, which is now no more, that the importation of Rosie may lead to good.'

'Very well,' said Canteloupe regally. 'Before you leave tomorrow I shall give you a letter for Mrs Malcolm, authorizing you to take Rosie to the Fens.'

At about the time at which the party in the King Edward VII Room was being served with its pudding, Len said to Provost Llewyllyn in the latter's Lodging: 'Ptolemaeos reckons he may have found out what Sheraton found out . . . the thing that bugged Sheraton so much he swamped himself in usquebaugh.'

'About the so-called soul? Presumably that it doesn't exist?'

'Oh no, Provost. Something much more annoying than that.'

Half an hour after breakfast, Sarum of Old Sarum was paraded in his pram in the Rose Garden for inspection by Max de Freville and Fielding Gray. Daisy the nurse manoeuvred the pram under command of Lady Canteloupe.

'Hail to my godson,' said Max, approaching the pram.

'If all goes well, my boy, I shall have a very pretty present for you later on.'

'Oh how nice,' said Baby. 'What?'

'Wait and see, my dear.'

'What about you, Fielding? Shall you be making him a present?'

'I have already made him one . . . that nobody else has.'

Baby kicked him under the pram.

'That gold mug for his christening,' continued Fielding, 'with all his names on it. Tullius, Fielding, d'Azincourt – '

Baby kicked him again.

'Would you like to hold him?' Baby said to Max, who was peering into the pram.

'No,' said Max, backing slowly. 'You know where I last saw his eyes?'

'Max . . .'

'In the face of that boy of Lyki's in Venice. Piero,* that cunning whore of Venice. You must remember, you met him, you both met him,' Max said, swivelling his gaze to include Fielding, 'at dinner in our Palazzo.'

'I remember him very well,' said Baby with admirable aplomb. 'He was a nice boy and very kind to me. Although he was lame, he showed me over the roof of the Palazzo.'

'Then he showed you what you had no business to see,' Max snarled, almost hissed, at the pram. 'He was Lykiadopoulos's whore,' Max said. 'Your son has the eyes of a whore.'

'I want to get back to her,' Donald Salinger said to Carmilla and Theodosia.

* *The Survivors* by Simon Raven (Panther Books, 1977)

'What nonsense, Da,' said Carmilla. 'Now look at the late Mr Getty's lovely antique sofas.'

The three of them were in the Getty Memorial Museum on the Pacific Coast, having driven to it down Sunset Boulevard, in a hired car the size of an aircraft carrier, from the Beverly Hills Hotel, where they had arrived the previous evening.

'We've only just got here,' Theodosia said. 'This is our holiday with you, Da; first we've had together in years.'

'I want to get back to Vanessa.'

'You're as near to her here as you would be anywhere,' said Carmilla, looking carefully at a Renaissance backgammon set with rude carvings round the rim. 'That thing reminds me: we must take up backgammon again. We used to love playing you when we were children.'

'Did you? I was taught by Max de Freville, you know. We used to play for fifty pounds a point. Max de Freville . . . the one that told me that story . . . about the filthy games Vanessa used to play. I must get back to her. I can only get back to her, Carmilla, Theodosia, if I return to England, to Green Oxley Laris. I've thought of a way of getting into her past, of punishing her, of humiliating her, there, in her past. There is said to be the ghost of an Abbess that haunts the forest round the chapel in Green Oxley Laris. Your mother looked for it as a child, with her cousin, but never found it. If I could somehow lure that ghost to her grave, now, it could mock her with her lost childhood, it could say, "You looked for me as a kind of joke, you never believed in me, you were mocking me, but now here I am, and where and what are you? Your cousin got the better of you in the end."'

'Look at this statue, Da. Eros and Psyche. Even as he makes love to her, she deliberately looks away, because she knows that though she may feel and touch him she may not set eyes on him, on pain of losing him. But we know, from the way her eyeballs are slanted in their sockets, that

283

very soon she will turn them on him, and that as a result she will be banished from his presence, and compelled to go forth, heavy with his child, into desolation.'

'Or look at this picture,' said Theodosia when her sister had finished. 'Helen on the Walls of Troy. She sees her rightful husband, as he and his brother are reviewing the Greek army beneath, and she weeps and cringes with grief and loathing, loathing of herself.'

'What are you saying, both of you?'

'That every crime carries its own punishment. Whatever Mother may or may not have done, she has been punished enough in her own lifetime, if only by the manner of her death. There is no need to pursue her now.'

'She mocked me, she deceived me,' shouted Donald. 'She promised to tell me the whole truth but she withheld whatever she pleased. She poisoned both our lives by making light of my love. She did not have to return it, nor even to be faithful to me, but she should have recognized it and respected it for what it was. She should have told the whole truth when I asked it of her, for that was *all* I asked of her, and she swore she would. But she did not even care about me enough to do that: I might have been a worm beneath her feet.'

Donald started weeping, silently but violently.

'I think,' said Carmilla, 'that it is getting rather hot in here. Altogether too much Art. A drive up the coast? What do you say, Theodosia?'

'A very good idea, Carmilla. The sight and sound of the sea are very soothing. Yes, I think that we should take Da to the sea.'

There had been considerable delay in bringing Rosie Stern and Jakki Blessington down to the Fens, as both girls were in the middle of their school examinations at Collingham's, and Betty Blessington was in any case reluctant to send Jakki. The upshot was that after much talk on telephones Fielding Gray had proceeded directly to the Fens from Wiltshire, and Rosie and Jakki were driven down from London some days later by Betty Blessington herself, who had now been persuaded that the scheme was, as her husband put it, *thik hai*.

'I'm not at all sure what's going on,' she told Ptolemaeos. 'When Major Gray asked me to bring Jakki here, I refused him. But my husband says that Canteloupe says that it's all quite harmless and could help that little Stern boy, Marius.'

'I hope so, Mrs Blessington.'

'Caroline is madly jealous. Why did you only want Jakki?'

'Because I'm told she's in love with Marius.'

'There's been a lot of soulful sighing, if that's what you mean.'

'As plain a symptom as any. Do you want to stay here? There's plenty of room.'

'So I see, and thank you,' said Betty. 'But my husband and Caroline need me in London. Everyone says you're a fit person to have charge of young children, because you were such a marvellous guardian to your niece when she was orphaned.'

'Jo-Jo and I got along very well.'

'So that's all right, and I'll be saying toodle-ooh.'

'Don't you want to say good-bye to Jakki?'

'Why should I? I'm not leaving her for ever. She's quite

happy in your garden with Rosie,' said Betty Blessington, 'and doubtless delighted to see the back of me for a bit – which goes for me too with knobs on.'

The first thing which Ptolemaeos did after Betty Blessington had gone was to introduce Jakki and Rosie to the sarcophagus in the Library. Fielding Gray was spending the day with Tom Llewyllyn in Cambridge, while Jeremy and Marius had been packed off for the afternoon to Newmarket Races. This left a clear field for Ptolemaeos, who intended to have his plan of procedure firmly formed and ready for immediate operation by the time everyone else came back. To this end he asked the following questions:

Of Jakki, in the presence of Rosie, he asked first, 'Does it frighten you to be lying in that huge bath?'

The answer was 'no' without hesitation.

'Why,' Ptolemaeos then asked, 'do you love Marius Stern?'

'I don't know,' said Jakki. 'All I know is that I want to hold him very close and that I would do anything, however dangerous, that he asked me.'

'Would you ever ask *him* to do anything for you?'

There was a very long pause.

'I might,' said Jakki at last, 'if he ever said that he liked me. But until he says that, I shall let him do all the asking.'

'Right,' said Ptolemaeos. 'Out you get. Dry yourself. Put your clothes on and go to the kitchen, where Mrs Gurt, the dumpy one, or Mrs Statch, the wiry one, will give you some tea.'

'I'd sooner stay here.'

'Do as Mr Tunne says,' said Rosie levelly. 'I'm sure he has good reasons.'

'Of course,' said Jakki, absolutely accepting Rosie's premiss and command. She retired behind Fertility Cults to take off her bathing drawers and dry herself. Then, when she had put on a soccer shirt and grey shorts (remnants of her father's schooldays preserved by her grandmother for reasons more of sentiment than economy, though both applied), she walked out whistling 'The Girl I Left Behind Me'.

'She likes dressing like a boy,' said Rosie, who was in a neat little tartan skirt with jumper and tartan knee socks. 'It makes her feel closer to Marius.'

'What's wrong with Marius, Rosie?'

'Don't you want me to get into that bath like Jakki?'

'No.' Ptolemaeos pulled the plug and let the water swirl slowly out of the sarcophagus. 'I've finished with it. For weeks I've been on the edge of finding out what I want to know, and now I have – or at least I'm as near to it as I'll ever be. The last man who was working in this way drank himself to death – and now I know why.'

'Why?'

'Did you hear the various tones of voice which Jakki used when she answered me?'

'I noticed that she sounded different when she was answering difficult questions.'

'Yes. Different. According to whether she was answering the questions straight from her brain . . . or from some deeper part of her *mind*. Do you understand the distinction?'

'Yes, Mr Tunne. The brain does automatic things like adding. The mind does arguments. And then there is the soul, which tells you what is right or wrong . . . and also about love.'

'Good girl. Who told you all that?'

'The teaching at Collingham's is very good, Mr Tunne. And so it should be, as the school is very expensive.'

'Well, the crucial question was, "would Jakki ever ask

Marius to do anything for her?" Before she could answer that question, which was a question for the *soul*, Rosie, she had to consult her *memory*, which is in the *brain*, to find out whether she had ever felt like making requests of Marius in the past. And when this happened (during that long pause) I suddenly realized something. Something which had been staring me in the face ever since I started this investigation, but which I was too stupid to grasp finally until just now. Whenever memory is needed, the question is always referred to the memory cells in the physical brain before being passed on to the immaterial mind or soul. Why, Rosie?'

'Because neither mind nor soul has its own memory, Mr Tunne. They depend on the material brain to store all the information they need. All this is really elementary, you know. If you wanted to find out about the soul, you had no need to go to all this trouble with Roman coffins and tape recorders. The few simple experiments which we do at Collingham's would have told you everything.'

'What would they have told me, Rosie?'

'Thought and love depend on mind and soul,' said Rosie in a sing-song voice, as of one who repeats a well-learned lesson. 'Mind and soul depend on memory. Memory depends on the physical brain. When the body dies, the brain dies, and with it the memory. Mind and soul may possibly be left, but since they have no memory they have nothing on which to concentrate their powers. Love can call to mind no object, thought can conjure no problems – without memory. So the soul drifts away for ever, conscious that it exists, but of nothing else at all.'

'Yes, that is what I finally realized just now. I have been near to it, going round and round it, for days, for weeks, and now at last I have it. Alas, poor ghost. Are you not sad for it, Rosie, as it drifts hollow and empty through eternity? The man who started me off on this scheme of research drank himself to death, through fear or horror, when he understood the truth.'

'How very silly of him. Even though mind and soul exist on a non-physical plane, we cannot be certain they survive the death of the body to which they are so closely related. Non-existence,' said Rosie, 'is hardly a state to be regarded with fear or horror. And even if mind or soul do survive, they will not suffer. To suffer,' said Rosie, as if rehearsing a litany she had loved since her earliest childhood, 'you must know. To be guilty or lonely, you must be able to remember what evil you have done, or what it was like to have friends. A bare state of consciousness, of being conscious but knowing or remembering nothing, must be almost the same as unconsciousness. When this person of yours drank himself to death, it must have been, not because he was scared or horrified by the state which his soul might assume at death, but because he thought it preferable to the agonies and uncertainties of life.'

'Also blindingly obvious. Out of the mouths of babes . . .'

'You were going to talk to me about Marius, Mr Tunne?'

'In a moment. Please excuse me. Read a book while I'm gone.'

Ptolemaeos went to the kitchen, where Jakki was drinking lemonade and tea in alternate gulps, and Mrs Statch and Mrs Gurt were putting on their hats to go home.

'Likes hot and cold together,' sniggered Mrs Statch. 'Rum little bit she is.'

'Dressed like her brother,' said Mrs Gurt.

'I haven't got a brother,' said Jakki.

'Good-night, sweet ladies,' said Ptolemaeos, opening the back door for them. And when they were gone, 'Jakki. Do you, at Collingham's, have lessons or do experiments which concern the relation between the material brain and the immaterial mind or soul?'

Jakki looked blank. Then, 'We have biology,' she said.

'The human brain has been described to us, and compared with that of an ape, a dog, a rabbit, and a lobster.'

'But there is no talk of the mind?'

'At Collingham's they seem to think that the mind and the brain are the same thing.'

'No talk of the soul then?'

'At Collingham's they are not religious.'

'Thank you. Will you be all right on your own for a bit?'

'I shall explore the house, if you don't mind.'

'Help yourself.'

Ptolemaeos returned to Rosie, who was reading William James's *Varieties of Religious Experience*. As soon as Ptolemaeos entered the library, she put the book carefully down on the arm of the chair in which she was sitting, stood up, and saluted Ptolemaeos with a curtsey.

'Sorry,' she said. 'I should have done that when I arrived. So should Jakki. We were so excited that we forgot. Please don't tell anyone at Collingham's.'

'I shan't,' said Ptolemaeos, 'if you'll now tell me the truth about Marius.'

'Tessa meant him no harm. None of it is her fault.'

'I dare say not. Nevertheless there is something which has not yet been told. Something which neither of you told Major Gray when he came to London the other day, but which you will now tell me.'

'I promised Tessa not.'

Ptolemaeos sat down on a hard chair near Asiatic History.

'Come and sit on my knee, Rosie.'

'No.'

'Come and sit on my knee, or else I shall tell them all at Collingham's that you are a disobliging and ill conditioned little girl.'

'And *I* shall tell them that you asked me to sit on your knee.'

'Only they will believe me and not you, because I am

rich and could give them a lot of money if I wished. Come now. I'm not going to hurt you.'

Rosie came and sat very demurely, feet and knees clamped tight together, on Ptolemaeos's gigantic thigh.

'You have beautiful hair, Rosie. Beautiful black hair. It shines. When I stroke, it will shine even more.'

He began to stroke her from the forehead, back over the crown of her head, and down to her shoulders. After he had done this three or four times, Rosie relaxed and placed one cheek against his breast.

'You have kind hands, Mr Tunne.'

'Sweets to the sweet, Rosie. Why did you tell me you learned about the brain and the soul at Collingham's?'

'I did, in a way.'

'But there were no experiments there. No instruction on the subject.'

'Sometimes Daddy used to come in the summer evenings, a year ago, to collect me from Collingham's and walk with me in the Park. He has not done it this year, because Mummy and he have been away; but last year he came quite often, when he was not too busy, and as we walked away from Collingham's through the Park, he talked to me about the mind and the soul. So it was all connected in my own mind with Collingham's, and it was easier, I don't quite know why, to tell you that I learned it there.'

'So you were telling me what your father believes?'

'Yes, Mr Tunne.'

'When did he last talk to you of these matters?'

'In the garden at the christening party. He was telling me that there is now a theory, though it can never be proved true, that the soul might somehow be equipped with its own memory after all and not be wholly dependent on the memory cells in the brain. This would mean that it could have a proper existence if it survived after death. But I said that anything as detailed and mechanical as the processes of sorting and storing and reproducing memories would have to be operated by the physical brain and could not be possible in an immaterial soul.'

'I agree, on the whole. Did your father?'

'He was called away to talk to someone.'

'And then Marius came, and you quarrelled?'

'He called Tessa nasty names.'

'Which brings us back to your secret. What is it about Marius and Tessa, Rosie, that you have not yet told me?'

'I promised Tessa that I would never tell.'

'Why?'

'Go on stroking my hair.'

'Why did Tessa make you promise not to tell?'

'Go on stroking me, Mr Tunne.'

'Tell me what I ask, Rosie.'

'I shall tell you after you have stroked my hair twice more, and I shall stop telling you as soon as you stop stroking.'

'Very well. It is shining beautifully.'

'It is not only your stroking that makes it shine. It shines when I talk about Tessa. Tessa is unhappy, Mr Tunne, because she has no father or mother. She loves her Aunt Maisie, and she loves Major Gray, who often lives with them, but that is not the same. To make up for not having a mother or father, she needs more than that: she needs a brother and a sister. I am her sister. She wants Marius as her brother; then everything, she says, would be all right. But Marius refuses. He refused to give her the kiss which would have made them brother and sister, even after she had shown him things that an elder sister might show a brother she loved, like how to defend yourself against unpleasant people.'

'She also showed him a peculiar painting in the National Gallery. Marius might reasonably have felt that she was being . . . rather more than sisterly. In any case, he found that he was in danger, if he responded, of being more than brotherly.'

'If he had loved Tessa as she wanted him to love her, he would have trusted her. She would not have minded some . . . some tiny little accident. She is very understanding.'

'Do you know – did she know – what kind of accident it would have been?'

'I think so. I have watched Marius, sometimes, when he thought no one else was in the room; and I have told Tessa what I saw. How could anyone mind a silly little thing like that, just a few tiny white drops?'

'But Rosie, Marius thought it was some power coming out of Tessa that made him feel like that. He was frightened.'

'Whatever he thought or felt, if he had loved Tessa as she wanted him to love her he would have trusted her and kissed her. When he refused, he spoilt everything. Later, when he was horrid about her at the christening. I decided it was time for revenge. I wished him a rotten cricket season, because I knew he was very sensitive, that such a wish would upset him so much that he probably *would* have a rotten cricket season.'

'Is that all, Rosie?'

'No.'

'What else?'

'Stroke my hair, Mr Tunne.'

'What else, Rosie?'

'I have told lies. I have told everyone that of course my spiteful wish could have no effect on Marius's cricket, nor did I want it to, it was just a thing of the moment. But as I have just admitted to you now, I knew that it might have the effect that it did . . . and I was glad, not sorry, when this happened. And again, I have said to everyone that I did my best to persuade Marius that I had no power to spoil his cricket, that in this way I tried to help him: but really I did it, not to help him at all, but to make a good impression on Tessa and other people. I was delighted

293

when he didn't believe me at first and his punishment was continued.'

'*But Rosie*. Why did you go on wanting to punish Marius? It was Tessa whom he had insulted, for whose sake he was being punished, and even Tessa wanted it to stop. Why did *you* want it to go on?'

'If you will stroke the hair over my ears . . . yes, just there, just like that . . . I will tell you.'

Jakki went stomping round the house. Downstairs she found a dining room with a round table, which did not seem to have been used for a long time, and a large, crumbly, dusty, cosy drawing room, through which she had been taken into the garden when she first arrived. The kitchen she avoided because she did not relish the memory of Mrs Gurt and Mrs Statch, and although they had gone home she thought their presence might linger. The library was out of bounds as long as Mr Tunne was in it talking to Rosie. There was a billiard room, a gun room with chained shotguns, a loo with groups of undergraduates on the walls, and a room full of files with many telephones of different colours on a large desk.

She went upstairs, wondering which bedroom would be allotted to her. Would she and Rosie be in the same room? Or even in the same bed? Sometimes children were packed into the same bed to save trouble. She would not mind, she thought, being in the same bed as Marius. Which was his room? She opened several doors: there were two dismal and rather mouldy rooms, then a grandiose affair (with sphinxes holding up the bed) which was probably Mr Tunne's, and then a smaller but still spacious room with a school trunk at the end of the bed. Marius, she thought.

But the room gave out an air of being unoccupied. The wardrobe was open and she could see no clothes in it. There were no towels by the basin, no tooth things or hair brushes. Perhaps, she thought, it was just a convenient place to dump Marius's school trunk . . . which, she found to her annoyance, was heavily padlocked.

The next room she came to had a four-poster bed. To the left of the top end of this a door led into a bathroom with a loo. Jakki wondered whether she would have her own bathroom with a loo, and thought probably not. In this one there seemed to be two of everything. Two tooth mugs, with brushes and tubes of paste in both of them. Two nail brushes. Two sponges. Two large towels, two medium, and two small. How odd, thought Jakki: I'm sure there's no one married in the house. She returned to the bedroom. One pair of pyjamas under each pillow. A pale green poplin pair under the left-hand pillow near the bathroom door, and a blue silk pair under the pillow near the window. Neither pair was marked. But some of the suits in the wardrobe were marked. Investigation revealed that a large suit of light checks had been made for Jeremy Morrison, Esqre, by Philby Talbot of Clifford Street, and that a much smaller suit of dark grey flannel belonged to M. O. B. Stern of Oudenarde House.

'So you see, it just wasn't fair,' said Rosie, as Ptolemaeos stroked her ears gently through their covering of glossy jet-black waves. 'Mummy loved Marius more than she did me because he was a boy.'

'Mothers love their sons. Fathers love their daughters.'

'Yes. Daddy loved me more than he loved Marius. But Mummy loved Marius more than she loved me by a much larger amount. Daddy preferred me; Mummy *adored* Marius. They had special words and jokes, special ways of holding hands and linking fingers, almost as though Marius had been Mummy's boy-husband.'

'I saw no sign of this at the christening.'

'You hardly saw us at all. You left so early. Anyway,' said Rosie, 'that was in public. It is in private that it all comes out. Mummy kissing his face with the point of her tongue. Marius nestling against her breasts as if he were still a baby and wanted to suck them. I couldn't bear it, Mr Tunne. I wanted revenge on Mummy as well as on Marius, revenge for me as well as for Tessa: so I wished what I wished, knowing that it would hurt both of them, Marius because he was so vain and Mummy because she doted on him so much and hated him ever to fail.'

'But since she has been away and knows nothing at all of his failure, your efforts have been wasted as far as she is concerned.'

'She will come back and find out.'

'Indeed she will,' said Ptolemaeos, who was gazing over Rosie's head, through one window of the library and out on to the drive, where Gregory and Isobel were climbing out of Isobel's Lagonda.

When Jeremy and Marius arrived happily back from Newmarket (having made a killing on Lover Pie, which won a long distance race at 33 to 1) they saw Isobel's Lagonda in Ptolemaeos's drive.

'Bugger,' said Marius. 'They're back. Everything will be spoilt now.'

'You'd better come and get your things out of my room before anyone comes nosing around.'

'I suppose so. Oh Jeremy, what shall I do if I'm taken away from you? It's only you that keeps me safe.'

'Your parents won't swallow that. I wonder where they are?'

'Talking to Ptoly, I expect. We'd better go upstairs and you can help me move my stuff back.'

But when they reached what for the last few days had been *their* room, they found Jakki, who was sitting on the bed in her shorts, hugging both pairs of pyjamas and crying. 'I hate you both,' she said.

'What are you doing here?' said Marius politely.

'Rosie and I came this afternoon.'

'Oh, did she?' said Marius with venom.

'Then your mother and father arrived. Mr Tunne took them and Rosie off somewhere, so I came back up here.'

'*Back* up here?' said Jeremy.

'I'd already been once and found out. I ran away, it was so horrible. Then I came back to make sure it was really true.'

Marius sat down by Jakki and put an arm round her shoulders. She sniffed boisterously and wriggled away. '*Beast*,' she said.

'Why?'

'Sleeping in the same bed with him.'

'I get frightened at night. He keeps me safe.'

'I know what people do when they sleep in the same bed. Mummy told us. It's meant to be a man and his wife. How can you be like that . . . with *him*?'

'I'm not . . . like that . . . with him. I just like being with him.'

'Even if that's true, it's still horrid.'

'Are you going to sneak?' asked Marius.

'Of course not.' She wriggled back towards him and hugged him. 'Lovely Marius.'

'Then help me and Jeremy take my stuff back. Before

anyone else finds out.' And to Jeremy, 'I don't suppose Ptoly Tunne will tell them?'

'Hardly, since he encouraged it. Would you mind,' said Jeremy to Jakki, 'not wiping your nose on my pyjamas?'

'They're lovely. So are yours,' she said to Marius. 'I was hugging them to pretend I was in bed with you both.'

'I thought you just said that was horrid.'

'Not if I'd been there too. Just friendly.'

'That's how it was anyway. Just friendly.'

Jakki smiled at the blue pyjamas and put them back under their pillow. Then she inhaled deeply from Marius's green ones and got off the bed.

'Righty,' she said. 'Where do I take these now?'

Baby and Jo-Jo were playing backgammon by the pool in the centre of their grove. Since they had been playing for twenty pounds a point Jo-Jo had won a further four thousand. It had been agreed that Baby should pay up when and if the figure reached ten thousand. If it didn't they would just play on till Baby won it all back. Since Jo-Jo wanted this to happen she was making a lot of mistakes on purpose, but Baby kept correcting them for her.

'You must take my piece and make the bar point,' Baby said.

Daisy arrived, wheeling Sarum.

'A note for you, My Lady,' Daisy said.

Baby opened it. After a minute or two, 'It's from Canty in the House,' Baby told Jo-Jo. 'Len has telephoned from Cambridge. He thought Canty ought to know that his old cricket chum, Donald Salinger is dead. Carmilla Salinger rang up from California to ask if she and Theodosia could come into residence for a while during the Long Vacation . . . now that they no longer have to look after their father.'

'How did he die?'

'Coming out of some museum. According to Canty according to Len according to Carmilla, a workman on the roof dropped a tile, which hit him on the head. And there's a PS. Len says that Tom and he have just been summoned by your Uncle Ptoly to witness the last act of the *affaire Marius*. Apparently Gregory and Isobel have turned up safely, just after Ptoly discovered the vital clue to the whole thing, and it will all be settled this evening.'

'How mean not to invite us.'

'No. Ptoly deliberately hasn't let us know earlier, because he says what is going to happen could be bad for Alexandre and turn my milk sour.'

Fielding Gray, Tom Llewyllyn and Len had all been spending the day doing an architectural tour of the more obscure colleges. When they arrived back in the Provost's Lodging for tea, there had been two telephone calls, the first for Len from Carmilla.

'We're going to have him buried here,' Carmilla had said. 'Just as well to have a continent and an ocean between his grave and mother's. We've commissioned a statue of a man batting to stand on his stone, but the Americans are finding this difficult.'

Then she had gone on to ask permission for herself and her sister to come into residence in Lancaster in a few days' time.

Finally she had told Len what a relief Donald's death had been to her and to Theodosia.

'Thea and I were on the point of taking him down to the

sea and arranging something,' she said. 'He was no good any more, Len, to himself or to us. Even so, we shouldn't have cared much for the job of putting him down ourselves, and we're very grateful to that workman on the roof. The museum people are amazed that we're not going to sue for a zillion dollars, but that would be sheer hypocrisy. What have we lost?'

The second telephone call had been for Sir Thomas Llewyllyn.

'Gregory and Isobel are here,' Ptolemaeos had said, 'and I'd like you and Len to join the party. Fielding still there?'

'Yes.'

'Tell him I want him back as soon as possible. You and Len follow in time for dinner. Isobel's going to be cooking that.'

Ptolemaeos put down the receiver of one of the many telephones in his office, and surveyed Gregory, Isobel and Rosie.

'So I'm cooking the dinner?' said Isobel.

'Rosie and Jakki will help. Women's work.'

'You promise,' said Isobel, 'that I shan't miss anything?'

'Cross my navel. You'd better get going.'

Isobel nodded meekly. 'Come along, Rosie,' she said.

Ptolemaeos led Gregory down the passage to the library.

'Very handsome,' he said, pointing to the sarcophagus. 'But for the purpose for which I bought it, a sheer waste of money. My idea was that people would tell me the truth if they were utterly relaxed, floating weightlessly in warm water. In fact if you want truth you've got a better chance if you use some kind of stimulus . . . sensuous or sensual

300

. . . as I've recently found out from – er from one of my assistants.'

'What conclusions have you come to?' said Gregory with polite distaste. 'I gather that you were seeking to establish or disestablish the existence of the soul.'

'I have simply established what Sheraton established many years ago, and what, for that matter, any intelligent child could have told me: that whereas the functions of the brain are maintained by a kind of electricity, the operations of the soul and the intellect are fuelled by we know not what and never shall. Now that we've got rid of Rosie, tell me what you've been up to.'

Gregory told him. 'Though I'm not absolutely certain where we were, not even now. Isobel got a pash, she says, on one of her wardresses, who had no trouble in persuading her to persuade me to give in. What they have demanded, Ptolemaeos, on pain of further unpleasantness or disruption, is that I should write and publish a personal statement to bring ridicule and contempt upon the Jews, and in particular to repudiate, radically, their right to occupy Israel.'

'An invidious undertaking?'

'Yes. But since in my view Jews *are* contemptible and ridiculous, and since their right to occupy Israel is indeed very questionable, and since, as a Jew myself, I understand all this very well, I shall be able to do the thing with conviction . . . and even, at times, with pleasure.'

'And the outcome?'

'There will be bouquets as well as brickbats. In any case, what can I do? What do I care about the rights and wrongs of this grotesque war? All I care for is my freedom to return to and remain with Rosie and Marius. I do not think Canteloupe should have sent them to you,' he said with a sudden show of hostility.

'You said that he could.'

'Under pressure. Your pressure. Blackmail.'

301

'You said that he could, and he did. I think you're going to be grateful. I have sorted out Marius.'

'What is the matter with Marius?'

'He thinks, or affects to think, that he is, or soon will be, possessed of a devil.' Rapidly, Ptolemaeos provided chapter and verse.

'But this is madness,' Gregory said.

'No. You will know what it is presently. Very soon now everyone I need will be assembled – '

' – I do not like Marius to be treated as a public entertainment – '

' – A few friends are going to assist him. That is all.'

'Indecorous. I protest and I forbid.'

There was a sharp knock on the door, and Greco Barraclough came in with Nicos.

'On our way back from Peterborough Cathedral,' said El Greco. 'We called to find out exactly when you are expecting us during the vac.'

'Good.' Ptolemaeos eyed Nicos. 'Both of you stay to dinner,' he said.

'I am tired.'

'Go to the summerhouse at the end of the lawn, and rest. *Kyrie* Nico, you stay here.'

'What do you want with him?' said the Greco crossly.

'His help.' And to Gregory, 'You go with Barraclough.'

Gregory hesitated, then stood his ground.

'Go with Barraclough, Gregory,' said Ptolemaeos, 'or else I may feel compelled, in the interests of anthropology, to treat him to a long discourse on the peculiarities of my Yiddisher Momma.'

'What on earth are you talking about?' said the Greco.

'You can ask Gregory, though I don't think he'll tell you. Didn't he publish that book of yours about the Mani? I suggest you discuss your royalties with him.'

Ptolemaeos went to the door and politely held it open.

'Ai-yai,' said Gregory as he left with Barraclough. 'I do not think *that* discussion will take very long.'

'I tell you, Angie,' said Max de Freville over tea and toast for two in his club, 'he had the eyes of a Sicilian whore. Lyki's Sicilian boy, Piero. That is why Lyki is not with us this afternoon. I did not wish him to hear me make the comparison. It would have hurt him.'

'I died too soon to know Piero,' said Max in Angela's argumentative voice, 'but I'm sure Lyki had enough taste not to take on a boy who was an obvious prostitute.'

'I saw it in his eyes when he smiled,' said Max, 'the look of a greedy, cringing whore. Sarum has that same look . . . and he shall have no money of mine.'

'Aren't you being rather precipitate?' said Max in Angela's most annoying tone of presumptuous deprecation.

'I tell you he shall have none,' shouted Max, rising and kicking the tea table across the room. 'A whore, a baby whore. None, *none*, NONE.'

When all Marius's 'stuff' had been taken back to the room where his school trunk was, Jeremy told Marius and Jakki to go and find Marius's mother, and himself went to the library to consult Ptolemaeos. With Ptolemaeos was a boy whom he knew slightly, an undergraduate (if rather an obscure one) of his own college, Nicos Pandouros. They nodded to each other politely and distantly. Then Jeremy turned to Ptolemaeos. Seeing the question in Jeremy's eye,

Ptolemaeos said: 'Everything is in order. Please wait here with us. At any moment Fielding Gray will arrive. Then we can begin.'

When Marius and Jakki eventually found Isobel in the kitchen with Rosie, Isobel wiped her hands, held Marius's face between them, and kissed his nose with the tip of her tongue. Rosie pretended not to notice. Jakki watched her with fascination and wondered whether Marius would accept such a tribute from her.

'Where have you been, Mummy?' Marius said.

'Having a nice change,' said Isobel, thinking of Artemis, 'of which I probably took too little advantage. Now you and Jakki can help with the dinner.'

When Fielding Gray arrived, Jeremy came out to him in the drive and led him off to the library.

'I shall drive to the Peloponnese this September,' said Fielding, 'and back again before the beginning of your Full Term. Do you want to come?'

'Very much.'

'I shall ask you to do much – most – of the driving. In return I shall pay for everything connected with the car, and your passage, both ways, across the Channel. But I shall expect you to pay your own hotel bills, which will not always be moderate. Do you still want to come?'

'Yes. Providing that Marius is all right.'

'You cannot wait on Marius for ever, or indeed for very

much longer. You must tell me now, quite definitely and *now*, whether or not you will accompany me.'

'I shall come, Fielding.'

When they reached the library, Ptolemaeos said, 'Action to cure Marius must begin at once. It will be sudden and quite pitiless. Please listen carefully while I give you all your instructions.'

'Len and Tom won't be here for some time,' Fielding said.

'They will be here quite soon enough.'

'Please, what is this?' asked Nicos.

'Young Marius Stern. You don't need to know the details. Just do as I tell you.'

'I said at that christening that he would come to no good. Boys of that beauty never do.'

'It has yet to be seen what he will come to,' said Ptolemaeos. 'Now, pay attention if you please . . .'

Daisy the nurse wheeled Sarum of Old Sarum across the lawn and through the sticky evening towards the house. Baby and Jo-Jo walked one each side of Daisy, while the backgammon set, folding table and chairs were piled on the pram, Sarum's face being just visible beyond the barricade.

'Max was quite right,' said Baby. 'He has got Piero's eyes. And of course Piero was a whore, though a very superior one. But he did *not* have a whore's eyes. He had a whore's smile, but then he hardly ever smiled. I rather adored him.'

At this stage Daisy and Sarum peeled off for the nursery entrance.

'I was thinking of Piero,' said Baby, 'while Fielding was

getting Sarum on me. I should have preferred it to be Piero, but of course he went into that Franciscan convent on the Island of Francesco del Deserto, and one can't go whistling up Franciscan friars to make one pregnant.'

'Can't one? Have you never read Boccaccio?' Jo-Jo said.

'Anyway, it wouldn't have been fair. He went into that convent to get away from the likes of us.'

Canteloupe came out of a glass door.

'We were just talking about what Max said about Sarum,' said Baby, 'that he had that Sicilian boy Piero's eyes.'

'Funny. Someone's been on the telephone about Max. He's been breaking up the club.'

'*Breaking up the club?*'

'Shouting. Punting the tea things about. Pulling down the pictures. Luckily there was a doctor in the place who had a needle handy and stuck something into him.'

'Why did they telephone you?'

'He happened to have his passport on him; so they looked at that bit where you write down the names of people who might help in emergencies, next of kin or whatnot. Max had written down Mrs Angela Tuck, with the British Cemetery in Corfu as her address, and Stratis Lykiadopoulos, c/o The Island of San Michele, Venice.'

'Oh, dear. I thought he was a bit peculiar when he came down here, though in one way he was quite right about Sarum's eyes – '

' – Luckily he'd written my address in as an afterthought. Slap in the middle of the Special Currency Section.'

'So what help could you be?'

'I told them to contact a character called Doctor La Soeur, an old chum who used to clear up our medical muddles back in our gamy youth. He has a kind of private nursing home where he'll be able to manage Max – if he's manageable.'

'And if he's not?'

'St Bede's . . . where Nickie Morrison is.'

And my mother is, thought Baby, but said nothing.

Yet Jo-Jo heard her through the silence.

'Sweet Jesus Christ,' said Jo-Jo, 'God has a lot to answer for.'

Fielding Gray came into the kitchen, ostensibly to ask Isobel Stern if there was anything she needed. She needed nothing, and he stayed there chatting, telling her and the children (Marius, Rosie and Jakki) about his visit to the Canteloupes in Wiltshire.

'Max said Sarum had Piero's eyes,' he told them. 'Piero was a boy in Venice we all knew, who became a monk. Or a friar. Not much difference in his case, as he was going to stay in the Franciscan convent on an island in the Lagoon. I think Max was right about Piero's eyes. A very bright green – like Marius's.'

'Marius has the eyes of my old boy friend, Mark Lewson,' Isobel said.

'That fits,' said Fielding, 'from what I remember of Lewson. Lewson's eyes, Piero's eyes . . . and Marius's eyes. When Max saw them in Sarum's face, he said they were a whore's eyes.'

Everyone was very silent, as even Jakki and Rosie (being true children of the age) knew what a whore was.

'But whores have to be ladies,' said Jakki tentatively.

'A whore is anyone who sells himself,' said Fielding, looking at Marius.

'I have not sold myself,' Marius said.

'Just what are you doing?' said Isobel to Fielding.

'Yes, you have,' said Fielding to Marius, ignoring Isobel. 'You have tried to pass yourself off, before Mr Tunne and Jeremy and others, as something which you are not. That

307

is prostituting yourself, Marius: that is being a whore: making a dud sale. A whore sells fake love, i.e. a false version of him- or herself, in exchange for money. You have sold a fake fear, i.e. a false version of your own self, in exchange for love.'

'I do not understand,' said Marius, very white.

'Neither do I,' said Isobel. 'Whatever you're doing, Fielding Gray, you'd better stop now.'

'What I'm doing is quite unstoppable,' said Fielding. 'Come to the library, all of you.'

They all came. In the library were Ptolemaeos Tunne and Jeremy Morrison. Nicos Pandouros came in just after Fielding, Isobel and the three children.

'I have spoken with the *Kyrios* Barraclough,' Nicos told Ptolemaeos. 'He understands your request and will detain Mr Stern in the summerhouse.'

'Detain my husband?'

'So that he shall not be distressed,' Ptolemaeos said, 'by what is to happen here. But first let us be very clear about one thing: will the dinner be safe for the next half hour without your supervision?'

'Yes,' said Isobel crossly. 'It's nursery stew. Just been put on a low flame.'

'Good. It is important that you should be here, Mrs Stern, since you are to blame for the situation (as you will see) and must be confronted with your guilt accordingly. Nicos will see that you do not make a nuisance of yourself.'

'And the children?'

'Witnesses, whose evidence will be required of them. Now,' said Ptolemaeos: 'first, a little history.'

He rose from his chair and went to stand near the tape recorder.

'Marius,' said Ptolemaeos, 'on the day after the night on which he arrived here, claimed that he *knew* some emanation or efflux from Tessa Malcolm was going to come to him in a very short time and take possession of his whole being. He had realized this, he said, as soon as he awoke in the early morning. I asked him who or what had told him this, and the following conversation was recorded.'

He pressed a switch on the flank of the tape recorder.

'IT has told me this,' said Marius's voice from the machine.

'That was in your dreams' (Ptolemaeos's voice) 'which have stopped. Who has told you this *since you have been here*? When you woke up this morning?'

'I told you. I just know.'

'I am giving you the lie, Marius. For your own sake, I am giving you the lie direct. You did not "just know". Somebody or something told you. *Who or what?*'

For answer came from the machine a long howl, which gradually and despairingly faded into little more than a sigh.

Ptolemaeos switched off the tape recorder.

'So,' Ptolemaeos said to his audience, 'I knew that the situation was rooted in falsehood and desperation. But I did not realize what had produced these until I heard a chance observation of Rosie's.

'But first let me go back a little. Marius claims, or claimed, that something was coming out of Tessa, like a kind of invisible cushion all round her, which produced lust in him. He claims, or claimed, that this something came to him in his dreams and made him have seminal emissions, thus weakening him and causing him to play rotten cricket. Lastly, he claims, or claimed, that this something was going to come to him and take him over completely, and this he finally knew on the morning after the night on which he arrived here. Although Rosie, as he believed, had persuaded Tessa to stop sending this some-thing to him in his sleep, he said that it was getting out of Tessa's control and would shortly come to possess him entirely regardless both of her wishes and Rosie's.

'Now then: this something, this emanation; It. It has

nothing to do, Marius says, with Tessa's minor deformity. It is an emanation from her inner being. But has anyone ever actually *felt* this emanation, except for Marius (as he claims)? Jakki? You know Tessa well. Have you ever felt anything . . . emanate . . . from her? Flow out of her?'

'No, of course not. Except kindness.'

Which is all very well, thought Fielding: but how do we explain that long lack of guests at Buttock's in the spring? True, *I* noticed nothing come from or out of Tessa; but something there must have been to send them all away, something from somewhere or somebody.

He was about to obtrude this problem on the assembly, but decided to hold his peace. Ptolemaeos's reaction, should he be interrupted, would be ferocious; when all was said he, Fielding, had nothing palpable to offer; and although the problem could not, in honesty, be forgotten or suppressed, its discussion could, for the time being, be very well deferred. He himself would take it up with Maisie again . . . in due season.

'Rosie?' Ptolemaeos was now asking. 'Have you ever noticed anything out of the ordinary which was coming off or out of Tessa? Tell the truth, girl, and your mother will love you as she loves Marius, for helping to save him.'

'Will you, Mummy?'

'I shall try.'

'Then there is no spirit or influence or emanation or whatever you may call it,' said Rosie, 'coming out of Tessa or out of anybody. I made a wish and Marius believed in its power and that is all.'

'He did not even believe that much,' said Ptolemaeos. 'He knew perfectly well why he was not making runs. It was not because he had the occasional wet dream, or because you and Tessa were sending a succubus to drain him, or even because he was upset by your malice (though that is the nearest to a rational explanation we have come yet): *it was because of his own bad habits*, because of his shame and disgust at them, and because of the debilitating physical effects which, perhaps with some exaggeration, he attributed to them. Tell us, Rosie, tell us what you have seen . . . when Marius thought he was alone.'

Marius made for Rosie with clenched fists, but Jeremy gathered him up, set him down at a safe distance, and stroked him down the arms to soothe him.

'He played with himself,' said Rosie. 'He has been doing it since he was very young, when he thought I wouldn't notice or wasn't there; but he didn't do it all that often until about a year ago. Then he started doing it much more, sometimes two or three times in a single hour. Recently some little drops of stuff have started to come out of him when he does it, and it is longer than it used to be before he starts doing it again.'

Marius spat at her from across the room.

'My dear Marius, you should not be so angry and ashamed,' said Ptolemaeos. 'None of it is your fault. I know that you try very hard to control yourself, I know that you are *fastidious*. You deliberately refused Tessa's kiss so that you should not embarrass her. You asked for Jeremy to be with you all the time because you knew that in his presence you would never touch yourself lest he should see you and despise you.

'Marius thought,' said Ptolemaeos to his audience at large, 'that Jeremy was the only person that could save him. But what Jeremy protected him against was not . . . It . . . but a habit which was threatening to possess him as totally and fatally as It (had it existed) would have done. He may have tried to deceive himself, for a time, into thinking that the habit was connected with, or caused by, It, but in fact he knew the truth quite well for what it was. When he announced, on his first day here, that It was on its way to him, he was really saying that the temptation to masturbate, *to masturbate excessively*, after a temporary lull caused by the events at Oudenarde and the subsequent movements and distractions, had returned to him more fiercely than ever.'

'I couldn't help it,' screamed Marius. 'I had to pretend that it was Rosie's fault or Tessa's, and I wrote begging them to lift the curse, but all the time I knew it was me. And I knew that if I was with somebody I really loved, like Jeremy, I could, *just*, make myself not do it. So I made up that story of Tessa's face at the window to make Jeremy agree to go on sleeping with me and to make Mr Tunne allow it.'

'Little beast,' hissed Isobel.

'Your fault, madam, entirely your fault.'

'What nonsense. I've always taken the greatest care of him.'

'When Marius was asleep in here the other day,' said Ptolemaeos, 'not on the occasion played back by the tape recorder just now, but some days after that, Fielding Gray and I examined his body.'

'Filthy pigs,' said Isobel.

Nicos edged a little closer to her.

'To confirm that he was uncircumcised,' continued Ptolemaeos blandly, 'despite his Jewish paternity.'

Len and Tom came in.

'It seemed to me,' said Ptolemaeos, 'that the ridge of the bulb of the penis was much too sharply outlined and bulked much too large under the prepuce. For a time, however, I thought no more of it; but later on, after Rosie had told me about her brother's masturbation, I had an idea, and rang up one of my acquaintance who is polymath in such matters and might be able to make some contribution to the dialogue.'

'You certainly picked a winner,' said Len. 'You see, ladies and gentlemen, like Marius here, and at his age, I too had not been cut. And my foreskin was, quite simply, too tight. It itched and irritated. So I used to put my hand down there to soothe it – and before I knew where I was I was having myself off. After the performance was over, the irritation would start up again immediately, if anything rather worse than before, so I put my hand down to soothe it, etcet, etcet, etcet. Finally I got round to telling a sympathetic doctor – a certain Doctor La Soeur, who did a lot of dodgy work for rich people, but also held surgeries for the poor in his part of London, on condition that he was allowed to use his patients in the interest of his researches. He was quite amused by my complaint – bubomania, he nicknamed it – and proposed an easy cure. Cut it off – the foreskin, I mean. So off it came, and right away little Lenny stopped jiggering his piece all day long.'

'You see, Mrs Stern?' said Ptolemaeos. 'Your Hellenophilia nearly cost Marius his sanity. You didn't trouble to notice that his uncut little foreskin was too tight. The result was, when he began to get bigger, compulsive masturbation, more and more compulsive, to relieve discomfort; and the result of that was the construction of a diabolical fantasy by which he sought at once to symbolize his situation and to shift the blame from himself, and which he used to blackmail others, notably Jeremy Morrison, into giving him the help he needed. This fantasy took the form of a succubus, operated by the innocent Tessa Malcolm of all people and directed by his sister Rosie, which threatened to engulf and to destroy him entirely, just as he thought, not altogether without reason, that his immoderate self-abuse might do.' And to Marius: 'Have you understood all this?'

Marius nodded. He went to his mother, kissed her gravely on the eyes, and linked his left hand little finger with her right hand one.

'Darling Mummy,' he said. 'Please may I be circumcised?'

'I have no doubt,' said Isobel superbly, 'that your father will know how to arrange it.'

'And that's about it, Maisie,' said Fielding Gray to Mrs Malcolm in her office in Buttock's Hotel. 'No one really to blame, in the end.'

'All too tidy,' Maisie said: 'someone's always to blame in the end. What about that Isobel Stern? She should have noticed that something was the matter.'

'But should she, Maisie? Should she have noticed anything so tiny? A little boy's prepuce that was just too tight . . . by a matter of millimetres. So small a thing to lead to such misery and violence and fear. But if you come to think of it, it is always the small things that have the greatest results, because they can stay unnoticed until they have done their work . . . for good or ill.'

'I see what you mean. "Great oaks from little acorns grow."'

Fielding giggled.

'If only it *had* been an acorn,' he said, 'nothing would have grown.'

'Whatever do you mean?'

'Small boys at prep schools call a circumcised penis an acorn. Or they did when I was Marius's age. So if Marius had only had an acorn . . . and he would have done from birth if it hadn't been for Isobel . . . then there would have been no trouble. Or at any rate, not *this* trouble. But one thing is certain, Maisie: whoever might or might not be to blame, it certainly isn't Tessa. So do I get my reward . . . for helping to clear her?'

'What reward are you hoping for?'

'It's time you kept your promise and told me who Tessa's father was.'

'Was . . . and is,' Maisie said. 'My promise had no definite date, remember. When the time is right, I said.'

'And isn't it?'

'No. You haven't earned a reward, Fielding, because although my Tessa is in the clear with your friends, with the Sterns and Tom Llewyllyn and the rest, she's not yet in the clear with me. You see, you still haven't explained – nobody has – what sent all our guests packing in the spring. For several weeks the place was like a morgue without even any corpses. The clients noticed something which we and the staff didn't. Well, what? Something to do with the way Tessa was growing up could be the answer.'

'I know. I thought about that when Rosie and Jakki told us, down in the Fens, that they knew of no emanation or anything like it that came from Tessa. But there must have been *something*, I thought to myself, to turn all Maisie's guests away last spring . . . I nearly raised the point there and then, but it hardly seemed wise to interrupt Mr Ptolemaeos Tunne.'

'I dare say we'll find out sooner or later, love,' said Maisie. 'In fact I'm working on a new little theory of my own, but I'd sooner not tell it to you until there's some sort of proof.'

'Oh, come on, Maisie darling . . .'

'I'll tell you what, then. I'll tell you my theory, *and* I'll tell you all about Tessa's father, and how I came to get into the club with her, if you'll promise to cancel your trip with that Jeremy Morrison in September.'

'Then I shall just have to remain in suspense a little bit longer. I'm looking forward to the Peloponnese with Jeremy, and I've no intention of cancelling. Greco Barraclough has given me some handy tips.'

'I don't trust him. Not one little inch of him.'

'Greco Barraclough?'

'Young Morrison.'

'You don't even know him.'

'I remember a few tales about his father – some of them yours.'

'You don't have to trust a man – let alone trust his father – in order to like him, Maisie. And I reckon I'm a match for any tricks which Master Jeremy might think up.'

'You just watch out,' Maisie said, 'they've invented a lot of new games since you were young.'

'I suppose one lesson that has come out of all this,' said Baby to Jo-Jo in the shade by the pool in their grove, 'is that we must have our boys circumcised.'

'But one does see Isobel's point,' Jo-Jo said: 'aesthetically, circumcision is an absurdity. Just think what those statues of Apollo or Hermes or Eros would look like if you chopped off the foreskins. Surely the thing to do is to establish whether it is really necessary in each individual case.'

'I think the trouble with that scheme,' said Baby, 'is that you can't tell, when boys are very little, whether it will be necessary or not. But if you leave it till they're big enough for you to be able to tell, and you then find it has to be done, it hurts them horribly.'

'Poor little Marius. Who's doing him?'

'Some rabbi Gregory's dug up – '

' – *A rabbi?* With all these things he's saying about the Jews? There was a long piece in the *Decimator* last week about their greed, their bigotry and goodness knows what. And a footnote said that Gregory was preparing a whole book of the same to follow.'

'So in the end the only rabbi who consented to take on

316

the job was highly suspect, and Gregory allowed Isobel to engage an old chum of hers – Doctor La Soeur.'

'Canty's old chum too, he said?'

'Yes. They all went to him at one time or another. That's why Max has gone into his home.'

'How is Max? I hope he'll manage something about that present he promised for Sarum.'

'He rather seemed to go off Sarum. Anyway there's no hope at all now – unless he'd arranged it before he blew up. He just lies there without talking or moving, Canty told me last night. Gives no trouble – except that he needs potting from time to time.'

'But look,' said Jo-Jo, switched back by Baby's idiom to the problems of infants, 'if circumcision hurts boys when they're grown, then it follows that you have to have it done when they're babies. But for all you know then it might never be necessary, so that you may be committing a very nasty aesthetic boob for absolutely no reason.'

'All very difficult,' Baby said. 'What about a game of backgammon? If you win a hundred and twenty more, you've got me over ten thousand.'

'Not just yet. Read to me, please, darling. Dear, restful Mrs Gaskell.'

'First tell me what you'll do about Alexandre.'

'Jean-Marie won't want him cut. The French hate it. But I shall do whatever you do about Sarum. What will that be?'

'Copy-cat. On balance, I think after all that I shall leave him be and hope for the best. But oh green eyes, green eyes, oh my poor fallen Lucifer.'

'But surely he's going to be all right now?'

'He can never be all right after all the horrible things he's done. Even if he never does a wrong or unkind action for the rest of his life, every time I look at him I shall think: he's the one who nearly killed a friend at school, he's the one who accused an innocent girl of being a vampire.'

'But you'll still risk it with Sarum?'

'Yes. The case of Marius is too . . . extreme to be a good example. The same thing must be happening to little boys all over the world, but they don't get up their own personal live horror shows on account of it. Where were we in Mrs G?'

'Chapter forty-eight. Poor little Molly Gibson is accused of guilty meetings with horrid Mr Preston. But she's really doing it all to protect Cynthia.'

'I wonder, Jo, whether we'll get to the end before Alexandre arrives.'

'Sometimes I wish he would never arrive. Sometimes I think I should like to sit here for ever under the trees, playing backgammon with Baby my Baby, and being read to out of Mrs Gaskell, and hearing the little ripples washing in the reeds.'

The world's greatest novelists now available in Panther Books

Simon Raven
***'Alms for Oblivion'* series**

Fielding Gray	£1.95	☐
Sound the Retreat	£1.95	☐
The Sabre Squadron	£1.95	☐
The Rich Pay Late	£1.95	☐
Friends in Low Places	£1.95	☐
The Judas Boy	£1.95	☐
Places Where They Sing	£1.95	☐
Come Like Shadows	£2.50	☐
Bring Forth the Body	£1.95	☐
The Survivors	£1.95	☐

Other Titles

The Roses of Picardie	£1.50	☐
The Feathers of Death	35p	☐
Doctors Wear Scarlet	30p	☐

Paul Scott
The Raj Quartet

The Jewel in the Crown	£2.95	☐
The Day of the Scorpion	£2.95	☐
The Towers of Silence	£2.95	☐
A Division of the Spoils	£2.95	☐

Other Titles

The Bender	£1.95	☐
The Corrida at San Feliu	£2.50	☐
A Male Child	£1.50	☐
The Alien Sky	£2.50	☐
The Chinese Love Pavilion	£2.50	☐
The Mark of the Warrior	£1.95	☐
Johnnie Sahib	£2.50	☐
The Birds of Paradise	£1.50	☐
Staying On	£1.95	☐

To order direct from the publisher just tick the titles you want and fill in the order form.

GF381

All these books are available at your local bookshop or newsagent, or can be ordered direct from the publisher.,

To order direct from the publisher just tick the titles you want and fill in the form below.

Name _____

Address _____

_____

Send to:
Panther Cash Sales
PO Box 11, Falmouth, Cornwall TR10 9EN.

Please enclose remittance to the value of the cover price plus:

UK 45p for the first book, 20p for the second book plus 14p per copy for each additional book ordered to a maximum charge of £1.63.

BFPO and Eire 45p for the first book, 20p for the second book plus 14p per copy for the next 7 books, thereafter 8p per book.

Overseas 75p for the first book and 21p for each additional book.